Fluff 3

Fluff 3

RavensDagger

Podium

To warm blankets, fresh socks, scalding showers,
snappy winter air, and friendly hugs—
as well as all the other things that make life worth living

Cover design by Nana Qi

ISBN: 978-1-0394-8624-9

Published in 2026 by Podium Publishing
www.podiumentertainment.com

Podium

Fluff 3

PROLOGUE

~~~~~~

Emily genuinely disliked moving.

Not that she'd moved much. Once, when she was too young for the memories to be entirely clear, her family had moved to a nearby town. Her dad had gotten a new job away from Eauclaire and the commute would be better. She didn't really recall living there, though her mom had once pointed out the house when they were driving through that little town, and she had seen pictures here and there of a baby Emily in an unfamiliar home.

No, the home she grew up in was the only home she'd known her entire thinking life. It was . . . home.

So really, her dislike of moving was more recent.

First, moving from home to the dorm a little over a month ago. That had been kind of awful. It meant a hard disconnect from her life at home, a loss of her comfortable bedroom and her own private little space.

And then there was moving now.

"Teddy, no," Emily said without looking up from the box she was repacking. She didn't have much, and yet it felt like a lot when she had to fit it all into a few boxes to be carried across the city.

"What? C'mon, Boss, you didn't even look up!" Teddy complained.

Emily did look up this time and turned to find Teddy standing, her eyes distinctly not meeting Emily's gaze and her hands tucked at the small of her back. Two of Trinity's three bodies were on the floor, as if they'd recently been shoved, and the third was clinging on to Teddy's back while trying to look innocent.

"What were you doing, then?" Emily asked.

"Nothin," Teddy said.

"Mm-hmm," Emily replied, extending a hand toward Teddy. "Sure. Give me that."

"Don't got anything to give, Boss," Teddy said.

"Teddy," Emily warned.

Teddy's cheeks puffed out, and she finally deigned to surrender . . . what looked very much like half of a slice of pizza, covered in a fine dusting of hair and mold.

Emily flinched, and the pizza splattered onto the carpeted floor.

"Mine!" Trinity said as she leapt down to grab it.

"No," Emily said as she caught the nearest Trinity by the scruff of her shirt. "No, absolutely not. Where did you even *find* that?" she asked.

"It was under the bed!" Trinity said. "Everyone knows the five-second rule!"

"Five seconds? This looks like it's been there for weeks!" Emily said. "Was that what was causing that smell?"

"I thought it was Teddy's socks," Athena said from where she sat nearby. Athena and Maple, at least, had been helping. The two of them were taping the boxes Emily packed with great enthusiasm and not-so-great skill.

"If you want to smell my socks so bad, I can stuff them into your nose," Teddy shot back.

Emily clapped her hands twice, catching everyone's attention. It was a trick she'd picked up from Mrs. Headerson, the kindly woman who taught her sisters and somehow managed to corral them into something approaching orderliness. "Let's not turn this into a fight," she said. "Teddy, Trinity, you can't have the, uh . . ."

"Floor pizza?" Trinity asked. "But the five-second rule!"

"I don't see how that rule applies here," Emily said.

"It's been more than five seconds, so it's mine," Trinity said.

Emily considered that, then dismissed it. "No. No, absolutely not. Athena, put the floor pizza in the No-Trinity-Trash-Can."

Athena made a face, but she ripped her arm away from a big bundle of tape, then tugged another piece from around her leg and made her way across the room to pick up the pizza slice. She held it out at arm's length and then tossed it into the No-Trinity-Trash-Can, which was just a normal trash bin with a sticky note on the side that had an X over a cartoony doodle of a raccoon.

Trinity pouted, and Teddy grumbled, so Emily decided to distract them.

Her dorm room was nearly empty already. Her books were in one box, her other belongings in a few others. Fortunately, a number of things from home had never been unpacked to begin with, so she didn't need to worry too much.

The rest was all stuff she'd accumulated in the month since her semester had started. Mostly there were a few toys, lots of small Maple inventions that did all sorts of things, and a number of necessities for her sisters.

There were a lot of blankets and clothes still left to pack away, but it was coming along. Enough so that Emily did a count of the boxes that were . . . mostly taped shut thanks to Athena and Maple's efforts.

"All right," Emily said. "Trinity, you have the most hands, so you can grab three times as many boxes as anyone else. Take those there, there, there, and there. Teddy, you take that one there, the heavy-looking one, since you're so strong."

"You hear that?" Teddy asked Trinity. "I'm strong."

Trinity rolled her eyes, all six of them, which was a rather impressive amount of eye-rolling from a single girl. "Yeah, but there's more of me, so blergh!" She stuck her tongues out at Teddy, and Emily worried that it might all turn into a scuffle.

Her sisters were rather excited about the move. As far as they were concerned, it was all fun and games, but then again, they didn't have to worry about the logistics of it all.

"What do you want me and Maple to grab?" Athena asked, her voice raised just loud enough to cut off Teddy's rebuttal.

Emily knew that she shouldn't play favorites with her sisters, but sometimes . . .

"Just grab that one there," Emily said. "I'll take my school bag, and this, and . . . Maple, do you think you can handle that box there? It's all of your gizmos."

"Okay!" Maple piped up. She looked up at Emily and smiled. Then she winced as she tugged a strip of tape away from her hair.

Emily grabbed a box of her own, then looked around the room. It was almost entirely empty except for her chair and a few bits of furniture that were too big to move easily. She'd need to grab those with her dad's help, but he didn't have time off for another day or two.

In any case, the room was essentially empty now.

It felt a little strange but not that bad. This room had only been her home for a month and a little bit, but . . . a lot had happened here. It was where she met her sisters, where she gained her powers.

But now it was too small. She had four sisters and, including herself, that made seven bodies squeezed into a room meant for one college student to sleep in. The rooms here weren't even supposed to be living spaces. There was a shared living area on each floor and a kitchen on the ground level for that kind of thing, apparently so that more rooms could be crammed into the building and so that people would have to socialize to get things done. Emily had avoided socializing at all costs, though, and had done a pretty good job of not even learning the names of the people who lived right next to her, with one exception.

Emily filed into the elevator with her gaggle of sisters, then trooped back out once they were on the ground floor. She had to pause to help one of Trinity pick up a smaller box that had fallen, then it was out the front of the dorm.

Sam was waiting for her there, eyes on her phone and back leaning against her brand-new car.

After their last big . . . adventure, Sam's car had been totaled and the insurance company had written it off as a loss. But Sam, being clever and prone to fraud, had gotten the best insurance she could afford a few weeks prior, including a hefty insurance payout that only kicked in if the car was damaged by Heroic or Villainous actions.

Which was exactly what had happened. Never mind that Sam had used her car to stop some bad guys from getting away on purpose.

Now Sam was the owner of a seven-year-old mint-green minivan.

It had seating for eight, more if the passengers were small and prone to ignoring the law, and plenty of room for all of Emily's boxes.

"Heya, Boss," Sam said as she lowered her phone. "Got all your stuff?"

"Yeah," Emily said. "Think it'll fit in the trunk?"

"Can I fit in the trunk?" Trinity asked.

"Oh, um . . . can I be in the trunk too?" Maple asked.

"No one's going in the trunk," Emily said. "The only thing going in the trunk is our stuff. Now come on, let's sort this all out. We might have to keep a few boxes closer to the front."

She was always a little worried that they didn't have car seats or whatever, but then her sisters would probably rather die than have to use a booster seat.

Emily shook her head as she closed the trunk, the last box packed away and her sisters fighting for the best seats. She looked up at the Quantum Mothman House, then smiled to herself. It was time for a new—hopefully calmer—chapter in her life.

One that was, unfortunately, going to start in an underpass.

CHAPTER ONE

~~~~~~~~~

Smoggy

The worst part of living under an underpass—other than the constant rumble above and that persistent smell of exhaust fumes from all the cars—was that Emily always felt terribly self-conscious when they arrived at the entrance of their base.

Sure, this one underpass wasn't in the trendiest part of Eauclaire. But it wasn't like anyone was around to notice. Any traffic would be *on* the underpass, not beneath it. The road it was on curved out a bit, so it wasn't even like people in the nearby apartment buildings could see that their van had stopped in the maintenance lane on the side, and this particular part of town was relatively quiet.

It was close to the college, but not so close that it was surrounded by dormitories. It was situated in just about the weirdest little nook, and that was probably what was best about it. No one would go looking for them here, or so she hoped.

Emily opened the side door of the van and jumped aside as two Trinitys spilled out. "Were you wearing your seatbelt?" she asked.

"I was wearing one of them," Trinity said as she jumped to her feet.

Emily decided not to pursue that line of inquiry. "All right. Girls, help me with the boxes?"

Soon they had the van's trunk open and Emily was handing out boxes to her sisters. She took a few of the heavier ones for herself, then made sure she could juggle them one-handed for a moment.

"I'll go park while you take all of that down," Sam said from within the van.

"That sounds fair," Emily said. "Will you come down after?"

"Yeah, sure, I can spare a few minutes. Besides, I've got your cash."

Emily nodded, then closed the trunk of the minivan and told Maple to shut the side door. Then she guided her gaggle of sisters to the interior wall of the overpass. A splash of old graffiti—with words she'd rather her sisters not learn but feared it was too late—hid the entrance, but the door into the base was still relatively easy to open . . . if she had more than one free hand.

Emily popped open a little panel, pushed aside the wires within, then wiggled her key into the lock and twisted the handle.

The door, a flat panel of concrete with its edges so tight that they were almost invisible, hissed open, sliding back and away from the wall.

Her sisters, of course, had no fear of what might lurk inside and eagerly pressed into the base. The corridor beyond had been a dusty, gray passage once, but a couple of weekends spent exploring the place had improved it . . . somewhat.

The walls were now a lively pastel green. The paint had been on sale at the local hardware store in large enough quantities to cover everything.

Splotches and speckles dotted the floor where Emily had failed to cover it with enough newspaper, and the edging was . . . not fantastic. But it was better than the flat gray it had once been.

The door at the end of the corridor, which led to the main part of the base, now featured a surprisingly well-done painting. Trinity had some real talent when it came to drawing and painting, and with six arms and three heads, she was quite quick as well.

The painting featured a large bear, three raccoons, a beaver, and an owl, all smiling and all wearing domino masks. It was cute. Less cute was the large image of a blond woman in the background wearing what looked like a windswept toga with her arms spread wide. Sunrays splashed out of her and onto the backs of the animals, giving the entire background an almost . . . religious feel to it that always made Emily uncomfortable.

Maple got the painted door open, and soon they were in their new home.

The base's main section featured a dormitory of sorts, with several rooms that were each just large enough to hold a bed and a small desk. Farther in was the kitchen space and a single larger room that Emily had taken as her own.

The middle of the base had several pillars rising to the ceiling, big stout ones that looked strong enough to support the world, which was comforting whenever a semitrailer rumbled past on the highway above. There was a recess in the floor with a big wraparound sofa—all made of concrete. They'd purchased a number of bright cushions, however, and the girls had added stickers to their doors, and some curtains had been placed at the entrance of the kitchen to split it off from the rest.

Her dad had donated an old TV from his workplace, which now sat on a shelf to one side. They didn't get any signal down here, but they had a DVD player and Teddy had several nature documentaries she could put on to fill the space with a bit of ambient noise.

It wasn't . . . home, not the way the dorm had been. It was still too sterile for that. But maybe it would be something like a home soon.

In any case, Emily set down her boxes with a sigh and rubbed at the small of her back. "Okay, let's unpack everything," she said.

As much as her sisters had hated packing, they seemed to love tearing their boxes apart. Maybe they felt like it was opening presents? Even if they'd been the ones to pack everything away just a bit ago.

Emily found herself smiling as they made a mess. She'd get them to clean up afterward, of course, but sometimes it was nice seeing all four of her sisters just having fun.

Maple met Emily's eyes, then smiled shyly. For a moment, Emily figured that things were looking up.

Sam opened the door then and looked at the mess, one eyebrow perking up. "You know, someone's going to have to clean that up," she said.

"Not me!" Athena said.

The others all jumped to say the same, but then an argument broke out about who called dibs on not being the one to have to pick up, and Emily tuned it all out.

"Did you find a place to park?" she asked Sam.

Sam nodded. "Oh, yeah. There's a corner store just around the bend near the exit ramp. It's one of those combo gas-station ones. Terrible coffee, lots of overpriced snacks . . . they have these little hot dogs on this machine that rotates them that taste way better than they should."

"I think I know the one," Emily said.

"Yeah, anyway, I parked there. The guy manning the counter said it was fine after I buttered him up a little."

"Buttered him up?" Emily asked.

"That's when you put butter on someone," Teddy said. "So they taste better, right?"

Sam laughed and rubbed the top of Teddy's head so that her ears wiggled. "Sure, that's one definition. Once you're a little older and start thinking that boys look like more than just snacks, ask me again and I'll tell you about the other."

She was talking about flirting, Emily realized, a subject she knew less than nothing about herself. "Let's hope that's not for a while," Emily said.

"Boys are disgusting," Athena said.

"They've got cooties," Trinity agreed. "I heard about them on TV."

"What are those?" Maple asked.

"It's a sickness they've got that makes them stupid and gross," Trinity said. She stopped picking her nose to cross her arms.

Sam laughed and nodded. "That's exactly right."

"Maybe we can cure them?" Maple mumbled, just loud enough that Emily could hear. She had that vacant look in her eyes, like she always did before taking something apart. Emily decided to leave her to it for now. It wasn't like cooties were an actual thing, so she figured Maple would just spend some time building and having fun.

"Wanna talk finances?" Sam asked.

"Sure," Emily said. "The kitchen?"

They wandered over to the kitchen, the sisters having some fun on their own, properly distracted by the TV as Teddy turned on one of her nature documentaries.

"So, we've got a lot to cover," Sam said as she pulled out her phone and opened, of all things, an accounting app. "Expenses are actually pretty low, but I'm totally counting gas costs in all of this, and I set aside an amount for costuming. The girls will need new clothes, and even if the laundromat is technically paying us protection money, we still need to use their services discreetly, which costs a premium. Otherwise, though, we're making bank."

"Really?" Emily asked.

"Well, in a manner of speaking. A couple hundred a week? It's enough to keep ahead of the food bills and such. Not even a fraction of what a real Villain would need to operate, I don't think. But hey, this is Eauclaire."

"Yeah, we don't have real Villains here," Emily said.

And thank goodness for that.

CHAPTER TWO

~~~~~~~~

Kevin

Kevin revved the engine on his bike, leaned forward, then zipped around the car ahead of him while it was still slowing down. The traffic on these highways was way too much for such a nowhere city like Eauclaire.

But maybe he'd have to get used to it.

As he zoomed past congested traffic, riding on the line between the bus lane and the innermost lane of traffic, Kevin got a decent view out over the city itself.

Eauclaire wasn't all that big. Just a few bridges, a handful of distinct sections, the school, and the downtown. It was more suburb than city, really. It didn't even have a proper crop of skyscrapers in the middle. Kind of pathetic, for a city.

Still, this place was going to be his soon enough.

He rode down an off-ramp, then navigated his way through the city, aware the entire time of the hustle and bustle around him. Despite never having been here before, with a power like his, it was easy to drive around and avoid the worst of the traffic. Hell, he could do it with his eyes closed.

Kevin wasn't some nobody. He'd been in the business for two years now. But all that time, he'd been held back, forced into some pitiful role on the sidelines.

He kind of even understood it, now that he had a year or so under his belt.

The first gang that he joined didn't want him on the front lines, and it had chafed. He was strong, he could prove it. Now he knew that it had been a bit of arrogance on his part. Sure, he was strong, but he hadn't known how to use it yet.

After a while, though . . . No, if anything, Kevin deserved to be the head honcho, the big Villain that made all the others quake in their boots and who kept the Heroes up at night.

He'd been held back, time and again. But that was over now.

The last group of idiots he'd been part of, Skeever's Crew, had tried to hold him back. He'd turned their base into a pile of rubble the day he left. Even beat the crap out of Skeever himself.

Kevin was done being held back.

It had hit him a few weeks ago. Power Day came, and with it a whole new crop of Heroes and Villains, all ready to play the game again. They were all so . . . weak. Sure, he'd been one of them, once, but now, with two years under his belt, he could snap the best of them over his knee with hardly any effort.

So then, why was he still listed as some C-tier Villain? Why was he not even the second-in-command of his own gang?

What had he been doing those last two years?

He was a little young for a midlife crisis, but then, Villains didn't live all that long to begin with, so maybe he was overdue.

Kevin had decided to turn over a new leaf, to set out and take what he wanted. But he couldn't do that in the city he'd been living in. That city had proper Heroes, established gangs of Villains—quiet and loud— and while Kevin was confident in himself, he had a good idea of what his limits were.

No, if he wanted to start fresh, he'd need to do it somewhere like here. A place that barely deserved the moniker of *city*, but which also had no competition. The Heroes were weak and fat, the sorts pushed to the edges, toward safe little havens where their weakness wouldn't cause any issues.

The city wasn't rich, but it wasn't poor. Plenty of college kids, plenty of money flowing in and out. Yeah, he could work with it.

Kevin found an empty alleyway to park in and kicked the stand out of the side of his bike. Her name was Charlotte, and she was a classic Espa motorized scooter, all done up in black and chrome.

Kevin stepped off Charlotte and stretched his back out. Then he got to work, pulling Charlotte's bench up to reveal the compartment where his costume was hidden.

He had gone through a few Villainous identities. Shaker when he was new, then for a long time he was known as Tremble.

But Shaker was a nobody who no one remembered, and Tremble was a C-lister whose Villainpedia page had little information on it. Even his pictures there were distant and blurry.

Because no one trusted him to stand in the limelight.

He shrugged on a coat. An expensive leather piece, with reinforced panels on the inside made by some gadgeteer he'd run into. It was supposed to be bulletproof to a ridiculous degree. A bit too heavy for comfort, but he didn't mind that.

Then he put on his new mask. It was bone white, a lower jaw meant to look like it had been torn off the face of some poor skeleton. It was fixed to his head in the back, with a cushioned plate there that would be disguised by the collar of his coat.

It wouldn't protect his upper head, but that was fine. Sometimes sacrifices had to be made in the name of looking the part.

Kevin pulled out a mirror and fixed his eye shadow, then adjusted the fit of his mask. Now he was stuck in a perpetual grin.

The last piece of his kit was an aluminum baseball bat with all of the markings shaved off. Nothing fancy, nothing complicated. He tapped the bat against his palm, feeling the vibration running through it and up into his arm. It would do.

He closed Charlotte up, tucked her keys away into an inner pocket of his coat, and set off walking with a twirl of his bat and a whistle on his lips.

He hadn't quite decided on a new name yet, but he thought he should settle on something appropriate. Maybe Rattles? It fit his new theme.

"Rattles," he said. "Rattles. *Rattles*. Yeah. I'm Rattles and I'm gonna shake yer bones . . . no, no, that's . . . no," he muttered, "that's way too much."

He noticed a few people on the sidewalk giving him looks, but no one was running away screaming yet. Back in some of the cities he'd lived in, the presence of anyone who *might* be a Mask would have everyone running for cover.

Eauclaire was going to be so easy to take.

He let his bat drag along the ground behind him, the end of it clanging against the sidewalk. Then it was a simple matter of picking up on that and making it *more*.

The noise grew and grew, and soon people were noticing that something was deeply wrong.

Windows started to vibrate in their panes in time with the rattle of his bat, and Kevin—Rattles—grinned under his mask.

Ahead of him, at the end of the street, was the Heroic Response Force headquarters for Eauclaire.

He picked his bat up, twirled it once for show, then rammed the head of it into the ground.

A wave, invisible to most, radiated out from him with a loud *clang*.

Windows exploded, people screamed, a car driving by turned sharply as its driver was sprayed with broken glass and it rammed into another parked car. Their alarms joined the cacophony.

Rattles continued to walk along, laughing under his breath. Yes, this was what he was capable of! This was what he could have been if he hadn't been held back for so long!

He spun his bat around and rammed the side of it into an HRF van parked on the side of the road. The hit did little, but the vibrations running through the van grew stronger and stronger until the entire vehicle was shaking itself apart. Metal crumpled, bolts sheared themselves apart, and tanks ruptured.

He laughed harder and started to hit every car he passed, turning them into no more than scrap metal on the roadside.

The HRF headquarters was finally starting to respond, agents in armor rushing out of the front doors. Rattles laughed harder. Did they think a few nobody cops could stop *him*? He stomped a foot down and a wave of power traveled along the road. It was a terrible conductor for his power, the asphalt cracking and snapping, but it still reached the officers and robbed them of their footing while he ran closer.

He was going to show Eauclaire who their new boss was, and he was going to do it in as spectacular a way as possible!

The HRF was useless. Their guns vibrated apart in their hands and their armor shattered easily under the lightest of his blows. Then he turned his attention toward their headquarters. It was a big old building, all brick and mortar. Tricky, for its size, but he figured he could work with it.

Rattles ran past the fallen HRF troopers and kicked the building itself. Then it was time for him to make himself scarce. He was tough, but he didn't want to be there when the entire building came tumbling down.

So he'd leave it there as a monument and as a warning that there was a new boss in town.

CHAPTER THREE

〜〜〜〜〜

Gossip

"Did you hear?" Sam asked.

Emily felt a little strange here, like she didn't yet belong, even though she was in the right age range and was a student at the college. Sam, on the other hand, looked like a veteran collegiate. She was in joggers and a loose blouse, her sports bra showing and her many colorful earrings catching the light. Basically, she exuded the kind of confidence and lack of care that Emily only wished she could show.

The two of them were meeting in one of the college cafeterias. Well, technically there was only one "college" cafeteria, right near the center of the campus, but it was widely considered a boring place to be. The food was about what one would expect from a place that accepted vouchers instead of cash, and the room hadn't been renovated since the early nineties and it showed.

Instead, they were right on the edge of the campus, where an enterprising businessman had bulldozed a couple of lots and then built a ring of restaurants around the now open space. It was packed with tables that had umbrellas hanging above them, and the air was filled with a dangerous amount of fatty oils from the various restaurants all around the outdoor food court.

It was, in essence, the perfect place for college kids to hang out if they had a bit of money to spare, and Emily happened to be one of those at the moment.

"I don't exactly keep an ear open for all of the local gossip," Emily said before biting into an Ubway sandwich she'd just bought. It was too much for her to finish, but she had a lot of eager sisters who'd want her leftovers. She'd have to pocket the cookies for later.

Sam grinned as she shifted forward in her seat. "Okay, so this isn't confirmed, but Sparkles hasn't shown up today, and there's a second rumor that says she's in the hospital."

"What?" Emily asked. She wasn't exactly friends with Spark—with *Glamazon*, she mentally corrected herself—but the older woman was a friend-like acquaintance, which was basically the closest thing to a friend Emily had ever had.

"Mm-hmm! So, you know the Villain attack on the HRF headquarters yesterday?" Sam continued.

Emily lowered her sandwich. "There was a *what*?"

"Oh. My. God. How can you not know that?" Sam asked. "Girl, you need to spend more time listening to the news. It was all over." Sam pulled out her phone, and with a few taps placed it in front of Emily, who tugged it a bit closer to read the article Sam had placed on it.

It was from the *Eauclaire Gazette*, a small but pretty okay local paper. Emily wasn't sure if that would make it more trustworthy than one of the big media outlets, but for local news she figured it wasn't a bad place to look.

New Villain Attack Defaces HRF Headquarters!

Yesterday, at around 4:50 p.m., an unidentified Villain attacked the local HRF headquarters in downtown Eauclaire. The Villain announced their presence with several loud thumping noises that locals reported left them dizzy, then destroyed several parked vehicles before moving on to the HRF building itself.

The attack lasted no more than a dozen minutes, but in that time our brave local Heroes responded, successfully scaring off the Villain.

Injuries were reported among several civilians caught in the crossfire, and an undisclosed number of HRF troopers were incapacitated as well. HRF spokesperson Chuck Warner had this to say: "It's unfortunate to see anyone turn to Villainy, and worse to see them try and disturb such an otherwise quiet and peaceful place as Eauclaire, but the HRF is doing their utmost to investigate and apprehend this Villain before they can cause any more harm."

At the moment, Main and Third are both blocked as construction crews and inspectors assess the damage left behind from the clash. The city gave a statement suggesting that it may be several weeks before repairs begin in earnest, as Eauclaire isn't a town that has to deal with such difficulties with any regularity.

The Eauclaire Gazette *will continue to follow this story and update its readership in the coming days as more information surfaces.*

"Whoa," Emily said.

"Yeah, did you see the word they used?" Sam asked. "Villain. With a capital V."

"Does that mean that they're, you know, an actual *Villain* villain?" Emily asked.

Sam shrugged. "Maybe. Could be that they're just on that end of the spectrum. The news likes to blow that kind of thing out of proportion, but usually it's *after* they've caught the bad guy. If they haven't caught them yet, then it just makes people skittish and worried."

"I'm starting to be worried right now," Emily said. She wasn't sure where to begin. A new Villain was . . . a problem, probably. Her current income stream came from some not-quite-at-all-legal sources, and it was entirely possible that a new Villain would edge into that.

For that matter, a new Villain might see her as competition.

She could barely handle any of the Heroes as it was. The Cabal was very much too big of a problem for her to handle, and she wasn't sure if she could keep her operations at the level they were on, or if it was even possible for her to downscale. Not to mention everything she should be doing to prepare for the nebulous future.

And then there was one other, smaller, more annoying worry that she tried very hard to squash.

What if her sisters thought that this Villain was a cooler Villain than her?

"What do we know about this . . . Is it a guy or a girl?" Emily asked. "The article didn't say."

"Not much is out yet," Sam said. "No videos. But it is a guy, according to some stuff online. Mostly it's rumors of the aftermath of his moving by."

"No videos?" Emily asked. That sounded unlikely to her. "He was on Main, there are shops and stuff there, and people with phones."

"All broken," Sam said, and Emily blinked. "Yeah, I know. My bet is that it has something to do with his power. Maybe some sort of EMP effect? But power didn't go out in the city or anything, so your guess is as good as mine. We do have one picture."

Emily frowned. "You said there were no videos."

"A picture's not a video, Emily," Sam said. She grinned and took back her phone. "Apparently he's called Rattles. Here."

Emily took the phone back and squinted at the picture. It was clearly taken from some ways away, with the zoom quality she'd expect from a cell-phone camera. Still, the image wasn't entirely blurry.

In the center was a man in all-black gear, his leather coat straining against his biceps and his shoulders covered in a brace of metal spikes. It reminded her a bit of old-school punk clothing, but this guy was actually pulling it off instead of looking like someone who spent too much time at Ot Opic.

He was clearly looking in the direction of the camera, but his features, other than darkened eyes and a few artfully messy curls of black hair, were hidden by thin, vaporous smoke. His lower face stood out in sharp contrast, a grinning face full of bone-white teeth.

He was in the center of what almost looked like an explosion crater, cars crumpled, the ground cracked, a few HRF troopers flung behind him as if they'd been propelled backward by the shiny bat he held by his side.

"Oh no," Emily said.

"What?" Sam asked.

"He looks cool."

Sam blinked. "And that's . . . a problem? He's just a Villain, and let's face it, Villains have it easy when it comes to looking cool, especially compared to Heroes. A Villain who tries too hard just becomes an edgelord, which is still kind of scary. A Hero who tries even a little too much becomes a tryhard, and that's lame."

"Right," Emily said. She was *not* about to admit to Sam, of all people, that she had insecurities about how cool of a Villain she was. Sam knew about so many of Emily's other insecurities that she didn't think it was wise to add more to the ever-growing list. "Do you think we can find out more about this guy?"

"I can only think of one person who might know more," Sam said.

"The information broker?" Emily asked.

Sam blinked. "Okay, two people. I was thinking of Sparkles. Hospitals have visiting hours, you know."

And asking her wouldn't cost Emily anything. Unlike asking Handshake or even Melaton, who might also know something. "I suppose," Emily said. She needed some time to mentally prepare herself to visit someone in a social way.

Fortunately, she still had classes left for the day. After wrapping up her leftovers, buying some extra cookies from the shop—because otherwise she'd have to deal with a few disappointed sisters and Emily was weak—and then packing up her things, Emily walked with Sam back to campus until the two split up along the way to get to their respective classes.

Sitting down for an hour and a bit was exactly what Emily needed to get her mind into the right headspace for a potential hospital visit. By the time classes were over, she had texted Mrs. Headerson and gotten the okay to pick up her sisters an hour later than usual.

That gave her . . . a fairly short window to visit the hospital, but a window all the same.

Maybe, Emily figured, she would be lucky and Jezebelle wouldn't be taking visitors today. Then she'd be able to honestly claim that she tried without having to suffer through the awkwardness of an actual conversation.

A twenty-minute bus ride later, she was going up an elevator in the Eauclaire General Hospital, no such luck in sight.

CHAPTER FOUR

~~~~~~~

Hospital Visit

Emily knew that a lot of people disliked hospitals. She could understand that.

They all had this *smell* to them, like a weird mix of antiseptics and warm plastic. And she imagined that most people's hospital-related memories weren't the best. It wasn't somewhere people went for fun, after all.

Emily was a little more ambivalent about them. She'd never been hurt or injured before (hard to get injured when your favorite pastimes all involved strenuous amounts of lying in bed and staring at a phone), and she had always gone out of her way to avoid having to visit people.

Now she was on a mission to visit someone and grill them for information, and she wanted nothing more than to leave, but it wasn't the hospital's fault.

When she'd asked the secretary lady by the front desk where she could find Jezebelle, she'd been given a room number and was informed that visiting hours ended at seven. Oh, and she had to follow any floor-specific instructions with regards to wearing masks, gloves, and those weird backward scrubs that patients wore.

Fortunately, Jezebelle's floor wasn't under any sort of restrictions like that.

Less fortunately, there were *people* next to the room with the number she'd been given. Two people, both men in casual clothes, standing on either side of the door in a very un-casual way.

Emily paused at the end of the corridor and stared at them. Maybe that was the excuse she needed to leave. Were they guards? Would she have to talk to them? Emily wanted to pace, but maybe that would make her look suspicious. But then, wasn't standing in the corridor and staring not also suspicious?

One of the men looked at her, and Emily jumped, eyes darting to the floor so she wouldn't have to meet his gaze. Then she shored up her bravery and walked over. "Um, hi," she said.

"Hello," one of them said.

"Can I see Jezebelle?" she asked with a faint gesture toward the door.

"Are you family?" he asked.

"Um . . . no? I'm a classmate. I was worried?"

"What's your name?" he asked. "I'll see if she wants visitors."

She swallowed. "Emily," she said.

There was a very, very long pause where nothing happened. She looked up, meeting the man's expectant gaze.

"Emily . . . what?" he prompted.

"Wright?" she asked.

"Uh-huh," he said. Then he opened the door and slipped in, leaving Emily in the corridor to pray that the floor would open up and swallow her whole. The other guy just crossed his arms and stared while she waited.

Then the first guy returned, and he gave Emily one of those side-nods boys did. She squeezed past him into the room.

Unsurprisingly, Jezebelle had a room all to herself, with a hospital bed in the middle, a bathroom to one side behind a door, and a window with a nice view of the parking lot. The woman herself was, obviously, in the bed, with a few beepy machines and an IV stand next to her that had tubes and wires trailing to Jezebelle.

Jezebelle looked . . . not great. She wasn't wearing any makeup, and her eyes looked sunken and tired, her skin pallid and sickly. Emily couldn't tell what was wrong with her exactly. It looked like she still had the correct number of arms and legs. Jezebelle was usually very attractive and always put together well. Now . . . not so much. "Hi," Emily said.

Jezebelle's eyes opened, and then she blinked. "Hey," she said. "Grab a seat." She waved vaguely to a chair next to the bed, then reached for a remote next to her. A long press later and her bed hummed as the back rose, letting her sit up.

Emily sat down on the edge of the old pleather seat that squeaked uncomfortably beneath her. "So, uh, I heard you met a Villain?"

Jezebelle chuckled darkly. "Yeah, I met a Villain. It wasn't all that fun."

Emily winced. "Yeah, uh, I can imagine. I was . . . worried?"

"You don't sound so certain," Jezebelle said. "Ah, were you worried that you'd run into him too?"

"A bit of that, and a bit of worry for you," Emily said, expertly parrying the foot on its way into her mouth. "I wanted to see if you were okay. And I guess, uh, ask about the Villain."

Jezebelle rolled her eyes. "Yeah, you and everyone else. Urgh, but at least you have good reasons to want to know. You can't believe how many gossips came here just to . . . you know, do gossip things."

"Yeah, sure," Emily lied. She didn't know. She didn't want to.

"So, right to business? You know, the HRF would probably tell you a bit if you asked them."

"I don't know," Emily said.

"Eh, yeah, fair, they did just get messed up by the guy, and I wouldn't trust whatever sanitized crap PR says after that. What do you know so far?"

Emily shrugged. "Not very much," she admitted. "I only found out about everything a few hours ago. All I really know is that he's a man called Rattles. I don't even know what his power is."

Jezebelle hummed. "That's such a stupid name."

Emily decided to keep her opinion about the name "Glamazon" to herself.

"Anyway, he has some sort of . . . shaker power." Jezebelle made a wobbly gesture with her hand. "When I fought him, the ground shook under me the entire time, and whenever he hit someone with that bat of his, they'd . . . shake a bunch. I haven't seen the official reports on it—they'll have proper, professional speculation—but I can tell you what it felt like."

"Did he hit you?" Emily asked.

Jezebelle nodded. "My attacks distracted him a bit, but they weren't working on him very well. So I got in close. I'm pretty good in a scrap, and it didn't look like he was enhanced or anything. Then he slapped me here." She touched her chest. "Right under a breast, too. What a jerkwad. It felt like . . . urgh, you ever ride on a school bus down a bumpy road?"

"I . . . I think I know the feeling," Emily said.

"Yeah, everything shook a lot. Felt like someone was hitting me with a jackhammer but all over. My costume got torn up pretty badly, and next thing I know I'm waking up in an ambulance with a concussion and the biggest bruise you've ever seen."

"Is it . . . bad?" Emily asked. She didn't exactly consider Jezebelle a friend—after all, the woman was a Hero, and if she discovered Emily's Villainy they'd have problems—but she didn't dislike her either, even if she was both a Hero and worse, an extrovert.

"They're treating me for blunt force trauma, even if that's not quite the right thing to call it. More like . . . I guess it wasn't one single hit? More like lots of tiny ones? I don't know exactly, but my insides got shaken up, and that's apparently not healthy."

"I can imagine, yeah," Emily said.

"But hey, I lived." Jezebelle shrugged. "Might be transferred to a bigger city to see a Hero who has healing powers."

That reminded Emily of something. "Um . . . maybe I can try to help?" she asked.

"By capturing Rattles?" Jezebelle asked.

Emily shook her head. "I have a healing power."

Jezebelle stared for a moment. "Huh. Yeah, you'd mentioned it. Would it work on me?"

"It's very weak. More for, uh, boo-boos." She realized what she'd said a moment later and wanted to die all over again. "It works via headpats?"

"Well, I've got more than a boo-boo to deal with, but I'll take whatever help I can get."

Emily flushed, then walked over to Jezebelle and patted her on the head. She focused on her Healpats ability, and fired it off between pats.

"Huh," Jezebelle said. "I think that . . . might have worked . . . maybe?"

"It's not very strong," Emily said. This was a better use of the skill than most. Usually she only used it to top up her sisters' health, just in case. She'd heard a lot of stories about how often kids caught colds, and she'd seen how many weird things ended up in Trinity's mouths.

"Well, thanks, in any case," Jezebelle said. "Anything that gets me out of here sooner helps. But I think we should keep this between us? You couldn't imagine how pedantic the HRF gets whenever you do something they haven't tested a million times."

"Ah, that would be for the best, yeah," Emily agreed. "Thank you for the information, about Rattles, I mean."

"What are you planning on doing now? Track him down to beat him up?"

Emily frowned. "I hope it doesn't come to that."

"Hey, me too," Jezebelle said. "Be careful with that guy, okay? He doesn't seem like some two-bit nobody. It feels like he's got some experience under his belt. No one just decides to attack the headquarters of something like the HRF just for fun, you know? There are easier, softer targets out there."

"Yeah," Emily agreed. "I'll be careful, I promise."

CHAPTER FIVE

Predictable

The Heroes were, for the most part, predictable.

He hadn't always seen it. Not before he had his powers, when he watched TV and saw all the propaganda about how being a nice person was good and all the movies where the good guys always won.

No, back then he hadn't seen the wider picture. It wasn't until after he gained his powers and had been part of some gangs for a while that he started to notice things.

This one guy, in the first gang he joined, was an absolute lunatic. Obsessed with conspiracy theories and the like, and while Kevin was pretty sure that there wasn't anything in milk that reduced a person's chance of gaining powers, he did listen to the guy sometimes, and sometimes he was right.

As time went on, Kevin started to notice a pattern.

Heroes always followed the same predictable moveset.

In this case, the moves they'd make were so easy to anticipate that they were probably lifted right out of a textbook.

He shook his head as he watched the TV bolted to the wall. He was staying in a motel on the edge of the city. Just a temporary spot for now. He didn't exactly have a ton of money to burn on nice accommodations. At least, not yet.

That was going to change soon.

On the TV, the leader of the local HRF, some thin, tall woman with graying hair and a mean look to her, was telling a gaggle of reporters the usual platitudes. The HRF was on the case. The Villain would be caught soon. No one had to worry about anything. Blah-blah.

He could have muted it and still understood the whole thing.

Point was, they were trying to reassure people, and that meant that they were playing things by the book.

He noticed that the camera often panned to the right, where three Heroes stood. He only recognized one of them: Silver Fox. The same guy whose masked face was on Kevin's shampoo bottles.

Small world, he thought. Just a day or two ago he'd been beating up the guy's apprentice at the HRF city headquarters.

Oh well. He got up off the motel bed, finished his lunch in a couple of bites—he was eating microwavable meat pockets, with the edges on fire and the centers somehow still cold—and then got dressed.

He was going to head out in costume again, though he'd wait to put his mask on until he was closer to his objective. He left the room with the TV still going, the news milking the local event for all it was worth.

Charlotte was waiting for him outside, the bench a little wet from a bit of early evening rain that had just started to calm down. He sat down, kicked up the kickstand, then took off.

The Heroes, if they followed their playbook—which they would— were all going to be at that press conference. They were probably hoping that he'd move while they were there, maybe attack the gathering.

Which would be stupid.

So he was going to hit something else.

Not too far from his motel was a small bank. It was the only Eauclaire branch of a major nationwide chain. There were plenty of other banks with plenty of other locations, but for this one bank chain, this was it when it came to this little nowhere city.

Kevin drove past the bank and eyed its front. The building had clearly been someone's home before being converted and modernized into the bank. It was made of the same kind of orangey-red brick as most build-ings around Eauclaire, and it looked perfectly boring on the corner of a busy intersection next to a road filled with restaurants and little shops.

He parked Charlotte in an alley a little ways down, one where he couldn't see any cameras. Then he put his helmet on and pulled his trusty baseball bat out of Charlotte's back compartment and thumped it against his palm a couple of times. Yeah, he'd need a new one. The bat had a small kink in the middle, and it didn't resonate as well when he struck stuff with it.

Well, it'd be usable for this job, he figured, so that was all that mattered.

Fixing his mask on, Rattles headed to the bank.

Not the front, obviously. He wouldn't mind taking on the cops and the HRF and even the local Heroes again, but not in such an open space. That would be stupid when they knew what to expect and might have contingency plans in place. But he didn't think they'd show up. At least, not quickly enough.

Nah, he walked around to the back of the building and studied the undecorated rear wall. He looked up at a camera and winked at it, then, putting his full body into the swing, he smashed his bat into the wall like a striker aiming for a home run.

The vibration rattled his teeth until he bit down on it and *pushed* against the tremors. They rammed into the wall, and he saw a ripple cascade across the bricks as if they were no more than water.

Of course, bricks weren't designed to ripple at the best of times.

Mortar came spitting out from between the brickwork, and he stepped back as bits of masonry came crashing down around him. The wall now had a large circle crushed into it. The center was no bigger than a quarter, but its impact spread out to the edges of the wall with fewer and fewer cracks as it went.

He judged it to be a decent hit. So he struck the wall again, then again, each smack of his bat accompanied by more cracks and snaps as the entire brickwork came apart. The moment a few bricks broke completely, the rest came crashing down all in one go.

He stepped out of the way, letting them pile up at his feet. When the dust cleared, he found himself looking at a chubby woman staring back at him with wide eyes and a phone in hand. She was crouching next to her desk. "Yo," he said.

She whimpered and pressed herself farther back. He shrugged. Most of the time people ran, but whatever. He walked over the pile of bricks and into the bank proper. Or at least its rear section.

Already, he could see secretaries and bankers and . . . other office workers, cowering. He was actually kind of impressed by how quickly they all ran to hide; usually he had to threaten them a little.

Twirling his bat around, Rattles headed for the front where the vault was located. It would be a simple matter of vibrating the front door until its locking mechanism gave out. And if that didn't work, then he could probably crack the metal of the door the same way he'd destroyed the wall. Though thick steel would take considerably longer to break through than a few old bricks.

"And who might you be?"

He stopped, then turned around to stare at a man standing on the counter at the front of the bank.

A man in a costume. He was dressed like someone out of a ren faire, with a poofy shirt and tight pants, his face covered by a cloth mask. He was also holding a long, narrow sword. A rapier?

"Are you a Hero?" Rattles asked. His grip tightened on the handle of his bat.

". . . I was in the middle of robbing the place, so no, I daresay I'm not a Hero at all."

Rattles blinked. "Really?"

"The actual Heroes are busy on the far end of the city, so yes."

"Right, same reason I came," he said with a gesture over his shoulder toward the hole in the wall. "Well, this makes things awkward."

"Nonsense," the man said. "I am Fabien the Fabulous. Swordsman extraordinaire and Eauclaire's greatest bandit. You must be Rattles. The nefarious Villain who recently fought the Heroes at their own base."

Rattles grinned, then bowed to Fabien. This guy was putting on a show, and he could appreciate that. "Well met, Fabien! Now, how do you want to do this? We fight over the winnings?"

Fabien stared at him for a long moment. "No. Let us, instead, split them equally between us. Do you have a way into the vault?"

"I do," Rattles said.

"Well, I have a way into the registers."

Rattles nodded. He would trust this guy as far as he could throw him. But something told him this Fabien was a new Villain on the scene, and Rattles liked his chances if it came down to a fight. Besides, it would be nice to make a few friends in a new city.

"I like the way you think, Fabien. Come on, that money ain't gonna rob itself."

CHAPTER SIX

Banking, the Villain Way

Rattles didn't have to work as hard as he expected to get the vault door open. The door itself was a monstrously heavy thing, all steel and reinforced metal, but the lock on it had a plastic cover that he ripped apart with ease, and that gave him access to the interior of the door, which he let his powers loose on. Whatever cheap lock they had wasn't resistant to his abilities.

With a grunt of effort, he pulled the door open to reveal a closet-sized safe with several shelves. Most held papers in neatly stacked folders, and only the centermost row had any cash on it, which was all in little canvas bags with zippers and small combination locks.

He pulled the bags out, tossing them into a garbage bag he pulled out of his back pocket. "Good to go," he said.

"I have the cashiers' money as well," Fabien said.

Rattles paused. This would be the moment for Fabien to betray him. Hit while his back was turned and he had already opened the vault. It would be the perfect time . . . if Rattles wasn't expecting it.

But Fabien didn't try anything. "Out the back?" he asked.

"Yeah, bet they're rushing over already."

The great big hole blown out of the back of the bank was still right where Rattles had left it, so he led the way out, Fabien a step behind him.

"Where did you plan on going now?" Fabien asked.

"Dunno," Rattles said. "You?"

Fabien seemed to hesitate for a moment. "If you want to split things fifty-fifty, then follow me. I wouldn't begrudge you wanting to run off on your own, however."

Kevin didn't care. He'd gotten a load of cash, enough to keep him going for a long time even split in half. More importantly, he'd made the Heroes of Eauclaire look like incompetents, which was worth more than all the money in this little hole of a city. "Sure, whatever. You got a bolt-hole?"

"Something like that," Fabien the Fabulous said. "Just a place to lay low for a few minutes while the heat dies down. Come!"

Rattles slung his garbage bag full of cash over his shoulder and followed Fabien through the alleys, keeping a mental map of where Charlotte was parked the entire time. He wasn't about to abandon her in this gutter for any longer than he needed to.

Then Fabien stopped next to a sewer grate in the middle of a tight alley and casually pulled the grate up and aside. "This line was disconnected a while ago," he said. "No stink."

"Huh," Rattles said. He supposed this was one of those advantages to being a local. They got to know the ins and outs of their little city a lot better than someone like him.

It looked like the perfect spot for an ambush, but if anything, he was even less worried inside the sewers than up on the street. The small enclosed space, supported by old concrete, would be perfect for his powers. As long as he didn't go overboard and bury himself alive.

Fabien was already turning on a flashlight, which he used to scan the tunnels. The tunnels looked pretty mundane. They weren't quite tall enough that either of the men could stand up straight within them, and there was an ankle-deep pool of stagnant water at the bottom. "That way," Fabien said, pointing with the light.

Rattles snapped his fingers and the noise echoed out far ahead. He closed his eyes for a second and felt at his surroundings. He didn't quite have a bat's echolocation, but one of his minor powers did give him a fantastic sense of what was around him, especially after his vibrations bounced off those things. As far as he could tell, there wasn't anyone ahead, just a tunnel that branched out in a few spots.

"I don't intend to stay down here for long," Fabien said as he walked. "Just long enough to ditch that bag you have."

"My bag?" Rattles asked.

"Those little pouches you picked up. They have trackers in them. They'll lead the police right to us."

He hadn't known about that. That would have been a nasty surprise, to get his door knocked in while he was counting his cash at the motel.

They pushed through the tunnels for a while, then stopped at the base of a ladder. Rattles dumped his bag down and fished out one of the pouches. It didn't take much effort to rip the zipper off, and then he had a handful of five-dollar bills and a small metal puck about the size of a dollar coin with a little LED in the middle. All it had written on it was a serial number, but it was pretty suspicious-looking.

"That's it," Fabien said. "There should be one in each pouch."

"Right," Rattles said. Fortunately, he had brought several garbage bags stuffed in his coat pockets. They transferred the loose cash—including what Fabien had grabbed from the registers—into a new one, then tossed all the empty pouches and trackers back into the other and flung it out the top of the sewers, where it landed in some random alleyway.

"Come on, there's a dancers' bar just around the corner. I've reserved a private room already," Fabien said.

"You do a lot of planning, huh?" Rattles asked.

Fabien paused for a moment, frowning. "Earlier on in my admittedly short career, I didn't plan ahead, and that ended with me in a lot more trouble than I wanted to be in. I've learned that overplanning is better than underplanning."

The dancer's bar was about as sleazy as any Rattles had seen. They were let in through the back, and Fabien led him to a room with a few plush seats and a pole in the center of the room.

They unceremoniously dumped the cash onto the raised platform around the pole, and Fabien immediately started to sort through the bills. Rattles helped. After all, counting out his winnings was one of the more fun parts of this kind of thing. "That's . . . twelve thousand two hundred and forty dollars," Rattles said. "Not much."

"Six thousand one hundred and twenty for both of us," Fabien said. "If you're still amenable to splitting it fifty-fifty."

Rattles shrugged. "Yeah, sure." The robbery had already let him finish a couple of minor quests, which was fantastic. The cash was a fun bonus to rubbing the Heroes' faces in the muck, and it would get him a place to stay for a long while. He would have gone to a proper hotel, but those required ID. Maybe some awful apartment somewhere near the school? Some of those had to be more . . . ambivalent about the law.

Fabien nodded. "I'll take six. You can take the extra on top of that. You broke into the safe, which I couldn't do, so it's only fair."

"You're surprisingly nice for a Villain," Rattles said with a grin. It wasn't quite fair of him. He'd met his share of Villains that were surprisingly helpful to their own sort.

"I'm a Rogue, actually. Just . . . somewhat leaning toward the other side of the spectrum. And you're a full-fledged Villain?"

"Yeah," Rattles said. "Eauclaire needed a proper Villain, I think."

Fabien paused mid-motion, then glanced up. "You don't know."

"I don't know what?" Rattles asked.

"About the Boss."

"There's a Villain org here?" Rattles asked.

Fabien nodded. "Sort of, yes. It's small, very discreet. I've only run into them a couple of times, and that was enough for me to know that I shouldn't push things too hard."

"Never heard of them," he said. "Some Rogues banding together or something?"

Fabien shook his head. "As far as I know, they're nearly all Villains. Proper ones. Their leader is this woman called the Boss. She's . . . the mastermind sort."

"Ah," Rattles said. He felt something twist in his gut, but then he suppressed it hard. Mastermind types were always the worst. "It is just the Boss, then?"

"The Boss and about five minions. They look harmless. Until they don't," Fabien said. He met Rattles's eyes through his mask. "I don't think Eauclaire will be as easy pickings as you might expect."

Rattles snorted. "I can handle a mastermind and their pathetic little minions."

Fabien shrugged. "Well, can't say I didn't warn you. I won't go telling her about you. We're not exactly friends. Not enemies either. I do robberies and their kind of Villainy is more . . . white-collar, I think."

"Hmm," Rattles said. He was becoming less impressed by the Boss by the minute. He'd met that kind of cowardly Villain before. Always playing it safe and careful, avoiding any kind of fighting, and only hitting targets that were significantly weaker.

They hadn't been worth his respect.

He doubted this Boss deserved it either.

He leaned forward and picked up his stack of cash. "Want to grab a drink for the road?" he asked.

He might not have respected this Boss, but that didn't mean he wouldn't pry what information he could out of Fabien.

CHAPTER SEVEN

～～～～～

Minion Hunting

So, I've been talking to Head Minion Sam, and I think it's about time we start recruiting more minions," Athena said.

They were at their new home, the bunker under the underpass. The place was a bit cold, and a little small, and it could really use some more windows, but Athena wasn't going to complain.

Mostly because it was a hidden bunker with secret entrances, and the entire place's aesthetic was so cool that she'd have to be an idiot or some sort of Goody Two-shoes to actually complain about living in such an obvious Villain-like base.

Her sisters didn't complain either.

Teddy had taken over one room and filled it with blankets and pillows to create what she called a "bear cave" and what Athena had heard her big sister call a "fire hazard." Trinity had decided to only take up one bedroom but also claim the janitor's closet. She hid all the best junk in the closet and kept her room mostly clean-ish . . . for now.

Maple's room had quickly turned into an itty-bitty workshop, with some tools and lots of strange noises, and Athena had decided not to go in there because anything that entered Maple's room was unlikely to come out of it in the same shape.

And Athena herself had turned her bedroom into a proper study room, with a lot of secondhand books and plenty of notes taped to the walls linked to one another by red yarn and tacks with all sorts of information that Athena thought was useful. Sam had given her an old laptop, and Athena had plugged it in at her desk (the battery was broken and she was afraid to ask Maple for help) so she could go online and look up all sorts of stuff about how to be a proper Villain.

There really wasn't much, so she relied on looking at the "how to be a Hero" sites and doing the opposite of what they said.

Anyway, right now her big sister was back from another day at school. The next day was the start of the weekend, so it was a perfect time to get up to some Villainy.

"You want me to what?" Emily asked.

"To get more minions," Athena said. "Look, I made a flowchart about it."

She reached into a small file folder she had borrowed from Emily's school stuff and removed a page with her flowchart drawn on it.

"See, this is us here, right now. We have three important tasks to do. First is cuddles and family time." She tapped that one. It was circled twice. "Second is doing basic maintenance Villainy."

"Maintenance Villainy?" Emily asked. Athena had caught her in the kitchen, so she was only glancing over every so often while paying a bit of attention to the water she was boiling.

They were going to have mac and cheese.

"Yeah. Maintenance Villainy. That's the kind of Villainy that Sam does. Extorting money, putting up gang signs, blackmail, sabotaging the Heroes. You know, the little stuff."

Athena brought her finger down and double-tapped the next point on her list.

"The last thing is real Villain stuff. That's like . . . robbing banks, attacking the Heroes, monologuing darkly, kidnapping sexy reporters."

Big Sister paused, cheese packet in hand. "Kidnapping sexy reporters?" she repeated.

"It's traditional," Athena said. "Sexy reporters make up sixty percent of all Heroic love interests, so it's normal that a Villain will want to kidnap them to hurt the Heroes as much as possible."

Emily nodded along while stirring the pot. "Makes sense," she muttered. "As long as you don't start shipping me with anyone."

Athena made a mental note to look up what that meant later. "Anyway. A lot of your precious time is spent on maintenance Villainy, right?"

Her big sister turned her way, a long wooden spoon in her mouth. "Hmm . . . nhot that mhuch thime. Sham mhostly takes chare of it, honestly."

"That's because our operation is tiny," Athena said. "But look at how many Villains we have! There's you, me, Teddy, Trinity, Trinity, Trinity, and now Maple. Plus we have Alea Iacta, who . . . I guess counts as a minion more than a Villain. But anyway, that's seven! Or at *least* five if we only count Trinity once. Most Villain organizations never get that many members to begin with."

"I think I'd rather keep our operation tiny," Big Sister Emily said.

"You're just saying that because the maintenance stuff is a lot of work!" Athena said. She pointed to the next bit of her flowchart and smiled big and wide. "See. If we get more minions, then we won't have to do nearly as much work, which means less time spent on this." She touched the maintenance Villainy bit. "And more time spent on cuddles and monologues."

It was foolproof.

"And where, exactly, would we find minions to begin with?" Big Sister asked. "It's not like I can put an ad in the paper for it."

"I sent Teddy out to get some already," Athena said. She puffed her chest out. "She said that she was real good at convincing people."

Emily froze. "You sent Teddy *where* exactly?"

"Uh, I think she said she was going to go look in a place where she could find people who would be easy to convince to join our cause."

"Teddy!" Emily called out, and predictably, there was no response. "Oh no," she said. Her hand flicked out and turned off the stove, then she started to move.

The pan moved, too, and Emily squeaked as she caught it mid-fall and spilled a bunch of cheesy noodles across the side of the stove and floor.

She used a few of the forbidden words, then ran out of the room.

Athena paused for a moment, then ran after her. She noticed one of Trinity staring, then running into the kitchen only to gasp. "Floor food!"

"Where are we going?" Athena asked.

"To find Teddy," Big Sister said. She ripped her coat off the couch and shrugged it on in a hurry before pulling her phone out. She stared at it for a moment, then looked toward Athena. "Where *is* Teddy, exactly? Is she somewhere that I can use Sisterportation on her without it looking suspicious?"

"You don't need to worry so much, she brought a minion with her," Athena said. She . . . could kinda see where she might have messed up, a little. Big Sister, despite being a Villain, worried a lot about her sisters. Which was nice, and it made Athena feel warm. But sometimes it was a bit much. They could take care of themselves. They weren't babies, and they were all Villains!

"A minion?" Big Sister asked. "Which one? Is it Sam? Please tell me it's Sam."

"Uh . . . no?"

"So, Teddy is out in the city with Alea Iacta, then?"

Athena nodded.

"And she's looking for new minions to recruit."

"Yup."

"From . . . where?"

"Well, we thought about it a lot, and we figured that we should start with the usual sort of person for new minions."

"The usual sort of person?" Emily asked.

Athena nodded again. "Yeah. You know, lonely people, with no friends, bad social skills, lots of anxiety. They're like, prime material for joining a cult or becoming a minion."

Big Sister pinched the bridge of her nose. "And where will Teddy find these people?"

"That's the tricky part," Athena said. She was pretty proud of their solution for this bit, actually. "Most of those kinds of people are probably holed up in their homes minding their own business and trying not to go outside, which means that finding them is gonna be really tricky."

"Please tell me Teddy isn't going door-to-door talking to people about joining our . . . our gang," Emily said.

Athena snorted. "No, that wouldn't work. She's just going to nerdy places with Alea Iacta. She's putting his powers to good use finding desperate, vulnerable people."

"That's . . . that's not a good thing," Emily said.

Athena grinned. "I know! I thought about it after reading about it on a Hero site. See, the Heroes go around looking for that kind of person all the time to tell them that everything's okay, and to get them to do, like, volunteer work or whatever. You know, good stuff. But I thought to myself, hey, Athena, you're a smart bird, why wouldn't you turn this into a Villain thing instead? And now we're going to get so many new minions you won't know what to do with them. Uh . . . after we do the intro."

Emily stared at her, then looked at her phone, then back up. "What intro?"

"For the new minions," Athena said. "You know. We invite them all to some secluded place, then turn on the lights, like *pash pash pash*, and then you're sitting on a throne of skulls and then you give them a monologue and then they're your new minions."

"We . . . There's several problems with that," Big Sister said.

"I've got Trinity looking for skulls already. She found six!"

Big Sister seemed to give up. "I'm calling Alea Iacta. Next time, Athena, just ... *tell me* before you start planning something like this. Please. I don't know how much of this my heart can handle."

~~~~~~~~

CHAPTER EIGHT

Recruitment Drive-By

I have told you that this is a bad idea, right?" Alea Iacta asked.

Teddy rolled her eyes. It wasn't the first time he'd said that. In fact, it wasn't the second time either. She didn't bother to keep count, but she was sure that if she had, she would be impressed by how often the minion repeated himself.

"It'll be fine," Teddy said. "You know what they say. A bear always knows."

Alea Iacta's brows drew together above the big sunglasses he wore. "I don't think that's something anyone says."

"Well, they would if they knew how much a bear knows," Teddy said. "Besides, if things go wrong, the Boss can Sisterportation me out of trouble."

Alea Iacta looked down at her. "And what about me?" he asked.

She shrugged. "Minions are expendable. That's just like, basic Villain stuff. And that's why we're getting more minions today. Think about it, these new minions will be under you in the totem pole. So when it comes time to expendableate a minion, they'll be expendabled first."

"Those aren't words," he muttered, but that didn't stop him from walking.

They had emerged from the subway network into an area not too far from their base. It was an old capitalist failure, a place with a bunch of storefronts, a good quarter of which were closed down with FOR RENT signs hanging on the windows.

These had been stores owned by small families and run by locals, but then a few bigger, boxier stores had opened up and now they'd been put out of business. Capitalism doing as capitalism did.

The remaining storefronts were a bit of everything. There was a Chinese food place, a flower shop, then another Chinese food place with a different name, then at the end, an ice-cream parlor with a big terrace.

None of those was their destination.

"That's the place," Alea Iacta said, pointing across the street toward a shop nestled in between the rest. It was called *Silver Specter: Comics and More*, and the front of the store featured several larger-than-life cardboard cutouts of strange characters. A woman in a skimpy fantasy outfit, a big hulking guy in power armor. That sort of thing.

"Looks weird," Teddy said. It wasn't like a normal store, she didn't think. From the window displays, it looked like they mostly sold card and board games, and like, dice and stuff.

"It is," Alea Iacta said. They reached an intersection, and he sighed as Teddy grabbed his hand while they crossed the road, but those were the rules, so he didn't complain any more than that. "That's the nerdiest store around. You won't find anyone more desperate and socially awkward than in there. Or at least, when that kind of person is outside of their bedroom."

"Uh-huh," Teddy said. "I guess that'll make it easy to recruit them, but then I'm not sure if I want weird people as minions."

"Because you and your sisters fill that role already?" Alea Iacta asked.

Then he hissed as Teddy kicked him in the shin. Not very hard, but enough for it to smart. "We're not weird. We're *dangerous*," she said.

"Yeah, yeah. Anyway, this bunch is pretty nerdy. Like, very nerdy. It might be hard to, uh, communicate with them."

"You're not that way?" Teddy asked.

"What? No. I'm not a geek or a nerd or anything."

"I thought you were in a theater group," Teddy said.

Alea Iacta let out a long breath. "Low blow," he muttered.

They crossed the parking lot (Teddy wasn't sure if that counted as a road, so she didn't let go of his hand, just in case) and then slipped into the store with a jingle of the bells over the door.

The place had a *smell* that Teddy wasn't used to. It was warm cardboard, flat soda, and sweat, all covered in a thick perfume. The store was divided into two sections. Right when they walked in was a section with a few stands of games and little figurines and a bunch of toys, with a long counter running the length of the room behind which were more displays with card packs.

The other section ran next to the main one. It looked like they'd opened up the wall into the store next to this one and converted the space into a play area with a bunch of tables. One of the tables was occupied by a group of four who all seemed busy playing cards.

A guy was behind the counter, sorting through a box and putting new card packs onto a wall-mounted rack. He glanced back, seemed a little worried when he saw Alea Iacta, then relaxed upon seeing Teddy.

Weird.

"Hey," Alea Iacta said. "Just here to meet the others. Uh, is there like an entrance fee or something?"

"New here, then?" the guy asked. "Nah, you're good. Just keep an eye on your daughter." He turned back to put more cards into place.

Teddy looked up at Alea and noticed that his expression had gone weird. It was like he'd just bitten into a lemon, or something that Trinity had found on the floor.

"That's them?" Teddy asked with a gesture toward the four at the card table.

"Yeah, that's them," Alea Iacta said. "I found them online. They're a group of Mask enthusiasts. Big on the whole Heroes and Villains scene."

"They work for the Heroes?" Teddy asked.

"No, no, they go where Heroes went and take selfies and stuff, and they spend hours online speculating about which Hero could beat up which Villain, or vice versa. Oh, and they hound people for signatures on merch and stuff. Basically, they're big on the fan-scene part of the Mask world."

"Oh," Teddy said. She nodded as if she understood. These people were knowledgeable about Heroes and Villains and things, which meant that they were basically perfect. They'd already know that the Boss was the best. "This is gonna be so easy," she said before confidently walking over.

The group paused as Teddy approached, but that was okay, since it gave her some time to check them all out. Of the four, there was only one girl. A shorter woman, about the Boss's age, with bright green eyes and a lot of freckles. She had a T-shirt on with a smiling Silver Fox on it.

Next to her was a short, chubby guy in a hoodie and jeans with messy black hair. He had almost as many zits as the girl had freckles.

And across from them were two more guys. One was tallish with darker skin and was wearing a cardigan. He smiled at Teddy but seemed as confused as his friends. The guy next to him was even taller, with red hair, and he looked like his shirt was a size too small for all the muscles he had.

Teddy narrowed her eyes and judged them for a while. Then she shrugged. The Boss could decide if they were worthy. "So, which one of you wants to become a minion?" she asked.

The zit-faced boy chuckled. "Hey kid, that's one hell of an opening."

Teddy crossed her arms and stared at the group, unamused by the boy's laughter. "I'm serious," she said with determination. "We're looking for minions."

"Hi," Alea Iacta said as he came up behind her and gave a little wave. "How are you doing? She's, uh, entirely serious."

"Yeah, I am. The Boss is looking for help, and Alea Iacta said that you bunch know a lot about Heroes and stuff. So if you want to be part of our crew, now's your chance."

The group exchanged puzzled glances, trying to gauge whether Teddy was joking or not. The girl with the freckles leaned forward with curiosity in her eyes. "Are you for real?" she asked, her voice a mixture of disbelief and excitement.

"Absolutely," Teddy replied, nodding firmly. "So, who's in?"

Then they started laughing even harder than before and Teddy felt her cheeks getting all warm and angry. She turned toward Alea Iacta, locking eyes with him. This wasn't how things had happened in her head!

He sighed. "I don't think they believe you," he said.

Teddy held back a gasp, then turned back to the four. "You think I'm lying?" she asked.

"Kid, who even are you?" the muscular guy asked. "Now, unless you brought a deck and want to play in the next round . . . we're a bit busy."

Teddy worked her jaw. This wasn't working out at all! She had imagined that they'd be falling over themselves to work for the Boss, not . . . this. No, that wasn't fair at all! She had to impress them, properly.

So she did the obvious thing, and turned into a bear. A stand of comic books crashed to the ground, soon followed by a tumbling cascade of model kit boxes.

"Oh boy," Alea Iacta said.

All eyes widened in shock and disbelief as they stared at the massive apex predator in front of them. The group around the table scrambled to their feet, knocking chairs over in their haste.

Teddy, still in her bear form, stood on her hind legs and growled. "Now," she began, her voice deep and guttural. "Who wants to be a minion?"

CHAPTER NINE

~~~~~~~~~~

Train Station

Emily put her hand over the receiver on her phone and took a deep, deep breath. She needed it to recenter herself. Then she spoke into the phone once more. "What do you *mean* she's bringing them home?"

She had calmed down a little after Athena's revelation and had settled on calling Alea Iacta so that he could explain himself.

Sure, this was probably . . . definitely Teddy's fault, but she was a preteen, and he was more or less an adult.

"Would you believe me if I said she threatened me?" Alea Iacta asked.

Emily thought about it for a moment. "I would," she said.

"Really?" Alea asked, sounding somewhat surprised. "I mean, yeah, that's definitely what happened. Anyway, we're heading back now. Teddy's insisting that we bring them to the train station."

"The train station?" Emily asked.

She had to duck a moment later as a spray of water missed her head.

Turning, Emily fixed the girls (minus, of course, Teddy) with a *look* that froze them on the spot. Trinity was fighting Maple and Athena for . . . something. Emily hadn't paid attention to the root cause of their fight. All the girls had Maple-modified water guns and they were taking turns firing at one another while using the couches as cover.

The water guns had been stringently tested by Emily, of course. All they did, as far as she could tell, was hold a lot more water than they realistically ought to, and that water tended to instantly evaporate about three seconds after hitting something.

She was pretty sure the water was returning to the water guns, somehow. Maple explained that it was because she had put a sponge in the guns' little tanks. Emily decided not to poke at the impossible solution too much.

The toys were letting the girls have fun splashing at one another without making an actual mess, and that was worth a lot as far as Emily was concerned.

She shook her head and refocused. "Which train station?" she asked.

"Uh. You know where the train base was parked before?" Alea said. It seemed as if they weren't trying very hard to be inconspicuous anymore. "The platform next to that. There's an entrance to it not far away."

"Okay," Emily said. "But *why*?"

"She said we needed to impress the new minions with how awesome their new boss is," he explained.

Emily suppressed a groan. The last thing she wanted to do was to let more people in on her secrets, or complicate her Mask life. Yes, more help would be welcome, but more helpers would mean more people who could betray them and cause a bunch of issues. It was a miracle that she had found Sam already, and she was sure that Alea Iacta was only helping because she had so much blackmail material on him, and because he was a little bit scared of her.

"Okay. Can you put it off?" she asked. "Or . . . cancel this whole thing outright?"

"Uh . . . I don't know about that. Look, you haven't seen how excited Teddy is about this. She's kind of already revealed . . . more than she should have."

Emily was gaining a pounding headache.

"Okay, I'll be there," Emily said.

She didn't want to. She very much didn't want to. She would much, much rather not have a last-minute social event with no time to plan and less time to grow anxious and then calm down about it, but here she was.

"Girls," she said after hanging up. "Get in your costumes. We have a thing."

There was a cheer, then a mad scramble for costumes. Emily dipped into her room (the only one with a bigger bed, which she needed because she inevitably woke up with every sister piled on top of her each morning, even if she locked her door) and got her costume out.

At some point Sam had gotten it to a laundromat, one that was paying them in protection money, so the costume itself was actually pretty clean. She suited up, tied her hair back, and then looked at herself in the mirror.

The Emily in the reflection—the Boss, she supposed—was a confident-looking young woman in a tailored black suit with a small black tie over a white button-up and a brimmed hat that she could hide her tied-back hair in, giving the impression that she had much shorter hair.

Sam had stapled two thin black bands to the inside of the hat, and when Emily adjusted them, it gave the impression that her hair was black . . . or maybe brown? She suspected that Sam had used two different wigs to make the disguise.

Adding a domino mask hid her face a bit more, and then she inexpertly, but carefully, applied some red lipstick. Another layer of obfuscation.

Not that she suspected she had any real hopes of hiding her identity if someone got a good photo of her face.

There had to be ways of identifying people just from their chin.

Maybe she could invest in a full-face mask?

And armor?

. . . Power armor.

Remote-controlled power armor? So that she could do all of this from home, in her pj's.

She made a mental note to ask Maple about it.

On leaving her room, she found the girls already waiting, though one of Trinity's bodies was still wrestling her shirt on.

Trinity was dressed like a cartoon bandit. Black-and-white shirt over black cargo pants and black boots, with some army-style face paint on (which she always got everywhere) and a bag with a dollar sign tucked into her belt. She was so comically Villainous that it wrapped around to being somewhat Heroic.

Or so Sam, and a few internet forums that had bought the "we're actually all Heroes" ruse, said.

Athena's costume was a little simpler. A leather jacket over whatever she felt like wearing that day. Today that was a cute sundress.

Maple's costume was still somewhat undecided. The girl had on almost comically large goggles, which had some lights sticking out of the sides that flickered on and off seemingly at random, and a surgical mask to cover her lower face. The rest of her costume was pretty much made up of her lab coat and a few bandoliers of random items criss-crossing her chest.

Looking at her gaggle of Villainous little sisters, Emily could truthfully say that they . . . were not very intimidating.

She picked up her phone and sent two texts. The first was to Sam, telling her to meet them, if she had the time, at the old train station. The other went to Alea Iacta, telling him to take his time. They'd only arrive there in ten or fifteen minutes, and that was if they rushed through the tunnels.

Messages sent, she turned to her sisters and eyed them all. "Okay. Here's what's going on. We're going to go meet with some people. Teddy and Athena have decided, without informing me, that we need more minions. Then, without discussing it with me, Teddy went out to recruit some people. I'm . . . not very happy about all of this, but I'm going to live with it. So I need all three of you to be on your best behavior."

Athena at least looked a little chastised about what she'd done, but Emily wasn't sure if that was all an act or not.

"Are we gonna scare them?" Trinity asked.

"I . . . I can make something for that," Maple said.

Emily was about to suggest that they didn't do that when she had an idea. "Can you make something that'll help us see if a person is loyal?" she asked.

"Can't I do that?" Athena asked. "All I need to do is look in their eyes for long enough and ask a few questions."

Emily hadn't considered that. Athena was a decent counter to any planned betrayals.

That made the idea of hiring more assistance (she didn't want to call people *minions*) somewhat more palatable.

Emily slowly nodded, considering the idea. "All right, Athena, you'll be in charge of checking their loyalty. Maple, do you think you can find a nonlethal way of subduing them if they turn out to be . . . problems? Trinity, you'll be the muscle."

"Ah, yeah!" Trinity cheered. "Teddy's gonna be so angry!"

"I'll be the one deciding if we actually accept anyone into our group. We're not trying to scare them away, but we do want to see if any of them will be a good fit. Understood?"

The girls nodded in agreement. There was a bit more excitement there than Emily was comfortable with, but maybe that was just because it had been a while since the girls had gotten out and done . . . Mask stuff. She hoped this impromptu recruitment session wouldn't lead to more trouble than it was worth.

Taking a deep breath, Emily began to lead her sisters out of the bunker and through the tunnels of the subway network. She couldn't help but wonder how much more complicated her life was going to become, and if this choice would ultimately be a blessing or a curse.

~~~~~~

CHAPTER TEN

Minion Meeting

Lucas was excited, nervous, and, he supposed, a little apprehensive about all of this. He rubbed the palms of his hands against the lap of his jeans for the fifth time in an hour. This was insane for him.

While Liam and Ethan were both prone to trying to drag their little group to different events and such, it was mostly to hang out in sports bars, or maybe go and watch a college game in a nearby city for an afternoon.

Normal stuff, but it still made him a little uncomfortable.

He wasn't an introvert—if he was, he wouldn't be hanging out with his friends as much—but he did enjoy his quiet time. Chloe was the same, outspoken and enthusiastic about what she cared about, but otherwise mostly disinterested in social . . . stuff.

And now all four of them were in what looked like an abandoned underground train station that he knew nothing about.

He wasn't an Eauclaire native, but he'd been living here for three years now for college and this was the first he'd ever heard of there once being a subway in the city.

Worse (better?), they were here because they'd been half threatened, half recruited by a preteen beargirl Heroine.

This was leagues outside of his usual comfort range.

"Did we seriously just follow a bear into a dark tunnel that leads underground?" Ethan asked.

"Shh, she might hear you," Chloe said.

"We could probably outrun her," Liam said. "She's like . . . twelve."

Lucas made a *so-so* gesture. "Kids have lots of energy. You'd probably get away, but my overweight behind isn't going to make it more than a block before I get a stitch and you know it."

Liam chuckled, flashing Lucas a knowing grin. "Told you to come to the gym with me, man."

"Oh, shut up," Lucas said, though he was kind of regretting not taking him up on the offer now. "Besides, can *you* outrun a grizzly bear?"

"If we all run in different directions," Liam muttered. Then he chuckled and bent away from Ethan, who tried to punch him in the arm.

"She seems mostly nice," Chloe said.

"Yeah, real nice," Ethan said. He shivered. "I think I nearly soiled myself when she turned into a bear."

"It was awesome," Liam said.

Ethan considered it for a moment, then grinned. "It kinda was, yeah."

The girl—Teddy—had untransformed herself after getting their full and undivided attention, then had explained that her boss, the Boss, who was a "Hero" (Teddy made finger quotes every time, and Lucas wasn't sure what that meant), needed new minions and that she'd heard that they were fans of that kind of thing.

Which, yeah, they totally were. They'd been playing *Heroes: The Spreadening* when she interrupted them.

They were about as big of Mask fans as could be. But that didn't mean that they were all ready to sign up and become . . . well, minions.

Didn't *minions* have a more Villainous connotation to it in the first place? Lucas wondered about that.

In any case, Teddy, the girl who could turn into a bear, had gone on to explain that the pay was terrible, the hours were weird, and that the biggest benefits of the job were that they'd get cool stories to tell and free selfies next to an actual grizzly bear. Not that she'd couched anything in those terms, exactly, but Lucas could read past the girl's . . . frankly hilariously bad doublespeak.

The guy with her was a little suspect too. Lucas hadn't caught sight of his face yet. He was just a guy wearing a baseball cap, a hood, and a pair of shades over a plain blue face mask. He could be pretty much anyone under that disguise, but something about him twinged Lucas's memory.

He leaned in close to Chloe, who was probably the best in their group at celebrity Mask sightings. "So, who's tall, dark, and broody?"

"He's not that tall," she said. "Also, I'm pretty sure that's Alea Iacta. The Luck Thief Villain."

Lucas stood up a little taller. A Villain? Well, a B-rated Villain with a rather lame title.

The forums loved Masks and Mask culture, but some of the Masks were . . . not great at coming up with names for themselves. So the forums gave them titles, which were often somehow worse. But they made for fantastic memes.

"The Boss is coming!" Teddy said. She rushed over to Lucas and his friends, hands going to her hips. "All right, minions. Now, just follow the rules."

"You didn't tell us the rules," Ethan said.

Teddy's mouth opened, then shut. "Crap," she said. Then she started counting off on her fingers. "Don't use cuss words. Don't make up new cuss words. Always pretend to be a Hero. Don't fight with your sisters. Go to the bathroom before leaving the house—"

"*Pretend* to be a Hero?" Chloe asked.

"Yeah," Teddy said. She was staring at her hands in confusion. "The Boss gave us ten commandments, but I can't remember the other five. Uh . . . I think one of them was don't kill people. And don't put trash in your mouth unless the Boss says it's okay. Anyway, just do your best and it won't be that bad."

Teddy gasped, and all four of them jumped.

"Hold hands while crossing the road!" she cheered. "That was one of 'em too."

"Hey, Teddy, the Boss is here," the still-disguised probably-Alea-Iacta said with a thumb pointing down the tracks.

Lucas found himself rubbing his hands on his jeans again.

The first he saw of the Boss was probably not the Boss at all. Not unless she was a child. There were actually a lot of children coming. Well, a relatively large number for the inside of an abandoned underground subway station, he figured.

"That's the whole Brat Brigade," Chloe said.

He'd heard of them! Only a little, since he wasn't paying too much attention to the local, smaller-scale Mask scene, but they had made national news for a blip a few weeks ago.

"The Boss is their leader," Ethan said. "She's worked with a few Heroes. Took out a whole Villain base a couple of weeks back. I don't think she has a title on the forums yet."

Lucas was determined to start reading up on the local scene a lot more. With that attack at the bank a day or two ago, and that other attack at the HRF, plus what seemed like a large team all arrayed out in front of him right now . . . Yeah, things were finally getting interesting in Eauclaire.

And then the Boss appeared, walking up the stairs at the end of the platform. She stood tall above the kids around her. A lean figure that blended in with the shadows behind her. All at once, he felt like she was almost forcing him to pay attention to her as she walked closer.

The young woman stopped some dozen steps away from them, eyes scanning over Lucas and his friends, and he suddenly felt awfully under-dressed in a Tar Ars T-shirt and jeans. His friends weren't dressed much better, and that didn't help him settle his nerves.

This girl, this woman, had a *presence* he'd never felt before.

She let out a sigh, and he wanted to either run or start fixing his hair. Why hadn't he visited a barber this week? Was he sweating? He was defi-nitely sweating.

"Teddy," she said.

"Yo!" Teddy said. "These are the minions I found, Boss. What do you think?"

The Boss glanced at them all, then back at Teddy. "Teddy, we're going to have a little talk later." Her attention shifted back onto the group and Lucas stood taller. "Um . . . hi?"

And then his shoulders slumped a little. That sounded . . . awkward.

"Hey?" Ethan said, one hand rising in a little wave. "Big fans?"

Lucas decided not to point out that they weren't.

"I'm sorry Teddy dragged you down here," the Boss said. "She can be very enthusiastic about things. She means well, though. I hope you won't be, uh, too distressed by it all?"

"It's fine," Chloe said. "She's cute."

The Boss nodded slowly. "Yes."

Lucas wasn't sure how far being cute would go to protect someone from the consequences of their own actions, but so far it seemed to be working for Teddy.

"Anyway, I've been thinking about it on the walk over. And I guess the offer is somewhat valid," the Boss said. "Do you, uh, want a job?"

Lucas looked to his friends, and they all spent a moment sharing glances. There was a lot of uncertainty here. Mostly because this was, on the whole of it, a completely wild scenario. This was like something out of a comic book.

Which meant that, in the end, there was only really one answer he could give.

"Yeah, sure," he said. "I'd love a job."

~~~~~~~~~

CHAPTER ELEVEN

The Pizza Place

Emily wasn't expecting unanimous agreement from her new . . . minions. Did they know that they were minions yet? They had agreed to the job, but she'd hardly given them much of a description at all.

Then her phone buzzed, and Emily slipped it out of her jacket pocket. She had a text waiting for her.

Sam: U went and got new minions?
Sam: R u trying 2 get rid of me?

Emily started typing a quick reply while rolling her eyes.

E. Wright: No. This is Teddy's fault. Now what do I do with these new minions?
Sam: I want to meet them. Where r u?
E. Wright: Train station.
Sam: All right. Pizza place, two blocks over. They're on our payroll. I'll be there in 5.
E. Wright: See you there.

"All right," Emily said, and whatever conversation her new minions had sparked up died pretty much instantly. "We're going to one of our more . . . open places for discussion."

"Which place?" Athena asked.

Emily restrained a sigh. "The pizza place."

There was a general cheer at that, from all of her sisters, and even a couple of the minions. Emily resisted the urge to pull out her wallet and check to see how much money she had left. Certainly it would be enough for a couple of pizzas and some drinks for her sisters.

The minions would have to buy their own drinks, she decided.

Glancing at her sisters, all of whom (with the exception of Teddy) were in costume, she realized that there would be no making this trip inconspicuous. Reaching into one of her pockets, she pulled out a small stack of domino masks and gave one to Teddy, then handed the others off to the minions.

She made a mental note to actually learn and remember their names at some point. It would be horribly humiliating to call one *minion* to their face one day just because she couldn't remember their name. "Here, to protect your, uh, identities," she said.

"Thanks," the one girl in the group said. "Not sure how good these will be."

"It's more the principle of the thing," one of the boys said. The shorter, more rotund one. "If you're making *some* effort to hide your civilian ID, then it means that anyone digging into it is doing so against your consent."

"Does it matter that much?" the tall one asked.

"Of course it matters. It's like the bikini-panty principle."

Emily found herself staring. "The what?" she asked.

The boy flushed, then rubbed at his nose. "Uh. Right, so . . ." He looked at the crowd of impressionable onlookers staring up at him and his flush deepened. "So, it's okay to stare at someone, a little, if they're wearing a bikini out in public, right?"

"Thin ice, Lucas," the girl muttered.

Lucas, ignoring that, moved on. "But looking at a girl wearing panties is wrong. That's because there's an understood level of consent being given."

"I'm wearing panties right now," Trinity said. She frowned. "I think at least one of me does. Does that mean looking at me's wrong?"

"Uh," Lucas said.

"Just pretend he didn't say anything," Emily advised Trinity. She understood what he was trying to say, but his analogy could use some work. A lot of work, even. In fact, maybe this minion could be a silent minion. "So, should we get going?"

With that, she started to move, then froze up as she realized that she'd just sort of expected everyone to follow her. She turned, and discovered that everyone had, in fact, started to follow her, but now they had stopped to stare at her, staring back, and . . . and Emily turned and kept on moving toward the exit while fighting back an anxious blush.

"Athena," she said, and her sister ran over to be closer. Maple was hovering nearby as well while Trinity and Teddy lingered around the group behind them.

"What's wrong, Boss?" Athena asked.

Emily pitched her voice low so that the potential minions couldn't hear. "Can you use your Parliamental skill to see if they're trustworthy?"

Athena bobbed her head. "I've been trying already, and they don't seem to be bad. But if you could give me some time sitting across from them, then I'll be able to dig in deeper. I can tell when someone's lying, you know?"

"That'll come in handy," Emily said. She reached down and patted Athena on the head, which of course got the girl preening. At least for a moment. "But I still remember that you're the one who started all of this mess."

Athena stiffened, but she stayed by Emily's side as she led the entire gaggle up a staircase and into the darkened interior of the main subway station building. Then they filed out of the side door.

Emily turned toward Teddy. "Did you take the key to this place with you?" she asked. The padlock on the outside of the door was unhooked.

"No, should I have?" Teddy asked.

"Oh," Alea Iacta said. "It wasn't locked correctly when I tried it."

Emily frowned. This entrance should have been more secure. It did lead into the underground where she and her sisters basically lived. Then again, how secure could they make something against Alea Iacta's luck-based powers?

Azzip's Pizzeria was only a few blocks over, but with an entire gaggle of sisters trailing after her, not to mention the four new minions and Alea Iacta taking up the rear, the trip over was . . . somewhat complicated.

It was made more complicated by the minions insisting on doing small talk. "So, um, Boss," one of them said. The tall guy. "Boss is your name, right?"

"That's my, ah, Mask name," Emily agreed. "What are your names?" she asked. It seemed like a good time to do that, and she couldn't think of a way to engineer a conversation to get there on her own.

"I'm Liam," the tall, muscular boy said.

"Ethan," the guy next to him replied. He was rather handsome, too, though not in the same *works out a lot* kind of way.

"Chloe," the girl said with a little wave.

"And I'm Lucas," Lucas said. "Are we going to use our actual names if we do work for you?"

"Um," Emily said. "No, I guess you don't have to. We could come up with something."

Lucas nodded. "We'll have to be careful. We don't want names that make people think we're Masks."

"Minion names?" Chloe asked. "Or . . . wait, *minions* has too Villain-ous a connotation to it. Sidekicks?"

"I don't think we count as sidekicks either," Liam said. "Hired hands?"

"That's not right either," Lucas said. "Anyway. We could have themed naming, like . . . fruit or something."

Chloe laughed. "I guess that would make me Miss Pear, huh?"

"Dibs on Eggplant," Liam said.

Ethan snorted. "Cucumber, then."

"Maybe fruits and vegetables weren't that great of an idea," Lucas admitted.

"Guys, not in front of the kids," Emily said. The minions glanced between one another and winced.

Teddy tilted her head back. "What's that mean? No eating veggies any-more? Because I'm all for that."

"What?" Trinity complained. "Vegetables are great! They get all mushy and smell strong, so it's super easy to find them!"

Emily decided not to wonder too deeply about what Trinity meant by that. They were almost at Azzip's Pizzeria, and she could see Sam's mini-van parked out in the alley next to the place. They'd gathered a few strange looks on their walk through the city, but not too many. It was midday, just a bit before most people would be out and busy, so things were rather quiet, which she definitely appreciated.

Sam was waiting for them behind the pizza parlor, wearing a bright red half-face mask and leaning against one of the old brick walls. "Boss," she said. "And the new recruits too. Pleased to meet you. I'm Minion Red."

"Oh, color themes," Lucas said.

"Do we get to pick?" Chloe asked. "Because I have *opinions* about being pink."

"You'd rather not?" Sam guessed.

"It's way too girlish a color," Chloe agreed.

Emily decided to stay out of any conversations relating to fashion, Mask or otherwise. Her concerns when it came to clothes mostly involved blending into the crowd, going unnoticed, or which kind of pajamas felt nicest.

"Sa— Minion Red, I was hoping you could do the, ah, talking," Emily said. "For the, ah, onboarding? Athena will help you."

"Yeah, sure," Sam said. "I ordered two extra-larges. Rose has a little break room in the back. It'll be tight, but we can have our chat there. Or in the alley, but that's a bit . . . lame."

"Great," Emily said. "How about you, ah, take care of that, and I'll stay out here and keep an eye on some of my sisters. So that we're not too crowded."

Sam gave her a *look*, and Emily knew that she knew that Emily was just trying to get out of having to socialize.

"I'm sure we'll all fit, no worries," Sam said with a grin.

Sometimes, Emily wondered who the real Villain was in their little organization.

~~~~~~~~~~

CHAPTER TWELVE

Head Minion

Sam leaned against the wall, because getting a seat at the moment wasn't in the cards, even if her feet were killing her.

The back room of Azzip's Pizzeria was far too tight for this kind of clandestine event, but at the same time, the decor *worked*. The room had several fridges and racks for packages of cheese and flour and a few huge floor-to-ceiling stacks of unfolded cardboard pizza boxes. There were two small tables, one near the door where they'd stacked the pizzas they'd bought (and where Emily's brats were congregating to grab as much food as they could), and a bigger table in the middle of the room with some seats around it.

They'd put four seats on one side, and one opposite. That's where Emily was sitting, looking intimidating as hell and yet also exuding anxious energy. It didn't help that she was sitting on a tall stool, which made her tip forward a little bit and which made her knees brush against the underside of the table. She towered over the new minions in a way that was making all four of them lean away.

Sam had grown rather fond of Emily, in a sort of big-sisterly way. Which was somewhat ironic, she supposed, considering how much of a big-sister role Emily herself played.

The girl was a mess of contradictions. She was a social disaster the likes of which Sam had never seen. It was a miracle every time Emily managed to get through a conversation without having a panic attack. And yet, when push came to shove, Emily was . . . vicious.

The girl had the confidence of a kitty facing a wolf, but sometimes, when she was in costume and things were going wrong, she'd suddenly move and act with terrifying efficiency.

Emily might not have wanted to be a Villain, but the more time Sam spent around her, the more she could see why Emily had landed in that position.

It was less about the clichéd Villainous need to do evil and to do things that were morally reprehensible, and a lot more about Emily not conforming to what the world expected of her.

Sam blinked, then pulled out a small notepad from her back pocket and scribbled that down. That'd be a nice tangent to explore in her thesis, actually. The link between Heroism and conformity, and Villainy and a lack of conformity. After all, Heroes more often than not worked to keep the status quo intact, even if that status quo was patently unfair.

Yeah, that would be a nice topic to pad things out.

Happy with herself, Sam flipped her notepad to a new page and looked up. The interview, insofar as they had one of those, was about to begin.

As the newly dubbed Minion Red (Should she dye her hair? Buy a wig?), Sam was something of a senior member in the Boss's Villainous organization. She was also the one mostly keeping it afloat, because Emily was kind of useless sometimes.

Emily cleared her throat, then looked to her side. Athena was standing there, a long slice of pizza sticking out of her mouth and her cheeks puffed out.

There was a fresh grease stain down the front of her dress, and Sam just knew that Emily was going to be annoyed once she noticed.

She made another note in her pad. *Get a used washing machine for the base.*

"So," Emily began. She always pitched her voice a bit deeper when playing the role of the Boss. At least for a sentence or two. Then she would forget and her voice would return to normal.

Sam was waiting for a good moment to point it out. It would be fun to see Emily die a little inside when she learned that.

"How do you handle high-pressure situations?" Emily asked.

Sam's eyebrows rose. Emily was going right for the jugular. At least it wasn't "Where do you see yourself in five years?"

The minions looked between one another, and then seemed to decide who would be going first. Sam made a little note of that. They were communicating nonverbally without too much difficulty. That suggested that they were all used to one another. She'd had an inkling that the four were friends already, but this cemented it for her.

"Well," Liam, the redhead who Sam suspected worked out, said. "I'm not sure about high-pressure Mask situations, but I think all of us have handled some impressively stressful things while working together."

"Liam, I don't know if tabletop games count," Chloe said.

Sam almost smacked herself in the face. Yes, of *course* the people Emily somehow managed to find and convince to work with her for this long were all Mask geeks. That . . . that only made sense. Who else would want to take the risk and work with an unknown?

"I see," Emily said. "Uh, let's count that. So, our, um, organization isn't affiliated with the HRF or any other Heroic or Villainous group. If you work for me, for us, then I'd expect you to be able to keep some secrets to yourselves. I don't want to ask people to do things they're not comfortable with—"

"What? That's not true!" Trinity said.

Emily half turned to give the raccoon girl a look.

Trinity pouted right back. "You're always telling me not to put stuff in my mouth," she grumbled.

Emily turned back to the new minions. "I mostly don't ask people to do things they're not comfortable with, but I still need to know if you're able to be, ah, loyal."

"That feels a bit, uh, loaded. No offense, Boss," Lucas said. "Just asking for that much loyalty without offering something in return feels a bit off?"

"That's . . . fair, I guess," Emily said. "I can't promise anything too big, but I think that if you agree to help me, then I can help you in return. We don't make that much money, but we do make some. And, uh, the experience might be worth the effort?"

"She's not wrong," Ethan said. "Where else are we going to get to spend time with an actual Mask? It'll make for an awesome story."

"Stories don't pay rent," Lucas pointed out.

And wasn't that a painful truth, Sam thought. She loved working with Emily and the kids, and she had her own ambitions for why she was doing all of this, but it *was* a little costly, especially at first.

Still . . .

"We do pay, a little," Sam said. "Part of our . . . protection system means gaining monthly donations from local shopkeepers in exchange for keeping them safe from Villains and the like. That money goes toward a lot of expenses, of course, but some of it goes into pay. Not that it's, ah, *taxable* pay, exactly."

Of all the somewhat legally dubious stuff Sam had been up to lately, not paying taxes was pretty low on the list.

She was mostly coasting on the firm hope that it wouldn't catch up to her.

"Pay is nice," Lucas said with a nod that was mimicked on the heads of his friends.

Emily seemed ready to go on when her phone rang.

Every eye turned to her, and Sam held back a laugh at the red crawling up Emily's neck and to her uncovered cheeks. "One moment," she muttered as she finished her phone out of her pocket with some difficulty.

Everyone was still watching as Emily frowned at the screen, then answered right then and there while standing up. "Hello?"

Emily's frown deepened.

"Glamazon, slow down," she said.

The minions perked up at that. Probably at the casual name-dropping of another local Hero's name. This bunch was going to be so easy to sway with a bit of celebrity.

"Oh . . . that's . . . right, that's not good," Emily said. "Yes . . . uh-huh . . . um, well, yeah? Maybe?" The girl winced. "I'll see what I can do? But no promises."

Emily lowered the phone and hung up, then frowned at nothing in particular for a moment.

"What's up, Boss?" Sam asked.

"Um. You know that new Villain who showed up recently? The one who beat up Glamazon? He's back again."

Sam blinked. "And what is he up to now?"

"He's robbing a money truck downtown," Emily said. "Glamazon didn't have all the details, but it sounds like he tipped the truck over and is just taking everything?"

"That'll be an issue," Sam said. "Some of our *clients* are downtown. That's their money he's taking."

"Right," Emily said. Sam could see the discomfort that she was trying to hide. The Boss needed to respond to this, and since they were nearby, and in costume, there was little she could do to squeeze out of this one. "Okay. Minions, girls, let's head out. We're going to see if we can't stop this Rattles Villain before he causes too much trouble."

"All right!" Teddy cheered loudest of them all. "Let's show that punk that he shouldn't mess with our turf!"

~~~~~~~~~~

CHAPTER THIRTEEN

Run-In with Rattles

The Villain was only a few blocks away, but that still meant that they had to run along the full length of a road, and Emily found herself short of breath about halfway to the nearest intersection.

Her sisters, obviously, had the kind of endless energy that kids had and were keeping up without any issue.

Emily glanced over her shoulder and winced. Her minions were spread out behind her. Liam and Sam were the only ones keeping up. Liam wasn't even breaking a sweat, but he clearly looked like he was an athlete of some sort.

The other two . . . weren't doing so well. She figured they got about as much exercise as any other college student her age, only they didn't have the dubious advantage of having to run after a gaggle of brats all the time to make up for the missing cardio.

Still, she figured she could do much better, and made a mental note to maybe, somehow, find the time to hit the gym.

Also, she'd need to start carrying a stick of deodorant with her. Her costume didn't have a purse, so she only had what could fit in its rather slim pockets, and that wasn't much. She could already feel sweat collecting on her back, and she knew she'd have no choice but to clean her costume again.

And she also realized that she was distracting herself from what was coming up. Slowing her run to a jog, then coming to a panting stop, Emily tried to call out to her sisters, didn't have the breath for it, then just snapped her fingers a few times as if calling for a dog's attention.

It worked, as her sisters slowed down too.

Not wanting to look weak in front of her minions, she resisted the urge to bend down with her hands on her knees to catch her breath and instead just huffed as much air as she could and hoped that her face wasn't too red.

"Trinity, one of you run ahead and tell me what you see," she said. "But be subtle about it!"

"Got it!" Trinity said with a quick, sloppy salute. Then she ran across the road without looking both ways and Emily choked on a scream. Somehow she made it to the other side safely, narrowly avoiding an ice-cream truck that swerved out of the way. Emily was going to have words with Trinity later . . . again.

"Girls, stay close. We don't know what this guy can do . . . do we?" Emily turned toward Sam, who came to a stop next to her. "He has some sort of vibration power."

"We don't know much," Sam admitted. "His name, Rattles, is public, and I read that his powers make things shake a lot. Don't get in close, basically."

"Right," Emily said. "Athena, hit him with whatever you can. Maple, do you have any ranged options?"

"I left the toaster at home," Maple muttered.

"That's okay, we'll . . . figure something out. Trinity, Teddy, be careful when you get close to him, all right?"

"Yeah, sure thing, Boss," Teddy said.

Emily swallowed. Her heart was still racing, but it was getting better. "Okay. Sam, can you keep the minions back? I don't think anyone wants to actually get into a fight."

"Yeah, we'll stay out of the way," Sam said. "Also, Boss, it's Minion Red today."

"Oh," Emily said. "Right, sorry." She wanted to make excuses about how much she had on her plate at the moment, but she had too much on her plate to find time to do that.

"I'll keep everyone safe, no worries," Sam said with a thumbs-up and a wink.

The others caught up around then, but Emily had her plan—of sorts—worked out already, and she really didn't want to have to go through the awkwardness of explaining it all to her new minions. "I'll leave it to you," Emily said before turning and crossing the street with her sisters' hands in her own.

They crossed another street at the next intersection, and that's when Trinity spoke up. "Ah, okay, so the me that's ahead can see what happened. There's a big brown truck on its side and a bunch of security guys are all knocked out. That other Villain's there too. He keeps walking back and forth from an alleyway nearby. He's taking all the money."

Emily frowned. "Any police?"

"Nope!" Trinity said. "There's some people hiding, and lots of cars stopped."

So, they'd have a crowd of onlookers to deal with. Emily didn't like that at all, but there wasn't much she could do about it.

She made sure all of her sisters were masked up at the next intersection, then she patted her cheeks and tried to shore up her bravery. It helped that things were moving so quickly, because she didn't have time to second-guess herself. "Let's do this," she said.

Emily came around the corner with her sisters spread out around her.

It was a smaller street, two lanes only with wide sidewalks on either side. Most of the buildings here were residential, with a few notaries and barber shops squeezed in for good measure.

As Trinity had said, a truck was tipped over onto its side in the middle of the road—a road that was massively cratered. At a glance, Emily guessed that the armored truck had hit the fresh crater wrong while moving too quickly. Momentum and gravity had done the rest of the job.

However, there were clear signs that this was more than just a freak accident.

The top of the cab was ripped apart, and two men in security-officer uniforms were laid out on the street, knocked out—or so Emily hoped.

The back of the truck was opened up, one door lying flat on the road. Even as she looked, a man stepped out of the back of the truck with a large bag slung over a shoulder. He was wearing biker leathers and a mask that looked like a grinning skull.

There was no doubting who that was.

"All right, comrades, let's mess him up!" Teddy shouted before she sprinted across the street.

Emily gasped, her hand reaching out uselessly to grab at Teddy. Trinity was already rushing ahead as well, and Athena was squinting hard at the other Villain.

He turned, watching them come. "Who the hell are you lot?" he asked.

His answer was having Teddy turn into a roaring grizzly bear that leapt forward, a huge paw swiping out at him.

Rattles jumped back, then ducked under a second blow. He flipped the money bag over his shoulder and threw it at Teddy, who grabbed it with a powerful chomp of her jaws and shook.

Bills flew everywhere, which was all the distraction Rattles needed.

He stomped a foot down and Emily felt the ground quake underfoot. Those closer to him had it worse, and two of Trinity's bodies tripped.

Then the road caved in before the man and Emily gasped as Teddy started to fall into an opening chasm.

"S-sisterportation: Teddy!" Emily gasped.

An entire bear flumped onto the ground right in front of Emily with a deep grunt. She coughed, and the money bag fell down at her feet. The contents, Emily noted quickly, were covered in bright blue paint. A security feature?

She stepped around Teddy and searched for Rattles, only to find the man in the act of spinning around. His booted heel crashed into Trinity's chest, sending one of her bodies flying back. It fell into the crack running across the street and then poofed with a burst of smoke only to reappear next to one of her other bodies. Fortunately, still in costume.

Rattles stumbled back as the other Trinity that had made it across rammed into his legs, but it didn't take much for him to grab her by the face and shove her back.

Something he regretted when Trinity bit him.

That body puffed into smoke as well as the air around Rattles *trembled* and Emily found herself stumbling as her entire body vibrated.

When she glanced across the street again, Rattles was slipping into an alleyway.

"Should we go after him?" Teddy asked.

"No," Emily said. "No, that's a bad idea." A power like that, in the tight confines of an alleyway? She didn't want to risk it. Besides, things hadn't worked out as ideally as they might have. There were civilians all around, too. They'd panicked and run initially, but now they were whipping out phones and pressing their faces to windows to look out onto the street. She didn't want to start using too many powers out here, and she didn't want to have anyone see her sisters hurt.

Emily looked to her sisters, checking on Teddy first, but her injuries were superficial at best. Trinity had been hurt, but all of her hurt bodies had popped and so she was as fresh as ever, and rather proud of herself for having gotten a bite out of Rattles.

Athena was frowning, and Emily noticed that Maple was half hiding herself behind her owly sister.

That . . . would need to be addressed, but after all of this was handled, because in typical HRF fashion, the good guys were showing up when the action had already finished.

~~~~~~~~~~

CHAPTER FOURTEEN

Mapley Mood

Maple watched her sisters cheering and bouncing around happily. Trinity was very happy because she'd helped a bunch, and so was Teddy, even if Big Sister had needed to teleport her out of trouble and give her a bunch of pats for her boo-boos.

Maple . . . wasn't feeling so nice about things.

A squeeze of her hand had Maple looking up to meet Athena's eyes, and her slightly bigger sister smiled at her. "It's okay," she said.

Maple tried to smile back, but it was hard. There was a big pit in her tummy that felt like it went on forever, and Maple was afraid that it might swallow her up.

She had ideas, of course. The moment she started thinking about it, her brain came up with all sorts of ideas on how to fill up a hole, even one that went on forever. She'd need crayons, some paper, at least six cans of soda (dark), and some sort of small explosive, and then . . . Maple shook her head and shooed the ideas away. It wasn't time for those.

Glancing over to Big Sister, Maple saw that her own bad feelings were mirrored on her sister's face too. Big Sister was glaring at the turned-over truck and the alley where the bad Villain had gone. Then she looked over at the three vans rushing down the street and unloading HRF troopers. Those were the annoying people in full-body armor with big scary guns and face-covering masks. They were quick to spread out and cover the scene.

Maple felt like she should be a little worried about them. They were *Heroes* after all, her natural enemies. But then Big Sister was right there, and there really wasn't anything to worry about when she was around.

The Heroes would never get away with hurting one of Big Sister's little sisters, and Maple was one of those.

Even if she was the least useful of them.

A Hero jumped out of one of the vans, and Maple recognized him. An older guy with a sprinkle of gray in his hair wearing a very tight costume of blue and white that clung to him and made him look like he had a lot of muscles.

"Girls," Big Sister said. "All right, everyone come here. We're going to have to talk to the Heroes. Which means that you need to let me do all the talking, okay?"

Maple agreed to that one easily. She didn't like talking to people to begin with. She always fumbled her words and felt her face get warm and her eyes watery, and then she'd worry about what people would say and what they were thinking of her. Worse, she often got ideas while talking, and then she'd be distracted with those for a little bit.

Her sisters knew about that, and they didn't mind if Maple zoned out for a little bit, but strangers? Those were scary.

Of course, her big sister didn't have any problems facing a scary Hero because she was so much cooler and calmer and better than Maple at talking about stuff.

Maple clung to Athena, using her sister as a shield from the curious eyes of the Hero. Fortunately, Trinity and Teddy were both more than loud enough to distract him.

"Hello, sir," Emily said with a nod to the Hero.

"Boss," he said. "And your bunch. It's a pleasure to see you here. Doing good once more?" The Hero placed his hands on his hips and straightened his posture.

Was he posing? Maple looked around, and there were some people with cameras. She hoped they didn't capture her blushing. But . . . maybe she could do something about that. She'd need something reflective . . . maybe some holographic stickers, and a phone of her own to program the virus, and then . . . Maple blinked. Emily was still talking to the Hero, but she'd missed a line or two.

"Yeah, we came here as soon as we heard that Rattles was here. But we arrived too late. He was already on the way out. Bandit and Ursa

Minor"—she gestured to Trinity and Teddy, who was still in her bear form, since she didn't have a costume with her, but people would look at the big grizzly bear for a while before looking at Maple—"tried to fight him, but he was retreating already. We, uh, managed to snag one bag away from him, but that's all."

The Hero rubbed at his chin. "Too bad he wasn't captured. But I can't blame you for not doing so. He's been a real thorn in our side."

"I heard what happened to Glamazon," Emily said with a nod. "Is she better?"

"She's receiving great care at the moment. I can't comment on when she'll be back on the streets helping the fine people of Eauclaire, but I'm sure she's working as hard as she can to be back out here," he said.

A lot of that felt kind of . . . bland to Maple. It was like his words were oatmeal without syrup.

"Right," Emily said. "Do you have anything you can share about, uh, Rattles? We didn't set out to fight him at all. But he looks . . . strong."

"There's little I can share with someone unaffiliated," he said, sounding sad while shaking his head. "Unless you and your friends here would be willing to join the good guys? An endorsement from Silver Fox would get you a long way!"

"Ah, no thanks," Emily said.

Silver Fox smiled and looked at the others, but Maple and her sisters all shook their heads with varying levels of enthusiasm.

Join the *Heroes*? Maple felt yucky just at the thought.

"Right, we're gonna just . . . head on out," Emily said.

"We might have some additional questions," Silver Fox said.

Emily's eyebrows drew together, and Maple felt a little shiver running down her spine. Big Sister was going into scary mode. "Glamazon has my contact information. As does Melaton and any other Hero who I've found to be helpful. Have a good day, Silver Fox."

She turned on her heel and stalked off, and Maple hurried to keep up while still clinging to Athena's hand. Silver Fox was clearly caught a bit flat-footed, but that was his own fault for annoying the Boss.

Once they were a little ways away from the HRF, who were setting up a cordon around the street, Maple saw the tension in her sister's shoulders drop away. "Oh my god, what did I say?" Emily squeaked as she covered her face.

"You were awesome, Boss!" Teddy said while untransforming herself. She wobbled a bit as she went from four legs to two, but that didn't slow her down. "You put the fear of bears in him."

"That's not a saying," Athena said.

"I said it, didn't I?" Teddy said. "But you know what no one's said before? 'I'll put the fear of owls in 'em.'"

Maple smiled a little while staring down at her feet and the sidewalk passing below. Now that all the excitement was over, it was nice to just listen to her sisters having fun and threatening to hurt each other like normal.

"Girls," Emily said, the warning obvious in her tone. "Not now, please."

"We'll continue this at home," Athena said.

There was a deep sigh from Emily, but she didn't dispute it.

"We need to break down how that fight went. See what we can do better next time. Maybe prepare for Rattles specifically," Emily murmured. "He had some sort of . . . impact power? Vibrations or something? It's not what I imagined from how Sam and Glamazon described it."

"He was annoyed by us, but not afraid," Athena said. "Not even of Teddy."

"What? You're wrong," Teddy said.

"Nuh-uh, I saw his eyes, so I know," Athena said.

"I bet he was *so* scared that it wrapped all the way around to him not being afraid anymore," Teddy said.

"Was he thinking anything else?" Emily asked.

"Not much. He didn't even want the money, I think. Well, he wanted it, but like, not *want*-want. Like how Trinity wants whatever she finds on the floor, but she won't be upset if she doesn't get it."

"I'm mature that way," Trinity agreed.

Emily nodded along. Sam and the new minions were at the end of the street. Emily sighed, and Maple sympathized with her. She was happy that her big sister was the one who dealt with people for them. "Right, we'll go over things in more detail once we're finally back home. Maple."

Maple jumped, eyes going wide as she looked to her big sister. "Yes?"

"We're going to be relying on you a lot from here on out, okay?" Emily asked.

Maple bobbed her head up and down. Her insides were squirming, though. Half of her was super happy that she'd get to do something to help, while the other half squished and squashed itself with worry. What if she couldn't help good enough?

Emily smiled and patted Maple on the head, and she decided that either way, she'd do her best.

CHAPTER FIFTEEN

Rapscallion

Kevin kicked down Charlotte's stand and leaned the scooter to the side as he disembarked. He was parked in an alley between two buildings downtown. Kevin grunted with effort as he removed two bags from the back of Charlotte. One of them had opened a little bit, and a few twenty-dollar bills were poking out. He adjusted the bag, made sure it was properly zipped closed, then headed deeper into the alley.

He wanted to bring all of the cash home, but that would be stupid. He'd learned his lesson last time, from Fabien. He didn't want a tracker of some sort pointing the cops straight to his new place. So he walked over to a manhole, opened it up, and observed the flowing water below.

He had a duffel bag sitting nearby already. He brought it closer, then started transferring bills over with quick, efficient motions. Once that was done, he riffled through the cash, looking for anything that would let someone track him. Just in case, he picked out a large magnet and pressed it against some of the bills, looking for anything metallic, but there was nothing.

Shrugging, he tossed both empty bags into the sewers and watched them float away.

Work done, Kevin stood up, pulling the duffel bag up and slinging it over his shoulder after making sure it was properly shut. Then he got back onto Charlotte, pulled her out of the far end of the alley without a care in the world, and headed to his new home.

He'd actually changed motels yesterday, packing all of his stuff into his bag and moving halfway across Eauclaire to a second motel. This one he paid for in cash with the ID of some middle-aged man he'd . . . acquired a few days earlier.

He didn't plan on making it too easy to find him, and moving was part of that.

A bigger part was that this motel was closer to the middle of Eau-claire. That meant a shorter walk to get to several restaurants and places he wanted to visit, and . . . well, the place was just nicer. It wasn't a five-star hotel, but the water was hotter for longer in the shower, the TV came with a better cable package, and the rooms were bigger.

Sure, it was nearly twice as expensive, but, well, he wasn't sure how many thousands he'd made today, but it was probably enough to live a comfortable life for several months, even if he splurged a bit.

It would make up for not having any sort of steady job.

Arriving at the motel, he parked Charlotte out front, checked to make sure she was still fine (he'd need to do an oil change soon, and maybe wash her up), and then headed inside while fumbling for his keys.

He tossed the duffel onto the bed, then jumped backward onto it, landing with an "oof."

It had been a productive day. Setting up for the robbery had taken more time than the robbery itself. But it had been worth it. The truck's guards were caught with their pants down and didn't know what to do about a Mask showing up. It was like taking candy from a baby, only the baby was an overweight middle-aged guy whose knees were shaking.

Then those Heroes had shown up.

Kevin's eyes narrowed. He hadn't expected to have to kick the butts of some children today. Or of a damned *bear*. Where had that thing even come from?

Sitting up on his bed, he scooted back while kicking off his boots. He grabbed a remote off the end table and flicked on the TV. Immediately, the room was filled with cartoonish screaming as some loud kids' show started. Right, he'd been idly watching cartoons the night before.

Flicking over to the menu, he scrolled up until he found a local news channel and clicked on it. The screen changed to an image of a reporter lady in a nice dress with crow's feet in the corners of her eyes. "—closure on Seventh and Fifth for the rest of the day. HRF officers haven't given us any information as to when the road will reopen, but we were assured it would be relatively soon. Road repair crews are on the scene already."

The camera changed to an image of the street he'd messed up earlier. The money truck had been moved, he noticed. It was deeper in the image, hitched to the back of a tow truck. A few police cruisers were left on the scene, but it looked like the fun had finished.

Then the channel turned to ads, and Kevin rolled his eyes. "Typical," he muttered.

He took the opportunity to get his coat off and toss it onto a hook by the door, then found some Ot Ockets in the room's minifridge and shoved them in the microwave.

By the time it beeped, the news was going over the story again. He had the impression that his little stunt was the most exciting thing that had happened this decade and they were milking it for all it was worth. Eauclaire was too damn quiet.

The report moved on to an interview with a Hero he vaguely recognized. Silver Fox. That guy with the shampoo and the commercial voice. He was smiling while looking between the camera and the young reporter standing next to him. "Mister Silver Fox, sir, can you tell us a little about what happened today?"

He nodded. "It's an unfortunate incident that ended on a positive note," he said. "The rude rapscallion Rattles showed up and ambushed a money transport. He successfully broke into it, but a brave group of local Heroes appeared in time to scare him off."

"What!" Kevin shouted. "Lying jerk, I wasn't scared off!"

"Which Hero did the saving?" the reporter asked.

"That would be the Boss, Bandit, Owlwatch, and Ursa Minor, as well as a yet-unnamed new companion of theirs. I suspect she hasn't had time to make her proper debut. Working together, they managed to hold Rattles off until the HRF arrived. The Villain fled at some point near the end of the altercation, unfortunately. We'd ask that the kind people of Eauclaire pay close attention in case he makes a reappearance."

Kevin scoffed. He couldn't recall seeing a single HRF Hero on the scene. Not if the Boss and her brats weren't members, and he'd only heard sirens once he was four blocks away. Silver Fox was spinning things to make himself look good while just barely avoiding lying outright.

"Calling himself a fox was right," he muttered.

The report went on, with some cell phone footage thrown in for good measure because that kind of shaky-cam stuff was always popular.

He did like seeing himself on screen; it was good for the ego. He made note of a few things. His costume looked fine from the waist up, but the jeans he wore stuck out a bit. Maybe he could buy darker pants, and chaps to go with the rest of the leather in his look? He had the cash for it now.

Then footage of the fight itself was shown, and he found himself leaning forward to watch it closer.

There was a girl who turned into a bear. Right, so it *had* been another girl. Then the one with three bodies. Or three clones? One of them disappeared when he hit her, but she reappeared farther back.

The bear was teleported back, too, near the end.

So, there was some trickery going on there.

He couldn't say much about the other three. The one in the lab coat was probably a gadgeteer, but he hadn't seen any weapons or weird gadgets come up. A non-threat? Was she even a Mask? He dismissed her.

Another view from another angle showed the tall chick with the fedora chatting with Silver Fox, and while he couldn't hear what was being said, it looked like she intimidated the old man a little.

Plus she was kinda hot. Kevin could admit to himself that he liked the look of a woman in a suit. He wasn't sure what her gimmick was, but she didn't seem all that strong.

The little girl in the leather jacket he wanted to dismiss, too, but he'd caught her eye at some point during the fight, and . . . something about her worried him. Was she one of those Heroes with a too-lethal power?

That happened, sometimes. Someone whose power was *instant body explosions* or whatever who had to hold way, way back, to the point of being useless in any real confrontation.

He'd plan around that.

Maybe that would be his next outing? The next part in his master plan? He had enough cash to live nicely for a while. Why not use some of that *while* to put the fear of Rattles in the local Heroes?

"See if they call me a rude rapscallion again."

CHAPTER SIXTEEN

〰〰〰

Debrief

"Th-thank you all for coming," Emily said. She bowed her head a little, then made a concerted effort to meet the eyes of her new minions.

She was expecting . . . well, maybe not anger, but disappointment, or something like that. Instead, she found all four of them looking at her with something just shy of amazement. Somehow, that was worse.

"Anyway," Emily was quick to say. "Sa—um, Minion Red, will be in contact with you in the near future. We need to go, uh, debrief after that encounter. Thank you."

The minions seemed to want to linger around, so Emily decided to gather up her sisters. With a final quick goodbye, she headed out with the bunch of them toward the same subway station entrance they'd used earlier.

The walk was about as quiet as a walk could be with all of her sisters around, so Emily almost jumped when she felt someone tugging at her jacket.

Athena was looking up at her, a hint of worry in her eyes. "Are you okay?" she asked.

Emily sighed. "I'm okay," she said. "Just . . . thinking."

"Do you want me to help?" Athena asked.

Emily almost dismissed her offer, but . . . Athena *was* clever. Probably the sharpest of Emily's sisters. Teddy and Trinity were play-fighting a bit ahead of them, and Maple had stuck close to Emily's side and was being rather quiet.

"Yeah, okay," Emily said. "I'm mostly worried about . . . actually, I'm worried about a lot of things, but right now that Villain is bothering me."

"The Rattles guy?" Athena asked. "He was dangerous."

"You mean his thoughts were dangerous?" Emily asked.

"Yeah. He didn't mind hurting Trinity and Teddy at all. And he thought we were mostly annoying."

That was disheartening to hear. "He's stronger than us, isn't he?"

Athena shrugged. "Maybe. But there's a lot of us and only one of him."

That was true, or it was true so far. Emily hadn't been a "Villain" for very long, and already she had minions somehow, and at least one of those minions had a power of his own. It wasn't hard to imagine Rattles gaining a few followers himself, and then her numerical advantage might disappear.

She didn't think he was part of the Cabal. While they seemed totally okay with hiring and helping Villains set themselves up to make their own Heroes look good, this felt different. It was too chaotic and messy to be the Cabal.

So he was probably a lone actor, at least for now, and yet he still felt stronger than she or any of her sisters did. "We need to prepare, to get better," Emily said.

Athena nodded. "Yup! Maybe we can pool all of our quests together and find out which ones we can all do together?"

Emily blinked. She'd . . . kind of sorta forgotten about that. All of her quests asked her to do stuff she wasn't comfortable with, so she had decided to just not bother. But they *were* a direct and obvious way to grow stronger. "That's not a bad idea," she admitted.

She didn't currently have any outstanding quests that she really wanted to tackle. Her sisters might have a few, though. Being that they were . . . more or less created from whatever system gave people powers, they seemed to all have an instinctive grasp of how the quests worked.

"Let's look over that stuff once we get home," Emily said.

She felt another tug, this time from her other side. Looking down, Emily found Maple pinching her jacket between her forefinger and thumb, but her eyes were downcast, not meeting Emily's.

"What's wrong?" Emily asked.

"Um," Maple began. "I want to help too. I *can* help. But I need more stuff."

Emily nodded slowly. "Okay. That makes sense. Do you think we could get stuff for you by shopping for it? We could go together, just the two of us, and pick out a few things?"

Maple looked up, eyes wide and almost teary. "Yes! Please!"

Emily smiled and rubbed Maple between the ears.

Her sisters might have been a pack of little pests, but she could admit to herself, in the privacy of her own mind, that they *were* kind of cute.

Athena pouted at her from Maple's other side, an ineffectual glare that did nothing to intimidate Emily. "I'm not cute," she muttered. "I'm threatening."

They arrived at the subway station, snuck in, then walked along the tracks until they arrived at their train base, which was parked right next to the entrance to their current bunker home. It was probably not too wise to have the train parked next to the bunker, but convenience trumped caution.

"Home!" Teddy cheered as she ran ahead. Within moments, she'd catapulted herself through the air and crashed onto the couch.

"Take off your boots first!" Emily snapped. "If you get the cushions dirty, you're cleaning them yourself."

It took a moment to organize her sisters so that they weren't climbing all over. Mostly that meant promising them snacks for behaving, and then she had to actually go and make those snacks in the kitchen. She ended up dropping a tray full of chopped vegetables and some dipping sauce before them while ignoring Teddy's protests about how vegetables didn't count as snacks.

"Quests," Emily declared as she tossed her coat off and flopped back onto the couch. Almost right away, one of Trinity climbed up onto the couch behind her and had her legs around Emily's shoulders. "We . . . didn't quite lose today, but I think it was a near thing. If we want to win against Rattles, then we need to be stronger."

"So we pick up a bunch of quests, boost our skills, then kick butt?" Teddy asked.

"That's . . . essentially it, yeah," Emily said.

"We're gonna grind!" Trinity cheered.

Emily nodded along. "Yes. But we're going to do it in a *smart* way. Ideally we'll find a couple of quests that we can work on together. Something that will give us all a small boost. I don't want any of you running off to do your own dangerous thing on your own."

That, as it turned out, was harder to organize than she'd first imagined.

Her sisters started rattling off the quests they had, and Emily immediately lost track of who had what. So she put a pause on things and went to dig through her school supplies. She returned with a stack of rectangular index cards and a few markers.

Her sisters wrote down all of the quests they had available, then, with Athena's help, they sorted through the heaps until they got a matching set of potential quests.

New Quest!

Charitable Chaos

Organize a false fundraising event to steal from the well-meaning. Scoundrel +1 for successfully taking from the generous.

Reward: +1 Skill Upgrade point for every $1,000 donated. (Max 2)

Accept? Refuse?

And another:

New Quest!

Grand Theft Hero

Steal from a Hero. The more you take, the better.

Reward: +1 Skill Upgrade point for every $100 worth of items taken. (Max 2)

Accept? Refuse?

Neither option was great, but at the same time, they were both entirely doable. And, more importantly, they would help her sisters too.

Emily shuffled through the index cards with the quests her sisters had that overlapped. Trinity was the easiest. So many of her quests had to do with pickpocketing or stealing that it was quite easy to slot some of her options in. Teddy had it a bit harder, but one of her quests *did* fit the bill.

Honeyed Heist

Intimidate people into giving you what you want using honeyed words and not-so-sweet actions.

Reward: +1 Skill Upgrade point for every person intimidated. (Max 2)

Accept? Refuse?

That would slot in beautifully with the charity idea. Not so much with the theft.

On the other hand, Athena had a quest that fit in the opposite direction.

Psychic Pilferage

Use mind-reading to outwit a Hero and take their valuables without being noticed.

Reward: +1 Skill Upgrade point for every $100 worth of items taken. (Max 2)

Accept? Refuse?

Emily chewed on her bottom lip. It seemed like there was no perfect one-size-fits-all thing they could do that would fulfill every requirement for everyone's quests. At best, they'd need to do two separate operations. Trinity and Maple were the exceptions. They had quests that were generic enough that they fit regardless.

Maple's quests were *very* generic.

Ingenious Inventions

Create three functional gadgets to help you and your family gain an edge on the competition.

Reward: +1 Skill Upgrade point on completion of the final gadget.

Accept? Refuse?

And then there was one that was aimed a little more toward helping her siblings.

Gadget-Assisted Larceny

Collaborate in a Villainous action by creating specialized tools used in a successful heist, murder, or gang war.

Reward: +1 Skill Slot for every crucial gadget provided. (Max 3)

Accept? Refuse?

Emily really didn't mind giving Maple a bit of an edge here. She was the one with the fewest skills, and the skills she did have were at the lowest level. So doing more to help her would only get her up to speed faster.

As long as she planned this out carefully, there was a lot of potential here.

CHAPTER SEVENTEEN

Pulling the Funds out of Fundraisers

It was just Emily, Sam, and Maple. The other girls were currently having lessons with Mrs. Headerson, and Emily was discovering that it was surprisingly nice to only have to watch one sibling instead of a gaggle of them.

Maple was at Emily's side, one of her little hands clinging onto Emily's index and middle fingers. Sam was walking to Emily's right, dressed in what passed for casual wear for Sam.

That meant that unlike Emily's own very sensible calf-length skirt and hoodie, Sam was in a tank top and jean shorts so tight that she had to carry her phone in her hand because there was no feasible way for it to fit into her pockets.

"You want to run a fundraiser?" Sam asked.

"You don't need to sound so surprised," Emily said. "It's a good way to build, uh, good . . . PR stuff with the city."

"I can think of a few other ways to *build good PR stuff*," Sam said, a teasing lilt to her words as she imitated Emily.

Emily pursed her lips, but she didn't know the terminology. "What would you call it, then?"

"A PR stunt, I guess. Though I think the HRF would call it something like a 'strategic visibility campaign' or maybe a 'brand awareness initiative.'"

"Wow," Emily said. "That makes it sound . . . kind of horrific, actually."

"Hey, it's the kind of stuff I need to learn, you know," Sam said with a wink.

Emily frowned. "Aren't you majoring in psychology?" she asked.

"Who do you think hires the most psychologists? Mental health places? C'mon, half the jobs are in marketing, and all of the well-paid ones are too."

"That's depressing," Emily said.

Sam shrugged. "So, a fundraiser of some sort. You want this to be big or something smaller? Do you actually have a cause you care that much about? Do you just want to bring attention to it, or is the plan to just make yourself look good?"

"Uh, well, honestly, the plan is to steal from the fundraiser. Teddy and Trinity both have quests that could be done during that kind of event, and . . . well, I guess Maple does too. Right?" Emily asked, that last part aimed at Maple.

Maple jumped, her hand squeezing Emily's harder for a moment before she nodded. Maple was wearing a bright yellow raincoat, mostly because it was the only long piece of clothing they had that could hide her rather obvious tail without making her uncomfortable, and the hood hid her ears too.

It hadn't rained in a couple of days, but who was going to comment on a preteen's fashion sense? Besides, the bright yellow made her easy to spot.

"Right, well, that's the goal, to finish as many quests as possible. Which means, uh, that we need to steal from the event, a little. Not too much, but . . . yeah. Maybe we can return the money after?" She wasn't sure if that would negate the entire quest or not.

Sam shrugged. "All right, yeah, I can work with that. So . . . hmm, any event where a bunch of Heroes show up is going to be a success. We could really go big with this."

"Big means more attention," Emily pointed out. And more attention meant more people she might have to talk to, not to mention more responsibility when one of her sisters did something she absolutely wasn't supposed to. Overall, Emily didn't want that kind of trouble.

"Big means more money," Sam said. "But you're probably right. So, something medium in scale? Do you have a particular theme in mind? We could have it be like . . . to raise money for kids in hospitals?"

"I'm not going to rob money meant for sick kids," Emily said.

Sam rolled her eyes. "Okay, Miss Good-hearted, what kind of charity *would* you be okay robbing from?"

Emily flushed. "Well, when you put it that way," she said. "I don't know. Maybe . . . maybe something to help the city fight Villains?"

Sam blinked, then started to laugh. "Oh! That's fantastic! Yeah, we could raise money to help local Heroes fight local Villains. Then you can take all the money. It's perfect!"

"I'm glad you like it," Emily said.

"No, no, it's really good. How about we go slightly bigger in scope? We could have you make the charity look like some neighborhood help thing? To help the stores that were damaged by Rattles. If you take three-quarters of the money for yourself, give each store enough to fix one window, and call it a day," Sam said.

"I could make a window fixer," Maple said.

Emily looked down at Maple, but all she could see was the top of the yellow hood. Maple's eyes were downcast, focused on the sidewalk. "You could? Hmm. Do you think you could make something to help fix up local shops?"

Maple finally looked up, big eyes blinking. "Um. Maybe? Like a cleaning bomb?"

"I don't like those two words being together," Sam said. "Actually, it's mostly the 'bomb' part that I'm not fond of."

"It's . . . yeah, maybe we can avoid bombs for now. But it might be cool to have some gadgets to help local businesses. It might convince them that we're, uh, not just stealing from them."

"I can think of some things," Maple said. "But I'm supposed to be making stuff to help the others first, right?"

"That's right," Emily said. "I don't know exactly what would help them, though. Buy whatever you need, as long as it doesn't cost too much."

They had parked Sam's van in a lot not too far away, so they'd be able to carry things back to it. One of the big advantages of moving from the dorm to the bunker was the added space they now had. Maple had started to set up a little workshop where she could make stuff. At the moment it looked like an arts and crafts station, if Emily ignored the toaster railgun hanging off the wall.

Emily and Sam came to a slow stop at the next intersection. They'd arrived close to a bunch of stores, but now they had to decide where to go.

"What do you need first?" Emily asked Maple.

"Um," Maple said. "I had a few ideas. But they'll each need different stuff."

"What're your ideas?" Sam asked.

Maple nodded. "Well, I was thinking I could make one tool for each of my sisters? Teddy needs a hammer and a sickle, she keeps talking about those. But I think I want to start with the hammer first? So I need a hammer for her. Um, for Athena? I actually have two ideas for her. One's a thing that'll improve her range, and another is a notebook that can send notes back in time."

"That's . . . broken," Sam muttered.

Maple blinked. "But how can it be broken if I haven't made it yet?"

"No, I meant . . . Never mind, go on," Sam said.

"Okay. Well, Trinity . . . I think I can make her a poncho of invisibility. She'll need three, though."

Emily didn't like that idea. Trinity was . . . Trinity, and her being invisible would make her a nightmare at home. On the other hand, Trinity being invisible would also keep her safer, and make her an even bigger nightmare for Villains to deal with. "Okay," Emily said. "What else?"

Maple blushed a bit. "I wanted to make you business cards, so that people know who you are," she said. "I had an idea for a little card maker?"

"Aw, that's cute," Sam said.

Emily nodded. "That's a very nice idea," she said.

"And . . . and I have two more ideas," Maple said. "For Steffie, Mrs. Headerson's daughter. Um. She doesn't like her wheelchair, so I thought I could make her something better. But that's a big project."

Emily felt a little twist in her heart, and she gave Maple a hug to relieve it. "That's a very sweet idea," she said.

"You think I should give Steffie a warmech too?" Maple asked.

"Uh . . . we'll work out the details on that with her mom, maybe?" Emily said.

"Okay," Maple said. "And my last idea was a weapon to deal with Rattles."

"A gun?" Sam asked.

Maple shook her head. "No. Something to counter his powers. I think they work by vibrating things. So I want to make an Anti-Vibrator."

Sam snorted, and Emily felt herself flushing a little all over again.

"Well," Sam said. "As long as you don't set it off near my room, we're golden."

"Sam," Emily hissed warningly. Maple stared at her, a bit confused. "Anyway. Let's head over to the hardware store first. You need a hammer, right?"

Maple bobbed her head up and down in a quick nod. "Yes, please!"

Emily took Maple's hand in hers again, and off they went, continuing their quest to find the stuff Maple needed to bring Rattles down a notch or two.

CHAPTER EIGHTEEN

~~~~~~~~~~

Beaver Shopping

Maple wandered through the aisles of the hardware store, her head tilted so far back that she was developing a crick in her neck.

There was so much *stuff* here. Big power tools, hundreds of pieces of wood, furniture, plumbing parts by the bucketful, actual buckets, paints in cans and spray bottles, gardening supplies, and one section that was nothing but lights, all of them lit up so that it created a dazzling tunnel with dozens of chandeliers hanging from above.

Maple had a budget, though, and she didn't want to spend it all here.

So she focused very hard, and pushed the intrusive thoughts away.

Yes, she *could* turn that chandelier into a spinning strobe light machine if she combined it with that drill over there. And sure, she could make that power washing machine that was on sale be able to cut through cement with some of those plumbing things, but that wasn't what she was here for.

Her brain felt like a bunch of little streams, all pouring together to form a larger, untamed river, but she was working hard to dam all the thoughts and keep things flowing the way she wanted.

Big Sister Emily and Sam were behind her, pushing a cart along, and Maple knew that her flitting around from rack to rack was probably a bit embarrassing. She suppressed that too. She could be humiliated about her pitter-pattering heart *later*.

"So, what are we looking for?" Emily asked.

"Hammer," Maple said.

Emily nodded and they both pretended not to hear Sam's snort.

She found a hammer. Unfortunately, it was next to other, cooler-looking hammers. There were mallets, and sledge hammers, and rabbit-eared hammers with wooden shafts and rubber shafts and some that were vibration-absorbent.

Maple looked at all of them, her power leaking out and telling her all sorts of things that could be done with these. "I don't know which one to pick," she admitted.

Emily came closer, then squatted down next to Maple. "Hmm. How about that one?" She pointed to a smaller hammer with a wooden shaft. The back of it was angled slightly, without any ears for nail-pulling. "It looks nice?"

Maple bobbed her head and took the hammer, then she got onto her tippy-toes and dropped it into the basket.

She'd need more than a hammer to make what she wanted to make, of course, but it was the big part for Teddy's . . . weapon? Gift? Tool? For what she wanted to make for Teddy. "Okay," she said. "I need some springs and dials and a small pressure gauge too."

They ended up walking through the store for well over an hour, Maple picking up a thing here or there, always aware of the rather big numbers tied to some of the stuff she was getting. She could feel her budget shrink with each purchase.

It was a whole new kind of anxiety, but she was determined to push through.

In the end, the cart wasn't even a quarter full as they paid up and left, and still, it cost over half of the five hundred dollars Emily had given her.

"O-okay," Maple said. "I still need more stuff." A lot more.

Fortunately, the next stop was a dollar store. Unfortunately, nothing was a dollar there. She still picked up a couple of clocks, some simple wind-up toys, and a few cleaning supplies. Another chunk of her money disappeared in exchange for two bags that Sam lugged around for her.

They started the long trek to an electronic hobby shop, and Maple was worried that things there would be the most expensive.

Maple decided to push her stress aside for the moment, and the best way to do that was to allow herself to be distracted. She was walking between Big Sister Emily and Sam, so she tilted her head back a bit and listened in on their conversation.

They'd moved on from talking about their plans for the charity thing and were now chattering about training, of all things.

"It's really not a bad idea," Emily was saying. "We keep running into these situations, and then I have to think of what to do on the spot. It's hard, it's stressful, and I never know if I'm doing the right thing. Some-times I lie in bed and come up with these wild scenarios and try to think of what I'll do in them, but that's never been too helpful."

"Is that normal for you?" Sam asked.

"Lying in bed and stressing?" Maple's big sister shrugged. "Yes? I used to daydream all the time about talking to new friends or whatever. I'd have entire conversations planned out. Surprisingly, I don't do that as much anymore. Being a . . . Hero is so much more stressful that I don't have as much time for my old social anxiety, you know?"

"I can only guess," Sam said. "It's an interesting solution to having dif-ficulty talking to people."

"I don't think it's a *good* solution by any means," Emily said. "Any-way, training. I think if we make a game of it, they'll all join in with no problems."

"Depends on what you're training for," Sam said. "But yeah, I think most things could be turned into games. Hide-and-seek for stealth train-ing, tag for cardio and to learn how to run better. I think one of the new minions is really into fitness. He could do a crash course on muscle training."

"Is that good for, uh, kids?" Emily asked.

"I have no idea," Sam said. "There's jungle gyms at the park. Could be good for learning basic parkour."

Emily shook her head. "Do you think we'd need parkour?"

Sam glanced at Emily. "Obviously. You'll want to participate too, you know. I saw how winded you were the other day."

Big Sister Emily groaned, but she didn't deny it. Maple thought that Sam's idea of training sounded like fun. She wasn't sure what a parkour was, but the rest seemed nice.

"I think I could get your entire group signed up for a martial arts class for fairly cheap," Sam said. "There's a few for girls around the college. Self-defense stuff. It's not exactly martial arts, but like, very basic self-defense stuff. I think they're free? Or at least pretty cheap. And if that works out, you might want to do grapple training and stuff like that."

Emily nodded slowly. "Yeah, that makes plenty of sense. I'm just not sure I want to subject myself to that, but . . . yeah, I also don't want to get hurt. And the girls will love it."

"Hey, on the plus side, it'll tire them right out," Sam said. "Maybe. Fifty-fifty odds that if they get tired enough, they'll go right to sleep once you get back."

"Oh, that does sound nice," Emily agreed.

"I could make something to make people fall asleep," Maple said.

Emily blinked, then smiled, shifted her bags around to free a hand, and patted Maple on the head. "Thanks, Maple. But I think we're all right. I don't think your sisters need help sleeping. Though one of these days it'd be nice to not wake up to everyone piled up on my bed."

Maple didn't understand. Sleeping while cuddled with her sisters was the best way to sleep. It was warm and safe.

Unless she woke up and had to pee. Then it was the worst, because there were so many sisters to climb over. Especially if Teddy was hugging her. Then it was almost impossible to get out because it was impossible to wake Teddy up, and she was very strong.

Also, if she woke up one of Trinity, then all of Trinity woke up, and that was kind of annoying.

But it was worth it.

"Hey, let's stop and grab something to drink for the road," Sam said with a gesture to a smoothie place.

Maple wasn't going to disagree with that. So the three of them slipped into the smoothie place, and she got a medium strawberry thing that was very cold and sweet, and it made her head hurt a lot when she sipped it until Big Sister Emily told her she needed to slow down, but that was nice too.

The electronics store was a lot less stressful after that, even if nothing had really changed. She picked out a few things, then winced at the register as they went five dollars past her budget. But Big Sister Emily didn't even blink as she paid that little bit more.

Maple held on to her drink with one hand and Emily with the other as they left the store. Part of her mind was on all the stuff she'd get to make once they got back home, but another part was just happy.

Today might have been a little stressful, but it had also been very nice.

She'd bet her sisters would be so envious when they found out, but then Maple was going to make them some awesome gifts and that would make it all better!

CHAPTER NINETEEN

~~~~~~

Charity Case

Emily imagined that hiring someone like Sam would either be entirely impossible, or cost far, far more than Emily could ever afford.

In under a week, Sam had set up and created . . . basically an entire charity.

Emily had helped, of course, but she felt entirely rudderless next to Sam, who seemed to always know what the next step was. Most of the time, Emily's job was to just *be there* when Sam was doing the actual work, and while that was occasionally very intimidating, it was still doable.

What was less doable was keeping up the pace that Sam set.

Every day, right after classes finished, Emily would join up with Sam and they'd get to work on *something*. That either meant getting into costume and working with her other minions while keeping only the thinnest veneer of having a secret identity, or doing endless paperwork to make sure that everything was set up and ready for the big event, or worst of all, going from shop to shop asking for help setting up the charity.

They'd visited most of the places paying them for protection and a dozen more shops besides, and Emily was . . . a little overwhelmed by how generous people were.

Just for the price of a shop being allowed to advertise themselves as helping, they were willing to give Emily (well, Sam, really) all sorts of things. Tables and chairs, coolers and mobile stoves; a printing shop helped them make some decently professional-looking banners and a local bakery agreed to provide the cakes and muffins they were going to throw out anyway.

It was all coming together at about the same speed as Emily was coming apart.

The schedule they'd kept up had been insane. Five or six hours of work a day, on top of school, homework, and taking care of her sisters.

Emily was burnt out by the time Friday rolled around, but she'd borne it without any complaints, because complaining would have required that she tell someone that she disliked something and it might have brought down the mood.

"Damn, I'm pooped," Sam said as she crashed back onto Emily's couch.

"Uh," Emily said. She was in casual clothes now, because as nice as her costume was, it wasn't exactly comfortable for any longer than an hour. She was considering an upgrade at some point, for herself and her sisters, but that would be expensive.

But she was about to get a lot of money . . . from robbing a charity she was working to set up.

Emily gave in and crashed on the couch opposite Sam. "I'm also pooped," she declared feebly.

Sam chuckled. "Well, we're nearly done. I'll send out some messages tonight. Lucas is pretty good with computer stuff. He said he could post things on a few forums and message boards and whatever. Plaster ads all over Acebook and Yspace, you know?"

"Yeah," Emily said. Her eyes were closed and her head was tilted way back to stare at the ceiling. She heard something clang in the kitchen, and she knew that Trinity was over there making a mess, but taking care of that was for someone with more energy than her. "Sunday, right?" she asked.

"Sunday," Sam agreed.

It was the best time to do anything. More people would be off from work and school. If they aimed for early afternoon, around noon, then it would be too early for people heading out to party or whatever, and just in time for the big lunchtime rush.

The plan was relatively simple. They would put up some decorations on one of the closed-off roads usually used for farmer's markets. It was a block away from an elementary school, a few of the oldest churches in Eauclaire, and a couple of nice restaurants.

Both sides of the road had parks, one with gravel and a bunch of jungle gyms and the other a dozen old trees with some well-trod paths between them.

It was a fantastic place to get people to show up . . . if they had anything to attract people there.

And unfortunately, they only really had one thing that could convince the average Joe to show up.

"So, did you practice your autograph any?" Sam asked.

Emily whimpered. It was a bit dramatic, but that was how she felt.

The entire thing was a "charity signing for the benefit of Eauclaire's Heroes." As far as anyone was concerned, they were raising money both to help the reconstruction of the shops damaged by Rattles, and for the HRF.

The idea of doing the charity for two groups was Liam's.

By saying they'd donate the proceeds to two different groups, they could short both of them, and then claim that it wasn't a fifty-fifty split.

It was devious, and a small part of Emily was both thrilled and horrified that she, a Villain trying . . . somewhat not to be a Villain, was going to steal money meant to help fund the local Heroes.

"I'll figure something out," Emily said. "It doesn't have to be nice, does it?"

"You could do like you did for the kids," Sam said.

That had been Chloe's idea. Mostly after she saw Teddy and Maple's signatures.

Maple wrote like she had a doctorate in scribbology, and the less said about Teddy's signature the better.

Athena's "Owlwatch" was nice. A cursive but clearly legible scrawl, and she liked turning the O into a birdlike eye. And Trinity was actually a fantastic artist. She liked adding some flourishes to "Bandit," but they were usually pretty cute and somewhat inoffensive.

So for both Teddy and Maple, they'd gotten a set of stamps made in a hurry with their Heroic names on them. Ursa Minor, with a hammer and sickle overlay for Teddy (she'd insisted), and for Maple . . . well, she lacked a Heroic name, but after much debate, back-and-forths, and a few arguments, they'd settled on one.

Eager Beaver!

They'd even added a few little flourishes to her stamp, turning the end of "Beaver" into the eponymous animal with a pair of buckteeth.

It was a much, much better name than some of the suggestions Emily had vetoed. *Dam Hammer* and *Bark Stripper* had been awful ideas from the start.

"I think I'll just practice writing 'Boss' down a few dozen times. It's four letters, how badly can I mess up?" Emily said.

She knew, deep down, that she shouldn't have been so lazy, but she was exhausted at the moment and didn't have the energy to care.

Then there was a loud clang that made her jump. It had come from the kitchen, of course. She sat up and met Sam's eyes. Neither of them wanted to check.

The sound of Trinity laughing had both of them bolting to their feet and turned Emily's stomach into knots.

"Trinity," she said as she jogged into the kitchen.

What she found was a scene of utter chaos.

All of her sisters were there, and only some of them had the good grace to look guilty. Maple was staring at the floor, and Athena was slowly backing away as if she could get out of there without being noticed.

Teddy and Trinity, on the other hand, were caught white-handed. One of Trinity was holding an open bag of flour that she and Teddy had clearly been emptying by the handful. There was a cloud of flour lingering in the air.

"What," Emily said.

"We're testing!" Trinity said. She threw a handful of flour toward the middle of the kitchen, as if to show what she meant.

Emily was wondering if the thing Trinity was testing was her nerves when she noticed the flour hit something and then . . . fade away. Some of it wafted out into the air and . . . and there was a pair of legs on the ground that led up to nothing at all.

"I'm flour-proof!" an invisible Trinity said, the ends of her hands poking out from thin air as if she had her arms spread wide.

Emily pinched the bridge of her nose. "Whose idea was this?" she asked.

Teddy put one handful of flour back in the bag. "Uh," she said. "It wasn't mine."

"Don't put the flour back in the bag," Emily said.

Teddy blinked, then threw the other handful at the invisible Trinity.

That hadn't been what Emily meant either, but she decided to surrender while she was ahead. "Um, it was my idea," Maple muttered. "I'm sorry. We needed to test if the cloaks would still work against airborne particulates and things that could stain them."

"That's actually kind of clever," Sam muttered. "I mean, fights get dusty, right?"

"I saw it in a cartoon," Maple said with a bit more confidence.

Emily pinched the bridge of her nose again. After this weekend, she decided she was going to take a vacation.

~~~~~~

CHAPTER TWENTY

Gift Giving

Maple was nervous, which wasn't unusual for her, but it was a whole new sort of nervous she'd never felt before. She was happy-nervous. Or maybe it was more that she was nervous that what she was going to do wasn't going to make others as happy as she hoped?

In any case, she'd asked Big Sister Emily to take her and her sisters out to somewhere where she could give them their gifts, and Big Sister Emily had more than provided.

They were about an hour's drive out from the center of the city, in a nice wooded area with a few huge rocky hills and a large clearing.

Big Sister Emily had said that her family came here to camp once or twice. It was between Eauclaire and where she'd grown up with Grandma Boss and Grandpa Boss.

They parked Sam's van next to a clearing, and everyone stumbled out of the car in a rush.

Maple loved her sisters a lot, but she didn't love them so much when Trinity and Teddy had a fart-off in the back and when Athena spent the entire trip sitting *on* Maple, because while Athena was Maple's second-favorite sister, she did have a very bony butt and hair that whipped into Maple's face.

Still, they were here now, and Maple found herself immediately liking the place. It was open, but there were trees, and a small creek nearby that she really wanted to explore, and rocks, and dirt, and it smelled much nicer than the city did.

The best part was that there was no one else around, just her and her sisters and Sam.

She decided that the next time Big Sister Emily decided to make a super-secret base, they should make one out here.

But then it would be hard to get to the city . . .

Unless she built a secret underground tunnel from here to the city? She had the plans in her head already! Though she'd need a few machines to make the machines to make the tunnel-boring machine, and then she'd need lots of tracks, and a train to put on them, but she was sure she could manage it all given about a year.

Then she could start building a cool forest base! Maybe in one of the trees? Tree houses seemed like a nice idea. Especially if the tree was on its side and blocking the flow from that little creek.

"Maple?" Emily asked, and Maple jumped. Her big sister was looking at her curiously. "Did you want to get the things out?"

"Yes, um, I was, uh," Maple said, hesitating. She wanted to ask something, but it was a bit strange, and she wasn't sure how her sisters would react to it, or if they'd think it was weird or something.

But Big Sister Emily patted her on the head between the ears in the way that Maple liked. "What is it?"

"I kinda wanted everyone to be sitting and waiting so that they could all see the gifts I made for them," Maple said while focusing on her sneakers.

Emily laughed. "Sure, give me a minute to round everyone up."

Maple nodded, then ran to the back of the van while the heat in her cheeks burned away. She opened up the trunk, which was kind of scary because the trunk's door had hissy hydraulic pistons and she was always afraid that if she didn't let go of the door, it would lift her right off the ground.

The gifts were all there. She'd counted them twice before leaving home.

Maple now had to decide which one to give out first, which was very hard.

She chewed on her lip for a bit with her buckteeth (Emily said they were cute, even if Athena made fun of her for them) and then decided that she'd just start with whatever was easiest to grab. Which, at the moment, was the thing at the very top of the pile.

It was in a small box, with some gift-wrapping paper taped to it, but the contents of the box still clattered a bit as she walked around the van.

Teddy and Trinity had gone off running as soon as they arrived, but Emily had wrangled them back closer, and now everyone was sitting on a big grassy patch nearby, even Sam, who had laid down a big blanket and flopped back in the sun.

Emily saw Maple, and she smiled and nodded. "All right, everyone, this is why we're here, so pay attention, please."

Maple nodded back and then took in a deep breath. These were just her sisters, her annoying sisters who she loved a lot, and who were annoying. She could do this.

"Whatcha got?" Teddy asked as she sat up.

"Um. So, to help everyone fight that other Villain, Rattles"—she paused for her sisters to finish booing the other Villain—"Big Sister Emily asked me to make everyone some new gear. Uh, I couldn't make too many big things, because there was really not that much time, but I made everyone at least one thing that I think will help you bunches. Ah, Athena, this is yours." She pushed the box toward her sister. "I hope you like it."

Athena got up and took the box, but then she was crowded by Trinity and Teddy until Big Sister Emily stepped in and had everyone sit down.

Somehow, having everyone sitting down and watching Athena open the package up was worse for Maple. "Oh," Athena said. "Are these binoculars?" she asked as she lifted Maple's creation from the box.

"Um, no! They're monoculars."

"But it has two tubes," Athena said as she lifted the device up. It did have two tubes, with a bunch of wires running from one to the other. There were a bunch of straps, too, so that the binoculars could be mounted onto Athena's head and all she had to do to look through them was flip them down.

"Only one of them works. The other has all the parts. Um, it's a power range-extender. And if it works right, then you won't need to see someone's eyes to read their minds!"

Athena grinned. "Oh, that's neat! What else can they do?"

"They allow you to see things that are far away," Maple said.

That had been really tricky to make, after she broke all the stuff inside the binoculars to make space for her gizmos.

Maple was happy that Athena was happy, so she ran back to the car and grabbed the next gift. This one was in one longer box, and she gave it to the nearest Trinity, whose other bodies jumped for joy. "You made three?" she asked.

"I did," Maple said.

The packaging was opened very carefully. Trinity was going to save the wrapping for later, she knew, so she hadn't used too much tape. Within the box were three bright yellow ponchos. Trinity immediately started to fumble all three of them on at the same time, then, all at once, she pressed on the buttons on the edge of the ponchos, and all of a sudden the only parts of her that were visible were her face, the ends of her hands, and her legs sticking out beneath.

Trinity cheered, then started to run around the field, which was fun to see when there was only a bit of her showing.

"That's . . . going to be something," Big Sister Emily said.

"It uses double-A batteries," Maple said. "I don't think they'll last very long."

"What'd you make me?" Teddy asked.

Maple smiled, then ran back to the van and returned with a small box that Teddy tore apart with ferocity. It revealed a hammer, with a small box taped to the handle and a bunch of wires leading to the head.

"Whoa," Teddy said as she lifted it up. "A hammer!"

"Yeah!" Maple said. "See that little box? It has lights, and when you hit things enough, the green light will go on, and when you press that little trigger, it'll take all the energy you made smacking things and fire it all off at once."

"Cool!" Teddy said. "I don't know what you mean, though."

Maple blinked. "Try hitting something," she said.

"*Not* some*one*," Emily said right away.

Teddy went and found a rock, and soon she was banging her hammer against it with wild abandon until, finally, she figured out how the hammer worked and the entire rock exploded.

And so did Teddy. She flew away from the rock and came crashing down to roll across the grass.

"Teddy!" Emily shouted.

But Teddy just climbed to her feet, then grinned. "That was awesome!" she said.

Maple grinned too. She had one last gift to give, and this one she'd been hiding in her pocket this whole time. She fished it out, then gave it to Big Sister Emily.

Emily smiled, then shook the little box. "What is it?" she asked.

"A collapsible cane!" Maple said. "So that you can look cool while Villain-ing!"

~~~~~~~~~~~

CHAPTER TWENTY-ONE

Chi-cane-ry

Emily pressed the little button on the cane and it snapped out to its full length with a distinct crack that reminded her a little of two pool balls striking each other.

The cane itself was matte black, without any real decorations except for a small silver cap on the bottom. The head was slightly curved, to fit nicely in her hand, but that was it. Just a rapidly retracting cane that clearly couldn't fit into itself but did so anyway.

It was also a gun. Maple had noticed that Emily had . . . mild issues with the toaster-based railgun she'd built, so she had made a smaller, more compact railgun just for Emily.

This one fired a metal rod (Emily suspected that it was the sleeve of a pen) at speeds that Maple had said were "very fast."

She hadn't dared test it.

Emily had never been very fidgety, but she found herself triggering the cane to open and close repeatedly.

The day out in the little campsite had been fun. Emily had encouraged Teddy and Trinity and even the more reserved Athena to run around. They played tag, hide-and-seek, and generally got exceptionally messy while exploring the woods.

Athena got lost at some point, but Sisterportation came in handy and brought her back without any issues.

They also practiced with the tools Maple had made. Trinity needed to learn how to coordinate while partially invisible, Teddy needed to learn how to time the use of her hammer, and . . . well, it didn't take Athena too long to figure out how to use her monocular, but her tool was relatively simple.

There was one more thing that Maple had made, but this one she didn't box up and wrap in flower-print wrapping paper.

It was a small device. Emily could recognize the parts for a remote, as well as a metal box with a few little metal rods sticking out of it and bent in strange angles. It was all held together with hot glue and a generous application of rubber bands.

It was Maple's anti-vibration device.

"It stops things from shaking," Maple said with a self-satisfied little smile. "But don't worry, I made sure it doesn't stop people-stuff from shaking, because I don't know if that would be bad for you. Do parts of the brain need to shake to work?"

"Right, that's a good idea," Emily said. Then Maple earned herself a few more pats on the head for not creating something that might accidentally kill everyone around her when she activated it.

Emily loved all of her sisters, but she was also afraid of all of them. So much power concentrated in such little, remorseless packages was kind of terrifying.

Coming back home from their little trip was much easier than heading out.

Maple had drained her social batteries and was extra quiet, and all the others had run around for hours. They were stuck somewhere between starving and exhausted, so the drive back to Eauclaire had been blissfully quiet.

"We should get them to run around like that more often," Sam murmured.

"Yeah," Emily agreed. "It's nice."

She turned in her seat and looked into the back of the van.

The girls were sleeping. Or some of them were, in any case. Teddy had her head tilted way back in a way that would lead to the worst crick in her neck if she were an adult. Her mouth was wide open and she was letting out small gargling sounds.

One of Trinity was lying on Teddy's lap while another had her head on Teddy's shoulder. The third was lying on the floor, nestled between Athena's knees.

Athena and Maple were more or less awake, talking to each other in low voices, but it was mostly Athena who was chatting, and even then, her head kept falling forward and then jumping back up as she fought against sleep.

Emily took out her phone, positioned it against the headrest, then snapped a picture. Her mom would like it, even if the girls had a concerning amount of mud clinging to their shins.

They got home soon enough, and then Emily had to herd her sleepy sisters into the bunker. She insisted on showers for all of them, no matter how much they complained. She said goodbye to Sam while cooking a very large pot of mac and cheese, then fed her gaggle of sisters and sent them to bed.

Emily found herself standing in their living room, the exhaustion catching up with her now, but there was still so much to do. She had schoolwork to look over, plans to verify. So she sat down with her laptop, went to Outube, and started watching videos of cute animals being cute.

She was particularly fond of videos of kittens trying to jump but missing because they were so small and couldn't judge their jumps yet.

Emily startled when she looked at the time and noticed that it was half past ten. It was hard to tell the time in their bunker, especially with no windows to the outside. She slapped the laptop shut, regretted not doing any work for the last couple of hours, then showered in a hurry and slid into her bedroom to find that all of her sisters were already stacked up on her bed.

Rolling her eyes, she found some extra blankets and a soft sweater to use as a pillow and returned to the couch.

She woke up several hours later to a knee jabbing her in the kidney. She shifted, suddenly aware of a heap of deadweight on her legs, and several warm bodies squeezed in between her and the back of the couch. She was so close to the edge that it was a miracle she hadn't rolled off while sleeping.

Groaning, Emily wrestled an arm free, found her phone, and stared blearily at the screen. Nearly six thirty. Early enough to rise, she supposed.

The problem was actually getting out of the tangle, but that was something she'd gotten a lot of practice doing lately.

She stumbled to the washroom, brushed her teeth (she had to set an example), then did her morning routine in a hurry before she started on breakfast. Usually she let her sisters figure that out on their own. Cereal wasn't rocket science (unless Maple got involved), even if her sisters did tend to discover new ways of making a mess with nothing but milk and Orn Lakes every morning.

But today was a big day. So she cracked some eggs and got out a box of pancake batter as well as a few breakfast sausages.

At one point, she turned around to discover the entire gaggle had sleepily snuck over to the table and were staring at her while she cooked.

The food was served in the order it was done, so it wasn't a perfect breakfast, but they scarfed it all down anyway like a pack of rabid hounds discovering leftovers.

"All right," Emily said as she sat down with her own breakfast. "Today's a big day, and we have a lot of goals to hit, so, do any of you have questions?" She smacked Teddy's questing fingers away from her breakfast sausage.

"Nah, we're all good," Teddy said with confidence while shaking her fingers.

Emily didn't believe her. "Let's do a recap anyway," she said. "Trinity, what's the goal today?"

"Uh," Trinity said in harmony. "To get stronger?"

"Essentially. The goal is to have all of you, and myself, complete a couple of minor quests so that we have more skill upgrades to work with. Teddy, how are we doing that?"

Teddy rubbed at the underside of her nose. "We're doing a charity?"

"Yes," Emily said. "But go on."

"We're going to convince people to give us money for stuff, then we're gonna steal it."

"That's essentially correct," Emily said. "Maple, what is your job during the charity event?"

Maple flushed, stared at the table, then gasped. "Oh! Sam said we just had to look cute."

"That's right," Emily said.

Maple's hand rose, as if asking a question. "Big Sister Emily, how do we look cute?"

"Don't worry about it," Emily said. "Just act naturally. You'll be fine. Athena, what are the contingencies?" That was a harder one, and one she wasn't sure her other sisters would remember.

"If another Villain shows up, we stick together and run away. If someone touches us too much, we kick their shins in, and if someone asks us too many questions, we go get you or Sam," Athena said.

"Fantastic," Emily said. "Sounds like you're all ready for today."

They were so not ready.

But she expected that even given a year to prepare, she still wouldn't feel ready for what was going down today. So moderately ready was the best she could hope for.

Besides, the event was relatively simple. She didn't expect too much to go horrifically wrong.

CHAPTER TWENTY-TWO

Three Jobs

Trinity had three important jobs to do, which was great, because that was her favorite number.

Her first job was that she had to watch out for bad guys and trouble-makers. That was good and easy. The place where they were doing the charity thing was a blocked-off road between a tiny park and a play area with a huge sandpit.

Trinity wanted to climb to the tippy-top of the jungle gym and use that as a lookout, but that would have been too obvious. Besides, Emily had asked her not to be "too silly," and the jungle gym, with its cartoon drawings and fun pee smell, was definitely a bit silly.

So, almost as soon as they arrived, she gave herself a boost up the side of a tree so that she could grab some of the lower branches, then the her that was up there climbed higher and moved some branches aside so that she could see the whole area around her while she wrapped herself up in her poncho.

If anyone looked up, the most they'd be able to see was her face, and only if the angle was just right. Meanwhile, she had two of her eyes way up high, where she could see everyone.

Her second job was to "be cute."

Trinity found this one hard, and she suspected that her sisters found it hard too. Sam and the other minions had built a big pavilion thing on one end of the barricaded street. It wasn't quite a stage, but it sorta looked like one, and it was decorated with cardboard cutouts of animals just like them, and of the Boss looking cool.

There were some little spinning light things, and a table covered in baked stuff that people could buy.

And, of course, there was a huge bin in the middle of the area. It was made of clear plastic, and they were supposed to encourage people to put their money in there by being cute and signing stuff—as long as that stuff wasn't paperwork.

At first, the only people around were mostly just their minions, but it didn't take long before there were a lot more people, and soon those people started forming long, long lines.

Trinity blinked at the first person—an old lady, about the same age as Big Sister Emily or Best Minion Sam—who asked her to sign a postcard like the ones one of the other minions was selling. The lady had the postcard in one hand and a plastic cup of something blue in the other. It smelled sweet.

Trinity remembered her instructions to be cute, so she smiled at the lady and pulled out her stamp. "You want me to sign the thing?" Trinity asked.

The lady nodded and smiled right back. "That would be very nice."

"I'll do it for that," Trinity said, pointing to the cup. There was only a bit left at the bottom.

"You . . . want the rest of my slushie?" she asked.

"Nuh-uh, I just want the cup."

The lady seemed a bit confused by this. "It's just trash."

"Yeah, but it's your trash, and you're not me, and people say that another person's trash is your treasure, so if that's your trash, then it could be my treasure, so I want it."

The lady smiled, then gave Trinity the cup. She didn't even finish the rest of the slushie first! Trinity bounced in place, her tail doing its own little happy dance. She stuffed the cup partway into her pocket, then handed it off to her other body, which was behind the stage and next to the big garbage bag back there.

That her got to rip the top off the slushie cup and down the rest, and it was very nice. "Thank you!" Trinity said. "I can stamp your thing now."

The lady nodded and let Trinity put her stamp on her postcard, then leaned forward a little. "Can I pat your head?" she asked.

Trinity shrugged. "Okay. But don't pull my ears."

The lady pat-patted Trinity on the head, giggled, then left with her card, but not before telling Trinity that she was very cute.

Success! Trinity still wasn't sure what she'd done, but she'd been cute.

Was taking people's stuff cute?

Well, that worked well with her third job, in any case. That job was to pickpocket as many people as possible.

That wasn't hard at all. So many people were standing in line, not paying attention to what was in or not in their pockets, and with so many of them packed in close together, they were constantly bumping into their neighbors and blocking one another's line of sight.

At first Trinity thought that she'd need to be all sneaky and invisible for this part, but it turned out to be so much easier to just walk up to small groups of people, smile, and be cute while taking the stuff in their pockets.

She kept rotating around, the her up in the tree looking for groups of people to steal from while at least one of her kept moving to just behind the stage where she could stuff people's things in a big, specially marked trash bag.

A few of the people she was cute with eventually discovered that they didn't have their wallets in their pockets anymore and started asking around for help. So Trinity decided to pretend to be a big dumb Hero and helped them, holding their hands as she led them around and asked complete strangers if they'd seen this random person's wallet.

Usually people seemed to feel really uncomfortable about it, which just made it even easier to take their stuff.

The event was a lot of fun, even if it was also a lot of work. Trinity was happy that so much was going on all at once, because sometimes things were boring.

It took her a long time to understand that even people like Best Big Sister Emily didn't *get* how things worked for Trinity.

It wasn't just that Trinity had three bodies. Which she did. But Trinity also had three times more attention to give to stuff than anyone else.

Trinity could rub her head and tummy in six different directions all at once. She'd tried it, even! She had heaps and heaps of things she could do all at the same time, so when she got bored, she got three times as bored as anyone else.

That was a lot of boredom to handle.

But today wasn't boring at all! Trinity kept an eye on all the people, and another eye on her sisters to make sure they were okay.

Athena was basking in the attention, looking extra smug as she talked to some adults and they kept telling her how smart and mature she was, while Teddy had found a group of younger men and was grunting and trying very hard to make her bicep muscles look big.

Maple was hiding behind Big Sister Emily, only occasionally coming out to sign something before ducking away to hide again. The people who did get to interact with her seemed to really like making squealing noises.

As for Big Sister Emily, she looked a lot more frazzled than usual. She was barely paying attention to any one thing as she tried to look at everything all at once.

Things were going pretty well, which was why Trinity wasn't surprised when things changed all of a sudden, and the quality of the murmurs and whispers in the crowd went from normal discussions to a more exciting pitch.

Trinity squinted from her vantage point up in the tree and quietly wished that she'd brought something to chop off some of the branches blocking her line of sight.

Eventually, though, the person causing all the stir showed up, and Trinity found herself rolling all six of her eyes for effect.

It was Glamazon, in a brand-new all-blue outfit that was skintight and shiny. Exactly the kind of costume that Big Sister Emily insisted was the worst and that she'd never be caught dead in.

The Heroine smiled and waved, then paused to sign a few knickknacks and things, but mostly she pressed onward, skirting along the edge of the crowd until she reached the Boss. The Trinity nearest the Boss waited for the person she was signing stuff for at that moment to finish patting her head (There had been a lot of that for some reason. Was being patted on the head also cute?) and then dipped over to the Boss's side.

Glamazon was a bona fide, real-deal Hero. Which meant that she was a problem. Fortunately, Trinity gave herself good odds of being able to take her in a fight. Heroes were always worried about stuff like nearby civilians, and doing too much damage, and they never seemed to remember that they could just bite people, which was very silly.

She'd have to remind the woman if the opportunity came up.

CHAPTER TWENTY-THREE

Concern

Emily knew that the fundraiser might attract the wrong sort of person, so she wasn't all that surprised when Trinity tugged at her jacket and had her looking down. "What is it?" she asked gently.

"There's that explodey Hero coming here," Trinity said. "Glamazon, or whatever."

"Ah," Emily said. It really was an "ah" moment, too. Glamazon being here would complicate things. It was entirely possible that she'd catch on to what Emily was doing. Though it wasn't *likely*. She was probably just worrying for nothing, really, and she knew that, but it didn't stop a pit from forming in her gut.

The rest of the day had been . . . not great, actually, but she'd spoken to Sam earlier, who had gone on a small psychology rant about the types of fun. Fun in the moment wasn't the same as fun in hindsight, and this entire event felt like it might be one of those *fun in hindsight* moments.

She couldn't wait for all of this to be a hindsight moment, because it was really dragging on. "Okay, thank you," she said before rubbing Trinity between the ears. She'd noticed that a lot of people were doing that to her sisters today, and Athena for one had decided to market it, charging people a fiver for the opportunity to rub the feathers sticking out of her head.

People were paying, too, and Emily was slightly concerned about the amount of money being earned from changing for headpats. People had a concerning amount of love for her sisters' little animal ears.

But that was a concern for later.

She spotted Glamazon making her way through the crowd, but instantly pretended that she hadn't noticed her in the middle. That was helped by the Heroine being hounded for autographs by the already primed crowd.

Not that they had a *crowd* exactly. So far they'd gotten three, maybe four hundred people to show up, but that was over the course of an entire morning and afternoon. At the peak, the greatest concentration of people so far had numbered around a hundred or so.

Which was still an intimidating number, but nothing like the massive throngs of people she'd seen gathering just to glimpse at some of the A-list celebrity Masks. This was far more tame, which was exactly what she wanted.

"Owlwatch," Emily said, catching her little sister's attention. The girl jogged over, all smiles. "Hey, I'm gonna chat with Glamazon, can you keep your eyes on hers?"

It wasn't the most subtle way of asking, but Athena caught on right away and nodded. "No problem! I'll wanna see what she thinks of all of this."

Emily smiled. "Yeah, I'll bet."

Glamazon waved some fans off, then came to stand before Emily, hands on hips and back straight. "Good to see you again, Boss. And your gaggle of little gremlins too." She said the last with a winsome smile that probably made it look like she didn't mean it to any onlookers.

Emily imagined that she did, and that the smile was entirely fake. "Hi, Glamazon. It's, ah, nice to see you again. You're feeling better?"

"Much," Glamazon said. She stepped in a little closer. "I'll tell you about it once we have a bit more privacy, of course. But I had to get out and *do* something, and I thought this event might be as safe as it gets." She glanced around at all of their homemade stands and the now-empty concession stand. "Well, to be honest, I was expecting something . . . more?"

"Well, I guess you're used to, um, officially sanctioned events. This is a bit more . . . low-key."

"It's cute," Glamazon said with a shrug.

Sometimes . . . oftentimes, Emily wished that she had the kind of disposition to call people out on their obvious lies. But she was already working hard not to stare at the ground between their feet.

"I appreciate you being here," Emily said. "We were just about to wrap up. It's getting . . . well, not late, but the girls haven't eaten, and I don't want them to go hungry for something like this. Do you think you can distract the crowd while we start closing things up?"

"Uh," Glamazon started.

Emily didn't give her the chance to back out of it and immediately turned and headed back toward their pavilion. It was a matter of moments to tell her minions (mostly Sam) to start packing up.

The first thing to go, of course, was the big jar filled with donations. That was carried over to Sam's van, parked just out of sight, and the money was dumped into a nice, convenient large sandwich bag.

"So," Emily said to Athena as they started on the way back. The money was now safely hidden under the van's carpet. "Did you get anything from Glamazon?"

"She really didn't like that you told her what to do," Athena said. "She also likes you."

Emily tripped over nothing. "She what?" she asked as she regained her balance.

Athena nodded. "She thinks you're friends, because you're both Heroes, and because you were nice to her." Athena smiled, extremely smug. "Good job, Big Sister, you tricked the Hero real well!"

"Uh, right. She likes me as a friend, right? Just to be entirely clear."

Athena blinked. "Huh? Oh, yeah, she doesn't like you the way a sister would like you."

"Right," Emily said. She wasn't going to dig into that. In fact, she was going to forget all about it, because the other option was to mention it to someone like Sam, who would definitely want to dig into the psychology of her sister's interpretation of platonic and familial love.

They returned to find that the minions had been hard at work packing things up, and even with Glamazon distracting the crowd, the event *felt* over. She noticed Trinity helping herself out of a tree (was that where the third body had been the whole time?) and Teddy helping the minions by carrying an oversized stack of boxes. She was saying, "I can take more, put more on," but no one was around to hear her and she couldn't tell because the stack was too high already.

Emily checked up on the minions, told Athena to take some off the top of Teddy's pile so that they could actually carry it away, then slipped back over to Glamazon just as the Heroine was waving goodbye to some of the last bystanders. "Thanks," Emily said. "I'm not really good at ending events like this, I guess."

"Oh? Yeah, looks like this went fine. Did you have any trouble?" Glamazon asked.

Emily shook her head. "Nothing. It went . . . perfectly all right, actually."

"That's good to hear! It's nice of you to raise funds to undo what that jerk did," Glamazon said. "Like a little bit of peaceful payback."

"Uh-huh," Emily said, without mentioning that she was going to steal nearly all the proceeds. "Well, thanks for coming?"

Glamazon shrugged. "Like I said, I needed to get out. And the HRF was nearby anyway."

Emily felt her blood draining away. "What?"

"Oh yeah. This kind of thing? Prime target for Villains trying to make a name for themselves. So the HRF was on high alert, just in case *he* showed up."

There was no doubt who *he* was. Rattles had certainly left his mark on Glamazon's memory. "I'm happy he didn't," Emily said. "Even though we were a little bit prepared for it. It's still better that he didn't show up."

"Yeah . . ." Glamazon said, voice trailing off. "So, uh . . . do you do training?"

"Training?' Emily asked.

"Uh-huh. Like, getting better with your powers, mock fighting, martial arts, that kind of stuff."

"Not really," Emily said. That sounded expensive. And maybe a little bit painful.

Glamazon nodded, as if she'd expected that answer. Then she pulled out a card from a very slim pocket sewn into her costume. It was right next to a seam, so the pocket was nearly invisible. She, of course, couldn't have normal pockets because her costume was one of those skintight ones that did everything it could to make Glamazon indecent while still covering everything from the neck down. "Here. This is where I go. It's a little place, pretty quiet. I don't need creeps staring or taking pics while I'm working out, you know? Anyway, they have a big room in the back with padded walls for martial arts training."

Emily stared at the business card Glamazon was holding for a moment before she took it. There was the address for a gym on it. "Thanks?" she said.

"Come tomorrow, if you want," Glamazon said with a beaming grin.

"Okay, but why?" Emily asked.

"Because if I can't take that jerk down, then you're the next best thing, and you won't be able to do much if standing around for a couple of hours and signing some autographs was enough to make you tired."

Emily . . . had a hard time thinking up a counter for that one.

CHAPTER TWENTY-FOUR

Skill Check

Sam was the one to carry the cash into their base. She dumped the bag onto their kitchen table, then emptied it out.

It was . . . well, not immensely impressive, but there were lots of wads of disorganized bills scattered across the table. "Wow," Emily said.

"Not bad, huh?" Sam asked with a sly grin. "But . . . this is before expenses. Things aren't free, and remember, we're only skimming off this. We're skimming a *lot*, but we do need to hand some back out."

"Right," Emily said. All of this was in service of a quest. Or several. Which actually reminded her. Emily turned to her sisters, who were crowding the entrance to the kitchen and dining room. "Did any of you complete your quests?" she asked.

"I did!" Trinity said with a cheer. "I pickpocketed so much stuff!" Then she raised a garbage bag and dumped its contents onto the table. It was mostly wallets, small purses, a few crumpled-up bills, some keys, and half a submarine sandwich wrapped in wax paper.

Trinity gasped and swiped the sandwich away, one of her bodies running away with it.

Emily decided not to do anything about that.

"That's . . . six wallets and two purses," Sam said as she swept her arm across the table and divided things up. "Right, let's count that money separately, I guess."

Emily nodded. "That's fair. I think . . . Teddy, you had a quest to intimidate people, right?"

"Yup," Teddy said, sounding immensely proud of herself. "I scared a bunch of them."

Emily couldn't recall anyone being scared around Teddy, though she did seem to have gotten a disproportionate number of people asking her to sign stuff. Also, she'd turned into a bear a few times, which Emily supposed had maybe frightened a few people.

In any case, Emily was just happy that Teddy had accomplished her quest. She glanced at Athena and Maple. "Athena?" she asked.

Athena nodded. "I got a quest to steal people's secrets. I didn't tell you about it, though. Is that okay?"

"That's fine," Emily said. "Though, maybe let me know, next time?"

"Okay!" Athena said.

And finally, there was Maple. "Ah, um, I got some points from giving everyone their gifts," she said.

Emily nodded along. That was more than fair. So, as long as they'd made a decent amount of money with their little scam, then Emily would have gained a few points for herself as well.

So she started counting. Teddy got bored with that soon enough, and one Trinity followed her back to the living room. The other two parts of Trinity stayed, and she was surprisingly good with the counting. Maple and Athena, in the meantime, were eager to help. They stacked all the bills of a similar denomination into little piles and emptied out the wallets they'd collected.

"What are we going to do with all of those keys and wallets?" Emily asked. The pile was a little daunting. There were cards and driver's licenses and all sorts of stuff there that was probably important to people.

Sam grinned. "Well, how about we give them to the police?" she asked.

"Really? Like, anonymously?"

Sam shook her head. "I have a better idea. Hand it in, and claim that you discovered some thief's hideout or something while being all Heroic and found all of these. Easy rep."

Emily snorted. That was just plain cruel, and definitely the kind of Villainous thing that she didn't want to do. But . . . well, she did feel a little bad for the people who would now have to get new copies of all their cards, and car keys were expensive. They even had a passport. "Yeah, we can do that," she said. "Next time I'm out in costume, we'll dip into a police department and tell them there's some dastardly little bandit around, stealing people's wallets and any candy they have lying around."

Once the money was stacked by denomination, it wasn't hard to count the number of bills of each kind. Then it was just a question of doing a little bit of basic math on her phone. "Wow, this is just over four thousand," Emily said.

"Not a bad haul," Sam said. "Now, to stop things from looking too suspicious, we should probably hand out about a quarter of this."

"That's fair," Emily said. "Three thousand for us, then?"

Sam wiggled her hand in a *so-so* gesture. "About five hundred for expenses, and then you need to pay your minions." She split the piles as she spoke, and Emily noticed that hers was growing smaller with every split. "Which leaves you with . . . well, just a smidge over two grand."

Emily wasn't going to complain. It was a decent pay for a week's work. She wouldn't have minded making a bit more, though.

They divided the money into a few envelopes, and a grinning Sam left with a hefty chunk of their winnings. "I'll get a receipt from the HRF and the shops. And I'll try to imply that the others got a bigger chunk of the money. I bet they'll buy it," Sam said before she headed out.

Emily wandered to the couch and flopped down onto it. She was burnt right out. It wasn't even early enough for supper, but she felt like she'd been running around all day long.

"Are you okay?" Athena asked as she carefully sat down next to Emily. The others were currently hypnotized by cartoons on the TV.

"I'm okay," Emily said with a small smile. "Just a bit tired."

Athena nodded, then flopped onto her side, back pressing into Emily.

Maple noticed, of course, and she very carefully and shyly left, only to come back with Emily's pillow, which she tucked under her head. Then Maple climbed up behind Emily and wrapped one arm around Emily's waist. She didn't protest. It was actually comforting.

Still, there was a kernel of worry in her gut about not doing anything productive. So, for the first time in a while, she muttered the magical word. "Status."

Name: Emily Wright	
Alignment: Villain	
Alias: The Boss	
Level: 1	
Powers	

Sister Summoning	
Create Sister	Rank 9
Sisterportation	Level 1
Double Trouble	Level Max
Healpats	Level Max
Triple Threat	Level Max
Menagerie Family	Level 1
Quadruple Quirkiness	Level Max
Center of Attention	Level Max
Points	
Power Slots: 0	Skill Upgrades: 2	Skill Slots: 0

Her progress wasn't fantastic at the moment. She only had two points to invest into any of her skills. At the same time, only three of her skills *could* be invested in: Center of Attention, which she didn't love, Menagerie Family, which she didn't use nearly often enough, and Sisterportation.

That last one was probably worth putting some points into. She imagined that it might reduce the cooldown, which could be a lifesaver later on.

Still, maybe something would come up? She suspected that if she ended up being caught in some trouble and managed to win, then she might be able to gain another couple of Skill Slots. That'd mean more options in which to invest the few points she had.

Out of curiosity, she opened up her sisters' status screens as well.

Name: Teddy Wright	
Alignment: Villain, Little Sister	
Alias: Ursa Minor	
Level: 1	
Powers	
Were Bear	
Rip and Bear	Rank 5
Iron Bear	Level 6
Bearly Hurt	Level 1

Hibearnation	Level 1
Harder Better Fatter Stronger	Level Max
Points	

Power Slots: 0	Skill Upgrades: 2	Skill Slots: 0

Teddy had a few things she could invest in as well. It wouldn't be a terrible idea to use her points now. Emily made a note to tell her to do so. Unspent points wouldn't help anyone.

And then Emily realized how hypocritical she was being and subtly put her two points into her Sisterportation skill.

Sisterportation
Sister Summoning
Level Three
Allows you to teleport a sister from anywhere in the world to your side. Instant use.
Activation: Vocal Command
Cooldown: Three Hours
Max Sisters: One

Her cooldown dropped from twelve hours to three. That was a lot more manageable. Still too much to really be of tactical use, but it was getting closer. If every point dropped the time by half . . . well, it would only take a few more points before the skill became useful in a fight.

Name: Athena Wright	
Alignment: Villain, Little Sister	
Alias: Owlwatch	
Level: 1	
Powers	
Owl Seeing Eye	
Owl Alone	Rank 4
Who's Hoo	Level 1
Parliamental	Level 1
Scowl	Level 1

Points		
Power Slots: 0	Skill Upgrades: 5	Skill Slots: 0

"Wow, Athena, you have a lot of Skill Upgrade points," Emily said.

Athena nodded. "Yeah," she said.

"You don't want to use them?" Emily asked.

"My skills are pretty good already. I don't see the point in upgrading the ones I have. Once I get something really good, then I'll make it super good with the points I have."

"Right," Emily said. "Don't be shy to use your upgrade points, though. We have them for a reason, right?"

"Okay," Athena said.

Name: Trinity Wright	
Alignment: Villain, Little Sister	
Alias: Bandit	
Level: 1	
Powers	
Eternal Raccoon Hurricane	
Three's Company	Rank 5
Sticky Fingers	Level 1
Trinventory	Level 1
Raccoon-aissance	Level 1
Hide and Cheek	Level 1
Points	

Power Slots: 0	Skill Upgrades: 4	Skill Slots: 0

Trinity was accumulating some points too. And she had an impressive number of skills. Somehow, Trinity had a gift for stumbling into new skills quickly.

Name: Maple Wright	
Alignment: Villain, Little Sister	
Alias: None	
Level: 1	
Powers	

Builder of the Dammed		
Sticks and Stones	Rank 2	
Approximate Gnawledge	Level Max	
Points		
Power Slots: 0	Skill Upgrades: 3	Skill Slots: 3

And then there was Maple. Her youngest sister, and the one with the most catching up to do. But . . . well, she was getting there.

Things didn't seem all that bad, Emily thought.

CHAPTER TWENTY-FIVE

Masks Off

Y ou came!" Glamazon said. She spread her arms wide, as if expecting Emily to just . . . walk up and hug her.

Emily hesitantly decided not to. She didn't . . . *dislike* Jezebelle, even if the woman was a consummate extrovert, but she wasn't inclined to hug at the best of times and Jezebelle wasn't Emily's favorite person. "I came," she said instead. "A friend suggested that I come. Exercise is important for, uh, our line of work."

The gym was a rather modest little place, tucked into the side of one of those outdoor outlet malls. It was just out of the way enough to give the illusion of privacy. The big windows at the front looked out onto one of those enclosed golf ranges, with a row of residential homes across the street. The name, Masks Off Gloves On, was written in bold letters across the front.

"Yeah, you bet it is," Jezebelle said with a grin. "Silver Fox keeps saying that a good cardio regimen is the most important thing you can do, after having good hair, in order to be a good Hero."

"Because of all the running away?" Emily asked.

Jezebelle snorted. "Or the running toward problems. Can't forget that," she said. "Anyway, come on in. I talked to the owner, and we should be good for the day."

"Uh, even with all of us?" Emily asked. She gestured to her sisters, who were being surprisingly well-behaved. The promise of ice cream and snacks was keeping them in line for the moment.

"Yeah, don't worry. The owner's cool. He's an ex-Mask," Jezebelle said as she turned back toward the door and held it open.

"An ex-Mask?" Emily asked. "Wait, he *had* powers?"

"Huh? No, he still has them," she said. "Just that he doesn't really use them. It happens a lot more often than you'd think."

"Really?" Emily said. She could totally imagine herself getting powers and not ever using them. If her powers were closer to Glamazon's, for example, of summoning exploding balls of distracting light? That could be hidden. Never used and kept under wraps. Her powers were a lot harder to hide, however.

Jezebelle nodded. "Yeah. You remember visiting the HRF a while ago? Like, maybe a week after Power Day? I remember you being there with a bunch of others."

"Yeah, I remember that," Emily said. She'd gotten to meet Quantum Mothman, which had been neat. Then she'd worked with a bunch of new wannabe Heroes. Cheatah and Hindsight and Slaymaker. Had there been more? She couldn't quite recall. It was several eventful weeks ago.

"Well, Cheatah moved to a busier city, but the others basically quit or joined some corporation to do advertising or testing. The whole Hero thing isn't for everyone. Especially not the way we do things. Wearing costumes and fighting Villains. A lot of folk that get powers either keep to themselves, find work they can do with their powers, or just pretend that they're normal."

"Lucky," Emily said.

Jezebelle gave her a look at that, but didn't comment.

Emily's sisters stood by the entrance of the gym and stared around, slack-jawed and in awe of all the machines lying around the room. There were only two others using the room at the moment, an older man in denim shorts and a tank top and someone who looked like she might be an instructor or worker at the gym.

"Owner's not here right now," Jezebelle said. "Come on, there's a room off to the side we can use. There's equipment there. Do you need to get changed?"

Emily nodded. Teddy was carrying a duffel bag with all of the clothes that Emily had decided were gym-worthy. Mostly it was shorts and loose shirts. Cheap stuff that could get sweat-stained and would breathe easily.

Jezebelle pointed them to the locker rooms, and Emily made sure everyone was changed and ready.

She felt a little underdressed as she stepped out and looked Jezebelle up and down. Jezebelle had on some sort of tight pants and a shirt that exposed a slip of her stomach, all in the same color and clearly designed for exactly the kind of activity that they were going to get up to.

"All right," Jezebelle said, clearly unaware of Emily's sudden wave of self-consciousness. "There's medicine balls and jump ropes over here, and the room can be closed off. It'll be nice and private. Do your, uh, sisters know how to stretch?"

"I don't think so," Emily said.

Jezebelle smiled. "I'll show them, then."

So Jezebelle led the entire group through a series of stretches. Mostly lunges and bending this way and that. Emily felt awkward the entire time, but she was still somehow more coordinated than some of her sisters.

Seeing Maple stumble through everything was endearing, but Emily didn't say anything except to encourage her. Teddy was surprisingly flexible for someone so stocky, and Athena was all elbows, which Emily knew rather too well. Trinity, however, was practically a little gymnast, and Emily suspected that she was double-jointed.

Then Jezebelle split them up into groups of two. Trinity with one of herself, the third Trinity with Athena, Teddy with Maple, and Emily with Jezebelle. That was after she showed them what to do. Mostly they were rotating between jumping rope, doing floor exercises like push-ups and sit-ups, and tossing a medicine ball back and forth.

"This is . . . harder than . . . it looks," Emily said as she caught the heavy ball, grappled with it for a moment, and then tossed it back to a grinning Jezebelle.

"It's great for your arms, though, and your core. Spread your legs a little more, let the impact bounce through your knees. Yeah, like that."

Emily nodded along. Her back was already damp with sweat, and she was regretting not bringing something stronger to hold back her hair because it was slipping out of her ponytail and across her face.

"So, did you . . . want to talk . . . about something else?" Emily asked between panting breaths.

Jezebelle nodded. "Yeah, a bit. I mean, the workout doesn't hurt, right? The kids look like they have a ton of energy to burn through."

"You have no idea how much," Emily said wryly. Her sisters were treating this like a game, which was fair. They were having fun, and hopefully they'd be exhausted by the time they got back home. "They can be a handful."

Emily wanted to press Jezebelle, ask her what she wanted to talk about, but they'd already moved past the subject, and she wasn't sure how to turn things back around.

Then Jezebelle did it for her. "So, I wanted to talk about Rattles."

"The Villain?" Emily asked. She flushed. How many other people called Rattles were around? Obviously Jezebelle was talking about the Villain.

"Yeah, that as—uh, that jerkhole," Jezebelle said. She clearly wasn't over her anger at the guy. "So, you know that the HRF doesn't look past people's costumes, right?"

"Uh, they don't?" Emily said. She kinda knew that. People who wore costumes were usually tried as their costumed selves. It was like having a whole new, second identity, in many more ways than one. She'd always thought that the government didn't really care too much about that beyond the surface, though.

"Well, they don't, publicly. Some Villains have known civilian IDs, but everyone just pretends that they don't know. Mostly because a lot of Heroes have the same, and it's like . . . returning the favor, sort of. You don't reveal mine, and I won't reveal yours, and if we meet at our kids' ball game, we'll glare at each other instead of throwing fireballs around."

"Uh, all right," Emily said. It made a sort of sense, but she was pretty sure there were some glaring issues with that. "And what's this got to do with Rattles?"

"Well, Rattles has been around for a while, and he's changed masks. Anyway, the HRF doesn't spy on people, but they also totally spy on people," Jezebelle said. "And I . . . might have stolen some very private documents about Rattles's past."

Jezebelle reached into one of the tight pockets of her pants and tugged out a small thumb drive.

Emily looked at it for a moment, considered how illegal that probably was, then recalled that she was literally a Villain and took the drive. "Thanks," she said.

"Don't mention it. Literally, don't."

"Why are you giving me this?" Emily asked.

"Because it might give you an edge on Rattles. I didn't find anything, but there might be something that'll help *you* fight him. And if nothing else, seeing all of his life laid out as a series of increasingly awful crimes might give you the right motivation to do something about him."

"Oh," Emily said. That made some sense. She looked around, then darted over to their duffel bag and tossed the thumb drive in.

She wasn't sure what she'd do with the information it held, but she wasn't going to discard any advantage she'd been given so easily.

CHAPTER TWENTY-SIX

The Report

Emily was feeling sore in new and interesting places the next day.

She was sure the exercise had something to do with that, but she was also partial to blaming the weird stretches Jezebelle had made her do.

The entire day had been spent trying not to limp too hard from one class to another, and sitting down had been a lot harder than it should have been. She felt like she was a hundred years older.

Her sisters, on the other hand, seemed completely fine, even if they'd been running around and exercising with a million times more enthusiasm than Emily had been. Still, she managed to get through another day of lessons.

Her schoolwork was probably not at the same level it would be if she hadn't gained powers and a bunch of little sisters to look after, but it really wasn't that bad. So far she hadn't had big exams to worry about, so it was mostly a few essays and some additional reading materials.

Unlike high school, college seemed to work under the impression that people had lives outside of the school, so the workload wasn't that bad.

Or maybe that was just the courses she'd picked to start off with.

In any case, Emily felt like she was doing . . . acceptably. She wasn't going to graduate at the top of her class, but she'd never aimed that high to begin with. After picking up her sisters from Mrs. Headerson's place and bringing them back to the bunker, she read from one of her textbooks and took notes while boiling noodles on the stove, then cursed as she cooked some canned spaghetti sauce and little droplets of it stained her textbook.

That book had been one of the most expensive things she'd ever bought. She didn't need it covered in spaghetti stains!

Once the kids were fed, then threatened into taking showers, Emily finally, *finally*, had a few minutes to herself.

She decided to spend those on the USB stick that Jezebelle had given her.

First, though, she had to make sure that this wasn't any sort of trap. Emily dug out an old laptop, one that she really didn't care for and which they'd found collecting dust in one of the bunker's closets. It was at least ten years old, and as far as she could tell, had been wiped clean a long time ago.

Making sure that it wasn't connected to the internet, she plugged the USB into the machine, then opened its contents.

There were several files. Some text, others scans of papers, and a few dozen photos.

She started with the photos, of course. They were mostly of a young man and seemed to all be dated. Obviously, they were all of Rattles, but Rattles before he picked up the moniker.

The first was a high school yearbook image. An awkward, lanky-looking boy, with his hair done up in gel-laden spikes and pouches under his eyes as if he hadn't slept in a while. He looked . . . normal. Just some teenager Emily could have gone to school with. He didn't have an aura of evilness, or mean eyes, or anything.

She clicked through to the next images and discovered a full-body photo of Rattles as . . . another Villain that wasn't Rattles.

It was clearly the same boy. The same chin and eyes, the same color hair, but here he was in a costume that looked like something he'd just thrown together. Gloves and a ripped-up shirt and some cargo pants. He was carrying a large hammer, but it was clearly just a spray-painted store-bought sledgehammer of some sort.

There was another image of him in a similar costume, this time with a rough faux-leather coat on. He was with another group of Masks that she didn't recognize. They were clearly Villainous, though. Heroes didn't wear that much leather, or that many spikes.

The last few images skipped ahead about a year or so, according to the dates at the bottom. Rattles was now in a brighter costume, one that looked more professional. He'd discarded the hammer at some point. The images were rough, though, taken from afar and from what looked like security cameras that didn't have the best quality.

The last image was of Rattles as Emily knew him, in his leather jacket, looking thin and imposing with that half-mask he wore and his hair all slicked to the side.

He . . . wasn't the kind of guy Emily found attractive (she didn't have a thing for bad boys), but she could admit that he was handsome in a *plays in a rock band* sort of way. She imagined he was probably pretty popular online.

The text files were next. The first couple were all incident reports from a couple of years ago. They only mentioned Rattles, and his previous aliases, in passing, but he was mentioned as a person of interest, a lesser Mask in a group of them.

Then she found the most recent file.

HRF CASE REPORT
CLASSIFICATION: CONFIDENTIAL
This document is the property of the Heroic Response Force (HRF) and is intended for official use only. Its contents are classified under the HRF Information Security Protocol 102. Unauthorized access, duplication, or distribution of this document or its contents, in whole or part, is strictly prohibited and may result in disciplinary action, up to and including criminal prosecution.

File #: 2357-HRF-CAN-578
Subject: "Rattles"
Additional Aliases: "Bones"; "Shivers"
Real ID: Kevin Lebeouf
Powers: Level 1 confirmed. Kinetic energy manipulation with specialty in vibration amplification.
Affiliations:
Former: The Reapers
Former: Skeever's Crew
Current: Independent Villain
Rank: Villain (Confirmation Pending)
DETAILED ASSESSMENT
Subject Profile and Conduct:
Kevin Leboeuf, aged 21, is an unregistered metahuman, identified with the ability to control and amplify kinetic energy, with a particular emphasis on vibrational forces.

Leboeuf became affiliated with The Reapers (GOI-146-HRF-CAN), a small-scale criminal organization, shortly after Power

Day when he was 19 years of age. A subsequent escalation in his participation in criminal activities led to a parting of ways with The Reapers and an alliance with a more sophisticated criminal syndicate, Skeever's Crew (GOI-159-HRF-CAN).

Throughout his criminal career, Leboeuf has predominantly functioned in an auxiliary capacity, offering his unique abilities as a supporting force for larger criminal initiatives. He has never sought or accepted a leadership role within these organizations, and as such, has not previously been categorized as a primary threat. Consequently, comprehensive personality assessments of the subject have not been deemed necessary until recent events.

Leboeuf exhibits a pronounced aversion to authority figures and an inclination toward eventual independence. This behavioral pattern is postulated to be the driving force behind his voluntary departure from both The Reapers and Skeever's Crew.

In his independent operations, Leboeuf has been characterized by his unpredictability and sporadic activity, making him a significant challenge for surveillance and apprehension efforts. His criminal actions, despite varying in their scale and impact, consistently exhibit a pattern of disruption and chaos, a distinct signature of his extraordinary abilities.

Power Assessment:

Kevin "Rattles" Leboeuf possesses the powered ability to manipulate and amplify kinetic energy, with a pronounced emphasis on vibrational frequencies. This power allows him to produce and control vibrations of varying intensity and scale, from the microscopic level to vibrations potent enough to dismantle macro structures.

His power's impact ranges from minor disturbances to catastrophic damage, based on the level of kinetic energy he chooses to harness. At a low scale, he can generate vibrations to disorient adversaries or to produce infrasonic waves that can induce feelings of discomfort and fear. At a more destructive scale, Rattles can amplify vibrations to such an extent that they can compromise the structural integrity of buildings, cause vehicular malfunctions, and in some cases, even cause physiological damage to living organisms.

While his power output appears to be contingent on his concentration and emotional state, it is worth noting that Rattles has shown the ability to control his powers with a high degree of precision. This level of control, combined with his understanding of the physical properties of materials, allows him to target and exploit specific weaknesses in structures or individuals, leading to efficient and highly destructive attacks.

Please keep this power assessment confidential and restricted to authorized personnel only, as per HRF Information Security Protocol 102.

HRF Recommendation:

Due to Rattles's unpredictability and the potent threat his abilities pose to infrastructure and human life, he is designated as a Category 3 threat. Surveillance and intelligence-gathering are highly recommended for effective prediction and disruption of his activities.

Active engagement is not recommended without a specialized response unit equipped to handle vibration-based attacks. A special team of Heroes, preferably with energy absorption or manipulation abilities, would be best suited for direct engagement.

It is of utmost importance that all encounters with the subject are reported immediately and handled with extreme caution.

Emily lowered the laptop, then rubbed at her eyes.
She didn't know how she could use this to help herself.

CHAPTER TWENTY-SEVEN

Betrayal

Emily entered the Dark Cup the next afternoon, and for some reason, the place felt completely different.

The little café was one of the first places she'd visited as a new Mask some time ago, and she remembered it as a deeply terrifying place. In her memories, it was a place filled with suspicious people, unfriendly staff, and a palpable aura of danger.

Now she looked around as she entered it and found . . . a rather normal, if hip, café. There were some pastries behind a glass counter, a barista making some sort of drink with a loud machine by the back, and a single waitress taking care of the three occupied tables off to one side.

The people here weren't suspicious; they were just normal, boring people. Two of them were on laptops, their schoolbooks piled next to cups of steaming coffee. The others were chatting between themselves, occasionally giggling over their cups.

It was a friendly place, but she was usually too nervous to appreciate that.

This time, Emily was a lot calmer. She was visiting Handshake again, without telling him about it, and she was bringing enough firepower to cause a fair amount of trouble.

She decided not to reflect on the fact that her number one solution to her anxiety problems lately had to do with being surrounded by enough powered individuals to level a building.

Emily didn't linger by the entrance for long. Partly because she didn't want to give people time to react to her and her sisters moving through, and partly because she worried that if she stayed in the café for too long, her sisters would make a fuss about getting their own cakes or croissants or . . . maybe coffee? She didn't want to experience her sisters on caffeine; the occasional sugar rush was more than enough.

She moved toward the back, only to be flagged down by the barista, who waved at her. "Can I help?" they asked.

"Just going downstairs," Emily said. "I have business."

"Oh," they said. "Right, go on down."

Emily was just happy that she wasn't being questioned any more than that, so she slipped past and headed for the little closet-like room at the very back of the café, then ushered her sisters down ahead of her.

They filed down the stairs in a little bunch, chatting between themselves as they went. The current topic of conversation was the value of dolls over little toy cars, or something like that. Emily couldn't quite keep up with the chatter, especially when Trinity was holding up half the conversation defending the virtue of some action figure she'd found in the trash.

At the bottom, they spread out within the poorly lit basement area. The bar at the back was once again untended, and the entire place was practically empty except for one man, sitting and staring from behind the monitor of a laptop at a desk covered in papers and stacked books.

"The Boss," Handshake said. He put on a smile that Emily immediately pinged as absolutely fake. "It's so nice to see you, unannounced, on a weekday. With all of these familiar little faces. You didn't bring that new one that I've heard about? Well, that's disappointing."

"Hi, Handshake," Emily said. She walked across the room, then hesitated once she reached the end. Now that she was *here*-here, she wasn't so sure of herself or what she had set out to do. She pushed past it a moment later—not so soon that there wasn't a long, uncomfortable pause, but soon enough. "I have something for you," she said.

"Oh?" he asked, his attention sharpening a little. "I do hope it's not a knife to the back?"

Emily shook her head, not sure what to make of the comment. "It's information," she said as she pulled out a thumb drive containing a copy of the information Jezebelle had given her. She'd bought it at the college's shop, so it had the logo of a local electronics store emblazoned on the side.

He took it, then weighed the little device. "And what kind of information is this?" he asked.

"It's about Rattles. His entire dossier, I think."

Handshake's eyebrows rose over the rim of his glasses. "Well, that's interesting. Sit down for a moment. Do you want some water? And please, don't let your . . . sisters run all over the place in here. I pay a decent amount for the right to loiter here, I don't want to ruin what I have."

Emily nodded. She could understand that, so she turned toward her sisters and gestured for them to sit down at one of the booths to the side. The exception was Athena, who came over and sat rather daintily next to Emily. Her eyes were locked on Handshake and weren't wavering at all. Or blinking.

The information broker's smile twisted a little, but he didn't comment. "Right, give me just a moment. I'm not in the habit of plugging in random devices into my work computer without taking some minor precautions."

"That's fair," Emily said.

She watched him grab a small box with some USB ports on it and plug it into the laptop, then do something with the machine for a while. The light from the screen flickered across his glasses. Finally, he plugged the USB she'd given him into one of the ports and tapped on his mousepad twice.

"Huh," he said. "These certainly look like official reports."

"You've seen some before?" Emily asked.

"Here and there. Usually they'll be old, outdated things that trickle down and find their way online. I think some were leaked on purpose a few times. This, on the other hand, looks a lot fresher. Where did you get this?"

"I don't think I should say," she said.

Handshake considered that, then shrugged. "Fair enough. Even having this is a federal crime. Copying it and walking out of the HRF? That's enough to land someone in more hot water than you'd ever be able to swim out of."

The pit in Emily's stomach grew. "Did you want it?" she asked.

Handshake considered what to say for a moment, then nodded. "I do. Of course, now I *do* have it. You didn't think I would just look at the files without copying them, did you? No, no, don't worry. I won't be a jerk about it. This is worth a fair deal, and it would be bad business not to remunerate you for it. But . . . I have the feeling there's more to it than that?"

Emily nodded along. "Yes. Rattles is a problem. I need to take care of him, and what I got from that is not enough to really help. It's more than what I had, but, ah . . ."

"It's dry," Handshake said. "Raw information that tells you a bit about your target, but not enough to really work with. Unfortunately, this is also more than what I know about Rattles myself. I can maybe add one or two more dates onto the list here, some more photos, too, but that's about it. I don't exactly have access to our Villain friend's diary."

"I know," Emily said. "I was hoping you could distribute this, though? If it goes around, maybe it'll make things harder for him."

"Hmm, clever. He doesn't strike me as the sort to wage informational warfare, so you'd be getting ahead of him there." Handshake sat up a little from his slouch. "All right. Here's what I can do. Since I doubt just paying you for this would help all that much, sure, I can help you distribute this. Heck, I'll sell it to everyone at a steep discount." He steepled his hands, eyes narrowing. "And if you give me a throwaway email address, I'll send you literally everything I have on him the moment I get it."

"Are you expecting any more information to come in?" Emily asked.

"I sometimes know where he'll strike before the HRF even gets the call."

"How?" she asked.

He shrugged. "Dispatchers make very little money and are open to bribes."

"I'll give you a, uh, number you can text," Emily said. She glanced at Athena, who gave her a small nod. Emily wasn't sure if Athena had blinked at all yet.

"That works," he said. "I can pay you as well, if you want. Though I hardly carry piles of cash with me."

"That . . . won't be necessary, not now," Emily said. "But thank you."

Handshake nodded, then glanced at the exit. "Was that . . . all?"

"I think so," Emily said. She realized that she had probably overprepared for this, but that was par for the course. "Um, okay girls, let's head out. Handshake . . . bye?"

"Goodbye," he said easily.

As Emily started heading to the door, she checked the prompt for the latest quest she'd received, which was now completed.

Action Reward!

For betraying the trust of a friendly Hero, you have earned:

+1 Skill Upgrade point!

That, she realized, was going to weigh on her for a good long time, because something so mean shouldn't have felt so good.

CHAPTER TWENTY-EIGHT

Guilt

Emily came back home feeling . . . strangely energized. She'd walked into a tough social situation and it had all more or less played out as she'd wanted it to. She got what she wanted in the end—more, even—and she probably hadn't looked bad doing it.

It was refreshing, and it made her feel . . . both guilty and good. It made her . . .

Emily hesitated. Was this how extroverts felt? No wonder they spent so much time talking to people.

If only it wasn't impossible for her to act that way without ample preparation. She wished she could, but she was afraid that she hadn't been born with the right genes for that.

Her good mood helped her endure the extra rambunctiousness of her sisters. Teddy and Trinity were play-fighting all the way back, and Athena was loudly slurping from an empty slushie cup.

Emily was carrying a full one destined for Maple, who hadn't come with them to visit Handshake at the coffee shop. Instead, she'd stayed at home with Sam, who was mostly just there to have a quiet place to do some schoolwork and take care of a few projects.

Emily didn't mind that her super-secret somewhat-underground home base was becoming a hangout spot for her minions-slash-friends. It was enjoyable to have people around, mostly because they distracted her sisters and that meant more alone time for Emily.

She stepped into the house, slipping to the side so that her sisters could rush in ahead of her. Trinity spilled some of her slushie on the ground, but another one of her bodies immediately fell on it, tongue sticking out with obvious intent before Emily tugged her up by the collar. "Get a mop," she said.

Athena volunteered to help clean up the mess and Emily decided to leave her to it. She still had a lot of work and a lot of thinking to do.

The message she'd received just as she was leaving Handshake's place was weighing heavily on her mind. Worse, it wasn't even untrue. She *had* betrayed Glamazon. Jezebelle had trusted Emily, and Emily had used that trust against her.

She'd known long before she gave Handshake that information that he wouldn't just use it to help Emily, but that he'd probably sell it and use it to push his own agenda too. There was no way that was what Jezebelle had intended when she gave Emily the USB.

The chance that the HRF caught on to the spilled information was *probably* not too high—after all, the people who would buy that information from Handshake were *probably* not the kinds of people who'd spread it around themselves—but . . . well, there were a lot of *probably*s in play there.

The data was no longer in Emily's control and she had given it away entirely on purpose. There was no way to spin the situation that didn't make Emily look bad.

The fact that she was more worried about how bad it would make her *look* than how bad it actually *was* gave her heartburn and a bit of a headache.

Emily knew that she should feel guilty. And she did. A little.

She felt the guilt of someone who didn't push their shopping cart all the way to the cart corral. It was a temporary, weak sort of guilt, and the fact that she felt so little was bothering her more than the feeling itself.

Had she always been so mean, or was this a new development?

She wasn't sure. The truth was that she had spent most of her life without ever running into a situation where she had a difficult and overly complicated choice between doing what was wrong and right. Sure, she tried to be nice, but she also generally avoided interacting with people to begin with.

Had the system been right to assign her the title of Villain?

Emily certainly hoped not. While she'd never gone out of her way to do good, she'd also never gone out of her way to be bad, either. She'd never cheated . . . though that was mostly because studying usually took as much effort as cheating would, and she was terrified of being caught and having to endure a lecture from a teacher.

She'd never stolen anything, though! Not that she'd ever really had the opportunity or the desire to.

Emily chewed on her bottom lip and considered things while heading to the kitchen. She had Maple's slushie in hand, and she wanted to give it to the girl before it went warm and gross. She was about to go searching for Maple when Sam walked into the main room.

Something about the look on Sam's face immediately set Emily on edge. "Hey," Emily said.

Sam sighed, looking as if someone had just removed a ton of weight off her shoulders. "I'm so happy to see you," she said.

That didn't sound good. "You are?" Emily asked.

Sam nodded. "You need to tell Maple to calm down," she said. "Or get her to stop. I, uh, don't think she's listening to me."

"What's Maple doing?" Emily asked. She couldn't imagine Maple, of all her sisters, causing that much trouble. She was usually very quiet and reserved, respectful even. Unless . . . "What is she building?"

"Legs," Sam said.

"Legs?"

"Yeah," Sam said without clarifying anything.

"Where is she?" Emily asked. "And what do you mean by *legs*?"

"She's down in the train tunnels," Sam said. "She told me she wanted to start making something, and since it was bigger than she could fit in her room, we set up in the tunnels. There are a few little maintenance rooms, you know? So I figured one of those could be a workshop for her. They're not too far, and if she makes something dangerous, it won't be right next to the living room."

That seemed very practical to Emily. She could still remember the destructive power of the toaster Maple had made.

"I showed her the room. It's got a little bench and some old supplies, but not much else, and then I came back up to grab some stuff for her. When I came back down, she was already working, so I got my laptop out and didn't pay attention for a while."

Emily suppressed a wince. Not paying attention to her sisters was a recipe for disaster.

Which reminded her . . . she wasn't paying attention to them now. A glance revealed that Teddy was doing one of her post-sugar-rush naps while hugging one of Trinity's bodies on the couch. The other two-thirds of Trinity were trying to free herself.

Athena was splitting her attention between them and the TV.

"Girls, behave, we'll be right back," Emily said before following Sam out of the room. She gave it fifty-fifty odds they'd make a mess while she was gone, but there wasn't much else she could do about it.

Sam led her down the stairs to the tunnel beneath the base. The cavernous passageway was as empty and cold as usual, even though Sam and some of the minions had installed some battery-powered lights around the doorways that they used so that they could easily light up parts of the tunnel.

"She's over here," Sam said. There were several small maintenance rooms along the length of the tunnel. Emily supposed that they were there for workers to store tools and the like, but since the entire subway network had been abandoned before it was ever used, the rooms were mostly empty rat warrens.

Emily could hear Maple inside. Metal clanging against metal, the distinct sound of tape being unrolled, the usual sounds her little gadgeteer made when she was hard at work. The door was left ajar, but Emily knocked on it anyway.

It was one part politeness, one part self-preservation. Emily didn't need Maple to get startled and for one of her gadgets to go off by accident.

The banging didn't stop, however, so Emily carefully pushed the door open.

Maple was at the bench, tottering on a footstool so that she could reach the top where she was assembling . . . something. They were disturbingly leg-shaped, which didn't inspire much confidence.

"Maple?" Emily asked.

Maple paused, then turned to blink at Emily. She had some goggles on askew across her face and her hair was a tangled mess. "Oh, hi," she said. Her eyes locked on to the slushie in Emily's hand.

"Hi," Emily said. She approached, feeling a little more confident that whatever Maple was working on wouldn't explode. Legs usually didn't. "What are you working on?" she asked.

Maple turned back to her work. "Legs," she said.

"Legs," Emily repeated.

Maple nodded. "For Steffie. She has some, but hers don't work."

It all suddenly made sense. Steffie, Mrs. Headerson's daughter, was probably her sisters' only friend who were their age, and so far she'd been a mostly good influence.

She was a wheelchair user, which limited her in a few ways.

"Legs," Emily said again as she took in the start of what were clearly mechanical legs. "I see," she said.

Maybe she didn't need to worry about being bad all that much?

CHAPTER TWENTY-NINE

Steffie's Mom

"Oh," Mom said from the other room.

Steffie looked away from the TV. She was supposed to be doing some worksheets her mom had given her, and she definitely was . . . during the commercial breaks.

It was Saturday morning! She was allowed to have a bit of fun. Besides, the commercials were always super long and Saturday had all the best shows.

Mom slipped out of the kitchen and crossed the living room, but not before looking at the TV and tsking to herself. She didn't tell Steffie not to, though, so it was totally okay. Mom stopped by the window at the front of the house and tugged one of the blinds down. It happened to line up with the sun just right to splash a beam of light across the TV that made it impossible to see anything.

"Mom," Steffie complained.

"You have worksheets," Mom said.

"I always have worksheets," Steffie shot back. And it was true! She loved her mom a whole heap, but her mom also wanted Steffie to be "successful in life" or whatever. And that meant that Steffie had to be smart.

She knew that having to use a wheelchair made things complicated. She knew it all day long. It also meant that if Steffie was going to be successful, she'd need to be ten times as smart as anyone else. So, worksheets.

It had gotten a bit harder after she made friends. Now her lessons during the week weren't as strict or organized because her friends needed time to catch up. That meant even more worksheets, and most of those happened after "school" had ended.

Steffie bore it with good grace. Or that's what Mom said, anyway.

"They do know it's Saturday, don't they?" Mom asked. It was that tone of voice she used when she was mostly talking to herself.

"What is it?" Steffie asked, turning her attention away from the screen. It wasn't like she could see the TV well anyway.

"It's Emily and her sisters," Mom said.

"Oh!" Steffie disengaged the brakes on her chair, tossed the worksheets onto the couch, then rolled herself back and across the living room. "Are they here to play?"

"Without calling ahead," Mom said. "I hope that Emily doesn't need an emergency babysitter. I need to get groceries later."

"Mom!" Steffie whined. She never got to play with her friends. Well, that wasn't strictly true. They did a lot of goofing around and playing during and after class, but it wasn't the same as *play*-play. Mom insisted on letting everyone out into the backyard to play at least once a day (which hadn't been a thing before, for obvious reasons), but Steffie was mostly trapped in her chair.

Athena liked to talk, and Maple liked to stand nearby and listen to Steffie complain about stuff, even if her replies were usually monosyllabic. (Her current set of worksheets were vocabulary practice, and the word was on her mind and primed for use.)

So, most of her "playtime" wasn't really spent playing, at least when her friends were around. Which was why she was practically trembling in her seat with excitement as she heard the familiar sound of several pairs of feet coming up the front porch.

Mom opened the door, smiling and greeting Emily and her sisters and . . . another woman who Steffie didn't recognize, a tall, dark-skinned lady who seemed to be about the same age as Emily. "Hello, hi, welcome. I wasn't expecting guests, so I'm sorry if things are a little untidy," Mom said.

It was a silly thing to say. Mom was always picking up and cleaning things, so the house was as clean as it ever was. "Hi, Mrs. Headerson," Emily said. "I'm sorry for dropping by so suddenly. We had something to talk about and, uh, yeah, I wanted to talk about it."

Steffie gave Emily a once-over. Emily was weird. She was always super shy, like Maple was, but sometimes she'd be very . . . not shy? Darn, she'd seen that word earlier . . . Not *extroverted*, that was another word. *Commanding*? Yeah, that was the one!

"Steffie!" Trinity said. She ran forward, three pairs of shoes flying off behind her as she left them by the door.

Then she was swamped by Trinity hugs.

Steffie wouldn't tell her other friends, because it would be mean, but Trinity gave the best hugs.

"Hey," Teddy said. She stifled a yawn, then grinned, all teeth. "What're you watching?"

"Hero cartoons," Steffie said.

"Oh, yuck," Teddy said.

Steffie giggled. "I keep watching them hoping the bad guys win one day, but it never happens."

"Yeah, that's just capitalist proper ganders is what it is," Teddy agreed. Then she shooed Trinity off and gave Steffie a hug too. Teddy was a nice middle ground between cool and fun. She was easy to get along with, and Steffie really wanted her to turn into a bear even if Mom said she couldn't in the house, or in the backyard, or in the shed after that one time.

"Hi, Steffie," Athena said. She gave Steffie her hug too.

Of all the sisters, she was probably the one Steffie liked talking to the most. They had nice debates about stuff, and Athena was smart. She liked learning, and sometimes they did puzzles and things together, and Athena would always be the first to figure things out.

She was also, Steffie realized, the more . . . emotionally intelligent of her sisters. That was important, according to Mom. Also, she was a great gossiper.

"H-hi," Maple said from behind Athena. She didn't come up for hugs. In fact, she mostly stayed half-hidden behind Athena.

"Hi, Maple!" Steffie said. She always tried to be nice to Maple, even if Maple wasn't very talkative. "What are you guys doing here?"

Trinity had already mostly relocated to the couch, and the loveseat, and the big fluffy seat squeezed into the corner of the room, while Teddy had moved behind Steffie and grabbed the handles of her chair to move her around. "Maple made you a gift," Teddy said. Steffie didn't like it too much when people grabbed her chair like that, but she was kind of distracted by what Teddy said.

"A gift?" Steffie asked. She glanced at Maple, but all she saw was Maple's face turning red and her focus redoubling on the floor. Steffie knew a bit about the sorts of things Maple could make. Her sisters swore up and down that she'd really made a supersonic toaster, and Steffie had seen enough Hero cartoons to know that gadgeteers could make some pretty cool things.

She hadn't expected to get anything for herself, though.

"Yep. We need to convince your mom to let us give it to you, though," Athena said. "So put on the puppy-dog eyes."

"The puppy-bear eyes are better," Teddy said.

"Bears don't have puppies, you idiot," Athena shot back.

"I know that! They have cubs. *You're* a puppy."

"What?"

Steffie tuned the two out as they started bickering back and forth over her head. She was paying more attention to Mom and Emily and the other lady, who were all talking in the entranceway. "Are you sure it's safe?" Mom asked.

Emily grimaced. "Yes? Maybe? Maple hasn't made anything unsafe before." That earned her a look from the other lady. "Well, nothing unsafe that wasn't meant to be unsafe. We tested them a bit at the base. Trinity used them, and they work."

"You tested them on one of your sisters?" Mom asked. She didn't sound very impressed.

"I let Trinity try them," Emily corrected, that bit of commanding-ness coming out. Steffie was a little impressed. Mom could be very . . . Mom sometimes. "She's uniquely capable of surviving things without being hurt. I wouldn't risk one of my sisters like that."

"Right, sorry," Mom said. "It's just . . . This is a lot."

"We understand," the other lady said. She touched Mom gently on the arm. "It's a lot to take in. But it's . . . well, something. An opportunity, maybe? A chance for Steffie to walk?"

Steffie's ears were burning as she was wheeled closer. "What's going on?" she asked.

The adults turned their way, and the concern was replaced by smiles. The fake kind, mostly. "Hey, sweetie," Mom said. That was a very neutral sign. Mom usually called her Steffie when she was being serious, and "love" when things weren't good. "Emily here, and I suppose Maple, said that, uh, well, Maple made you something."

"Uh-huh," Steffie said. "Teddy said she made me a gift?"

Mom nodded. "It's up to you, I think. You're old enough to choose to try it or not. Emily said that Maple made you legs. Not actual, new legs, but . . . ah," Mom paused.

"Something like an exoskeleton," the dark-skinned lady said, filling in for Mom.

"I want to try!" Steffie said right away. "What do they do? How do they work?"

"Oh," Maple said. "They're worn over your legs. There's a belt too. It should be easy."

Steffie almost gawked. That was awesome! And also, more words than she'd ever heard from Maple in a single sentence. "I definitely wanna try!" she said.

There was no way she would skip an opportunity to kick Teddy's butt.

CHAPTER THIRTY

Bundle of Worry

Maple was a bundle of worry as she watched Steffie try to slip into her new legs.

The legs were a design that Maple had come up with well over a week ago, and one that she'd refined and improved (in her head) at length. It was probably the most complex project she had ever taken on. Nearly all of her school papers had doodles on the corners of servos and braces and notes about the control mechanism for the legs.

Now she was seeing a fifth of her life's work being put to use, and it made her even more nervous than she usually was.

"Oh, this is tight," Steffie said. She was frowning as she wiggled her unresponsive legs into the braces. Maple was there to help, but at the same time, she didn't want to just . . . grab Steffie's feet and stuff them into the right spots. That would feel way too intrusive and rude.

So she held on to the legs she'd built as Steffie squeezed into them, then showed Steffie how to hook the legs into place.

The legs were like pants.

Kind of.

If pants were really large, and made of wood and metal, and had joints and servos and a few trailing wires.

So, less like pants and more like . . . something that wasn't pants. They were designed to be worn around Steffie's normal legs, with a pair of large boots on the bottom for her to fit her feet into. Those were connected by a shaft (a cut-up hockey stick) to the first set of servos around the knees.

Then there was a brace (made of coat hangers and some utensils) that connected from the top of the knees all the way to the waist.

The topmost part of the legs was a thick worker's belt, one of those with some pouches for tools worked into it. Those had been handy since she had a bunch of parts that needed to be put somewhere. Batteries, a remote, some things that she'd built but couldn't quite recall what they did. Normal stuff, basically.

"Okay," Steffie said as she tightened the belt. "Now what?"

Maple swallowed. There was a lot of attention on her, but even more, there was *expectation*, and that was so, so much worse. "For now you can use the remote to move," Maple said. She grabbed a special controller from one of the belt pockets.

"Hey, that's from our Laystation," Trinity said.

"You broke the second controller?" Teddy asked.

"It's a spare," Maple defended. Honestly, she couldn't remember taking it, but they did have two.

"But we need it to play multiplayer," Trinity complained.

"Girls," Emily said, her voice a warning. "Enough. It's just a controller. Not a big deal. Maple, go on."

"Thank you," Maple muttered. She gave the controller to Steffie. "Forward goes forward, back goes back, the stick is to turn, and X kicks. Y is to jump, and B makes you sit and unsit. O is for crouch. There's a hat, too! But it's going to take some time for the hat to read your brain and know what you're thinking when you want to move." The hat was just an old baseball cap with some wires coiling in and out of it.

"Got it," Steffie said.

Maple nodded, then flicked the legs on using a small switch at the side of the belt. The legs twitched, and some of her sisters jumped back, spooked by the sudden motion.

The lot of them were outside, on the terrace behind Steffie's place. She was still in her wheelchair, though she was bent at an awkward angle to fit the legs on. If it weren't for Sam standing behind the chair and keeping it steady, she might have slipped off.

"Okay," Steffie said. She pressed B, and the legs moved. They folded at the knee joint, planted the boots down, then stood.

Steffie squealed in panic as she was raised up, then thrown forward, her legs moving on their own without her upper body coordinating with them. Her arms cartwheeled, but it didn't take long for her to find her balance. "Whoa," she said. "I'm so tall!"

"Careful," Mrs. Headerson said. She looked like she wanted to grab on to Steffie but was holding herself back.

Maple ran a few last-second checks while Steffie was standing. Her friend was actually a bit taller than Maple when she was standing up, which was interesting. Though some of that height came from the thick boots and the legs; they gave her a bit more height than she'd have naturally. The batteries were still over eighty percent, the wires were all connected at the right places, none of the strings or gum had come apart, and everything looked like it was working. "Okay," Maple said. "Um, try walking?"

Steffie snorted, then laughed. "Try walking. Thanks!" She pushed the controller forward, and the legs took a big, slow step in that direction. It was a little clumsy, and Steffie had to hold her arms out to balance the whole time, but it worked. "I'm walking!" she said.

Maple expected Steffie to be happy, maybe start running around with her sisters and playing ball or something. She didn't expect Steffie to start crying.

Maple swallowed, looking around for help. Had the legs pinched her? Was something wrong? But then Mrs. Headerson was there, hugging Steffie, and everything was okay, and then Emily was hugging Maple too and telling her that she did good, so things were all right.

She liked the warm feeling in her tummy. It was like pouring cool water on the burning inferno of anxiety always threatening to spill out of her.

She could get used to this, she decided.

Steffie was soon released from her mom's hug and was quick to wipe her eyes and blow her nose. Maple understood not wanting to look like you were crying in front of your friends. Then she was off, tottering across the backyard with big, awkward steps, laughing all the while.

They started an impromptu game of soccer, Athena and two of Trinity on one team, and Teddy, Steffie, and Trinity (but with a bandana) on the other. Steffie was . . . not good at it, and Maple wasn't sure how much of that was the awkwardness of her new legs and how much was Steffie just not being great at sports.

Maple hung back to watch. She didn't like sports much either, and she wanted to keep an eye on her new invention, in case it broke or she needed to make some changes to it.

"That's impressive," Sam said.

"It's incredible," Mrs. Headerson said. "But I'm worried . . . oh, I shouldn't be, but I'm worried it'll get to her head."

"How's that?" Emily asked.

"What if she wants to go to school next? I mean . . . maybe she can? Though . . . the legs don't look very, ah, professional."

Maple pretended not to hear that last part, and she pretended even harder not to feel the slight sting at the criticism. She supposed it was true, the legs did look a bit messy. She'd seen cartoons and shows and stuff where there were Heroes like her (in the power sense, not in the personality sense, she wasn't one of those yucky Heroes). Her inventions were a lot simpler, made of stuff she found around the house.

The Heroes on TV had cool high-tech-looking gadgets, with stainless steel and hard plastics and little LED lights.

She could do the lights, but the rest was tricky, and she wasn't sure if her stuff would even work with those kinds of materials.

"I think Maple could make something more . . . streamlined," Emily said. "But it might take a lot longer, and it might not be easy for her."

Emily placed a hand on Maple's head, then started to run her fingers through her hair. It was very nice.

"I think I could," Maple said.

"I'll pay you," Mrs. Headerson said over the sounds of Steffie and the others laughing as they kicked the ball around.

"You've done a ton for us already," Emily said. "I couldn't ask for money. But . . . maybe Maple could?"

Maple blinked. Ask for money, from Mrs. Headerson? That felt . . . hard. Especially with Mrs. Headerson looking at her right then. "Um," she said.

Sam laughed. "How about a compromise? Maple will need some materials. Usually her stuff's pretty inexpensive to make, but if we want legs two-point-oh to be nicer, then she might need nicer gear to make it. Gadget makers are like that, you know? So if you covered the material cost, within a reasonable budget . . ."

"That's more than acceptable," Mrs. Headerson said. "Besides, I spend more than you'd imagine on medical supplies already. A lot of it is covered by my insurance, but it's the basic stuff that's not covered that adds up."

"That seems fair," Emily said. She gave one of Maple's beaver ears a soft squeeze. "Is that okay with you, Maple?"

"It is," Maple said. It would be nice to have a big project to focus on. "Um . . . I also have some more points to spend?"

"Oh, right," Emily said. "Well, maybe when we get home. I'm sure you might find something that'll help you improve as a gadgeteer."

Maple wanted to nod, but she didn't want the ear scritches to stop. It was hard, sometimes, deciding what to do, but she felt like she'd done the right thing today.

CHAPTER THIRTY-ONE

Bears Just Wanna Bear

Spending a weekend day at Steffie's place was kinda cool. At least, Teddy enjoyed herself. Steffie was *really* bad at soccer, but it was fun to see her stumbling around, and the entire time, Steffie had a smile that was almost bearlike in its ferocity.

The playtime came to an end, though. Teddy was hungry, Steffie's robot legs needed new batteries, and the older people like Big Sis had decided to get out of the sun to chat.

Teddy and the others were herded into the living room and given snacks and juice boxes while the older people stayed by the kitchen to talk. Teddy found her attention somewhat split between talking with her friends and watching the filthy capitalist proper ganders on the TV. The between-cartoon commercials were loud and flashy and awesome-looking, but Teddy knew that it was all a terrible facade designed to trick her brain into wanting to buy all the cool stuff they had.

That didn't mean it wasn't working. She still wanted the stuff. She just didn't want to buy it like a happy little capitalist would. Maybe she could convince the Boss to burglarize a toy store?

Steffie wobbled over to a couch and her eyes narrowed in focus. Then she did a three-point turn so that the back of her legs hit the edge of the couch. She sat. It was clearly a bit awkward, with her legs at a perfect ninety-degree angle, but it worked well enough, even if Teddy wasn't sure she'd be able to un-sit.

"Do you think I could go to school?" Steffie asked.

"School?" Athena repeated. "With those legs?"

Steffie nodded rapidly.

Athena eyed the legs for a moment, then shook her head. "No, not those."

"Why not?" Steffie asked.

"They're too obviously made by Maple. People would know that they're special, and then they'd get all prissy about it. You know how adults can be. 'Is this safe,' 'What if it breaks,' 'Can she kick someone into tomorrow with those,' and a bunch of other dumb questions."

Steffie pouted, but the answer seemed to mostly satisfy her. The question itself, however, nagged at Teddy. "Why would you want to go to school?"

Steffie looked surprised at the question. "Why wouldn't I? Don't you want to?"

Teddy shrugged. She'd never given it much thought, and when she did, school seemed boring. She already had lessons with Mrs. Headerson, which were hard enough. Sometimes the Boss would teach her stuff, too. Who wanted to sit in some boring room when they could learn on the job, especially when the job was awesome stuff like pulling heists and fighting Heroes?

"Sounds boring," Teddy said.

"No way!" Steffie said. "Mom's a teacher, and she really likes school. There's a lot of people to make friends with, and you learn stuff together, and there's like, tests and recess and sometimes if you're good you get to watch movies."

"You can watch movies at home," Athena pointed out.

"Yeah, we do all of that already," Teddy said. "And without some non-Boss boss telling us to behave."

Steffie shook her head. "You just don't get it," she said.

Teddy agreed, she really didn't. But at the same time, something about all of this worried her. "Why do you want to go to this school thing so much anyway?"

"I . . . don't know, I just want to," Steffie replied with a shrug.

Soon after, the Boss, Minion Sam, and Mrs. Headerson returned from their chitchat. Unfortunately, Steffie had to step out of the new legs for the moment. She was disappointed about it but perked up when she learned that Maple was going to use the old legs to make newer, better legs. Soon she was back in her chair, looking a lot smiley-er than usual, and she wasn't an un-smiley person to begin with.

"All right, gang, time to go home," the Boss said, placing a hand on Maple's and one of Trinity's heads.

Teddy felt a little detached as they said their goodbyes, traded hugs with Steffie and Mrs. Headerson, and started the trip back to base. Once they were back in the van, with Teddy squeezed in at the back behind Sam, who was at the wheel, she found herself still wrestling with the concept of school.

Would it be . . . fun?

She figured it wouldn't be, but maybe it was something she could investigate? She leaned back in her seat and watched the world slip by outside. It struck her again just how many ads she was seeing all the time. Images of food that looked too tasty to be real, pretty women in nice dresses that wouldn't fit Teddy in a million years, smiling Heroes being all yucky and Hero-like.

She'd seen it all before, but it hadn't bothered her. Now she was feeling . . . something.

"You okay?"

Teddy looked up and found Athena looking at her. They were near the overpass, and Sam parked the van in a lot not too far from the base. The others were heading out already, but Teddy had zoned out. "Uh, yeah, yeah, I'm coming," she said, then clambered out of the car.

Surprisingly, Athena stayed by her side as she started walking toward the base. "What's wrong?"

"Nothing's wrong," Teddy said.

"Something looks wrong," Athena replied.

"Your face is wrong," Teddy shot right back.

Athena rolled her eyes, then she shifted to the side and bumped her shoulder against Teddy's. "Something's going on in your head. I can *feel* it. It's annoying you. If you tell me, I'll stop bothering you."

Teddy grumbled, but she knew that Athena could be super hard-headed when she wanted to be. There was no point in fighting her. "I was just thinking a lot. About like, school and stuff. I dunno."

"You want to go after all?" Athena asked.

"What? No. It sounds awful."

"Hmm. Then tell me what you're thinking, and then you can relax."

"Why would that make me relax?" Teddy asked.

"Because then I can do the thinking for you. I'm much better at it," Athena said without a shred of self-doubt.

"Just feeling weird."

"About school?" Athena asked.

"Kinda," Teddy said. She reached up and picked at the side of her nose. "It's like, I don't wanna go. It's stupid and boring. But Steffie *does*. And I guess I don't get why."

Athena was quiet for a moment as she thought. "Maybe she just wants to have a normal life?"

Teddy looked at her sister. "Normal? Like what we have?"

"I don't think we're normal," Athena said. "But we have the Boss, we do cool stuff, we're all Villains, so we obviously know better than anyone else. But I still don't think that's normal. Normal is what most people do, and we don't do that."

"I guess," Teddy said before going quiet. She hadn't thought of that before. Her life felt pretty normal. Sleep, wake up, poop, eat, sometimes beat up a Hero or another Villain or steal some stuff, do what the Boss said, then go back to sleep again.

"Our normal's not other people's normal," Athena continued. "And Steffie's . . . nice, but she's kind of *normal*-normal, you know? Except for the whole wheelchair thing, and she'd probably like to be even more normaler."

"Hm," Teddy chewed on the thought.

"Feeling better?" Athena asked after a while.

"Maybe. I mean, yeah. Just weird to think about."

Athena grinned. "At least you're thinking. Don't do too much of that, you might hurt yourself." She dodged Teddy's shove, then laughed. "Maybe we can do something fun instead of hurting your head?"

"Something fun?" Teddy asked.

Athena's eyes were glimmering. It was a dangerous look. "How about we go to school after all?"

"What? Why?"

"No, no, not the normal way. We can sneak into a school, then remind them how we're the best! I bet there's a lot of stuff worth taking in there."

"I'm in," Trinity said as she popped up between them.

"How long have you been listening?" Teddy asked.

Trinity blinked. "The whole time? But I forgot most of it. Except the bit about stealing from a school. That sounds fun!"

Teddy considered it for a bit. "We can't tell the Boss," she finally said. It would have to be a secret between sisters, but not Big Sis.

They hurried to catch up with the others. When everyone had arrived at the overpass, the Boss paused by the entrance. "All right, girls, I'm going to be heading out with Sam and Maple. We need some supplies again, and I figured that getting things now would be better than waiting. Can you behave yourselves while we're out?"

"Sure thing, Boss!" Teddy said.

Athena and Trinity nodded along, then slipped into the opening corridor of the bunker. The door shut, and the three of them looked at one another.

The timing was almost too perfect.

"We'll have to wait a bit for her to get farther away," Athena said.

"One of me can stay here," Trinity said. "I can make a mess so it looks like we were here the whole time. I bet I can stuff some pillows in Teddy's bed and say she's sleeping."

Teddy grinned, a lot of the worry she'd been feeling bleeding away. This was going to be fun!

CHAPTER THIRTY-TWO

Expendable in School

The school they picked for their research was called Beausoleil Elementary School, and it was about as lame as a school could be.

They didn't really pick it for its lameness, though. They mostly chose that school because it was only a few blocks over from the underpass where they lived.

"Oh man, that place looks awful," Teddy said as she looked at the school. Beausoleil was an old building, made of big chunks of gray stone with a large archway over the front doors. The blocky main part of the building was three stories tall and sat behind a pair of old trees growing in a small yard next to a little parking lot out front.

The wings to either side were much newer. They looked like they'd been added onto the main building a hundred years later or something.

"So, do we just go in?" Trinity asked.

"I guess so," Teddy said. "Can't be that hard, right?"

"It's Saturday," Athena said. "It might be closed."

The front door opened, and a mom and her two kids left the building.

"Okay, so maybe it's not," Athena said. "If we can just sneak in, then all we have to do is act like we're supposed to be there."

"Easy," Trinity said. Then she whipped out one of her big canvas bags with the dollar signs on the sides so that it filled with air and expanded to its full size with a *fwump*. "Let's do it so fast that they won't know what hit them!"

Teddy grinned and started to step onto the street, but Athena reached out and grabbed her—and the nearest Trinity—by the scruff of the neck. "Hey! What did the Boss say about crossing the street?" Athena asked.

A big moving van rumbled by. It wasn't moving all that quickly, but it was pretty big. "I'd have lived," Teddy said, but she sounded whiny even to herself.

Athena just gave her a Look. Athena was good at that. "Big Sis would cry if you died, you know."

Teddy pouted, cheeks puffing out as she broke eye contact. "Yeah, maybe, I guess," she said.

"I die all the time and she doesn't cry," Trinity said. Her smile slowly faded. "Wait, does that mean she doesn't love me as much?"

"Don't be an idiot, Big Sis loves you too, even if you're more expendable."

"Woo!" Trinity cheered.

Holding hands, they all looked both ways, determined that the next oncoming car wasn't moving quickly either, then bolted across the street. The woman behind the wheel honked her horn at them and slammed on the brakes, but she didn't run any of them over, so it was okay and they made it to the other side safely.

Then it was time to enter the school proper.

Teddy craned her neck back as they approached. The building was . . . just an old stone building, but there was something about it. A sort of aura of old authority that stuck to it. It reminded her a bit of a jail, even if she'd never been to jail yet.

Trinity pushed the door open, and they found themselves in a lobby with hallways that went off to the right and left. The front bit had an office where a secretary-looking lady was doing something on a computer. She looked up and frowned at them. "Hello?" she said.

"We're supposed to be here," Athena said with confidence before she started walking off to the right.

Teddy nodded and followed after her, then reached back to tug a Trinity along before she could reach one of those big stands with a bunch of pamphlets.

There was a staircase to the right, so they went up the stairs and away from the lobby area. They paused on the second floor. "Now what?" Teddy asked. Doors were open here and there leading into classrooms, which were all empty.

For some reason, Teddy had expected to find them all full of boring brainwashed kids, but she guessed that even those went home on weekends.

"I don't know, this was your idea," Athena said.

"Uh," Teddy replied. "I don't know. Maybe look for signs of capitalism?"

"What would that look like?" Trinity asked.

"Fat people in suits wearing monocles and top hats," Teddy said with confidence. "Maybe smoking cigars and carrying big bags with money and gold."

"I don't think we'll find that in a school," Athena said.

Teddy shrugged. "You don't know that."

Trinity had wandered off as they talked, but she caught Teddy's attention when both of her gasped. "There's an art room!" she said before darting into the room in question.

Teddy and Athena followed, of course.

"Look at all the colors!" Trinity said as she danced across the room. Teddy paused to stare at a wall covered in big pieces of paper with stuff painted on it. They weren't very good paintings. Trinity found a handful of paintbrushes and sniffed them, then stuffed them into her bag with a clatter.

The air in this room was thick with the scent of paint and clay and very strong cleaning products. Teddy wasn't sure she liked it, but Trinity seemed to be having fun.

"I'm gonna do a mural," Trinity declared.

"Really?" Teddy asked. "That sounds stupid."

"It'll be of the Boss kicking Heroes in the butt, and we can all be there, and you'll be a bear eating a Hero, and then the kids will come in and see it and they'll know how awesome we are," Trinity said.

Teddy changed her mind. "Okay, that sounds awesome."

Athena laughed and closed the door, then locked it. "Okay, we'll have to be quick, though. Where are you gonna paint it?"

Trinity blinked. "It's a mural. On the wall." She pointed to the wall at the front of the class. Teddy supposed that a blackboard would work well as a canvas.

One Trinity pushed a chair toward the board while another ran around grabbing tubes of paint and a plastic tray thing to mix the paint on. "Teddy, can you help?" she asked.

Teddy shrugged. "Fine, but I want really big teeth."

"Okay!" Trinity agreed.

Working together, they brought a few more chairs to the front of the class so that Trinity had something to walk on that'd let her reach the top of the board, then Teddy held on to the plastic tray while Trinity squeezed some fresh paint on it.

Athena, meanwhile, stood by the door to listen for adults and security guards and Heroes, just in case.

Trinity worked fast. She had a big brush in one hand and was painting large blobs of different colors. Teddy had no idea what she was doing at first, though she guessed that the big brown blob was a bear.

It took a few minutes before Trinity finished the bigger shapes. Then she went back and started adding more paint on top of her first layer, this time bringing out smaller details and adding shadows and brighter splotches.

The painting came together pretty quickly. It was the Boss, in her full costume, glaring at someone while her foot stomped on the face of a Hero. Athena was in the back, strangling someone, and Maple was there, too, with a big toaster gun. There were a few Trinities here and there, of course, and a huge bear on the right side of the painting, its mouth open and filled with bloody Hero chunks.

"Nice!" Teddy said as she took in the building image. It was starting to look great, but that was normal, because Trinity was good at painting and stuff.

Then there was a hard knock on the door. "Hello?" someone said on the other side.

The handle jiggled.

"Quick!" Teddy said. "Add the last details."

Trinity nodded and started to move faster.

Something that sounded a lot like a key fitting into a lock sounded from the doorway, and all three of them froze. Then Athena spun and hissed at them. "Look natural!"

The door opened, and they discovered an older woman standing there. She blinked, taking the three of them in, confusion writ large across her face. Then she noticed the mural. "What in the world?" she said.

"Oops," Athena said. "Is this not . . . outside? Our bad," she said.

"That's fresh paint . . . What are you three doing in here?" she asked.

"We're lost," Athena said.

"Did you paint that?"

"No," Trinity said. She was covered in droplets and splotches of paint. It wasn't very convincing.

The woman shook her head. "I can't believe this. All three of you, with me, *now*," she snapped. "We're going to the principal's office. When your parents find out about this, I swear."

Teddy grinned. Joke was on her, they didn't have parents!

CHAPTER THIRTY-THREE

~~~~~~~~~~~~~~

School Smarts

Stay in here," the lady said as she held the door open.

The room she was leading them into was a large-ish office with a big desk in the middle and some seats across from it. There was also a small sofa next to the doorway. The far wall had a few shelves with books and trophies on it and a handful of diplomas in picture frames.

"For how long?" Trinity asked. "I wanna go home."

The teacher lady huffed. "For however long it takes the principal to get here. I can't believe what you did in the art room. Your parents won't be proud of you."

Teddy was about to tell the lady where she could stuff her parents' pride, but Athena kicked her shin from the side. She looked down at the ground, trying to seem real pitiful.

"We're sorry," Athena simpered. "We'll behave, I promise. Just . . . don't tell Dad?"

The teacher lady huffed again, then gestured toward the seats. "I'll be back," she said.

The door clicked shut, and both Teddy and Trinity turned toward Athena.

"Dad?" Teddy asked.

"We have a dad?" Trinity replied, sounding shocked.

Athena snorted and shook her head. "I was just telling her what she wanted to hear. Should we leave now that she's gone?" There was a window overlooking the backyard of the school, where there was a big sandpit and some jungle gyms and slides and a bunch of space to run around in.

"I guess," Teddy said. "But we're here now, aren't we? This is, like, the school's boss's room."

Athena's eyes narrowed. "That's not a bad idea," she said. "Trinity, lock the door."

"I'll do it," Teddy said. "Trinity, open up the window so that we have a way out."

"Aye-aye, bear sister!" Trinity said with twin salutes. She ran over to the window and started wrestling with the latch.

Teddy, in the meantime, sized up the door. It opened inward into the room, so the best way to close it forever would be to block its path. She eyed the sofa next to the door. Shrugging, Teddy walked over to the sofa and started to pull on it, but it was a lot heavier than it looked.

So she did the obvious thing and turned into a bear.

"Hey!" Trinity said as Teddy's behind bumped her. "Watch it!"

Teddy rumbled back at her, then grabbed onto the sofa with her clawed paws. The soft leather made for great pawholds once her claws punched through the material. With a grunt of effort, she stood the sofa up on its side, then pushed it against the door. Now anyone trying to get in would have to shove aside the entire thing.

"Oh, wow," Athena said from the desk.

"What?" Teddy rumbled. She padded over around the room, chairs falling out of her way and the stuff on the shelves crashing down as her sides rubbed against the walls. She got to see the screen, though.

"The password was just the name of the school," Athena said. "This principal guy doesn't know anything about good security."

Athena squinted at the screen, then started to open up a few programs.

"It's open!" Trinity said as she threw the window open. Her other self dragged a chair over and tossed it outside, that way they'd have a place to step onto once they were out. A second chair served as a stepping stool from the inside.

"I found the school registry," Athena said. "And the grades."

"Perfect!" Teddy said. "Put all our names in as past students."

"What? Why?" Athena asked.

"So we can graduate and get diplomas and stuff. That way we can get jobs. That's how the capitalists think."

"But we didn't go to school," Trinity said. "Except for today. Does that count as enough?"

"Doesn't matter. We'll have the diplomas on paper, because we're not stupid enough to actually go to school," Teddy said.

"All right," Athena said. "I'll need a minute to figure out how all of this works."

"That means we've got a minute, right?" Trinity asked.

"I guess so," Teddy replied.

Trinity grinned, then started to rummage around. She started with the trash can under the principal's desk, flipping it over and spreading its contents out. She picked the best stuff and shoved it into her dollar-sign bag.

Teddy wasn't really much of a looter, but Trinity looked like she was having fun, so she decided to help by opening all the drawers of the principal's desk.

They were designed for weak humans, though, so Teddy ended up ripping them right out of the desk and dumping the contents on the ground.

Trinity giggled as she jumped on the loot spread out on the floor, stuffing heaps of pens and pencils and school stationery into her bag.

"Hey, do we use our real names or our Hero names?" Athena asked.

"Real names, I think," Teddy said. "Does it need a last name?"

"Yeah," Athena said. "Okay, that's me down."

"What about the rest of us?" Teddy asked. She leaned over the screen to stare at it until Athena grabbed her by the snoot and pushed her muzzle away. The screen was covered in boring text anyway.

"I'm doing us one at a time," Athena said. "Do we enter Trinity three times?"

"Nah, there's just one of me," Trinity said. "I can share it with myself."

"Oh, that makes sense," Athena said with a nod.

Teddy noticed something on the desk, a sort of microphone pointing toward the seat Athena was in with a large button at the base of it. "What's that?" she asked while pointing a claw at the thing.

"Looks like a PA system," Athena said. "To talk to the whole school . . . No, wait, don't," she warned.

"Why not?" Teddy asked.

"Well, first you should think about what to say. And second, I need to finish entering all of this. If you press that, then people will know we're here."

"And they'll be able to recognize your voice!" Trinity said. She was currently trying to stuff a potted fern into her bag. Its branches were sticking out every which way, but she didn't seem to care.

"I'll talk in bear," Teddy said, but she did wait. At least a little while. It felt like Athena was taking forever to type things up.

"Almost done," Athena said.

That was good enough for Teddy. She pushed a claw against the PA system's button, then grinned as a squeal sounded out across the school. She cleared her throat and could hear the sound repeated through the walls.

Now she just needed to figure out what to say.

"Comrades! I am Te— I am the bear of communism, and I'm here to tell you about the glories of the proletariat!"

"Yeah!" Trinity cheered in the background as she continued to steal stuff.

"Now, I might not know what communism means, exactly, but I believe in it. I know that it means that we should all share stuff, that we should be our own bosses, and that no one should take our stuff. Only we're allowed to take the stuff of others!"

"I don't think that makes sense," Athena said.

Teddy growled at her to shut up. "Comrades! Let's rise together! Let's bring down the fences that keep us out of the parks! Let's fight against those who say that we can't eat our fill! No longer will we live under the oppression of bedtimes and those stupid 'don't feed the animals' signs!"

There was a loud *thump* from the door, and the doorknob wiggled. "Hey! Hey, let go of the PA!" someone shouted through the door.

"Oops. Sorry, comrades, got to go!"

Teddy didn't know how to turn off the PA, so she flung it against the wall, where it embedded itself into the drywall.

"All right, let's go!" Trinity said. She ran for the window, one of her bodies leaping out and rolling to her feet while the other hoisted up her big bag. She helped herself maneuver it past the opening while Teddy and Athena made their way to the window.

The door opened up a smidge, but the weight of the sofa was keeping it closed for now.

Athena used the chairs to climb through, then it was Teddy's turn. She was tall enough as a bear that she could just leap right through the opening. But then her belly got caught in the too-small window.

Growling, Teddy turned back into her girl-self and tumbled out the other side. She was quick to roll back to her feet. The others were already sprinting across the yard toward an open gate in the fence, so Teddy rushed after them while someone finally managed to barge through the door, sending the sofa crashing with a loud bang.

"I like school!" Trinity said as she sprinted along the sidewalk. "We should come back more often!"

"We'll see," Athena said as she worked to keep up. "But we should get back home first, before Big Sis notices that we're gone."

"Nah, she won't notice!" Teddy said. "We were subtle about it!"

CHAPTER THIRTY-FOUR

Dreaming Big

Trinity was lucky she had so many ears. It meant that she could listen to TV and her sisters and Big Sis at the same time.

Two of her were sitting on the couch in the living room, while her last self was sitting next to Big Sister in the kitchen.

"I can't believe we got away with it," Teddy muttered.

"Shush," Athena said. "We *won't* get away with anything if you keep talking about it."

Trinity chuckled, and at the dining room table, Big Sister looked up from her work, one eyebrow raised. "Athena said something funny," Trinity explained.

"Oh," Emily said. She looked back down at her work. Trinity didn't know exactly what it was, but she was helping anyway! Her big sister had sorted out all of her different subjects' handouts on the dining table and Trinity was putting the papers away into their respective binders. She was placing little color-coded stickers on the top of the header pages and adding little doodles on the spines of the binders to make them nicer.

Big Sister had pirated some of her textbooks and printed them all out, which Trinity thought was a perfectly Villainous thing to do. Plus, Trinity got to help!

In the living room, Trinity paid less and less attention as Teddy and Athena bickered. The argument was silly, and anyway, the commercials were ending.

She was leaning back on the couch where a new show started. It was some sort of documentary on climate change or something like that. She just had it on that because it was playing on one of the channels they had. It was distracting noise. She'd have preferred something more fun, but Big Sister Emily didn't want them watching loud cartoons while she was doing work, and Teddy liked documentaries a lot.

Trinity was ready to just mindlessly watch the show when it switched to a panning shot of a place she'd never seen before.

Trinity sat up and squirmed forward until she was on the edge of the couch, all three mouths agape. She almost ran the body in the kitchen over so that she could see the TV with all of her eyes.

It was beautiful.

A kaleidoscope of discarded treasures, towering mounds of shimmering, sparkling steel and plastic and crushed aluminum. Trinity had never seen so much trash all in one place before. She absently reached up and wiped her lower lips free of drool. She could only *imagine* the smell.

"Landfills—a monument to human consumption and a near-permanent reminder of the consequences of our modern throwaway society. These behemoths of refuse contain a cocktail of hazardous waste leaking into the Earth."

Trinity nodded at the voice of the narrator. He didn't have to sell her on the idea, she was in love already, but his smooth Ritish voice continued.

"The skies above these mounds of trash fare no better. It's not just the smell that is noxious, but its impact. Decomposition releases a steady stream of greenhouse gases, notably methane, which contributes substantially to climate change."

The show moved on to talk about some recycling thing and about how landfills were bad, but it wasn't showing the landfills anymore.

Trinity pouted, increasingly frustrated at not seeing the pretty trash heaps full of treasure. There were a few more shots showing some lucky gulls picking away at the junk, but that was it.

She had never been so in love with something on the TV before. Balling up her fists, Trinity gave herself a triple nod of determination. She'd visit one of those landfills if it was the last thing she did.

She just needed to figure out how.

"Big Sis?" the Trinity at the dining table asked.

"Hmm?" Emily said.

"Can we go to the landfill?" Trinity asked.

"No," Emily said.

Trinity pouted harder. Plan A was a bust already, and she hadn't even started planning it!

"Boss?" Trinity asked from her self that was nearest the kitchen.

"Yeah?" Emily asked.

"Can I use your laptop?"

Her big sister looked up. "Hmm? I guess? What is it for?"

"I want to look at garbage trucks," Trinity said.

"Oh . . . uh . . . okay? As long as you do it from here." Her big sister leaned to the side and grabbed her laptop out of her school bag, which was laying on the floor beside her. She placed it next to the binders Trinity had been working on.

Trinity smiled and sat on her knees on one of the chairs so that she'd be tall enough. The laptop took a while to boot up, and when it did, it asked for a password. Emily entered it, fingers moving too quickly for Trinity to catch what she wrote. Then she turned the laptop around and Trinity had access to the internet.

It took a while because she had to type things carefully and ask how to spell *garbage*, but eventually she found lots of pictures of garbage trucks and an Ikipedia page about them.

Some skimming later, she had confirmed it. Garbage trucks *did* go to landfills! Perfect! It wasn't hard from there to discover the Eauclaire garbage schedule, and fortunately the trucks went around picking up trash five days a week across different parts of the city.

"Thanks, Boss," Trinity said as she found a neat video to look at. It was garbage trucks with big mechanical claw arms on their sides that could pick up entire dumpsters, and it was definitely one of the coolest things ever.

"You're welcome," her big sister said. She was still mostly focused on her schoolwork.

The Trinity on the couch jumped up and walked out of the bunker. She didn't try to be sneaky, because she wasn't going to do anything sneaky. Most of her wasn't even leaving the house!

Once a third of her was outside, she started down the sidewalk, keeping off the road because she couldn't cross without someone's hand to hold. Her mission was to find a garbage can that hadn't been picked up yet, which she figured would be easy. After all, the longer trash stayed out, the more enticing it smelled.

Unfortunately, the first ripe dumpster she found was too tall and had a big latch keeping its cover down. With only one of her bodies, she wouldn't be able to get in there.

After she had walked for a while, Trinity noticed someone in an alleyway next to a fast food place with two large trash bags in hand.

All three of her mouths grinned as she spotted it. Unfortunately, it was on the other side of the road. Fortunately, there was a big stranger passing by. "Mister," she said.

The man paused and blinked, then looked behind him. "Yes?" he asked.

Trinity pointed across the street. "I need to go over there," she said.

"Uh . . . okay?"

"I can't cross the street without holding hands."

"Where's your mom?" he asked.

She was about to tell him that she didn't have one when she realized that would be silly. "Over there," she said, pointing across the street to the fast food place.

"Then how did you get here?" he asked.

"Accident," she lied again.

The man looked around some more. "I don't know," he said. "I don't wanna look like a weirdo."

"If I don't hold hands, a car will hit me," she said. This time, it wasn't a lie.

The man said some words under his breath, then looked both ways. "Fine," he said.

"Your fingers are fat," she said as she held on to him. It didn't take long to cross the road, and Trinity waved at the man as she ran off. "Thank you, mister!"

The guy said something, but Trinity was already in the alleyway and moving toward the large dumpster at the back. It was even open!

With a "hup," Trinity jumped and grabbed on to the side of the dumpster, then scrambled up and into it, falling back-first onto a pile of bags that cushioned her fall.

Now all she had to do was wait!

It didn't take long for the person with the bags to come back. He didn't even look in the dumpster before flinging in a few more bags. One of them ripped apart, spraying Trinity with squished burger buns.

She'd get to wait with a snack! This was the best non-plan ever! She stuffed her pockets full of bread, then sent some to the hers back at home.

It didn't take long for Big Sister to notice her pulling out a squished lump of bread to chew on while she was looking at more garbage truck pictures. "Hey, don't eat over the laptop . . . Wait, where did you get that?"

"The trash!" Trinity said.

Emily sighed and got up. "Trinity, stop eating stuff from the trash, I swear. Is that mold? If you were hungry, you should have just told me."

Trinity gave away one of her buns without protest. There was a whole sackful of them, after all, and if Big Sister wanted some, she was more than happy to share!

Soon she'd be at the landfill and would have more trash than she could hope for!

CHAPTER THIRTY-FIVE

Landfill/Paradise

Waiting was boring.

Fortunately, only a third of her was waiting, so she was only one-third bored, which really wasn't so bad. Another third was watching TV (the documentary about landfills had ended and Athena had turned the TV over to news, which wasn't super fun but it was bright and there were sounds so it was okay), and the last third of her was in the kitchen.

She was helping make food!

"Can you get the butter from the fridge?" Big Sister Emily asked.

"Mm-hmm!" Trinity replied before jogging over and throwing the fridge open. The stuff stuck to the outside of the door clanged around, which was a sound she really liked to hear. Trinity found the butter, then ran back. "What are we eating?" she asked.

"Mac and cheese" was the reply.

They'd eaten mac and cheese twice already this week, so this would be the third time. Trinity raised her arms over her head and cheered. "Yeah! That's awesome! Can we have hot dog bits in it?"

Big Sister Emily smiled, then gave Trinity's head a rub. "Sure, get the pack out of the freezer. I don't think there's that many left, though."

While Trinity was helping Big Sister Emily in the kitchen, the part of her that was waiting in a dumpster next to the fast food place was cataloging the stuff from the bags around her. She was trying not to make too much noise, because people got very angry when other people went through their trash, even if they were literally getting rid of the stuff.

It didn't make any sense to Trinity.

Her patience was rewarded, though. She could hear a deep rumble through the metal walls of the dumpster as a truck pulled up next to it. Trinity shifted around inside, then slowly, carefully, pushed the heavy lid of the dumpster up.

What she saw on the outside made her gasp from all three mouths.

"Are you okay?" Emily asked in the kitchen.

"Yeah!" Trinity said.

The garbage truck was beautiful. It was white, with rust-brown streaks along its side, and even though she was sitting in a dumpster filled with festering fast food, she could still smell the truck. It reeked of diesel and years of accumulated trash.

A huge metal fork came down with a hydraulic hum, and Trinity squeaked back as it latched onto the dumpster. She grinned from ear to ear. Athena gave her a look in the living room, but she didn't ask any questions.

Trinity held back a squeal of excitement as the dumpster jumped, then it slowly rose up and she felt her world tipping back.

The lid flew open, and then Trinity spread her arms wide, like a bird taking flight (but it was a raccoon instead), a moment before she crashed into a heap of compacted trash inside the garbage truck.

The dumpster was moved away, and Trinity found herself half-buried in its contents.

"Nice," she said to herself.

Then the walls started to close in around her.

That . . . wasn't normal, was it? She stared at the inner walls of the garbage truck as they pushed closer and closer. A machine hummed, and Trinity found herself a little bit uncomfortable as the walls just kept coming.

It was like getting hugged too hard by Teddy, only worse.

Trash fell in around her, and she heard bottles popping apart. The trash shifted more, and her vision was buried away from the light. She grunted as the pressure continued, and continued, and then . . .

A brand-new Trinity popped into being in the living room.

"Dang," she said.

"Did you die?" Teddy asked.

Trinity sighed. "Yeah." Her new body trudged over to the kitchen, where she was helping Emily with the food. The laptop was still on the dining table, so she turned it over and opened a new browser tab before typing "garbage truck squisher machine" into the search bar.

She learned that garbage trucks sometimes came with big compression machines to squish in even more garbage (and poor raccoons), and that garbage trucks were even cooler than she thought.

"What are you looking at?" Emily asked.

"When I grow up, I want to be a garbage truck," Trinity decided.

"I . . . don't know about *being* one, but maybe you can work for the city as a garbage person? It's a respectable enough job, and I think the pay's decent. Plus . . . three bodies means you could probably do triple shifts."

Driving *three* garbage trucks at the same time? Or maybe she could be the driver and the person who picked up the trash cans, and her third self could be in the big container with the trash . . . as long as it wasn't one of those with a crusher.

"Cool!" Trinity said. "I'm gonna be a garbage person! Unless . . . Can I be a Villain at the same time?"

"I . . . guess?"

Happy with the answer, Trinity cheered and ran out of the kitchen, leaving one of herself behind to continue helping. The new body went running past the others, who barely paid her any attention, which was good, because she ran right out of the bunker again.

This time, when she was on the street, she knew exactly where to go. Garbage trucks had to stop a lot, so the one that had squished her couldn't be far!

It didn't take her long to find the white whale of a truck slowly making its way along one of the side streets and stopping to slip into every alleyway where a dumpster waited.

Trinity ran over to a still-full dumpster, then waited. Not inside it this time, but in the shadows behind the dumpster.

She didn't have to wait too long. By the time the truck arrived, Big Sister Emily had just asked her to set the table.

The truck rumbled over, then its big claw reached for the dumpster.

She jumped on. Not onto the dumpster, but on the claw. It rose up, and Trinity held on tight so that she wouldn't fall. Once she was at the very top, Trinity leapt off the claw, past the big hole where the trash was being dumped, and onto the roof of the garbage truck.

"Where's the rest of you?" Big Sister Emily asked as they all sat around the table.

Trinity had three chairs stuck together on one side. "That part of me is busy," Trinity said. She was more focused on the gooey, cheesy food in front of her. She'd gotten some extra hot dog bits for helping!

The her on the garbage truck laid herself flat on the roof of it, arms and legs spread out in case there was a lot of wind, but with the start-stop motion of the truck, there really wasn't much.

Other than the interesting smells, it soon grew kind of boring, but that was okay, she had food to distract her at home, and when that ended, it was time to wash up and she helped Big Sister Emily with the dishes, too.

"You're helpful today," Emily said as she handed Trinity a dry plate to put away.

"Uh-huh!" Trinity said. "I learned good things today, so it's a good day, right?"

"I guess so," Emily said. "Did you want to play a board game or something after? With your sisters, I mean. I'm mostly done with work and could use a break."

"All right!" Trinity said. She wasn't very good at board games, but a lot of them had nice art and she liked looking at the cards.

On top of the garbage truck, Trinity felt the vehicle make a turn, and then they rode on faster and faster. Soon, the garbage truck was on the highway, and Trinity pressed herself even flatter against the roof as her tail caught the wind behind her.

The ride felt like it took a long time, but eventually the truck went off the main road outside of Eauclaire and the road felt much bumpier and less smooth than the city streets.

She carefully propped herself up so she could take a look around.

They passed a big old warehouse building with a few other trucks parked out front, then through a gate into . . .

A landfill!

It was amazing, a huge open space filled with mountains and mountains of trash.

Back home, the dishes had been done for a while and Trinity had joined Athena, Teddy, and Maple in the dining room, where Emily was setting up a game of Onopoly. "Hey, where's your third body?" Big Sister Emily asked.

"Heaven," Trinity said.

Emily shook her head. "Never mind."

The garbage truck backed itself up toward one of the smaller trash heaps, then the entire container on the back started to rise at one end.

Trinity held back a cheer as she slid off the top and crashed onto a big heap of cushioning trash.

She'd made it!

CHAPTER THIRTY-SIX

Athena's Trashy Morning

Athena woke up because Emily was getting out of bed. She mumbled at her bigger sister to stay in place, but Emily didn't listen. Athena was always the earliest to wake up, though she wasn't always the first out of bed.

Mostly because Athena and her sisters liked sleeping on top of Emily, and that made it hard for her to squeeze her way out of bed sometimes. That wasn't the case this morning, though. Emily slipped out, let out a loud yawn, then stumbled out of the room.

Athena snuggled back in. The spot Emily had left was warm. Something felt . . . off, though.

Athena blinked her eyes open and looked around. The lights were off, but that wasn't a problem for her. Athena didn't make a big fuss about it, but she was actually really good at seeing in the dark. Better than her other sisters, at least. It's why she was able to tell that most of someone was missing.

Teddy had grabbed the prime spot at the top of the bed, where she was drooling on Emily's pillow, and Maple was pressed up against Athena's back, her face shoved into the space between Athena and the bed. Trinity was curled up at the base of the bed.

Just one of her, though.

Athena worked her jaw, then crawled her way off the bed. She squinted her eyes shut as she left the bedroom. The lights were on in the rest of the house.

There was water running in the washroom, so Big Sister was taking her shower, probably.

Athena checked her own bedroom. Her bed was undone, so she went over and fixed it up.

Every night, Big Sister Emily would tuck them all in to sleep. It was nice, and warm, and none of her sisters complained about it.

It was annoying having to untuck themselves from bed and sneak over to Emily's room to make a cuddle pile there, but that's just how things worked.

She went over to the kitchen, grabbed the stool, then set it in front of the fridge before climbing on top of it to tug open the freezer at the top. It was Sunday morning, which meant that it was eggs and bacon day. Athena—and somehow Trinity—were the only ones other than Big Sister who were allowed to do any cooking.

Maple could manage it well enough, but she'd often get distracted, and Emily had put her foot down when she discovered Maple turning the oven into a flamethrower.

Teddy just couldn't cook.

Athena hummed to herself as she pulled out a couple of cartons of eggs and set them on the table, and then she found a stick of butter and the milk.

Eggs usually meant omelets, because those were the easiest to make and no one complained much. She put the ingredients on the counter next to the stove.

She got a couple of plates, a trash can (for the eggshells), a spatula, and a butter knife. Soon Athena was watching the eggs start to sizzle. That was when Emily came in, hair still a bit damp from her shower. "Oh, you started already," she said.

"Uh-huh," Athena said.

Her big sister came over and patted Athena's head. "Good work. Thanks. I'll start on the toast."

Athena smiled and allowed herself to feel particularly smug. She'd already gotten headpats and it was still super early in the morning. Big Sister opened the fridge, then sniffed. She bent down, sniffing at the cool air coming from the refrigerator, then she straightened and sniffed at the air some more.

"What's that smell?"

Athena smelled the air, but her nose wasn't the best. She could smell the eggs, and maybe a hint of shampoo from Emily. There was something else. She sniffed a bit more. Rotting meat? "It's stinky," she said.

"Yeah. I thought that it might be some of the leftovers, but I don't think it's coming from the fridge." Emily went over and checked the trash bin, but it was mostly empty and didn't smell strong. "This is going to bother me," she said.

Athena clicked the stove off and set the pan on another burner as Emily left the kitchen. She hopped off the stool and followed her.

Emily stopped by Teddy's room, opened the door a crack, and sniffed. "Not here," she said.

She moved on to Trinity's room and popped the door open.

A cascade of *stuff* came pouring out into the room. Bottles, cans, a few electronic things, and several smaller bags. There were stained clothes and some very squished boxes.

"What?" Emily said. Then the smell hit, and both Athena and her big sister recoiled. It was a thousand times stronger with the door open.

A very dirty Trinity stumbled out of her room, trash clattering out ahead of her. "Hi!" she said.

"Trinity, what is all of this?" Emily said.

Trinity looked down. "Uh. Trash?"

"I know that! Where did you *get* it?" Emily asked.

Trinity's face blossomed into a huge smile. "The landfill!" she said. "It's awesome!"

"What do you mean, the landfill?" Emily asked. "How did you get stuff from there to here?"

"One of me is there now," Trinity said.

"You've been going back and forth all night?" Athena asked.

Trinity shook her head. "I've done nothing but teleport trash all night," she said. She stuffed a hand into her pocket, then tugged out what looked like half of a Rubik's cube. "See?"

Emily rubbed at her face. "Trinity, no," she said. "You can't just . . . you can't just teleport trash into your room from the *landfill*."

"No one wants it," Trinity defended.

"That's not the problem, you doofus," Athena said. "It's stinky and gross."

"But Big Sister said I could decorate my room how I wanted," Trinity said.

"Not with trash!" Athena said.

Emily opened the door some more while pinching her nose shut. "Oh, there's so much," she said as she took in the mess in Trinity's room. "Trinity, we . . . we need to have a talk."

"Uh-oh," Trinity said.

Athena almost patted Trinity on the shoulder in sympathy, but she really did stink.

"But first, I think we need to get rid of all of this," Emily said.

"*All* of it?" Trinity asked.

"I . . . yes?" Emily said. Trinity looked like she was on the verge of tears, and Athena could tell at a glance that her big sister was on the edge of taking it back, but she couldn't do that, because then Trinity would discover that Emily was weak to her little sisters looking sad.

That was a powerful weapon to have in her back pocket, so Athena didn't say anything. "I'll help you," Athena said. "Maybe there's something you can keep?"

Trinity sighed. "Okay. I guess it'll all just get back to the landfill, so it's not like it's lost forever."

"Right," Emily said. "Where are your other bodies?"

"One's in bed," Trinity said, then she stifled a yawn. "Only a third of me slept. This me was here so that I could get the trash, and my other me is at the landfill."

"Can you have that you come back?" Emily asked.

"Okay!" Trinity said. She smiled, then a moment later another Trinity popped into being next to her. She was covered in bits of junk and stank so much that Athena took a step back from her.

"Did you die?" Athena asked.

"I jumped off Mount Trash," Trinity said.

Emily sighed. "I'm going to go finish breakfast. Athena, if you could help in here, that would be really nice. I'll come help in a bit too. Just . . . put everything in bags and then we'll handle them from there, I think."

Athena nodded. She could manage that. Maybe she'd borrow a pair of gloves from Maple's room first.

After Emily left, the last of Trinity's bodies joined them from Big Sister's bedroom, so Athena had all of Trinity to boss around. "Did you think that the Boss would be okay with all of this?" Athena asked.

"I hoped?" Trinity said. "I probably should have guessed that she wouldn't like it. She's the best, but she doesn't get it."

And by "it," Trinity meant her personal appreciation for discarded stuff. Athena was afraid that nobody appreciated trash the way Trinity did. "Well, whatever. Let's get started. Can you go get the bags?"

One of Trinity ran off to do that while Athena went to get the dustpan and broom. There was a *lot* of trash. She paused on the way over, then changed directions and headed for Emily's room.

Maple might want some of the trash for her stuff. Besides, she could have Maple help in exchange for that, which would reduce the total work that Athena had to do.

She knocked on the door, then pulled it open. "Hey, Maple," she said.

"Mm?" Maple said. She was hugging Teddy, face buried into Teddy's tummy.

"Do you want some free stuff for your projects? Trinity just brought in a heap of trinkets. I bet there's stuff you could use!"

Maple rolled around, then reached up and moved her messy hair out of her face. "She what?" she asked.

Athena grinned. It was so easy to read her sisters. At this rate, she'd be the best of the little sisters in no time.

CHAPTER THIRTY-SEVEN

Big Sister Still Loves You

"Oh, you're finally up?" Athena said as Teddy stumbled out of the bedroom.

Athena liked being the first one up in the morning. Well, the first one up after Emily. She wasn't about to sacrifice snuggle time just to get out of bed a little early. Teddy was the exact opposite. On some days, when they had nothing going on, she would only crawl out of bed hours after everyone else was up.

"Yeah, yeah," Teddy said. She yawned so big that her jaw clicked. "Food?"

"Big Sister and I made breakfast," Athena said. "There's some left."

Emily had made a plate for Teddy, then covered it with another, upside-down plate so that it would stay warmish for Teddy. That was pretty normal morning stuff, actually.

"Oh, cool," Teddy said. She stretched her arms out, then scratched at her tummy. "Why does it smell weird in here?"

Athena glanced down the corridor. The door to Trinity's bedroom was open, and a strong scent of detergent and soap was wafting out of it.

A dejected pair of Trinitys shuffled out of the room, one carrying a mop and the other a bucket full of dirty water. "Trinity made a mess," Athena explained. "We helped her clean it. Then we discovered that her room was a *mess*, so the Boss made her clean it properly."

"Oh, that sucks," Teddy said. "But she shouldn't have let her room get so dirty."

Athena gave her a look. Teddy's room was hardly a bastion of cleanliness. It wasn't that bad, especially not compared to Trinity's room, but it was still messy. Teddy had about ten times as many blankets as everyone else, and they were all stacked on her bed in a big mound.

Sometimes Teddy would squeeze her way into the pile, like a fat worm wriggling its way into a heap of dirt, and then all that they'd see was Teddy's feet sticking out of the blanket pile. "It's whatever. Big Sister already gave her a talk. Trinity's kinda down right now."

"Hmm" was all Teddy said as she rubbed her chin. "Sucks."

"Yeah. I'm going to try to cheer her up a little. You go eat breakfast and then go take a shower."

Teddy glared. "You're not the Boss, you know."

"You don't want breakfast?" Athena asked.

"Of course I want breakfast. What I don't want is you telling me what to do," Teddy said.

Athena glared back. They were always butting heads, especially in the morning or when Athena tried to further her goals. It wasn't either of their faults, though. Athena knew that they were both fighting for the same thing, so of course they'd end up *fight*-fighting about it.

Athena wanted to be the best little sister so that Big Sister Emily would praise her, and tell her that she was the best, and so that she could get more pats and hugs and more attention. Teddy already thought that she was the best, and she did have a running start.

Teddy was the oldest and maybe the strongest of her sisters. It meant that she'd had a lot more time to build up credit and stuff with the Boss.

It wasn't fair, but that's how it was.

Athena would catch up, though, because she was the smartest of her sisters, according to herself.

She had a *plan*. It was a simple plan, which was the best, because complicated plans had more ways to fail. The first step was to become invaluable to everyone else. That meant helping the Boss as much as possible, which Athena was already doing. The second part was helping her sisters, which was by far the most annoying part.

"Just take a shower," Athena said. "Trinity did, and she's usually the stinkiest, which means that now *you're* the stinkiest."

Teddy pouted. "I don't like showers," she said.

"Too bad," Athena said. "Do you want the Boss to sniff-check you and tell you that you can't get in the cuddle pile because you smell?"

Teddy grumbled, then stomped past Athena. "Fine. Whatever. What are we doing today, anyway?"

Athena shrugged. "Nothing, I don't think? Emily has stuff to do later, but we're just staying at home."

"All right," Teddy said as she continued on past and headed toward the kitchen. Athena watched her head out before she turned back to her own work.

Her plan required that all of her sisters looked up to her like the paragon of intelligence and smarts that she was, but that was really tricky with some of her sisters. Actually, it was kind of tricky with all of them, but especially with Teddy. The two of them bumped heads more often than they agreed on stuff.

Athena shrugged to herself and decided to take the little victory where she could.

Walking over to Trinity's room, she poked her head in and found one of Trinity's bodies on her bed. She was sitting with her knees tucked up to her chest and a big pout on her face. She wasn't crying, but it looked like it wouldn't take much to get her to start sniffling.

Trinity looked up for a moment and Athena caught her eyes. It was always strange reading any of her sisters' minds. Trinity was probably the most "normal" of her sisters, except that there was so much information coming in all at once since she had so many more eyes and ears and limbs than anyone else Athena had met.

Athena didn't delve in deep. Just a quick skim of the surface was enough to know that Trinity was upset.

"Hey," Athena said.

"Are you going to tell me to clean the bathroom next?" Trinity asked. "Or will I have to . . . to take out the trash again?"

"No, nothing like that," Athena said.

Emily had already told Trinity off for trying to bring home every neat thing she found at the landfill. Athena didn't need to poke at Trinity any more than that. Instead, she climbed up onto Trinity's cover-free bed, then sat down next to her. Their combined weight created a divot in the mattress that made her shoulder bump against her sister's.

"That sucked," Athena said.

Trinity pouted harder. "Yeah. I was really happy at the landfill. I thought it would be okay."

"Yeah," Athena said. "But you know why Big Sister made you throw it all away, yeah?"

Trinity nodded. "Yeah. She said that everyone else might get sick, and that you thought it was stinky, and that there were cockroaches. Well, she didn't say that last part."

There had been a lot of screaming at the discovery, actually. The Boss did *not* like cockroaches. At all. Athena could mostly understand, since they were small and crawly and hard to kill. Like Heroes.

Emily had given Maple permission to turn the microwave into a cockroach-killing machine, and ever since then Maple had disappeared. So had most of the cockroaches once all the trash had been emptied out of Trinity's room.

"Big Sister will always love you, you know," Athena said.

It was even true. She'd seen it in Emily's eyes. She was annoyed with Trinity, even a little disgusted, but she still loved her.

Athena was working to make sure that she was the most loved, but she didn't mind sharing some of that. A little bit of it, anyway.

"Come on," Athena said. She leaned to the side and started rubbing circles into Trinity's back. "You know, it's not about being the kind of sister Emily expects us to be, it's about being ourselves so good that she'll like us anyway."

"But I *was* being myself."

"Well, yeah, but there's being yourself, and there's being your best self, and sometimes that means not killing us with the smell."

Trinity hiccupped. "I just wanted to go to the landfill."

"Ah, it's okay. I'm sure Big Sis would love to go with you, but you know how she is, she needs to do things at her own pace. Sometimes we do things too quickly, and that ruins her Villain plans. Plans in plans in plans."

Trinity nodded. "Yeah."

"I'm sure she just wants the best for all of us. And once we rule the world, I bet you could get an entire super-base hidden in a huge mountain of trash."

Trinity smiled. "That would be cool."

Athena nodded along, even if she wasn't sure she agreed. She understood Trinity's love for trash—it was hard not to understand people when she could peek behind their eyes—but it was still kind of weird. "Absolutely. But . . . yeah, you made a little mistake. Maybe if you'd asked the Boss about it, she wouldn't have been as annoyed?"

"Okay," Trinity said.

"Are you feeling better?"

Trinity let out a long sigh. "Yeah, I guess." She grinned. "I got to help Maple, though, so that's nice."

"Uh-huh," Athena said with a nod. Of course, if anyone else asked, she was totally taking credit for that idea, as long as she didn't hurt Trinity while doing so.

It was hard being the smartest of her little sisters sometimes.

CHAPTER THIRTY-EIGHT

No Worries

Athena looked up from her cards and scoured her gaze across the table.

Her sisters were quick to divert their eyes down, not meeting her gaze.

"Tsk," she said before returning her attention to the cards before her. Without eye contact, the game was a lot harder to play, but her sisters had wised up after the first dozen or so of her attempts to cheat.

Cheating was, of course, totally allowed. Unless they were obvious about it. She glanced at Trinity, who had two bodies on her wider chair. Trinity wasn't good at card games, because focusing was hard, but she was the best when it came to sneaking a few good cards into her hands, and when she did focus, her math skills were the best in the bunch. Trinity wasn't allowed to shuffle or else she'd just give herself the best hand. Athena couldn't catch it, but Trinity had clever little hands and was good at moving things where she wanted.

Athena turned her attention toward Maple. Maple wasn't as good at cheating, but she had a memory like a steel trap when it came to knowing who had picked up which cards and which ones had passed by already.

Then there was Teddy. Teddy wasn't that good at the game, and she wasn't that good at counting, but she'd turn into a bear and tackle anyone she caught cheating.

"Do you have a four?" Athena asked.

Teddy grinned. "Go fish," she said.

"Tsk," Athena said again as she picked a card from the pack in the middle.

The others went through their turns while Athena strategized. A familiar sound came from the front of the home and they all glanced at one another. "It's too early to be the Boss," Teddy said.

"Enemies?" Maple asked. She was wearing one of Big Sister's hoodies, which was way, way too big for her. Her hand snuck into the pouch-pocket at the front and came out with a gun.

"Could be Heroes, yeah," Teddy said. She raised her head and gave the air a sniff. "Doesn't smell like self-righteousness, though."

Trinity perked up. "It's Sam," she said.

Athena and the others relaxed. It was just the Boss's head minion. It was always safer to be cautious though, just in case. They were Villains in a Heroes' world, after all. They were always one do-gooder away from potential trouble.

Also, Emily might show up, and they all wanted to be the first one to get welcome-back hugs.

"Hey, brats!" Sam called out. "Oh, hey Trinity, how are you?" The two Trinitys across the table from Athena wagged her heads left and right as if an invisible hand was patting her heads.

"Should we pause the game for now?" Athena asked.

"You're just saying that 'cause you're losing," Teddy said.

Athena stuck her tongue out at Teddy (who was maybe a little bit right) and then she placed her hand down and leapt out of her seat. "I'm gonna go say hi to Sam!" she said.

She left the kitchen, her sisters trailing after her, and found Sam in the main room of the bunker. She was grinning while rubbing her hand from side to side atop Trinity's head so hard that her raccoon ears flipped and flopped up and down. "Hi, Sam," Athena said.

"Oh, hey, the whole brat squad is here," Sam said as she let Trinity go. "What are you up to?"

"We were playing Go Fish. Did you want to join us?" Athena asked. Sam didn't know not to look into her eyes, and she might unbalance the game a little in Athena's favor.

Sam laughed. "No, I think I'm okay. I just came to drop a few things off." She raised her off-hand, which was holding a few big grocery bags.

"I can help," Athena said. "Where does it all go?" She noticed a few other bags on the floor next to Sam, probably put there when Sam started petting Trinity.

"In the fridge. And no, it's nothing you can just eat like that. It's all stuff that needs prepping. Sorry, girls," Sam said.

Athena picked up a pair of bags, then smiled as Trinity grabbed the last one. They followed Sam into the kitchen, where she hefted the bags onto the counter and started emptying them. Trinity opened and closed the fridge while Athena and Sam sorted through the food.

"Did you just come to drop off the food stuff?" Athena asked.

"Nah, I've got some news for your big sis too," Sam said. "Do you know when she'll be back?"

"Ah, in about an hour, I think," Athena said. She glanced at the wall clock. "Maybe less than an hour?"

"Oh, that's all right. I can wait that long," Sam said.

"What do you have to tell the Boss?" Athena asked.

Sam clearly weighed whether or not to tell Athena for a moment, but then she shrugged. "Yeah. I think I know where Rattles will be next."

Athena perked up at that. "You do?"

"For the past couple of days he's been showing up at a few bars. He just pops in and talks to the guys there. It looks like he's recruiting some minions of his own. Not sure how well it's working out, though. He got into a fight at one place and got booed out of another. But eventually someone's gonna join up. He's got the money for it."

Athena scowled. Rattles wasn't supposed to have minions. He was the Boss's enemy. They had minions, not *him*. "We should tell anyone who joins him that they're in for a lot of trouble. Or we can tell the Heroes about them, get them all caught. Then we might learn where Rattles's base is."

"Wow, you'd do minions dirty like that?" Sam asked.

"Just Rattles's minions," Athena said. She patted Sam on the side comfortingly. "Don't worry. You're our minion, so we wouldn't let the Heroes take you."

"Wow, thanks, kid. You sure do know how to be comforting," Sam said.

Athena puffed her chest out. Yeah, she was the best at this sort of stuff. Maybe Emily would let her become the group's head of minion relations? "What kind of places is he recruiting at? Just random bars?"

"Nah, random bars have random people. Most Euclaire bars are near the college. Actually, it would probably make sense to recruit there. College guys are notoriously easy to string along."

Athena shrugged and filed that information away for later. "Where, then?"

"Biker bars, mostly," Sam said.

Athena stood up straighter. Biker bars? Like the one that she went to once? She glared at nothing in particular for a moment. How dare he try to get minions from the place she'd been to! That was *her* untapped source of minion fodder, not his. Even if she hadn't really done anything with the bikers in a while.

Maybe she should change that.

Athena finished helping Sam put stuff away, then Sam got distracted by the others. She ended up sitting at the table, half of her attention on her phone and the rest on Athena's sisters, who were all trying to impress the head minion in their own way.

Athena quietly slipped out of the kitchen and started to go back to her room. She caught a Trinity by the sleeve on the way. "Hey, I'm gonna be heading out for a bit."

"You are?" Trinity asked. "Are you allowed?"

"I'm not *not* allowed," Athena said.

That was good enough for Trinity. "Do you want me to come with you?"

She shook her head, then reconsidered. "Actually, maybe? That way if something happens you can tell the others."

"Yeah, I don't mind," Trinity said. "We're just playing cards, and I can do that without thinking very hard."

Her win rate certainly suggested as much, but Athena didn't mention it. She was the only one in their family who cared enough to keep track of who won and lost the most. "Let me get dressed, and I'll be with you," she said.

"Do we need our costumes?" Trinity asked.

"Hmm, probably not. But maybe bring a mask or something, just in case."

"Okay!" Trinity said. She darted into her own room to change out of her daytime pj's. Athena did the same. Her room wasn't all that big—none of theirs were—but it had a nice closet thing with some clothes in it. A lot of stuff had been donated to them by Steffie's mom, and from some of the new minions who happened to have old clothes. Oh, and the Grand-Bosses sometimes bought them clothes, too. Mostly socks and undies, but it was still nice to have new stuff.

She dressed up in a hoodie and loose cargo pants, then threw on her leather jacket. She'd need it where she was going.

She met Trinity by the door. "Are we going to get into trouble?" Trinity asked. By the wag of her tail, she didn't seem to think that was such a bad thing.

"This is my thing, and I never get into trouble," Athena said. "Besides, if we do, then it'll be on me. Don't worry."

CHAPTER THIRTY-NINE

~~~~~~~~~

Doing This

'm home!" Emily called out.

She secretly—or perhaps not so secretly—loved the reaction that those particular words caused.

There was the familiar sound of chairs scraping back, then the excited pitter-patter of feet as Emily put her bags down next to the door. By the time she stood back up, she had just enough time to brace for impact before Teddy ran into her at full speed.

"Oof!" Emily said as she half stumbled back. Teddy had wrapped her arms tight around her chest.

Then there was another, smaller impact as Trinity ran into Teddy, twice. The last to join was Maple, who hesitated for a moment before joining in the greeting hug. "Hi," she said.

"Hi," Emily replied.

"Do they do this every time you arrive?"

Emily looked up and felt her cheeks warm a little as she saw Sam leaning against the corner wall. "Yeah, they do," Emily said as she tried to suppress the blush. It was probably a little silly of her to enjoy the attention so much. Still . . . she gave Teddy's head a rub, then squeezed her back before moving on to Trinity, then she gave Maple a hug, too, then . . .

"Wait, where's Athena?" Emily asked.

"Uh," Trinity said.

"And where's your third body?" Emily added.

In all likelihood, the two of them were just doing something elsewhere in the house. It was probably not a cause for concern. But Emily had learned through harrowing experience that she couldn't just dismiss things because they were *probably* not trouble.

That way lay sleepless nights and migraines.

"Um," Trinity said. "Do I have to say?"

"Yes," Emily insisted. The more secretive her sisters were, the more trouble was in store for Emily.

Trinity didn't meet her eyes. "My other me's at the bar."

"What?" Emily asked.

"The bar," Trinity repeated.

"No, I heard. What are you doing at the bar? Which bar?"

"The one five blocks that way," Trinity said while pointing to one side and slightly up. "And me and Athena are having drinks."

"Wow," Sam said.

Emily shook her head. "You're having drinks at the bar? Wait, what are you drinking?"

Trinity smiled. "Soda! The nice bar lady gave it to us."

Emily relaxed, just a tiny bit. She did not feel like dealing with drunk versions of any of her little sisters. Then she unrelaxed because one and a third of her sisters were at a bar. "Why are you even there?" Emily asked.

"Oh," Sam said.

Emily's head snapped up. "Oh?" she repeated.

"Yeah, that might be somewhat my fault, maybe," Sam said. "Trinity, did you go to the bar because of Rattles?"

Emily was liking this less and less with each passing second.

Trinity shook her head. "I went because Athena was going, and I didn't want her to be alone. She went because it's a bar she likes and she doesn't want Rattles to steal the people there from Big Sister."

Emily had no idea what to say about that. "Okay, fine, can you come back home, please?"

"Okay!" Trinity said. She seemed like she was in a good mood. Probably because Emily hadn't seen fit to punish her for sneaking out of the house again. Emily realized that she hadn't exactly ordered her sisters to stay locked up indoors either, which was probably a mistake. She'd have to have a chat with them about stranger danger and leaving the bunker unattended. A very specific, carefully worded chat without any loopholes that they could sneak through.

"What's all that about Rattles?" Emily asked. She grabbed her schoolbag from the ground and placed it on the couch while moving deeper into the living room. She idly noted that the room needed another sweeping, and that someone hadn't listened to the *no eating on the couch* rule, again.

"He's been trying to recruit some minions. Mostly hitting up local bars, getting into fights there. He only hit two of them that I know of, but it's enough to guess at a pattern, I think."

"Are you sure he needs minions?" Emily asked. "He feels like more of a lone operator so far."

"He has the money for them," Sam said. "He robbed an entire bank, plus he's gotten away with more. The right kind of person probably wouldn't mind working for someone like him for the right kind of money."

Emily nodded along. Her own minions were . . . surprisingly cheap? It felt more like a mini social club that got together for random activities than something like a proper employment situation. Then again, she had the advantage that her little sisters were surprisingly endearing . . . sometimes.

"I think Athena was really fond of this one bar. She got lost and they took care of her. I guess she might be feeling protective? It's . . . a bit silly. They're adults."

Sam shrugged. "Tell that to Athena, then?"

"Uh-oh," Trinity said.

Emily spun around toward her raccoon-y sister. "What is it?"

"The bar lady won't let us leave."

"Why not?" Emily asked. Were they planning on hurting Athena and Trinity?

"Because we're too young to go wandering out in the city," Trinity said. "Which is weird, because we wandered our way over to the bar without trouble. Now she's saying that we need to call our parents."

Emily sighed. "Yeah, okay, that's . . . actually perfectly reasonable. Tell her that I'll be there in a bit."

"That's a bit suspicious, no?" Sam pointed out.

"Oh, right. Ask for a phone, and dial . . . wait, let me write the number down. It's the number to one of my burners."

What followed was a weird situation where Trinity called Emily's cell phone and talked to her while also standing right next to her in the room. Emily instructed her on what to say for both ends of the conversation, which was a little weird to do, but not that hard. As long as it pushed away any suspicion, then it was probably worth the trouble.

Emily hung up, then started to make her way to the door. "I'm going to go pick Trinity and Athena up," she said. "You girls stay here, all right?"

"That's no fair. Athena and Trinity got to go out," Teddy said.

"They *snuck* out. Which they weren't supposed to do," Emily replied. "It's not the same as just going out. We . . . can go out to the park or something later. I think we have time for that."

Teddy cheered, and even Maple seemed a little eager at the idea. Emily made a mental note to go out with her sisters more often. The bunker was a nice, secure place, but it was also windowless and indoors, and probably not the best kind of environment to be raised in, not when the only entertainment was one TV and card games.

"Let me put my shoes back on," Emily said. "Sam, would you mind keeping an eye on the girls for a bit?"

"Yeah, sure," Sam said. "You're going to walk?"

"I know where it is, and it's not that far," Emily said. Besides, she hadn't gotten that much walking done that day. Mostly she sat in buses and was ferried around, or sat in class. It would be nice to get some steps in.

She put her shoes back on, gave the girls some goodbye hugs, then darted out the door. She didn't want to run all the way to the bar, but she did walk with alacrity, pacing herself so that she'd make it there sooner rather than later.

Five blocks wasn't that much, but it was still enough to get her heart beating. Which was probably for the best; she needed the cardio if she was going to keep up with her little sisters and their endless fonts of energy.

She was three-quarters of the way there when her phone rang.

Frowning, Emily plucked it out of her purse and checked the number. It was Sam. "Hello?" she asked. Her first thought was that Sam needed her to pick something up on the way back. Or her sisters had done something, again.

"Rattles is there," Sam said.

Emily stopped mid-step. "Where?"

"The bar. Athena and Trinity just spotted him walking in. He's mostly out of costume, but they recognized him anyway."

"Are they okay?" Emily asked. She started walking again, this time picking up the pace until she was nearly at a jog.

"Yeah. I don't think he's noticed them, maybe? Or maybe he doesn't care. They are just kids, you know? What do you want to do? I can tell them to pull out, but the bartender is probably already suspicious."

"I'll be there soon," Emily said. "I . . . Can you grab my go bag? Tell the girls to costume up."

"Oh, we're doing this?" Sam asked.

"I guess so?" Emily asked right back. Rattles was slippery. They had no idea where he'd strike next. If they could grab him now . . .

"Make sure Maple brings her new anti-Rattles equipment," she said. "And have Teddy grab my bag. I'll Sisterport her over to me once I'm closer."

This was a chance that she wasn't sure she could pass up. Even if she didn't feel ready for it at all.

CHAPTER FORTY

The Angry Rattler

The booth was uncomfortable. Maybe that was because it was made of that same cheap fake-leather that bus seats were made of. Maybe it was the long strips of duct tape keeping it together, maybe it was the slight stickiness, or maybe it was his jeans being a bit too tight. Whatever the case, Kevin didn't like it.

At the same time, despite the awfulness of the booth's seat, it was still at least a little comfortable, not physically, but . . . he supposed it was an aesthetic choice? The booths fit in with the rest of the bar.

Dingy, a bit dirty around the edges, old but maintained. He nodded to a waitress and ordered whatever was on tap. She returned with a pint of something murky and brown with a layer of foam at the top.

He left a ten-dollar bill on the table, which she swiped away in passing. He didn't expect to see any change from that, and he didn't really care.

The place was the particular kind of dump that he enjoyed. It had character. The old men sitting around felt like they were part of the furniture here.

Kevin glanced up as the door opened and a man with a stooped back in a ratty old coat walked in. The man glanced around, then raised his arms a little. A chorus of "Hey!"s and "You're here!"s sounded from a nearby table, and even some of the people on stools by the counter half turned to say their hellos.

The old guy sat down, and the same waitress who had served Kevin placed a mug of something before him. He hadn't even ordered.

The atmosphere here was nice. Familial, almost. These folk weren't the richest in Eauclaire, they weren't fancy retirees or anything special, just working men and women with some time off, spending that time in their favorite pub.

He was going to hate ruining it for them, but needs must.

Or they'd must after his beer, and maybe a bite to eat. The smells coming from the kitchen in the back were making his mouth water. After all, a few minutes spent scoping the place out wouldn't hurt.

However, he was worried that he wouldn't find any minions here. The folk were either older, or looked like they were just normal civilians off work for whatever reason.

What he was looking for were gangsters and bangers and thugs with nothing better to do. Unfortunately, Eauclaire, being the nowhere city that it was, didn't have much in the way of criminal enterprises or losers that would be willing to join him.

His search so far had turned up nothing. A few drunks, maybe, but they'd need training and toughening up, and he wasn't looking to do more work. Some guys from the college nearby were options, too, but he found that those kinds of guys tended to be more . . . idealistic than thuggish.

Kevin figured he'd get lucky eventually. There had to be some people he could bully into working for him. It wasn't like he'd pay them poorly. He was just unlucky when it came to recruiting, at least so far.

He took a long pull from his pint while checking the bar over. If he couldn't find the right kind of people here, then he might as well make a little money. Emptying the cash register wouldn't hurt, especially in a place like this that dealt exclusively in hard currency instead of electronic money.

There were two kids sitting at the counter. One of them was looking back in his direction, and he caught her eyes. For a moment, he found himself freezing up, then the spell broke and he shook his head and refocused. Did he know her?

Kevin didn't exactly spend a lot of time staring at brats. They were usually harmless, if annoying, but he didn't like interacting with kids at the best of times.

The last time he'd seen kids was . . . that little fight with some Heroic brats who had tried to stop him from robbing that money truck.

He sat up straighter, then eyed the girls more carefully. There were two of them, sitting at the bar and sharing a plate of fries. They had sodas, with straws. They looked like normal kids, but what were kids doing in a bar?

Then he blinked as he noticed that one of them, the one in a gray hoodie who hadn't stared his way, had a tail hanging out the back of her pants.

He had seen it already, of course, but he'd dismissed it as some sort of childish costume or something innocent.

But a normal costume wouldn't be wagging like that.

Kevin stood up, the booth squelching a bit beneath him, then made his way across the room toward the girls.

The tailless one glanced back and saw him coming. She smacked her friend on the arm, and they both jumped off their stools and slipped out of the bar. The barkeep, an older woman, frowned as they left. "Hey!" she called after the pair.

She didn't move to follow them as they slipped out.

Kevin might have tried to go after them, but the bar was a little packed, and unless he wanted to barrel through people, it wasn't going to be easy to run out.

Instead he went to the counter. "What's up with those two?" he asked with a gesture to the door.

The barkeep turned to him, then looked him up and down with narrowed eyes. He felt a bit awkward for a moment. A guy asking about two unattended girls *was* a little suspicious, he supposed.

"They looked a bit young to be here," he explained, trying to put on a concerned-parent face.

"Yeah, well, they were waiting for someone to pick them up," she said. "Maybe she arrived."

"Yeah, okay," he said. He wasn't going to push it further than that. A glance around the bar again, and he decided that it was a bust. Plus, he was a little worried. What if the kids had come here to ambush him?

Then again, they'd been at the bar since before he arrived, and they left in a hurry once he started to approach them. It was probably just a coincidence.

But again, why were kids in a bar?

If it was just a coincidence, then it was a strange one. If the two little would-be Heroes were adult women, then he'd have dismissed it as just pure happenstance, but they shouldn't have been here to begin with.

Kevin sighed. And here he'd wanted to have some lunch before getting down to work. He stepped out of the bar, shrugging his coat on better. Charlotte was parked out front, looking rather sleek next to some grungy old motorcycles. He walked over to her and popped open her little side-saddle trunk. His Villain mask lay within.

He grabbed it and tucked it into his coat, then eyed the rest of the stuff in the scooter's container. He had a couple of guns, a retractable baton, and some pepper spray cans. Everything someone might need to cause some trouble.

He figured he wouldn't need any of it just yet, not for a couple of kids.

He patted Charlotte's container closed, then turned and searched the streets for his quarry. He found them relatively nearby: The two girls were being chastised by a third, with a fourth girl standing near them, arms crossed.

The two newcomers were in costume.

Kevin worked his jaw. This was definitely something like an ambush in the making. Maybe one that he'd foiled by being proactive.

He considered just leaping onto Charlotte and riding away. It would be the safer option.

He cracked his knuckles and started forward. Safer didn't mean better. If he wanted this to be *his* city, then he needed to put any sort of Hero in their place.

Walking toward the girls, Kevin allowed himself to grin. His heart was beating faster already, and his breath came quicker too. The fight hadn't even started and already he was getting excited for it.

The girls saw him coming, of course. The one with the crossed arms noticed him first, and she tugged the sleeve of the other costumed girl.

"Damn," he heard her mutter. "Owlwatch, Bandit, get behind me. Ursa Minor, play for time."

"You're on my turf," Kevin said. They wanted to play for time? That could only mean that they didn't expect to be able to pull a victory. He'd won already. All he had to do now was the fun part.

"This ain't your turf," the chubby one with the crossed arms said. She glared. "This is the Boss's city, so how about you wobble your butt out of here, Shakes."

"My name," he growled while reaching into his coat for his mask. He slid it easily into place over his face. "Is *Rattles*."

CHAPTER FORTY-ONE

Not One Bit

Emily didn't like the situation she was in. Not one bit.

Athena winced as she looked at the man who was slowly and calmly walking their way. "I'm sorry," she said.

"It's fine, sweetie," Emily replied.

It wasn't.

Emily and Teddy were both in costume, which was about the only thing that had gone right so far. She had Sisterported Teddy over to her side, and then went through the humiliating dance of getting dressed in an alleyway.

It wasn't something she enjoyed. Just the idea that someone might walk into the alleyway and catch her bare-legged, half-hidden behind some dumpster, gave her metaphorical hives.

She shook her head and pushed that thought aside. She was out here, on the not-so-mean streets of Eauclaire, and there was a known and dangerous Villain ambling his way toward her. "Trinity, Athena, get in the alley, go get changed," she said.

The two girls nodded, then darted away.

They'd be safe back there. She didn't want to say it to Athena's face, but Emily was mostly worried about her. Despite how terrifying she was outside of a fight, she wasn't really fit for frontline combat.

Then again, Emily wasn't fit for fighting either, and yet here she was.

"Ratt-les!" she called out.

Her voice cracked.

Emily considered turning around and following the others into the alley. Maybe she could just keep going after that. Leave town, maybe?

The Villain stopped some dozen paces away. "I remember you," he said. "And the beargirl too. Can't be bothered to remember your names, but you made me miss out on a decent payday. Didn't even make up for it by giving me a good fight."

Emily licked her lips. "What are you doing in Eauclaire?" she asked.

"Whatever I damn well want to," he shot back, grinning bright and confident before tugging up the skull-shaped mask to hide his expression. "Are you going to stop me, Hero?"

Emily balled her hands into fists at her side. "We will," she said.

"Yeah, you ugly, stinky-breath, no-moustache-having money-grubber!" Teddy added. She made a pair of rude gestures with her fingers toward Rattles that Emily had definitely not taught her.

"I . . . How old are you?" he asked.

Emily was grateful for the stall. She had a plan. It wasn't a very good plan, but it was *a* plan, and for it to work she needed some time. Or more accurately, Sam and the other girls needed time to get here. The entire plan hinged on Maple and her Anti-Vibrator.

"She's . . . young," Emily said.

"Do you think I won't smack her around just because she's a kid?" Rattles asked. He puffed his chest out and started toward her again.

She looked around, taking in the scene, looking for something she could use as a distraction. There was the bar behind Rattles, with a few bikes and a single moped parked out front. Next to the bar were some older shops and a few three-story apartment buildings. The area was semi-residential. There was a corner store not too far off, with an adjoining gas station, but that was about it.

They were just off one of the main roads in Eauclaire, which meant there was plenty of traffic . . . about a hundred meters away. The road they were on, however, was basically deserted. She had a few old homes to her left and the road to the right, and an alley behind her that she was still technically hidden in.

Nothing came to her.

"Boss? Can I kick his sorry butt around?" Teddy asked. She tried to crack her knuckles and failed.

"Hold on, Ursa Minor," Emily said. "Just . . . hold on." Teddy glanced up at her, confused, but she stayed put, tensed like a coiled spring waiting to go off.

Rattles chuckled. "Are you playing for time? Waiting for some of your Hero buddies to swoop in?"

Emily felt her heart sink. Was she being that obvious? "I'm . . . I'm giving you time to consider surrendering," she said. "Your reputation can't afford a beatdown by a girl. Can it?"

"We should find out!" Teddy added.

Rattles snorted. "Cute. Real cute."

"Damn right I am," Teddy agreed.

"That's not what I was saying, kid," Rattles said.

"Then who else were you calling cute? The Boss?" Teddy's eyes narrowed and she growled. "You can't have her. You're not good enough to date her."

"What? No," Rattles said.

Emily felt like she should say something, but this was successfully wasting time, and she could use that, so she kept her mouth shut while Teddy went on. "Well, if you're not calling me or the Boss cute, then who?" Teddy asked. "Yourself?" She snorted the kind of snort that spoke volumes about how unlikely the snorter thought something was.

Rattles glared. "You calling me ugly now, kid?"

"I called you ugly earlier. Now I'm gonna call you stupid for not remembering. And then I'll call you ugly again, just to make sure you remember this time."

"All right, that's enough," Rattles snarled. "You two planning to run away like cowards yet, or are you actually going to try something? The only reason I haven't ripped your ankles apart yet is because I'm giving you a chance to scurry out of *my* city."

Teddy looked up at Emily. She nodded slightly.

"Not your city, Rattles," Emily said. "Mine. Ursa Minor, plan B!"

Teddy's eyes lit up. "Finally!" She screamed a scream that turned into a roar as she transformed into a grizzly bear. "Plan Bear!"

The transition startled Rattles, giving Teddy just enough time to charge at him, her powerful bear muscles propelling her forward and into a huge swipe that could have tossed a car aside.

Rattles ducked under it.

He slipped backward and out of Teddy's chomping range. Then the Villain raised a foot and brought it down in a hard stomp.

The entire street shook, and Emily almost lost her footing as a wave of cracking asphalt slid past under her. A few windows burst around them, and Teddy had to quickly shift her stance to something wider to avoid getting knocked prone.

Rattles jumped back, unaffected by the quivering ground, and with each step, the entire street continued to do its Ell-O reenactment. Teddy, despite her best efforts to stay up, staggered awkwardly around like a drunk bear, and Emily was windmilling her arms around to keep standing.

Rattles chuckled. "You don't measure up, teddy bear."

Emily's heart, already hammering, jolted in her chest. Did he know Teddy's real name? No, no, that wasn't possible. It was just a coincidence. Emily watched the Villain dance just outside of Teddy's swiping range. Then he casually whipped his leg out, kicking Teddy in the snout and making her grunt with pain.

Emily winced as Teddy stumbled back. "Are you all right, Ursa Minor?"

Teddy roared, shaking her head to clear it. It was as close to a "yes" as Emily expected to get at the moment. She was going to have to give Teddy so many pats later.

Rattles sneered. "This is sad. You're not even stacking up to the Heroes. You're just standing there looking useless, and the bear's scarier to look at than to fight."

A car honked and Emily glanced back to find a familiar minivan coming down the street. It turned sharply, parking behind a small truck that would hide it away. It seemed like Sam wasn't ready to risk a second car to a Mask fight.

Emily turned back toward Rattles. Just a few more minutes and it would be over. Less, even.

And then a small miracle happened.

"What the hell is all this?" a woman shouted as she stomped out of the bar. She was followed by a good dozen older men and women in ratty old leather coats, a few plainclothes sorts, and a grinning Athena.

Had she gone around to get help? Emily hadn't noticed her slipping away, but she wasn't going to begrudge the choice, not now.

"Oh, now there's an audience. Fantastic," Rattles muttered. He spun, arms going wide as he took in the small crowd. "Looks like you're all here! My name's Rattles, and I'm looking for muscle."

Emily blinked. Was he . . . turning this into a recruitment pitch?

"Eauclaire is under new management. Mine. But I need minions. I have the cash, and it's the kind of work that comes with all the best sorts of opportunities. Like kicking the asses of little Heroes like these two."

The bartender spat to the side. "All I see is a punk with too much money and not enough sense. There's plenty like you around."

Rattles's jaw clenched. "Well, you're fired before I ever even hired you. Not that I want some old bag working for me."

That was probably the wrong thing to say. Emily wasn't great at reading people, but even she noticed all the bikers standing taller at the insult. She looked back again when she heard feet tapping on asphalt. Maple was here, with two more Trinities, and she had her device.

It was time to turn things around.

CHAPTER FORTY-TWO

~~~~~~~~~~~~~~~~

Bad Vibes

Emily glanced back to check on Rattles, then locked eyes with Maple. Her little sister was running over as quickly as she could while hugging their trump card close to her chest.

It was a black, cylindrical object, covered in dials and buttons, with a single blinking LED at the top. And a few stickers, of course. Emily wasn't sure if the dinosaur stickers were decorative or if they were integral to the device's functioning, but in either case she wasn't going to test it.

"I have it!" Maple gasped as she came closer and held the device over her head.

Emily nodded. Now they could put the plan into action.

It wasn't much of a plan. They'd discussed how to take out Rattles for some time. The Villain was, Emily suspected, stronger than any one of her sisters.

He wasn't afraid to tangle with Heroes that had years of experience, or to face off against the HRF right next to their headquarters. She didn't expect to be able to win in a straight-on engagement.

Even though Rattles wasn't exactly super strong, or super tough, his abilities made him nearly untouchable. But Rattles was all alone, and they had Maple.

"Just click?" Emily asked, just to be sure.

Maple bobbed her head in a nod. "The red button! It should work in a big sphere," she said as she handed the Anti-Vibrator up to Emily.

Emily grabbed it, switched it from one hand to another, then patted Maple on the head. "Thanks," she said. "Get behind, with Trinity, just in case. You have stuff to tie him up with?"

"I have stuff," Maple agreed with a big nod. She patted the pockets of her lab coat, which did look like they were quite stuffed.

Emily shifted her attention back to the fight. Rattles was still arguing with the people coming out of the bar. He was distracted, though maybe for good reason. Teddy was splayed out on the ground, legs stretched out every which way as she tried to stand up with some difficulty.

Emily clenched her fingers around the Anti-Vibrator, feeling the contours of the device dig into her palm. The crowd coming out of the bar was growing louder, a cacophony of disapproval, and even Rattles looked a little daunted by all the booing.

She walked toward him, then stopped as she slipped into the range of his ability. She didn't think his power had a fixed range, exactly, but it felt like she'd gone from stable to suddenly being shaken, very slightly, from all over.

She was struck by a sudden memory. Her dad owned an old acoustic guitar, and at one point Emily had wondered if learning how to play it could lead her to having friends. The vibration she felt now was similar to the warm rumble that the guitar had made when she'd hugged it close.

This wasn't the time for hesitation or second thoughts. It was now or never.

She pressed the button on the Anti-Vibrator with a *crick-click*. Instantly, a low hum emanated from the device, almost too soft to hear. Emily watched as the asphalt on the road, still rippling from Rattles's power, stilled almost instantly.

This was it.

"Plan B, round two!" Emily shouted.

Teddy, picking herself up from the ground, roared again. This time, the sound reverberated strongly; the Anti-Vibrator didn't mute it. Teddy's growl was almost happy as she charged at Rattles.

Rattles spun around and stomped a foot down.

He had just enough time to stare down at his foot accusingly before Teddy shoulder-checked him.

Emily had never seen a grizzly bear shoulder-check anyone before, but it was an impressive sight. Rattles was sent sprawling back onto his rear, coughing. He tried to stand, but Teddy planted a foot down on his chest and pushed into him, finger-length claws pressing into his shirt.

"Don't. Move," Teddy said.

Maple rushed forward, pulling zip ties and other restraints from her overstuffed lab coat pockets. She was halfway through binding Rattles's hands when he chuckled.

"You think this will hold me?" he sneered.

"Shut up," Teddy growled.

"It's over, Rattles," Emily declared, clutching the Anti-Vibrator in her hand as if it were a trophy. "You underestimated us. You thought you could waltz in here and—"

She was interrupted by a soft buzzing sound.

Maple stopped to stare, but Emily was quicker. She rushed over, grabbed Maple by the shoulder, and ripped her away from Rattles.

It was just in time. The Villain squirmed around and planted a boot into Teddy's chest. It shouldn't have done anything. A kick from such a poor angle, in the chest of a huge bear? But his foot was *humming*. It looked more like a blur than anything else, and she watched as Teddy's fur was displaced around the foot.

Teddy grunted, then lunged her head down, jaws opening wide to bite.

Rattles stopped vibrating, but there was a single loud *pop* and Teddy was sent reeling back, a large patch of fur missing from her front. Meanwhile, Rattles was pushed in the opposite direction, skidding and scraping his back across the asphalt as he slid away, out of Teddy's reach.

"No!" Emily cried, and ran as fast as she could toward Rattles. She wasn't sure what she was going to do once she reached him. Kick him, maybe?

It didn't matter. Rattles had climbed to his feet with a groan. The glare he turned on her froze her mid-step. Then Rattles was running toward her, and Emily found herself backpedaling away.

Not quickly enough.

The Villain slammed a palm toward her, his entire arm humming as it vibrated.

It struck her in the chest, and Emily gasped as the air was *rammed* out of her lungs. She saw stars, then the gray sky above.

"Boss!" Trinity roared. There was a chorus of screams as all three of her charged at Rattles.

Emily tried to call her off, to tell her not to, but at the moment she couldn't get air into her lungs and her chest was radiating an intense pain that was burning through her.

She gasped, lungs finally pulling in air as she rolled onto her front. The ground was vibrating.

Emily looked up.

Rattles was fighting Trinity off with ease. Smacking her into oblivion with casual backhands even as the ground started to vibrate again. The Anti-Vibrator was on the floor to one side, clearly crushed.

Rattles cursed as Trinity bit his hand, drawing blood. "You are so annoying," he spat.

Then a beer bottle froze in the air, vibrating like a crystal cup under the attention of an opera singer before it shattered above Rattles, raining down bits of glass onto his head.

Rattles bent forward, shielding his head before he turned toward the bar. There were more people out, big men and women in leather coats who didn't look pleased at what they were seeing.

Another bottle sailed just past Rattles's head and cracked apart on the road behind him.

Rattles hesitated, weighing his options. His eyes darted between Emily, who was now standing with Maple's support, the rest of her sisters, and the crowd. There was a Trinity still latched on to one of his legs, chewing on his boot as hard as she could.

He let out a growl of frustration, and, with his leg vibrating intensely, kicked Trinity off so hard she poofed on impact and reappeared next to her other selves. "This isn't over," he yelled. "And this is *my* city. Whether the idiots living here want it to be or not."

Rattles stomped toward the bar and the crowd screamed as the air thrummed with his power. More glass shattered, and the bar's sign rattled out of its frame and crashed to the ground, sending bikers scattering every which way.

Rattles started toward the line of parked bikes, then cursed again and ran off to dart down a nearby alley.

Emily tried to stand straight, but she gave up as the pain in her chest grew. "Are you okay?" Maple asked.

"Ye-yeah," Emily gasped.

Teddy shifted back into her human form and staggered over, looking like she was a little drunk and topsy-turvy. She immediately proceeded to double over and puke all over the sidewalk.

"Oh, that's no good," Maple said.

"Teddy," Emily staggered over. She patted Teddy gently on the head, healing her a little. Hopefully enough to undo any damage done by Rattles's attacks. "Why didn't . . . uh, why didn't it work?" Emily asked, turning back to Maple.

Maple swallowed. "I think it did? But not on him? Um. It stopped the vibrations outside of him, but not those within?"

"Mmm," Emily said. She supposed that made as much sense as anything.

"Heya, Boss, you good?" Sam asked as she jogged over.

Emily nodded, still not sure if she could straighten herself up. Her chest was throbbing and aching terribly. She glanced around herself. Her sisters had all rushed closer. Trinity looked like a mess, but she seemed otherwise okay. Athena and Maple were unhurt, and Teddy was looking a bit better. Emily herself was the one with the worst injuries, it seemed.

"You think we should go to the hospital?" Sam asked.

"I'd really rather not," Emily said. The day had been bad enough, and she didn't feel like adding unfamiliar nurses and doctors examining her, prodding, poking, asking sensitive questions, all while possibly in a crowded room or ER, on top of everything right now.

The street was a mess. Broken glass was everywhere, the sidewalks were cracked, and the road was even cratered in a few spots. All from a fight that had probably lasted no more than a minute or two.

She wasn't looking forward to explaining this one to the police.

CHAPTER FORTY-THREE

Bar Hopping

Emily had never actually been to a bar before. They were places for older people to hang out and drink, and she was neither old nor a drinker, and definitely not the sort of person to do *hanging out*.

She didn't expect her first time in a bar to have her sitting in the kitchen with her shirt off. She hissed as Sam pressed something frozen against her chest. "Ah, cold, cold," Emily squeaked. She grabbed the bundle of cloth, which unfolded a little.

It was a pack of frozen peas wrapped in a dishtowel.

"You need to keep the swelling down," Sam said. "Actually, what you should do is go to the hospital."

Emily groaned and pressed the bag to her chest again. It stung, but after a few seconds the coolness started to spread across the not-yet-visible bruises covering her front. It didn't make it hurt any less, but it was something. "I'll manage," she said. "I really don't want to go to the hospital."

"Maybe you should?" Athena asked. She wasn't meeting Emily's eyes, and Emily could almost feel the slight undertones of guilt coming off her little sister. The same little sister who Emily would have said was the smartest of the bunch just a day ago.

No, that wasn't fair. Athena was clever. It was just a coincidence that Rattles had shown up here today. Still, it wasn't the first time one of her sisters had run off and caused some trouble.

"Okay. New rule," she said, loud enough that all of the others heard.

Teddy and Trinity looked up. They had been picking pieces of meat out of a large pot of spaghetti sauce sitting on the stove. The evidence was all over their faces. Something else for her to clean before the nice bartender lady came back.

Maple, meanwhile, was sitting not too far from Emily, the parts of her anti-vibration machine laid out on the counter before her. She had been sorting through them for a while, as if trying to see what had gone wrong with her machine.

"What's the rule?" Athena asked.

"No more leaving the house without my *explicit* permission. Trinity going to the landfill was one thing, but running into dangerous Villains on your own is another. And I think it's also the final straw."

"There's a box here!" Trinity said. She plucked a brand-new box of plastic straws from her bag.

Emily sighed. "Put that back. The nice bar lady is helping us, so we shouldn't steal from her. Put whatever else you took back too, please. And Teddy, leave the sauce alone."

Teddy dropped the spoon she'd been using . . . into the sauce.

"So, wanna talk about what went down?" Sam asked.

Emily leaned back, then groaned as that pulled at the muscles in her chest. She looked down at herself. There was a large yellowish mark starting to appear over her ribs and the space between her breasts, all the way down to her stomach. It wasn't pretty. "I guess," she said. "Why did he run away?"

"Because we scared him off good?" Teddy offered.

"Maybe," Emily said. Losing his powers must have spooked him. She knew that she herself would be pretty spooked if her powers stopped working.

"There was also the bikers' reactions," Sam said. "Throwing bottles and such. If he came here to recruit and it failed, then there wasn't much of a reason for him to stick around anymore."

"Maybe," Emily said again. "But it still feels strange. He had us on the back foot. Especially after he hit me and broke Maple's device."

Maple looked up. "I can fix it," she said. "But I should probably make a newer, better one instead. This one didn't work as good as I wanted. I'm sorry."

"Don't be," Emily said. "It did exactly what you said it would. More or less. I don't think you could have expected him to be able to use his power the way he did."

"How did he use his power?" Sam asked. "I was a ways off, so I didn't see."

Emily shrugged, then shifted the pea bag around. "Maple's machine worked. It shut down all the vibrations in the area. But then he started . . . shaking himself?"

"His name *is* Rattles," Sam said. "Maple, how was your thing supposed to work?"

"Um. It stops things from vibrating through the air," Maple said. "But I didn't want it to be too strong, because the science man on the TV said that sound is vibrations too, and I thought everyone not being able to hear would be bad. Also, stopping all vibrations might stop people's hearts."

"Uh," Emily said. She hadn't considered that. "I'm glad you designed it the way you did, then. It *did* work."

Maple shook her head. "He got past it."

Emily sighed again. She was sighing a lot today, she realized. "We'll get him next time."

"Yeah!" Teddy said. "Rule of three!" The others nodded.

Emily met Sam's eyes, and Sam shrugged. "What's the rule of three?" she asked.

"It's when a Hero tries to fight a Villain, or a Villain fights another. If they don't beat each other up good enough that the fight's completely over the first time, then they gotta fight three times, and the third time's the last time," Teddy explained.

"Oh . . . kay," Emily said. She wasn't so sure how accurate that was. Was it something quest-related? Her sisters knew a lot more about the system that governed powers and abilities than she did. They probably knew more than almost anyone, actually.

Sam hopped backward to sit on one of the counters next to Maple and her pile of stuff. "So, you're going to take him on again? Isn't that asking for trouble?"

"We can't let him go," Athena said. "If he doesn't stop, soon everyone will think that he's the city's big bad Villain. No one will respect the Boss and the rest of us."

"Yeah, this city's not big enough for two big bad Villains," Teddy agreed.

Emily felt a weight settling on her chest. More stress added onto the heap that was already there. Rattles had gone from a challenge that she could choose to face to someone she absolutely had to fight, and win, against.

"What would happen if we lose again?" she asked.

Teddy scoffed. "We won't!"

The others cheered, adding their agreement.

"Okay," Emily said. "Okay, so we'll fight him again. Great. But next time, I don't want it to be like today. We rushed to get here, we didn't have much of a plan, and we only really won because Rattles didn't look like he wanted to carry through."

"I'll keep an ear to the ground," Sam said. "He'll pop up again eventually. The HRF have certainly proved that they can't handle him."

Emily nodded along. "We need a better plan. Maple, I think we're going to have to rely on you a bit more. The anti-vibration machine worked. Can you make one that's even better?"

"I can do that," Maple said.

"And can you make me something that I can fight with?"

Maple blinked. "I can. Why do you want something like that?"

"I don't want to be useless again," Emily admitted.

Sam grinned. "Well, you can start by hitting the gym some more. You need to learn how to actually fight, even if Maple gives you a railgun toaster or whatever."

Emily winced at the thought, but Sam wasn't wrong. "We should work with the minions too. Those bikers today actually helped a lot. I think Rattles's weakness might be his range. It's pretty good, but he can't handle things outside of it well."

"Yeah, I saw him get conked by that bottle," Sam said. "Do you intend to give the minions grenades or something?"

"M-maybe not grenades," Emily said.

"I want grenades!" Trinity said.

"No," Emily put her foot down. She adjusted the frozen peas again. The bag was leaking condensation all over. "We're not arming our minions, or Trinity, with grenades."

Trinity sighed in tune with herself.

"Can you make stuff that's nonlethal, Maple?" Emily asked.

Maple nodded. "I think I can. Nonlethal just means that they don't die right away, right?"

"That's a terrifying definition, but it's not entirely wrong," Sam said.

"I can do that."

"Sounds . . . good," Emily nodded. "We'll talk about it more at home." Groaning, Emily stood up, then tossed the peas on a table. She looked down at her chest again. The bruising was turning a little purplish. She prodded herself curiously, and instantly regretted it.

"You sure you don't wanna go to a hospital?" Sam asked.

"They'll ask questions," Emily said. She started to button up her shirt again, then tucked it back into her pants. "Maybe we can get armored versions of our costumes. It wouldn't hurt to be a little less . . . fragile."

"Add it to the list of things to do," Sam said.

"That list just won't stop growing, huh?" Emily shook her head. "Come on, I probably need to report what happened to the HRF, and then we can head out."

CHAPTER FORTY-FOUR

Powers

Talking to the HRF was an ordeal. She ended up facing some detective sort who was trying to get as much information out of her as possible, and Emily's social batteries were drained before the conversation even started.

Worse, some people had noticed Maple's device, and now the HRF was probing her hard about it. They wanted to know what it was, how it worked, whether it was dangerous to others. There were *forms* that gadgeteers needed to fill in order to bring equipment out onto the field. At least, if they happened to work for the HRF. If they didn't, then liability was entirely on the person who made the gadget, even if it was misused or stolen by a Villain.

Emily supposed that it made sense, at least from a legal point of view. That didn't mean that she enjoyed skirting around the law with the HRF at all.

Still, after a long couple of hours, she was able to return to her sisters, who were being entertained by the bikers in the bar.

Not exactly the kind of people she would have picked to babysit, but they were actually pretty decent. One big gruff guy showed off a knife to Teddy, then started telling stories about fights and adventures he'd been on. Another knew a few magic tricks that distracted Maple, Athena, and Trinity, and overall the entire lot of them turned from big, gruff, scary guys to a bunch of kindly grandpas the moment her sisters turned their attention on them.

It was kind of strange, but Emily decided not to poke at her good fortune.

Once she gathered her bunch up, they headed back out. Sam drove around to the exit of an alley a street down, and they loaded into her mini-van until it was filled to bursting.

The moment she was sitting in the van, belt buckled and butt firmly in the seat, Emily felt all of the tension drain right out of her. She sank into the seat and leaned her head back onto the headrest.

She felt a bit like crying.

"You okay?" Sam asked.

Emily gathered herself together. "Yeah, I'm okay," she said. The belt was pressing into her bruise, which didn't help anything. "I'll be fine."

She hoped that was true. At the moment, she felt far too weak for her own good. Rattles wasn't even a *smart* enemy. He was just powerful enough that she wasn't sure they could take him on again.

"Girls," she said, which quieted down the chatter in the back. Her sisters, at least, seemed to bounce back from the loss without any difficulty. "How powerful is Rattles?"

"What do you mean?" Athena asked. "Power's hard to measure. Do you mean his levels and skills?"

"I guess?" Emily replied. "What else could I mean?"

Athena shrugged. "There are powers, then there's power, and then there's the other kinds of power, too."

Emily still had no idea what Athena meant, and it must have shown, because Athena went on to explain.

"So, there's how strong you are. That's like, the power from your abilities and your skills. Teddy is the 'strongest' one of us because she's physically strong. But Maple, even though she's newer, could fight her and win because she has a power that's flexible, and I could beat Teddy because I'm smarter and my abilities are mental. Trinity can't beat Teddy, but she's hard to put down, so it doesn't matter."

"Okay," Emily said. "I guess I asked a question that was too . . . nebulous for a straight answer. Powers are like really complex rock-paper-scissors. There's no easy or direct way to compare them."

"Yeah," Athena agreed. "But then there's also 'power.'"

"What's that one?" Emily asked.

Athena frowned in thought for a moment. "You saw the bikers? They threw stuff at Rattles and annoyed him? They did that because we're more 'powerful' than he is when it comes to making people like us."

"That's a kind of power?" Sam asked. Her eyes were on the road, but she was clearly listening.

"Uh-huh. Usually it's a power that Heroes have a lot more of than Villains," Athena said.

"The power of the people!" Teddy added.

"We're much stronger than Rattles with that. No one likes him," Athena said.

"He didn't look very smart, and I bet he doesn't eat good food," Trinity said.

"He . . . he might stink, maybe?" Maple added her own two cents.

"Right," Emily said. "So, power-based power, and then societal-based power. I suppose he's strong with one and weak with the other."

"There's more kinds," Athena said. "Information is important. You can be very strong with that. And then there's allies, and stuff like having the law on your side, having lots of money, and knowing the right people. Power is complicated."

"Yeah, I guess so," Emily agreed. "So, in terms of *power*-power, how would you place Rattles?"

Athena thought about it for a moment while rubbing her chin like some wise man in a statue. "I think he's stronger than any of us, by a lot," she said.

"He's a lot uglier, you mean," Teddy grumbled.

"He only has one power, I think," Athena said. "But it's a lot stronger than ours. I guess he's been a Villain for a long time, so he had time to do a lot of quests and get lots of points and stuff. He might even have maxed out his power."

Emily sat up straighter. "You can max out a power?"

"Yeah," Athena said. "It happens. It's why there are Endgames, so you can go and get another power and keep doing quests and things."

"I've never heard of that," Sam said.

"Me neither. I guess it makes some sense. The Heroes wouldn't go around telling people that they won't be growing any stronger," Emily said. Now she had one more thing to worry about, though maybe it wasn't so close to happening for her that she needed to concern herself with it yet.

"We lost," Athena said. Emily glanced back and found Athena staring right at her. "But it's okay. Sometimes the Hero wins, sometimes the other Villains are tougher. What makes you a good Villain is that you get up again and do things that are even more evil than before to make up for the loss."

"Yeah!" Teddy cheered. "Let's rob a bank!"

"Oh! Can we?" Trinity asked in harmony with herself.

"No, we are not going to rob a bank," Emily said. "But . . . maybe you're not entirely wrong."

"Uh, Emily?" Sam asked. "Mind clarifying that one a little?"

"I mean, we lost because we were too weak. We tried improving a little, but it wasn't enough. I think we can push harder, become stronger. Learn how to work together better and just improve enough that we stand a better chance of coming out on top in any fights. And Athena isn't wrong about other sorts of power. I . . . I need to learn how to be less shy. If we can't beat Rattles in a fight, then we have to beat him elsewhere. We can outnumber him, we can turn the Heroes against him, we can spread information about him around. We might not have to beat him in a straight fight if we attack from another angle."

The van was quiet for a little while, at least until Teddy started clapping. "That was a good monologue, Boss!"

"That wasn't a monologue," Emily said.

"A little bit," Sam said.

Emily felt her cheeks warming up, and she turned to stare out of the window, refusing to engage with the others while she was this embarrassed. It hadn't been a monologue, just a little rant with maybe a tiny bit of inspirational speech squeezed in.

Sam continued driving the van through the streets that led to their hideout's underpass entrance while Emily's mind whirred. What Athena told her had struck something, though she wasn't sure what, exactly. It felt more important than a discussion in a van ought to be.

Her entire life, she'd been crippled by constant worry, a nonstop fear that she'd say the wrong thing, do the wrong thing, and end up a laughingstock. She'd seen others stand up and do presentations, or meet new people with smiles and laughter, and she'd always been envious. They could do something she found impossible.

That was a sort of power she'd never had. Until now, maybe. It wasn't Emily Wright who was intimidating and able to talk to people, but the Boss. That didn't matter, though, because she was the Boss when wearing that mask.

The bikers in the bar had been an excellent example. They'd had no reason to throw their weight behind Emily and her sisters, but they did it anyway. Was it the girls' innate likability? A shared disdain for Rattles? Or maybe they just rooted for the underdog. Regardless, it was a form of power, as real as any superstrength or gadget.

The van rolled to a stop alongside the road near the underpass. Emily sighed. That kind of thinking could wait. Her sisters were probably hungry, and there would be a rush to use the washroom, and then she had to see about her homework, and check out her class schedule, not to mention checking out her minions, and . . .

Emily slipped out of the van. One thing at a time.

CHAPTER FORTY-FIVE

Toy Soldiers

Maple knew it was her fault, even if Big Sister Emily said it wasn't.

Athena had cornered her that morning and said the same thing. It wasn't Maple's fault that Rattles had gotten away.

But Maple didn't feel that way.

All day she'd been a little listless and slow, only putting in some effort to pay attention to Mrs. Henderson's classes and to play a bit with Steffie in the afternoon. The rest of the time, Maple found herself retreating into her own mind.

Usually that was nice. She didn't tell her sisters, but Maple thought that she had the nicest powers out of all of them.

Everything she saw was a new idea, a new thing to try, a new experiment. Every cartoon gave her a million flashes of inspiration, and every time something went a little wrong, her power whispered a thousand solutions.

Right now, Maple was smacking down her power's little voice like a beaver slapping mud down. It could stop its yammering for a bit. It was her power that had given her the idea for the anti-vibration machine in the first place, and that had let Rattles get away.

Maple had seen it all from afar. She didn't mind not being in the thick of it. Fighting was kind of scary, and she wasn't as tough as Teddy, or as immortal as Trinity. It was a lot nicer to be on the sidelines, watching and thinking.

She got to see Teddy fight Rattles, and then Big Sister stomped up to the bad guy and talked him down. It was awesome!

Right up until Rattles broke Maple's machine and hurt the Boss. All because Maple didn't think hard enough and didn't build something good enough.

She should have made her anti-vibration machine better, so that Rattles couldn't have pulled that trick he did. And she should have made it tougher, so that a smack wouldn't break it apart and leave it useless.

Maple got home from classes and went to her room. She pushed aside the projects on her bed, then flumped down onto it, face smushed into her pillow.

It was a nice pillow. She'd taped an ice tray to the back, with a little fan and a small container for the spill-off, and then she put some hoses in, and a battery, and now her pillow was always pleasantly cool.

Maple picked it up and threw it across the room, where it rammed into the wall with the tremendous force of a feather carried by a mild gust. She wanted to be angry, but anger was hard. Instead she just felt a boring sort of sad.

If she told Big Sister Emily about it, she'd get hugs, and headpats, and maybe some nice words, and it would make her feel a little better, because all three things were good for that, but it wouldn't fix the problem. The guilt she'd feel from Big Sister being nice to her despite her mess-up would only paint the whole thing into something ugly.

She knew, because that's how she felt already.

Athena was good for talking to, but Athena would just also tell Maple that it wasn't her fault. It wouldn't help, and Athena didn't have Big Sister's knack for giving good headpats. She was all right at hugs, but Maple wasn't in a hugs kind of mood.

Puffing her cheeks out, Maple grumbled to herself, then rolled off the bed.

She was going to do something.

She didn't know what that thing was, but she sure was going to do it.

Stomping (gently, she didn't want to bother the others) out of her room, Maple looked around. It was just her sisters for now. Mrs. Headerson had dropped them off and they were waiting for Big Sister to come back from her own classes, but that wouldn't be for another couple of hours.

Maple glanced around, but whatever she was going to do, she didn't think she'd be doing it here. So, with a big sigh, Maple shuffled off to the front of the bunker. She didn't leave, though. She wasn't as adventurous as Athena or Trinity, and she didn't like leaving home besides. Also, it was against the rules.

Instead, she opened the door leading to the stairwell that went down into the train tunnel under their home. That was, as far as she knew, still "home," so it wasn't breaking any rules to go down there.

Maple picked up her flashlight from a little peg. It was something she'd made recently, a flashlight that was ten thousand times as bright because she'd placed a second bulb into the end bit. The first one was 100 lumens, and the second was also 100 lumens, and she used her calculator and it said that 100 times 100 was 10,000, which was really very bright.

It also never ran out of battery, because she'd connected the end of one battery back into itself so that the power went back around. Maple didn't know why they didn't just do that normally, but Teddy said it was because there was a secret cabal of capitalists making lots of money selling little batteries.

With the stairwell lit up better than if it had been open to the sun, she made her way down into the tunnel. For a while, she used to think that the train tunnel was a little spooky, which was silly. Big Sister was often here, so there was no reason to be spooked, and besides, she was a beaver. Beavers practically lived in tunnels. Still, the way it went on and turned dark at the end was always kind of spooky.

Now it was *bright*-bright, so much so that she had to shield her eyes a little. The brightness did reveal just how many spiderwebs there were, and it sent a few mice and such scurrying away to safety, but otherwise the tunnel was empty except for their train.

The train was still a big new rust bucket. Maple had plans for that. One day she'd turn it into a mecha, or a jet fighter, or a jet-fighting mecha. Then, when Big Sister needed her most, she'd exit (from a cool exit, like a giant lift that lifts a whole mountain up and then comes out of it) while piloting her giant jet fighting mecha and . . .

Maple frowned. She thought she'd told her power to shush up. Or had that just been her own imagination? Sometimes it was hard to tell where one began and the other ended.

There were some bikes parked next to the train, four of them, just leaning there. They didn't have enough dust covering them to have been in the tunnel for very long.

Maple wandered over and looked at them. She didn't recognize any, but she did recognize some of the voices coming from inside the main compartment of the train.

It was the minions.

Maple almost turned and headed back to her room, but . . . she hesitated. The minions weren't mean. They worked for the Boss, and so did she. Technically, she supposed she was their superior, but they were all big adults and loud and they liked talking and . . . and then she almost convinced herself to run back home.

Instead, Maple walked up to the door of the train car and flicked off her light, plunging herself into darkness. It took a moment for her eyes to adjust enough to see the dinosaur stickers she'd placed on the handles so that they glowed.

Maple really liked dinosaur stickers.

Tugging the door open, Maple stepped in, then hooked her light onto another peg. There was chitchat going on, and the occasional laugh, and then someone said, "That's not fair!", which set off more laughter.

"That's what you get for playing xenos!"

Maple poked her head into the main room, blinking at the soft light within. The minions were standing around a dining table that had been moved closer to the middle of the room. On the table were some little houses and tiny plastic ruins and a lot of tiny plastic figures, some painted, some uncolored gray.

The big strong one—Ethan, she thought—was grinning as he rolled a handful of dice onto a small tray. "Oh, that'll hurt!"

"No!" Liam said. "Come on, you've been rolling sixes all— Oh." He froze up on noticing Maple. She had been trying to hide, a little bit, but half of her head was still poking out from behind cover.

It was maybe too late to sneak back out.

"Look sharp, guys, one of the kids is here. Chloe?"

"What?"

"Well, say something to her," Liam said.

"Why me?" Chloe asked.

"Because . . . you're better with kids?" Liam tried.

"That's sexist."

"What? How?"

Maple slowly pulled herself into the light. "Um, hi," she said. The arguing stopped, then one of them—Lucas, she thought—came over and grinned.

"Hey. Are all of your sisters here too?" he asked. Maple shook her head. "We just . . . well, the game shop won't let us play unless we buy something, and that gets expensive fast."

"Only because you're cheap," Ethan muttered.

"So you came here?" Maple asked.

"Yeah," Lucas said. "What are you here for?"

Maple shrugged. "I just . . . needed time? Can I watch?"

∿∿∿∿∿∿

CHAPTER FORTY-SIX

Rolling

R oll!" Liam cheered. "C'mon, turn my luck around, kid!"

Maple counted the number of dice she had in her hand, made sure it matched the little plastic figures on the table, then dropped them into a tray where they rattled about. Eventually the dice settled and she read the pips at a glance. "Um, four of them are over four," she said.

"Yeah!" Liam cheered. "Eat lasers, Lucas."

The boys leaned over the table. The "fighting" of their little plastic models was done for now, so they started to go into the next turn or whatever. Maple wasn't sure she understood the rules, even though Liam and Lucas and Ethan had explained them to her. The problem was that they'd all explained them at the same time, and she wasn't sure which rule went with which part of the game. It was all rather confusing, but she was . . . well, she was happy that she got to participate a little.

Maple stepped to the side and picked up one figure. It was a little green guy in a little mecha made of bits and bobs. She wasn't too impressed. If she made a mech, it would have a lot more guns on it.

She put the model back, then stepped away from the table. Chloe was nearby, sipping from a can of soda. "Tired?" she asked.

Maple shook her head. She was a lot of things, but tired wasn't one of them. "I'm okay," she said.

"So, why did you come out here? You couldn't have known that we were here. Unless you did?" Chloe asked.

"I didn't," Maple said. "We probably should have cameras in the tunnels, and better security." Maybe she could have defense mechs? She really wanted to build a mecha or three, and having more security seemed like as good a reason as any. "I just came here because . . . I guess I needed to think?"

Chloe smiled, then gave Maple's head some pats, which was nice. "You've got a lot going on, huh?"

Maple started to nod, then stopped. What if that made Chloe stop the pats? "Yeah," she said simply. There really was a lot going on, with the Boss, with Maple, with her whole family. She had so much that she needed to do that she wasn't sure she'd be able to do. It was just a lot.

"You look too young to be so anxious," Chloe said. "But I guess there's no age for it, huh? Well, we'll be here for another few hours at this rate. I want my turn at the table too. You can hang out with us if you want? Hey, do you like painting? I've got so many minis to paint."

"I guess I do," Maple said.

It didn't take long before Chloe had whisked her over to one of the tables farther into the cabin. Then, she took out a small case with paints, little brushes, and some paper towels. Maple was shown some of Chloe's other models so she had an idea of what colors to paint, then was left to it.

Maple wasn't too sure if she even wanted to paint them at first. What if she messed them up? But Chloe said that it was fine, so she decided to give it a try.

It wasn't long before Maple was biting the tip of her tongue and smudging paint across a model and also her own fingers.

It was making stuff, which was what her power was all about, but she wasn't trying to make something too special, she was just painting a little figure. It looked like some sort of sniper character, with a big gun and a little cloak for hiding.

Maple dipped her brush into some paint, then concentrated as she painted the details on the figure's cloak. It was different than what she usually did. There was no problem to solve, no immediate need to fulfill. It was just painting for the sake of it.

It was nice, but also frustrating, because she couldn't stop the chatting of her power in the back of her mind. She refrained from doing what it suggested. Chloe didn't need her little figure to move, or for their little guns to fire actual lasers . . . Maybe she could make it so that their little cloaks *did* make them partially invisible, since that was easy, but no more than that!

So far, Maple and her power had an understanding of sorts going on. It would give her ideas and things it could do, and Maple would sometimes pick one of those to make something. The things she made had to be help-ful, though, either for herself or her sisters or her friends. It was a good power, Maple thought. They got along very well.

They could get along even better, though.

Name: Maple Wright		
Alignment: Villain, Little Sister		
Alias: None		
Level: 1		
Powers		
Builder of the Dammed		
Sticks and Stones	Rank 1	
Approximate Gnawledge	Level Max	
Points		
Power Slots: 0	Skill Upgrades: 3	Skill Slots: 1

That was three points of upgrades she was sitting on, and a single new, unused Skill Slot.

She had earned it while her sisters fought Rattles. They had used equipment she made, which fulfilled the requirements of a quest. It was enough to push her into gaining a slot. She really needed it. If she was going to catch up to her stronger sisters and be useful, then she needed to hurry up and get stronger!

Maple grabbed her open Skill Slot (metaphorically) and shoved her free point into it.

Sticks and Stones
Rank 1
The user is uninterruptible and cannot be stopped while they are at work. While in this state, the user generates heat and can become ill if the state continues for extended periods.
Cooldown: 24 hours

Maple blinked. That was . . . certainly a skill! She smiled as she thought of how best to use it. If they had that fight with Rattles again, then she could use this to fix her machine right then and there without having to worry about anything, at least until she was done fixing it!

Maple put two points into the skill, reducing the cooldown a little.

Sticks and Stones
Rank 3
The user is uninterruptible and cannot be stopped while they are at work. While in this state, the user generates heat and can become ill if the state continues for extended periods.
Cooldown: 6 hours

That was a lot more usable!

"You're smiling a lot," Chloe said. "Are you done painting?"

"Huh? Oh, yeah," Maple said. She blinked, then started looking for the model that she had been painting. Where was it? It took her hand brushing across the surface for her to find it. When she touched it, the model turned the same color as the skin of her hand. "Here it is," she said.

"Uh," Chloe said as she took it. The model changed, part of it the same beige as her skin, but there were some streaks of blue, probably from her nail polish. "Well, that's something. It's going to be tricky to play with this one."

"It's no good?" Maple asked.

"Oh no, this is super good," Chloe said with a grin. "It's kinda awesome, actually. I'm not going to be able to match it with the rest of my army, though, since it's so much better. Also, it might be easy to lose on the table."

"I can make it normal again, if you like," Maple said. She felt a little bit guilty about using her powers more than she'd intended on Chloe's model.

"No way! This little guy's special now. Plus, I can brag so much with this, you wouldn't believe it. Thanks, Maple."

Maple perked up as she earned more headpats. They weren't Big Sister pats, but they were still nice.

The games at the table were still going on, the minions having plenty of fun, but Maple was feeling a little tired. "I think I'm going to go home," she said. Spending time around so many people who weren't her sisters had really drained what Big Sister called her "social batteries."

Could she make something to recharge those?

An idea for later, maybe.

"That's all right," Chloe said. "Here, do you want to take some snacks back with you? Liam always brings too many and I don't know if I want to carry them all back."

"Okay," Maple said.

It wasn't long before she was holding a big plastic shopping bag filled with opened bags of chips and some cans of soda. She imagined that she'd be very popular once she got back home. Big Sister Emily didn't say that they couldn't have junk food, but she also didn't buy much of it.

Maple decided not to make a big fuss about saying goodbye. She just picked up her flashlight near the door and then headed homeward.

She was feeling a lot lighter than she'd felt earlier. The next time they fought Rattles, he'd be fighting against her sisters while they were equipped a lot better. He wouldn't stand a chance.

CHAPTER FORTY-SEVEN

Gyms and Abstracts

Sam glanced up from her laptop to stare across the room. She did a quick head count, something she'd become extremely proficient at in the last couple of weeks. One, two, three-four-five . . . and Teddy was over there, so that made six heads for four little Villains.

The girls were currently at one of the parks on the edge of Eauclaire, maybe a thirty-minute walk away from the school campus. The park should have been filled with people, but it had gained a bad reputation as a place where university students hung out and harassed any of the teens or whatever who came here.

Now it was a little overgrown, and the playground equipment was dated. That all added up to create a space where no one actually came to hang out.

It probably helped that most kids Sam knew would rather spend the evening online than running around a rusty jungle gym.

Sam stared at her computer again, then subtly shifted the screen over to some homework as she heard panting.

Emily ran by, breathing hard and covered in a sheen of sweat. She paused not too far from the picnic table that Sam had requisitioned for herself, grabbed a water bottle, downed half of it, then, with a pitiful groan, started running again.

Sam tabbed back to the document she'd had open before and reread a few lines. She had gone back to the beginning and was trying to work out her abstract.

Abstract

This is a confidential field study conducted to gain a better understanding on the psychological profiles, motivations, and personalities of a group of anonymous individuals engaged in Villainous behavior. This study's goal is to create a psychodynamic profile on these Villains while probing their mental states, beliefs, and the rationales for their actions.

Sam squinted at the screen. Was that too formal? Not formal enough? She needed anyone who read this to take it seriously from the get-go, because a lot of parts later on were far from serious.

Really, when she'd joined Emily's little band of misfits, she'd expected things to be a lot more clear-cut.

They *should* have been. Emily herself was . . . a hot mess, psychologically, but her little sisters? Oh, they should have been treasure troves! Living people, made by and for a Villainous power, with powers of their own.

They weren't born normally, and they shouldn't have been in any way nurtured into being anything but their natural selves. At least, not initially.

The perfect example of what "superpowers, or the system that gave out powers," considered appropriate abilities for Villains.

The study of superhuman powers was still relatively new. There were probably millions of dollars of grant money just sitting there, waiting for someone to come along and pluck it away. Not to mention the clout.

Sam stilled her beating heart. Later, later.

Her fingers hovered over the keyboard as she reread more of her text. She had very few examples of similar work to draw on. A few papers had been published tailing after Super Heroes, but those tended to be . . . too clean. They'd barely made a splash in the world of psychology.

She expected that something a lot more raw would do the trick, and that it might counteract some of the issues that came with having to be so secretive within her own reports. She couldn't give away powers, weaknesses, or anything like that. Not only would it be a betrayal of Emily, but it would make it way too obvious that she was clout-chasing.

There was a nice, fine line to everything. But Sam was good at finding those.

Plus . . . she kinda liked the brats. Emily, too. It had taken a while for them to grow on her, but now they felt like little nieces she'd never had.

Scrolling down a little, she stopped at a segment near the top of her report. Her methodology section was a *mess*, and she was determined to work on it . . . some other day. She kept scrolling.

Findings

Contradiction in Behavioral Expectations

One striking aspect that defies what the TITLE [Researcher? Student? Pre-PHD and Nobel Prize winner? I need a name here] *expected is the variance in archetypical Villainous behaviors. The subjects have a set of moral standards that are, on paper, archetypically Villainous. They have no respect for the authority of the government or law enforcement, care mostly for their own in-group, see no issues with theft, arson, or harming others, and find the suffering of others to be amusing.*

They find pride and joy in being as "evil" as possible and wish to dominate and control others, to be praised for their unkind deeds, and to be more powerful than any in their entourage.

On the surface, these behaviors paint the subjects as purely Villainous forces of evil.

Sam hummed to herself. Was she putting it on too thick? This was where she'd depart from what someone would expect to read, and no one, not even people who claimed to be scientists, liked it when what they read went against their preconceptions.

No, it was probably better to lay it on thick here.

She wiggled her fingers to make sure they were limber, then continued.

These Villainous tendencies conflict with observed behaviors. If asked, most subjects would admit to being evil, Villainous, and quite cruel. However, if observed, the subjects will display actions contrary to that self-description.

They show affection and concern for one another's well-being, worry about what others think of them, and are uncharacteristically loyal. Most of their actual, demonstrably Villainous actions are simple actions taken because they don't feel the need to fit into our wider society. These can be harmful—examples include petty theft, or what might be considered burglary, as well as making threats of physical violence—but more often than not, the subjects cause very little by means of actual harm.

In that regard, these Villains are no more immoral than an unlearned child might be. They are free of the moral constraints and rules that someone raised in a civilized, modern society might adopt, while also holding onto other moral elements with more tenacity than would be expected of someone who was born and raised in that same society.

Sam leaned way back, stretching her arms over her head and cracking her knuckles. She had a couple of good lines in there. She'd need to pretty them up, though.

The conclusion she was slowly circling was kind of trite and boring. The kind of first-year-sociology-major stuff that would have eyes rolling. She couldn't quite think of another, better conclusion to draw toward, however.

Looking up, she saw the girls swinging from old rusty bars. Maple was the odd one out, but she was over by the sand pit, building . . . a multi-floor sandcastle, with levering doors made of ripped-apart soda bottles and what looked like a missile silo to one side.

It looked like it was still just in the sandcastle phase, so Sam decided to leave it be.

Emily was coming around from another circle of the park. She was even sweatier than usual and looked like she was ready to faint.

"Having fun?" Sam asked as she tabbed out of her report.

"Yeeeagh," Emily said. It wasn't quite a word, but it still communicated a lot.

"Sounds like fun," Sam said. She didn't begrudge Emily's recent exercise kick. It would probably be good for the lanky girl to put on some muscle.

"Time of my life," Emily said as she came to lean against the table. She took the water bottle and downed the rest, then pressed a hand against her ribs. "Stitch," she groaned.

"Give it a minute," Sam said.

Emily wiped at her brow, then glared at nothing in particular. Sam liked to think that she was glaring at the concept of exercise itself. If Sam was "exercise," she wouldn't be very worried, though. Emily could be scary, but only in small amounts and usually at key moments. The rest of the time, she was about as spooky as a wet towel.

"It's good for me," Emily said, like someone trying to convince themself. "And the exercise is good for them too. Plus, it's cheaper than the gym."

The girls were running around. Someone had stepped on Maple's sand-base and now Maple was chasing them with . . .

"Is that a knife?" Sam asked.

Emily's head whipped around. "Maple! No knives! No, I don't care that you made it yourself. Yes, Trinity probably deserves it, but no stabbing your sisters!" Emily bent down and pulled a second water bottle from her bag. She ripped the cap off and drank deeply from it. "They're going to be the end of me," she said.

"They're quite something," Sam said.

"Yeah."

"You ever wonder what they could become? You know, if things were different?" Sam probed.

"Different how?" Emily glanced at her.

"I don't know. More . . . normal?" Sam tried.

Emily was quiet for a long moment, then she shook her head. "No. No, I don't think I can imagine them as normal." She set her water bottle down on the picnic table, then took off running again.

Sam grinned. "Not normal" was good, as far as she was concerned. It was more to write about.

CHAPTER FORTY-EIGHT

Cheater?

Emily stared at the paper, then stared harder. She was breathing harder than she should have been, and yet she couldn't get enough air. It felt like someone had a hand inside her chest and was squeezing her heart.

It couldn't be.

Looking up, she glanced around the room. This wasn't the usual lecture hall where they sat and listened to a professor talk for a while, but more of a traditional classroom, where each student had a small desk to work from, all facing a blackboard and the teacher's desk.

The room still had a number of students in it. Some had swiped their papers and left right away, but a few were lingering to talk. Emily had been paying some attention and noticed that there were several little friend groups forming within the class. Not that she was part of any of them.

Usually she was one of the students who was out of the room relatively quickly, but this paper . . .

It would be time for her midterms in a couple of weeks, and there was a palpable tension in the class as everyone started to get ready to cram and study for the upcoming exams. Her paper had a note at the top, right next to the field for her name. *Please come talk, Wesley Percyson.*

That was the name of the teacher's assistant, and it was right next to her grade on the paper. A big fat zero.

Another student moved past Emily's desk and she glanced up just in time to see them catch sight of the zero and look at her before walking on.

Emily's face felt unbearably warm all of a sudden. She snatched the paper off the desk and folded it in the middle. Standing on wobbly legs, Emily got up and quietly walked to the front of the class.

She'd been studying. She'd been doing her homework this entire time. And it hadn't been *easy*. She felt like a single mom, taking care of four to six children with only a little bit of outside help. It was a miracle that she was keeping up with her studies at all, and most of that came from her sacrificing sleep and leisure time in order to have even a minute or two to do her schoolwork every day.

A zero was impossible. Maybe she wasn't studying or absorbing as much as she might have if she wasn't a Villain, but to take in nothing at all? That was wrong. It had to be.

There was a small line by the teacher's assistant's desk, and Emily waited off to one side. Not quite in the line, but close enough to let people know that she wanted a chance to talk with Wesley at some point.

Finally, after a good ten minutes or so, the room was left entirely empty except for her and the TA. "H-hi," she said.

"Yes? Can I help you, Miss . . ."

"Wright," Emily said.

There was a flash of recognition in Wesley's eyes. "Right, Miss Wright. You're here about your results."

Emily nodded and placed the folded paper on the desk between them. She didn't want to unfold it and reveal that ugly zero again.

"You know, you're lucky that I gave you a zero," he said.

"What?" Emily squeaked.

"I could have you expelled outright."

Emily shook her head. "I don't understand," she said.

"Cheating isn't viewed well here. Nor is plagiarism."

She reeled back. "Ch-cheating? I didn't?"

Wesley stared at her, one eyebrow raised. "Really? Because your answers are identical to another student's."

Emily shook her head. That was impossible. She had never cheated before. It wasn't even that she was entirely opposed to the idea of cheating (well, she supposed that she was), but more that she couldn't help imagining what would happen to her if she was caught. That thought gave her cold sweats and nightmares, and now it was happening before her eyes without her even having cheated in the first place.

She swiped her paper from the table and looked it over. The answers were what she'd written. This wasn't a prank or anything. "No, no, these are my answers. I know they're right."

"Oh, they are," Wesley said. He stood up and started packing his things into a little briefcase, obviously done for the day. "That test scored the other student a nice ninety-four, which is well above the class average."

"But it's mine," Emily said. She felt a little faint, as if she hadn't eaten all day, and was on the verge of trembling.

"Look," Wesley said as he closed his suitcase with a final *snap*. "Next time, don't cheat."

"I didn't," Emily whined.

The teacher's assistant just sighed and picked up his case. He started heading toward the door. "Sure, sure. Look, I didn't get you expelled. Clean up your ac—"

Emily didn't remember moving, or grabbing onto Wesley's arm, but here she was, with a firm grip around the young man's forearm that stopped him in place. She blinked past the tears gathering in her eyes.

Her chest still trembled, and her hands shook, but now the panic was being burned away as if it were doused in gasoline. "No," she said. "I want you to tell me who cheated off me."

Wesley shook his arm, as if that would be enough to get her to let go. He frowned, but he did come around to answering her question. "It's the professor's niece. She's a straight-A student. I can't imagine why she would cheat, let alone off you. She has a number of friends in the class and is well-liked."

The implication—Emily noticed immediately—was that she herself wasn't well-liked in the same way, nor did she have any friends in the class. Or many outside of it.

"I didn't cheat," Emily said.

"Let go of me," Wesley said. He smiled smugly as he delivered his next threat. "Maybe I'll present your paper to the professor. Would you like that? Being expelled not even a semester in?"

Emily took in a quick breath. That would be . . . so unfair.

It happened often, though. Not accusations of cheating, but accusations of stuff that she couldn't defend herself against. People walked all over those who didn't have a voice to defend themselves with, and Emily was one of those. First putting pickles in her burger when she was too shy to ask for another, and now this whole thing.

"Listen to me, Wesley," Emily said. She used the same tone she unleashed on her little sisters when they really needed to listen. Soft, and calm, but with an edge. Her grip tightened, anchoring the teacher's assistant to her.

"You're accusing me without evidence. You made an assumption. You presumed that I'm guilty and another party, who isn't here, isn't."

"Let, let go of me," Wesley said. His smug smile had been wiped away, and he looked like he wanted out now.

Her eyes finally looked up and met Wesley's for the first time since this whole thing started. He looked increasingly uncomfortable. Somehow, seeing him like that made the grip around her heart loosen. "Did you do it because it was convenient? Because the professor's niece can't possibly be in the wrong? Do you like her that much? Did she smile at you? Did she say the right things? You say she's well-liked and has friends. Are you saying that I don't? Because you might be right. I've been doing all of this on my own. I've been juggling problems that you can't even imagine, Wesley. I haven't had a good night's sleep in months, Wesley. I have to do my homework while kids are screaming and starting fires all around me, Wesley."

Wesley tried to tug his arm free.

She didn't let go, not even when he started to speak.

"No. No, you don't get to talk, Wesley. You're going to listen to me, because you've been a very, very bad . . . man. You decided to ruin a perfectly good afternoon because I'm not as popular as someone else? Or was it because you're too lazy, sitting there at your tiny, pathetic desk, making judgments like you're some sort of academic god? Do you have *any* idea how much stress I'm under? Do you?"

"I—"

"Shut up, Wesley," Emily snapped. It wasn't the kind of language she'd use on her sisters. But Wesley wasn't one of her sisters. She felt a cold shiver run through her entire body before it was replaced by a fuzzy warm flush. "I didn't cheat. I studied for that test. I put in the hours, even if it wasn't easy. You made an assumption, and you were wrong. I will not be penalized for someone else's actions. I will not allow you to sabotage my education just because you can't be bothered to actively investigate. I am *tired* of idiots with a tiny smidge of power being too lazy to do their damned jobs."

Wesley finally managed to pull his arm free from Emily's grip. She was breathing heavily, and she was probably a little sweaty and disheveled. The adrenaline still spiking through her was the only thing that stopped her from folding into a nervous little ball to be swallowed up by the floor.

Wesley seemed to find his voice. "I'll . . . talk to the professor?"

"Yes, that would be nice, thank you," Emily said. She cleared her throat, then scampered out of the classroom, hugging her stuff to her chest. "No, no, no," she muttered to herself.

Emily slipped through the crowds outside, invisible as always, even though she was talking to herself the entire time.

"I am *not* a Villain," she said, even if it had felt spectacular.

CHAPTER FORTY-NINE

Wanna Go

I think I want to go," Emily said.

Sam looked at the page, then back up at Emily, and Emily knew what the other girl was thinking, even if she would usually consider herself a poor reader of faces. This was probably not a good idea.

"How did you even get this?" Sam asked as she waved the page around.

Emily sighed and melted onto the dining room table. "I got it from Glamazon."

"Really?" Sam asked. "This looks like it's from the HRF."

"It is. Look, the HRF knows that Glamazon, or Jezebelle I guess, knows who I am out of costume. Apparently it's pretty normal for Heroes to un-Mask to other Heroes without wanting to un-Mask them to the HRF."

"Makes sense," Sam said.

Emily glanced up. "It does?"

"Yeah. Look, un-Masking to something like the HRF is scary. They're a big governmental organization. They're kind of faceless, and have a bunch of rules and such. Anyone who's not, like, a paragon of Heroism probably worries that they might make one small mistake and then the next thing they know the HRF is knocking at their front door with a warrant."

Emily swallowed. That was a nightmare to consider.

"I've been looking into it. Do you know how many of the HRF's Heroes aren't entirely Heroic?"

"I . . . don't?" Emily said. She perked up. Was Sam about to tell her that the HRF accepted Villains, even inadvertent ones like herself?

"It's probably something like half," Sam said. She waved Emily down.

"They're not Villains. They're like, a tier or two down from all-out Hero. You know, anything above Anti-Hero."

"Right," Emily said. She'd looked at the rankings that Handshake had given her a long time ago for hours, which Teddy had once confirmed as sort-of-accurate. She was solidly in the black, all the way in the bad-guy section of the chart. The Heroic, good-guy section went on for a while too.

Most people who got powers probably started off somewhere in the middle of the morality chart. Stuff like Anti-Heroes, Rogues, maybe one of the stranger ranks like Merchant or Mercenary or Defender. There were lots of possibilities, though society at large tended to lump people into five broad categories: Super Heroes, Heroes, Rogues, Villains, or the exceptionally rare Super Villains.

"Okay, so the HRF recruits from the middle, then," Emily said.

"Yeah," Sam said. "And the people in the middle probably don't want to get lumped in with those who don't *mind* being in the middle. It's probably a lot harder to act all Heroic and do good when you have the word *Vigilante* hovering over your head. So the HRF understands when someone doesn't mind working with them but still wants to keep their ID under wraps."

"Do they think that's what I'm doing?" Emily asked. It had the benefit of being a little accurate.

"Probably. I bet they're assuming that you're somewhere in the middle too. Maybe a Mercenary instead of a proper Hero? Anyway, Masks chatting with other Masks is normal, and if they chat, they'll grow to trust one another a lot more than they'll trust a governmental org."

"Right," Emily said.

"It's called reciprocation. A Hero, like Glamazon, opens up to someone a few rungs down. That person might be worried about the HRF, but they'll open up to a friend who opened up to them. Then *bam*, the HRF has a way to get to you and send you awful spam letters." Sam waved the letter around some more.

Emily reached out and grabbed it before Sam could crumple it up with her gesturing. She flattened it on the dining room table, careful not to get it messy. The girls had eaten at the table earlier, so it had a few stains on it.

Dear The Boss,

It's with great pleasure that the Heroic Response Force of Eauclaire invites you to our annual Littlest Heroes event!

The youngest minds of our generation need Heroes to look up to, and we think that you're fit for the job of being a stellar role model!

The event will be taking place this Friday, at 6:30 p.m. at the Eauclaire General Hospital. Catering will be provided. Please leave all weapons or dangerous implements at home and RSVP to the following address.

Below the HRF headquarters mailing address, the rest of the letter had a bunch of minor legalese expertly disguised as pleasantries by someone who was probably underpaid.

In essence, it was a yearly event where a few B-list Heroes would show up at the local children's wing of Eauclaire's biggest hospital. They'd linger around, hand out merch, maybe take some selfies, and generally do PR stuff.

It was the kind of trite, boring do-gooder stuff that Emily had always hated.

She'd actually attended an event like that once. A couple of Heroes had shown up at her high school with merch and did signings and the whole thing. Emily had been determined to keep away, so she'd hidden in the library like a sensible person.

She couldn't remember the name of the Heroine, but she'd shown up in the library looking for "lonely souls" and had pestered a stuttering conversation out of Emily before getting bored and leaving.

The memory of her own fumbling had stuck with her for years now, one of the crowning jewels on her mountain of embarrassing moments.

"I think we should go," Emily said.

"Really?" Sam asked. "That seems like a terrible idea, but you're the boss, Boss. I'll hear you out."

Emily worked her jaw. She wasn't sure how to explain why she wanted to go. She herself knew why, but it was a little . . . mushy, and she was worried that Sam might not take her concerns seriously. "I think that we're maybe . . . a little *too* good at being Villains."

"I feel like this needs a better explanation than just that," Sam said.

"I don't want to be a bad person," Emily said. "I . . . Being a Villain is feeling so easy. It feels *good*. Maybe if I do morally good things, then that'll offset things?" She gestured to the letter. Attending the event was probably the most objectively good thing she could do at the moment. Helping sick kids feel better? That wasn't Villainous at all.

"Huh. All right, I think I can see that," Sam said. "You want to clean off the karmic slate, so to speak."

"Yes, exactly," Emily said with a firm nod. That's what she wanted. An opportunity to pull away from being a Villain.

Sam gestured vaguely at Emily. "Is this because of the whole cheated test thing?"

"No . . . maybe?" Emily said. She'd related the story already. Sam was the only person other than Emily's mom she was comfortable ranting to, and she didn't want her mom to hear about how she'd maybe lost her temper a little.

"You know that Weasel guy was a jerk, right? He totally deserved all the shouting you did at him."

"Wesley," Emily corrected. "And maybe? But it's not like me to act that way."

Sam shrugged. "If you say so. I think he's got a rep for being a lazy jerk, so I don't see the harm in putting him in his place."

"It's not that it was bad to shout at him, it's that *I* did the shouting. I've never done that kind of thing before," Emily said. She resisted the urge to sound petulant about it. "I'm going to the event. It'll be good for my sisters to see what it's like to behave. Maybe it'll set a good example?"

Sam didn't look like she believed that for one moment, and Emily secretly agreed with her. "Well, whatever. It's Friday, right? That gives us a couple of days to clean up our costumes and get the girls used to saying the right kind of pleasantries. I don't think you want to let them be their normal selves at a hospital, of all places."

"Yeah . . . no."

"Teddy would wreck the room as a bear to show off. Or attack the administration the moment she learns that they charge for anything. Athena would want to lord it over the doctors. Maple might turn the machine keeping someone alive into a gun, and Trinity would end up diving into a dumpster full of biohazards."

"Oh . . . oh god," Emily muttered. That all sounded exceptionally plausible. "Yeah, we're going to need to do . . . like, lessons on how to behave."

"Uh-uh, *you're* gonna do that. I've got other things to do this week, Boss. Being a minion is fun and all, and the pay's not half bad, but I've got a social life to keep up with and I've been neglecting it for a while. You can probably get one of the other minions to do the cleaning, if you ask." Sam languidly stretched her arms over her head.

"Right, of course," Emily said. She couldn't even muster any disappointment. It only made sense that Sam would have a social life where Emily had none. Besides, she was feeling a little guilty about all the time she'd stolen from Sam to begin with. "I'll figure it out. Don't worry."

Emily didn't need Sam worrying when she could worry enough for the both of them.

CHAPTER FIFTY

Sickly Sorts

Teddy squinted and tried harder to see out of her mask.

Her big sister had replaced the thin plastic strap holding the mask in place with the strap from a pair of goggles, hot-gluing the thicker strap to the inside of the mask so that it stayed on her face better. It made the mask much comfier. Then she'd poked a few dozen little holes into the mouth area of the mask, too, and put one of those disposable face masks on the inside with more glue.

It made her plastic bear mask feel a lot nicer and better, but it still didn't help with her vision. The little eyeholes made it hard to see from the sides, and Teddy was worried that a Hero might sneak up on her.

She had to turn her head all the way around to look up at the Boss. "Do we gotta?" Teddy asked. "I don't want to be all chummy with . . . you know, *that* sort of person."

Teddy was being careful with her words because at the moment, she and all of her sisters were riding on one of the city buses. They took up three whole rows by the front, and Teddy got lucky enough to have one of the aisle seats, the one right next to her big sister. She was the first one to see anyone walking onto the bus, so if they were a Hero, or a rival Villain, they'd have to deal with Teddy before they could try anything funny.

"Ted— Ursa," Emily said. "What we're doing today is a good thing. It'll help people who are hurt, like Steffie, and it'll keep our cover as Heroes. I expect all of you to be on your best behavior, all right?"

Teddy pouted, not that anyone could see it. Working with Heroes sounded so boring. Working in a hospital sounded even worse. Why would Teddy even want to be around sick kids?

She crossed her arms and harrumphed. If the Boss said it was important, then Teddy figured she should at least try.

The bus rode on for a while, and Teddy tried to have some fun with her sisters. Trinity was squished in next to her and was hogging the window, so Teddy half turned and played rock-paper-scissors-claws with Athena. It was fun, at least for Teddy, since according to the rules she made up, she was the only one who could use claws, and claws beat everything.

Actually, they only played three rounds. The rest of the time was spent with Athena complaining while Teddy laughed at her for losing three games in a row.

Finally, the bus rumbled to a stop, and Teddy turned to look out the window. They were in front of a great big building, all gray and white, with a big parking lot to one side and a spot with a bunch of ambulances parked in a row next to it.

A big sign by the front read EAUCLAIRE GENERAL HOSPITAL, so Teddy knew they were in the right area.

Unfortunately, next to all the normal cars and ambulances was a trio of ugly black vans with the HRF logo plastered on the side. The Heroes were here already. Teddy groaned, but there was nothing for it.

They got off the bus, and the Boss made sure everyone was accounted for. One of Trinity was still inside, so she had to go fetch her, but then they were all together, baking in their costumes on the sidewalk.

"All right," the Boss said. "I want everyone to be on their best behavior. What did I say about hospitals?"

"Even a Villain wouldn't rob them," Teddy droned without emotion in an echo of what her sisters said.

"Good! I'm very proud of all of you. And I'll be even *prouder* if we get through today without some sort of disaster." Emily nodded firmly, then reached down for a hand to grab. Teddy was fastest and closest, so she got to be the one to grab on first, then she had to hold on to Maple, who held on to one Trinity, and so on until they were all linked up.

There was a big show of looking both ways before they crossed the street and headed right for the HRF vans.

Halfway there, they were met by a clipboard person coming from one of the vans. "Boss? And . . . various little Heroes?" the guy said. He looked tall and reedy, not at all the mental image that Teddy had of HRF troopers, but pretty much exactly the image she had for bureaucrats, and those could be way worse than troopers.

"That's us," the Boss said with a wan smile. "Are we late?"

"Just in time," the clipboard-holder said. "We were wondering if it was okay to separate the girls? We have a few locations where we're having visitors."

"I . . . suppose. Could I rotate between the groups?" the Boss asked. "What are the locations, anyway?"

"We have three," the clipboard said. "One in the children's wing, one visiting patients across the hospital, and another in the lobby by the entrance, where we have an HRF kiosk for donations. Each group has one Hero assigned to it already. Glamazon is taking care of the entrance, Melaton is in the children's wing, and we have Silver Fox doing room-by-room visits. Soothe-Sayer is arriving soon, and he'll be rotating through the groups too. If you want, you can work with him?"

"All right," the Boss said. She looked over her sisters, and Teddy tried to stand taller and be more intimidating. Maybe she'd get the best job that way. "Um . . . Well, Bandit, you can have one of yourself at each, that much is easy. Maple, can you do the room visits with Silver Fox? Is Silver Fox . . . good with children? Shy ones?"

The clipboard nodded. "He's very charismatic, and he's been doing this for a while. We also have a PR expert with each team." The clipboard smiled. "Not every Hero is great at conversation, or handling awkward situations. It's fantastic just to have you here, so we can hardly ask that any of you be perfect at that kind of thing."

"Okay, good, good," the Boss said. "Owlwatch, you'll be at the entrance. Ursa Minor, you can handle the children's wing, right?"

"No problem, Boss!" Teddy said.

It didn't take long until they were all split apart at the entrance of the hospital. Teddy and one Trinity were told to follow another clipboard-holder, one that Teddy immediately decided she didn't like. The woman looked down at Teddy with a vacant smile and talked to her as if she were a twelve-year-old instead of a ravenous, hungry grizzly Villain in the body of someone about twelve years old.

It was annoying, but Teddy kept reminding herself that her big sister would be disappointed if she ate one of the HRF's clipboard people, so she just held on to Trinity's hand and continued after the woman through what felt like the entire hospital.

Eventually they arrived in a big room with a bunch of toys to one side. There were saccharine, boring paintings on the walls, and a number of chairs laid out here and there. Teddy felt herself growing a little more tense as she noticed a Hero in the middle of the room sitting on a chair and facing a bunch of kids who were sitting in a semicircle before her.

Teddy recognized the woman: Melaton, one of the very first Heroes Teddy had ever met. Not that she thought Melaton was a very good Hero. She was a violent, mean-spirited woman. Practically a step away from being a Rogue, which kinda made her all right in Teddy's books.

"Oh, hey, the bra—the kids are here too?" Melaton asked. "If you guys want, you can sit with the others. We're reading something." Melaton raised her hands, revealing some colorful superhero propaganda book.

Teddy scoffed. "We're just here to make sick kids feel better by being close to us," she said. "We don't want stories read to us. We're too cool for that."

"Yeah!" Trinity said.

There was a flash of humor in Melaton's eyes, and Teddy felt herself puffing out in pride as all the kids gawked at her.

"That's nice, kid. But you'll miss out on snacks and such in a moment."

"Yeah!" Trinity cried again, this time with more enthusiasm and hands in the air. She skipped ahead and plopped herself down on the floor with the other kids. "Hi! I'm Bandit, and I'm definitely a Hero. When's snacks?"

Teddy crossed her arms. They could bring her to places that were all lame and Heroic, but they couldn't force the Heroism out of her.

She noticed that not all of the kids were in front of Melaton, though. A small group of them was off to the side, hanging out by the couches. With a nod, Teddy went over to join them. They were all a little older and looked a lot more jaded.

"Hey," she said.

"Hey," one of the teens said. "Are you here to sell us some bull about Heroes being the best, because if you're gonna, then save yourself the time and don't bother."

Teddy scoffed. "No. Heroes are lame and stupid. Everyone knows that."

The teens looked at her with renewed interest, and Teddy grinned. This could be an opportunity.

"So, y'all are sick, right? But are you sick of capitalism and its terrible influence?"

CHAPTER FIFTY-ONE

Up to Something

Emily was, naturally, worried about what her sisters were up to. She was second-guessing splitting up Trinity the way she had. It meant that she didn't have any easy way to communicate with all of her sisters at once. At the same time, if she hadn't separated all three of Trinity, it might have meant splitting them unevenly, which would also mean concentrating a critical mass of trouble in one spot.

Her sisters could, individually, get up to a lot of trouble. As a group, that trouble was magnified tenfold with each additional sister. They were very good at reinforcing one another's bad habits that way.

Emily had to have some confidence that they wouldn't burn the hospital down while she wasn't watching over their every move, otherwise there was no hope that she could ever live an even moderately normal life.

"Miss The Boss?" one of the HRF agents asked. Emily was by the hospital's entrance, kind of awkwardly standing to one side in the same room as the kiosk the HRF had set up, but far enough from it that she had a plausible excuse not to walk over to Glamazon to greet her.

Besides, Athena and Trinity were keeping the table distracted already. The kiosk was doing a signing event of some sort, selling overpriced, generic merch with signs above claiming that all of the proceeds went right back to the hospital. It was the only way Emily could think of justifying the prices she saw.

"Sorry," Emily said with a shake of her head. "What were you saying?"

"Soothe-Sayer is here," the agent said. "He's waiting outside and preparing. Did you want to meet him?"

"Sure," Emily said before she started to follow the agent. "Um . . . so, who is Soothe-Sayer? They're . . . he's a Hero?"

The agent nodded. "It's not surprising that you haven't heard of them. Soothe-Sayer has been with the HRF for three years now. He's one of our very best Heroes, but he doesn't take on any combat-related jobs."

"Oh?" Emily asked.

The agent nodded. "He has a power that lets him help people in hospitals. So he's constantly rotating between cities and hospitals. He's a great example of a selfless Hero."

"Oh. A healer?" she asked.

"No, not quite," the agent said, but he didn't go into any further detail.

They stepped outside into the bright sun, and Emily squinted. There was a recreational vehicle, one of those mobile homes, parked out front. It was all black, with a subtle HRF symbol painted on the side.

The agent led her over to the RV, then left her there, alone, to greet the man stepping out of the vehicle.

Emily looked up, then up some more. "Uh, hi," she squeaked.

Her dad was a big man. He was six and a bit feet tall, and built wide. His work had kept him fit, even if he'd grown a beer belly.

Soothe-Sayer had a few inches on her dad, and he was broader besides. A lot of that size was muscle. He was wearing a pastel sweater over clean slacks, but the sweater looked like it was straining to stay on his muscular frame.

He blinked down at Emily, then smiled. Soothe-Sayer was only wearing a domino mask that covered half of his face, and Emily imagined that his identity wasn't all that well hidden. She didn't imagine that many people of his size were hanging around. Still, he was dressed like the host of a kids' show, and he almost immediately slouched his shoulders a little. "Sorry, didn't see you there," he said.

"It's fine," Emily replied quickly.

Soothe-Sayer had a rich, deep voice, soft and rumbly, and Emily imagined that if he wanted to, he could easily launch a career as a singer. There was something about his voice that just *made* her listen.

"You must be the Boss? Right, right. Give me just a second, I need to grab my coat and the plushies!" Soothe-Sayer reached back into the RV and pulled out a long patchwork coat. It looked like a blanket Emily had at home, one that her grandmother had quilted a long time ago, but as a coat with dozens of pockets.

It seemed terribly un-Heroic, as far as costumes went.

He moved over to the side of the RV, then squatted down to pop open a storage box built into the outside of the mobile home. "When I visit the kids' wing, I always bring some of these with me," he said in the tone of someone admitting a dark secret. "They get so annoyed with me when I hand too many of them out." He pulled out a small plush version of Quantum Mothman and wiggled it about.

"They? The HRF?" Emily asked. She accepted the plushie as he handed it to her.

"Yup. It's official merch, you know?" Soothe-Sayer grinned as he started loading his pockets full. "But I don't care. The kids remember their favorite Heroes. It gives them hope, you know? And I think that's the most important part of what we're doing here."

"Right," Emily agreed. Then she stepped back quickly as Soothe-Sayer stood up and hefted a large bag over his shoulder. It was lumpy and strange, and very clearly filled with more plushies and dolls.

"I was told this was your first time?" Soothe-Sayer said as he started to walk toward the hospital.

"Um, yes?" Emily tried. She had to walk quickly to keep up. He had a much longer stride than her own.

Soothe-Sayer glanced over his shoulder and grinned. "It's a nice thing to do. So, in case no one else tells you, thank you."

"Oh, uh, thanks," Emily said. She felt her cheeks warming up, then glanced away while hoping no one would notice. "So, uh, the agent said you weren't a healer?" she tried. It wasn't her best attempt at small talk, but it was far from her worst.

Soothe-Sayer sighed, and the sound immediately made Emily feel like an utter failure for a moment before he glanced at her and chuckled. She instantly relaxed at the sound. "No, no, I'm not a healer," he said. "My powers are a blessing, though. Or at least, that's how I like to see them."

"Oh, that's nice," Emily said. She frowned. Was his power messing with her emotions?

"I can make people feel things by talking to them," he confirmed right away, before she could even ask. "It's more of an amplification, really, and it doesn't last more than a second or two. But! But there is one big use. I can talk people out of their pain."

"I . . . don't know if I understand," Emily said.

"People suffer. People hurt. In places like these most of all. I can't heal them, but I can give them a kind word, and maybe for a day or two, the pain goes away, and when it returns, sometimes it's not so bad." He glanced her way and grinned. "So that's what I do. I go around, I chat, I do what I can to listen and help, and maybe at the end of the day, more people are happier than they would have been otherwise."

Emily swallowed. That power sounded more like a curse to her than anything else. Having to talk to people? That was asking for a lot. But . . . he did make it sound very . . . not Heroic. She wasn't sure what word to use to describe it, exactly. Kind?

"We'll start with the children's wing, if that's all right," Soothe-Sayer said. "I like stopping by there first and last. Some kids are a little shy, they take some time to gather up the courage to come and talk."

"That's . . . okay," Emily said.

"Fantastic!"

She expected to just walk on over to the other end of the hospital, but to her horror, that didn't happen so easily. Soothe-Sayer was immediately distracted by an older lady with a walker who needed a little bit of help, then he went to a nurses' station and complained with them at length about the quality of hospital coffee, and then he found an older gentleman in a wheelchair and they talked about the weather for a full two minutes.

Emily felt like she was ten years younger, trailing after her dad again as he met up with old friends and repeated the same joke over and over.

At last, they made it to the children's wing, and Soothe-Sayer took a deep breath as if psyching himself up before he burst through the door. "Melaton! You old stinker, what kind of boring things are you reading to these bright little Heroes today?" he asked, his voice booming across the room.

The kids jumped, momentarily scared of the big man until he softened.

"Now, I know old lady Melaton's a fantastic storyteller," he said, his voice like smooth, comforting silk as he took in all the children. "But I have something even better up my sleeve."

With a big, goofy smile, he reached into his coat's sleeve, then rooted around for a while, biting the tip of his tongue as he did. Then, with a flourish, he revealed an upside-down Melaton plushie. "Taa-daa!"

Emily wasn't sure what to think of this man, but she had the impression that she was meeting a real Hero for the first time. Not a crime fighter or a glory-hound, but someone who did what they could to make the lives of others just a little better.

CHAPTER FIFTY-TWO

Coiffed?

He's a weird one, isn't he?" Melaton asked.

Emily nodded and glanced across the room at where Soothe-Sayer was entertaining a gaggle of children. He'd been a little intimidating, initially. He was a big guy, and that was only more obvious when he was surrounded by children. But his silly pantomimes and childish jokes, not to mention the presents, won him a lot of fans.

"He's a little eccentric," Emily agreed. "I'd never heard of him before."

"Soothe's not one of those Heroes you hear a lot about," Melaton said. She leaned against one of the walls, arms crossed, and looked extremely unapproachable. It was the kind of unapproachability that Emily wished she could pull off. There was a gulf of difference between someone like herself, who was lonely and wanted to be able to socialize, and someone like Melaton, who could navigate social things without a care but just didn't seem to want to bother.

"I guess. Did you know him before? He seemed to know you."

Melaton shrugged languidly. "We've met. Honestly, I wouldn't be doing this whole hospital thing if it weren't for him."

"Oh?" Emily asked.

"He's got a way to make you feel real guilty without ever pushing an ounce of guilt your way. He ain't the kind of Hero I am. Probably not the sort you are either," Melaton said. She swiped the pad of her thumb across the bottom of her nose, then shook her head. "You know what I mean?"

"I . . . I don't know?"

"Hm. Well, it's like this: There's Heroes who are in it for the cash, some who are in it for the clout, some, like me, who are in it because it's something to do and because we damned well can, and then there's those who are in it without seeming to wanna be." She gave Emily a pointed look that made her want to squirm. "And then you have Heroes like Soothe-Sayer. No fame, no money. He gets paid about as much as any HRF agent. He does it because it's the right thing to do."

"That's . . . that's a lot better, no?"

"Sure. If all that matters to you is who does the most good, then at the end of the day . . . Let's put it this way, once we're all dead and gone, if there's such a thing as karmic scales, I don't want my heart weighed against Soothe-Sayer's feather."

"Uh," Emily said. She wasn't sure if that analogy worked, exactly, but she wasn't about to point it out.

"Might want to keep an eye on your bear brat," Melaton said. "Before she starts a revolution."

Emily's head snapped around and she locked on to her sisters. Trinity was . . . actually, just bouncing with the other kids around Soothe-Sayer. Some of them were playing with her tail, and she seemed to be behaving pretty well.

Teddy, on the other hand, was with a group of older kids, teens even, at the far end of the room. She was standing on a plastic children's table, her Little Red Book raised up by her side. "Oh no," Emily groaned before she rushed across the room.

Teddy's eyes were burning with fervor, and her audience was enraptured. "Listen, capitalism is like . . . like a Hero in the comics, but it's real. It exploits the weak, just like how the Heroes exploit us."

"But Heroes are good?" one of the teens said.

"No, they're not," Teddy said with finality. "Communism is good. It's like . . . being on a team where everyone has a say, and everyone gets an equal share of the loot and the headpats, and an equal amount of space on the bed! No more disgusting capitalists stealing all of your hard-earned credit!"

"Te— Ursa Minor," Emily said as she arrived behind Teddy. "Um, what are you talking about?"

Teddy turned, not even a shadow of guilt visible. "I'm teaching my new comrades how to be better citizens."

"Uh-huh," Emily said. "Uh . . . I mean . . . I guess that's not technically against any rules? I guess."

"Everyone, this is the Boss," Teddy said with a gesture to Emily. "She's the best."

"Is she?" one boy asked, sounding exceptionally sarcastic in the way only a teenager could.

"Yeah," Teddy said. Emily had the impression that she hadn't noticed the sarcasm.

She paused. Teddy proselytizing was . . . not against any rules, was it? It might annoy some people to have one of her sisters encouraging others to participate in politics, but at the same time, it was a free country, sorta. Emily wasn't sure if this would go horribly wrong, but it looked like Teddy had at least made something like fans, and it was working to distract the kids who were too old or who thought they were too cool for Soothe-Sayer.

"Uh, I was just checking up on you," Emily lied. "You keep up the, um, good work. But also, don't encourage people to rebel or anything, please?"

"Not in the hospital," Teddy agreed with a nod.

Emily didn't feel like she had time to dive into that, so she just gave Teddy a pat on the head. Soothe-Sayer looked like he was done with things, anyway. "Keep it up, okay?"

She walked toward Soothe-Sayer, who was nearing the exit. On the way, she stopped next to Trinity and bent down so that they could talk. "Keep an eye on Teddy, please? She's not doing anything wrong, but I'm still worried she might, uh, lead others into doing something."

"Okay, Big Boss Sister!" Trinity said with a thumbs-up.

Emily gave her a pat, too, then ran off to catch up with Soothe-Sayer.

"You're a busy one," he said when she arrived.

"Huh?"

"With the kid Heroes. Are they on your team?" he asked.

"Oh, yeah. We have our own team," Emily explained. "We don't really have a team name, or much else. I'm the oldest, and I'm trying to make sure that things are more or less safe."

Soothe-Sayer nodded. "I was thinking we could find the group making the rounds next? It shouldn't be too tough!"

"Yeah, of course," Emily said. "So . . . you know Melaton?"

"I do! I know a lot of Heroes. Not that I'm bragging, it's just that I spend a lot of time in hospitals, and so does the average Hero. At least those who don't have a power that makes them supernaturally tough. Even those ones will sometimes do events like this one, to raise funds and such. So I tend to run into everyone eventually."

"That makes sense, I guess," Emily said.

"I'd hope so," Soothe-Sayer said with a chuckle. "Melaton . . . I think I met her two years ago? She wasn't in the same costume back then. Believe it or not, she used to be even edgier. She's a very competent Hero, from what I've heard. But she's not one for the limelight. If you work with the HRF long enough, you'll learn that they have a certain . . . image that they strive for with their Heroes."

"An image?" Emily prompted.

"Bright colors and spandex," he said with a grin. "I'm not really fond of it, myself. I tried spandex once, and . . . no, it's not for me."

"I . . . no, I think I agree with you on that one," Emily said. The thought of being paraded out in public in one of those formfitting costumes was enough to give her hives. If she had to wear the kind of thing that Glamazon wore regularly, then Emily would lock herself up at home and never leave.

Soothe-Sayer nodded. "I'm trying to be personable, and I find that the more fantastical Heroes, while great role models, tend to be more . . . alien. They're working very hard to be more than human, but the people I'm trying to help are very much human. That's why they need the help. I don't want to come down from above like some savior. I want to be a good neighbor and friend first."

Emily listened and followed. She had the impression that she'd need to sit down and think later about what it actually meant to be a Hero.

"Well, well, well! Look who showed up," someone called from up ahead.

Emily blinked and glanced up, then almost froze. They'd run into the group doing their rounds of the hospital. It was Maple, Trinity, three HRF handlers, and, in the middle of them all, standing with his chest properly puffed out and his hair perfectly coiffed, Silver Fox.

"Fox!" Soothe-Sayer said. "Good to see you, my man."

The two met with a quick bro hug, and Soothe-Sayer and the veteran Hero started to chat right away about this and that. Emily slipped by. She was always worried around Silver Fox. The man gave her . . . strange vibes. He was too charismatic.

"Hi, Maple, hi again, Trinity," Emily said. "Have you two been having fun?"

Trinity nodded, but Maple shook her head slightly, all without meeting Emily's eyes.

"What's wrong?" Emily asked.

Maple finally looked up, and there were tears in her eyes. In an instant, Emily felt herself going on alert. Something was wrong.

CHAPTER FIFTY-THREE

Unhurt

Emily looked around quickly for a place to talk to Maple. It didn't take long to spot one, a little private hospital room with a bed and a TV and currently no one in it. She ushered Maple inside. The bed was without sheets, but there was a cart in the room, and it looked like whoever was taking care of it was just gone for the moment.

She squatted down a little, bringing herself to eye level with Maple. "Okay, okay," Emily said. She didn't think she was very good at this kind of thing, but her mom was great. When Emily was younger and even worse at communicating, her mom had always been able to tease out what was wrong.

It usually took a lot of yes or no questions, and some good guesswork. Emily hadn't appreciated it as much before she had to take care of so many little sisters.

"Are you hurt?" she asked.

Maple shook her head.

"Did someone say they were going to hurt you? Hurt me or one of your sisters? Did they ask you to do something you didn't want to do?" Emily asked. Her mind went to dark places for a moment. Emily didn't want to be a Villain, but she'd make a big exception if something that awful happened.

Maple sniffled, swallowed, then coughed a little. "It's nothing," she said.

Emily decided that it wasn't nothing, but she couldn't very well demand that Maple spill. "It's okay, it's okay. Do you want a hug, and then you can tell me all about it?"

That trick had worked a few times on a younger Emily, and it seemed to be working now. Maple pressed into Emily, and Emily patted the back of Maple's head as she gave her the best hug she could manage.

"It's the people," Maple said.

"The people?" Emily repeated.

"In the beds. They're sick, and old, and it hurts."

"Oh," Emily said.

"I said I could fix them. I can make stuff for that, but then the old guy said that it was normal. People get old, and they get sick, and they get broken, and then they *die.*" Maple was full-on crying now. The hug seemed to have done exactly the opposite of what Emily had intended.

"Hey, hey, it's okay," Emily said.

"No it's not," Maple whined. "Big Sister is old too. You can't get sick and broken, and you can't die!"

"Uh," Emily said. She was nineteen, and while she liked to think that she was levelheaded and somewhat smart, she had also not spent all that much time contemplating her own mortality yet. "I mean, I think I have a few years in me?"

"No!" Maple said. She shook her head from side to side, spreading snot and tears across Emily's shoulder. "No, no, you can't."

"Hey, hey, it's okay," Emily said. She decided that she'd have words with Silver Fox. Or maybe not. The man was kind of intense and charismatic and loud. So maybe she'd just think very rude things in his direction. "All right, so . . . um . . . I'm very bad at this."

"I know people can die," Maple said. She sounded a little petulant. "I'm not dumb. But it's other people who are supposed to die. Not us."

Emily took a deep breath, trying to find the right words to say and knowing she wouldn't. "Life is . . . complicated. And sometimes really unfair. But I think we just have to work hard to make sure that it's not us who does the dying, right? That means listening to your big sister, and eating your greens, doing your homework, and if any one of us gets really sick, then maybe we can figure it out then, right?"

Maple nodded slowly. "If you die, I'm going to bring you back," she said.

"Um . . . yeah, okay," Emily said. She wasn't sure if she should be agreeing to that. It felt a little risky, but at the same time, she didn't like Maple being sad.

"And I'll make you bigger, with more arms for hugging, and bulletproof skin, and you won't have to worry about the weakness of the flesh, because the machine is stronger. And you can have a retractable bed, and a freezer for snacks, and . . ." Maple continued, her words turning into a small litany under her breath.

Emily was no longer worried for Maple, but was instead worried *about* Maple.

"Just don't turn me into whatever you're thinking of the next time I take a nap, all right?"

"Okay," Maple said meekly. She rubbed her face against her sleeve until Emily reached into a pocket, tugged out a small ziplock baggie full of tissues and wet wipes and Band-Aids and fished out a tissue to help Maple blow her nose and wipe her face clean.

"You'll be just fine," Emily said. "All of us will be. I promise."

Maple sniffed one last time, then nodded. "Promise?"

"I . . . yes. Look . . . I think that sometimes, things don't go the way we want. Sometimes things don't work out. It happens . . . often, even. But I think that the best people, those who come through the worst things and are still able to keep on going, are the ones who have a lot of hope. Hope that no matter what, things *will* work out in the end."

"Oh," Maple said.

"Hope . . . or spite," Emily said more truthfully. "Spite can also work well. Sometimes you just need to hate all the bad stuff so much that you're able to keep on enduring it, even when you really don't want to anymore. So, have hope that you can come out on top one day, and have enough spite to keep you going."

Maple looked up, lips twitching into the hint of a smile. "Spite sounds very Villain-y. I think I like that."

Emily held back a cringe. "Well . . . maybe a little," she said.

"Hope and spite. Okay, Big Sis. I can do that."

Emily gave her another squeeze. "That's the spirit."

The two were silent for a moment, the quiet only swallowed up by the faint hum of the hospital and the occasional footsteps and calls outside. "I don't like hospitals," Maple admitted.

"That's okay. I don't think many people do. But we'll be out of here soon. Do you want to come with me? Instead of staying with Silver Fox?" Maple nodded, and Emily stood up straighter while tucking her little baggie away. "All right, then. Trinity can come too."

Emily took Maple's hand, and they left the room. It was just in time, as a nurse slipped by and went to make the bed. Emily found Soothe-Sayer and Silver Fox chatting by the nurses' station.

"Can you go get Trinity?" Emily asked. She saw Trinity farther in, entertaining a trio of wheelchair-bound older ladies. She was letting them pet her tail while . . . while she ate from one of the lady's lunch trays.

Emily sighed, but let it pass.

"Hey, you're back," Soothe-Sayer said. "Is everything all right?"

"Ah, it's probably nothing. I wouldn't want to be in charge of so many kids. It's trying enough when we need to do this kind of thing at schools," Silver Fox said.

"Yeah," Emily said. She was feeling a little fed up with Silver Fox. "She just . . . hospitals were a bit much for her. She'll be fine."

"Poor kid," Soothe-Sayer said with what sounded like genuine sympathy. "Yeah, it's not always easy, no matter how old you are. That's why we come here. It's so much harder to be in a place like this when you know that not only are you suffering, but you're suffering alone. If we can make people smile, take away the pain for a moment, and just give them a little bit of hope, then it's worth all the effort, right?"

Silver Fox scoffed. "Are you practicing that speech? There aren't any cameras around."

Soothe-Sayer shook his head. "It's not a speech. It's what I believe."

"That's . . . nice," Emily said. She felt a little queasy in the stomach hearing that. Soothe-Sayer was genuine in a way she'd never felt in herself before, not in a way that mattered. Emily wanted to be . . . well, not a Hero, but given all the options for powered people, Hero seemed like the best bet if she wanted a quiet life.

She had half expected the hospital visit to be little more than a performance, but also an opportunity to do a little good. Watching Soothe-Sayer made her wonder if there wasn't a kernel of true goodness in all of it.

"Are we going?" Trinity said as she bounced over. There was pudding on her face, and on her wagging tail.

Emily sighed, ditched the philosophical mental ramblings, and pulled out her baggie again. "Give me a minute, Mister Soothe-Sayer."

"No problem," he said with a chuckle. "I'll do my rounds up here real fast, then we can head back down. It's okay if you need time to take care of the girls. Family's important too."

"Thank you," she said.

This Hero was making the whole Villainy thing a lot more complicated than it had been before.

CHAPTER FIFTY-FOUR

~~~~~~~~

PR

"Oh!"

Teddy interrupted herself mid-rant and glanced over at Trinity. "What is it?" she asked.

Teaching her new disciples—even if some of them seemed to think they were too cool for communism—took a back seat to helping her sisters and the Boss with trouble, and Trinity would be the first to know if there was trouble.

Trinity bounced over to Teddy, waving off some of the kids who were playing with her. "Boss said that we're going now!" Trinity said.

"How did she say it?" Teddy asked. "Was it like . . . 'Hey! We have to go now!'" She tried to sound like the Boss when she was stressed and loud. "Or was it more, 'Okay, we're going now.'" That time she tried to sound like the Boss when she was just normal-stressed.

Trinity frowned, her head tilting to one side a little as she thought. "I think it sounded like, *'Trinity, can you tell Teddy to come to the lobby, please? And you come too. And don't steal people's food on the way. And tell Teddy not to start a revolution.'*"

Teddy sniffed. "Your Big Sis voice is awful."

"No it's not, yours is."

Teddy shook her head. "No. Mine's so good, you wouldn't even be able to tell us apart. That's because I'm related to her by being her sister."

Trinity blinked. "But I'm her sister too?"

"You're a third of her sister, so you're only a third as good at imitating her," Teddy said. The math was impossible to deny. Grinning, Teddy turned back to her disciples and jumped back onto the table she'd been using to proselytize. "All right. So, in essence, people who wanna sell you stuff are probably capitalist shills who want all of your money so that they can eat your food. Remember, those people aren't people, so it's okay to kick them around."

Teddy gave them a thumbs-up, then leapt off the table.

Trinity was pouting nearby. "I'm not a third of a sister," she said. "I asked the Boss, and she said that sometimes I'm three times as much trouble as anyone else, and that means I'm three times more of a sister than you are."

Teddy and Trinity started to argue back and forth as they began to make their way through the hospital. They only stopped for a moment to tell Melaton that they were leaving, and that was only because she happened to be nearby.

Melaton was pretty cool, for a Hero, but she was still a Hero, which by default made her very uncool. It wasn't her fault . . . Teddy frowned. Actually, powers were usually given with a morality that explicitly fit the person who received them. So, it totally was Melaton's fault.

She might have been trying to look cool and suave and kind of anti-Heroic, but deep down she was probably, no definitely, definitely a do-gooder. It didn't matter how dark and edgy her costume was, or how gruff and mean she tried to sound. She was still in a hospital reading books to sick kids, and that made her lame.

It didn't take long to find the Boss and their other sisters. Maple, Athena, and the rest of Trinity were milling around the entrance, doing signings for some fan-people.

Teddy wasn't sure what to think about signings. Her Villain name, Ursa Minor, was pretty long to write, and her handwriting was very scratchy. That, and people *paid* for her to write her name on stuff. It was weird, and sometimes she worried that it was a little too capitalistic.

Then again, she did like the attention. Sometimes she'd let the people touch her ears, which people seemed to really like doing.

"You're here," the Boss said. She seemed . . . not all that stressed, actually. That was probably for the best. Teddy had been quietly very proud of all the steps Emily had been taking toward becoming a better Villain, and gaining confidence in herself was one of the big ones.

Obviously, Teddy didn't need to worry about gaining confidence, or being stressed, because she was a bear.

"All right, we'll be heading out in a minute. I just want to say goodbye to Soothe-Sayer and let . . . the HRF agents know that we're heading out."

The Boss led them outside, where she talked with lots of gestures to one of the clipboards, and then she walked over to that Hero with the patchwork coat. Teddy followed, grabbing Emily's hand now that she wasn't paying too much attention.

"You handled today really well," Soothe-Sayer said. "I know you probably don't hear it enough, since being a Hero means that people just assume it of us, but I'm proud of you, Boss."

"Oh, uh, thank you," the Boss said.

Teddy looked up to her sister with narrowed eyes. Then gave her a sniff to be sure. It didn't look like Emily was in love with this guy, but she was very blushy. "Thank you. I appreciate it. I . . . being a Hero is hard sometimes."

Soothe-Sayer smiled. "We do our best, but I understand. These places can be tough. But hey, just remember that you made a difference today, and if you keep it up, you'll make a difference tomorrow, and the day after. If we all put some effort into it, some kindness, the world will be a better place. Or so I'd like to believe!"

Teddy snorted. This guy was, in her professional Villainous opinion, an idiot.

"Right, thank you again, Soothe-Sayer. Maybe we'll see each other around," Emily said.

It didn't take long before she was tugging Teddy away and back to the others who were waiting nearby.

"That guy's so wrong," Teddy said.

"You think so?" the Boss asked.

"Yeah. He's too optimistic, which makes him dumb. Heroes always think like that. That they can *save* people. But it's really just about keeping things the way they are. He wants to help people get better, but he's doing nothing about stopping people from getting hurt in the first place."

"I'm not sure it's dumb to want to help," Emily said.

Teddy shook her head. "If people are getting hurt because of cars, then you can either spend a lot of time fixing the people, or you can blow up any car that drives over the speed limit."

"Then you'd have blown-up people," Emily said.

"Only for a while. The non-blown-up people would start driving slower, I bet. If people are getting sick because of bad food, then you can either cure them, or you can burn down the factory the food came from. If people are getting old and dying, you can either sit back and let them, or you can fight against death. *That's* like, the core of being a Villain."

Emily glanced down at Teddy. "That's a very . . . uh, destructive view of things."

Teddy shook her head. "No, it's proactive," she said. "Heroes react. Villains act. That's what makes us better. Well, it's one of the things. We're also just cooler."

"I don't think all change comes from destruction. Sometimes people build new, good things for good reasons."

"Yeah, sure. But it's usually just to help them react more. Plus it takes forever for that kind of change to happen. Like, months and years."

"I think we can afford to wait sometimes. I don't think I want to become the kind of person who hurts others just to get what she wants."

Teddy shrugged. "You don't have to hurt everybody, if that's not the kinda Villain you wanna be. You just gotta hurt the ones who are between you and what you want."

Emily let out a long sigh, but she didn't seem able to contradict what Teddy had said. Which was obvious, because Teddy knew that she was objectively correct.

The two of them walked in silence for a bit, at least until they reached the rest of the group. "Okay!" the Boss said. "I hope everyone had a nice time?"

"It was all right," Athena said. "Networking isn't fun, but I guess it's good. Plus we did a lot of good PR."

"What's a 'PR'?" Trinity asked. "Can you eat it?"

"No, that's a pear," Maple said.

"Not a pear, *Pee Arr*," Athena repeated, drawing the word out.

"Your *pee are* stinky," Teddy said.

The Boss had to separate them because Athena decided to bop Teddy on the head for that one, and Teddy just laughed and fought her back because she was stronger and more clever.

"All right, break it up, you two," Emily said. "I think we were memorable enough for one day. I don't want a video of you fighting to end up on Outube."

"Teddy started it," Athena said.

"Her stink started it," Teddy shot back. She grinned. That had been a good one, but the Boss just sighed and started walking home.

One day, Teddy figured the Boss would learn how to Villain properly. Then she'd appreciate Teddy's fantastic sense of humor even more!

CHAPTER FIFTY-FIVE

～～～～～

In Want of a Plan

Kevin was enjoying his time the way time was meant to be enjoyed. He was in a hotel today instead of a seedy motel. It was one of the only ones in Eauclaire, just a few blocks over from the big college or whatever. At the moment, if anyone asked, he was . . .

Actually, he couldn't remember the name on the ID he'd stolen. He was some college guy who had paid for one of the nicer rooms in cash. That was all that mattered.

He was lying on a large, comfortable bed, pantsless, and watching a large-screen TV while enjoying a few beers he'd nicked from the mini-fridge of the room next to his. No way was he going to pay for the stuff in his own room's minifridge. The prices were just shy of Villainous.

Kevin reached under his shirt, rubbed a hand across his belly, then yawned. He'd done nothing all day, and it was exceptionally tiring.

He couldn't do this forever, of course. Eventually he'd run out of cash and need to head out. And overstaying his welcome wouldn't be wise. There was a chance the poor sap whose ID he'd stolen would notice something amiss, or the hotel would.

He doubted the latter, though. This hotel didn't seem like it was getting a lot of patronage at this time of year, so it was pretty understaffed. Still, it was possible that someone with too much time on their hands would want to look into Kevin, and that could mean trouble.

But that would be a problem for later.

What was the point in being a Villain if he didn't get to sit back and just relax once in a while? It was meant to be a way of life, not a nine-to-five job.

He shifted on the bed, then winced as the shifting pulled something along his side. There was a long, discolored bruise running up his calf. It was yellow and a little green on the edges. The bruise had been fading nicely for the past couple of days, but it was still present enough to hurt when he moved.

Another reason to stay inside.

Kevin didn't have any of that fancy self-healing stuff. He had a few tricks, though. Reaching down, he ran a hand over his leg. The whole hand started to shake, tremble, and then vibrate like a phone going off. The vibrations were redirected into his leg, and he could feel all the muscles and bones shivering.

It felt nice, like a massage. Most people wouldn't appreciate it, though. The vibrations were tuned so that they'd probably melt the flesh off someone's leg, but his powers didn't work on himself that way. To him, it was soothing. Like pressing a heating pad into a sore muscle.

The fact that he'd been hurt at all was what annoyed him.

Eauclaire was meant to be *easy*. It was some nowhere little city with nothing important in it. It should have been a piece of cake for him to waltz in, wreck the local Heroes a little, and then rule this little kingdom.

If he had to pick between being the king of a slum or being a servant of something bigger, he'd always choose the king.

Yet here he was, stuck in some hotel in his underwear watching cartoons. Not a single minion in sight.

This, he concluded after thinking about it for a while, was all that Boss chick's fault.

She'd popped up out of nowhere. Some brand-new Hero-type do-gooder who couldn't mind her own. Her and her gaggle of brats.

Kevin flung his empty can across the room, where it clattered against the floor. He picked up another and popped the tab with a satisfying hiss. He should have had a cool base by now. Maybe a bunker, maybe a nice club. Yeah, a club, with a DJ, and those flickery lights, and maybe a few hot minions who would serve him hand and foot.

He grumbled some more, then reached for the remote. The cartoons had turned to obnoxiously loud ads, and he didn't care to be advertised to. Flipping the channel forward, he flew past vapid sitcoms, re-re-releases of old movies, the news—

Kevin paused, then flicked back a few channels to the news.

It was playing some boring feel-good story about the local Eauclaire hospital. A bit of cell-phone footage taken from a parking lot.

There were a couple of HRF vans and a larger recreational vehicle parked out front.

His attention was mostly on one person in particular. The Boss, standing outside, the brats all around her while she talked to some patchwork-looking Hero.

The newscaster was going on about some big visit thing, raising money for charity and some sort of children's fund. Rattles wasn't paying the conversation much attention.

There she was. Looking alive and smug and unbothered that she was in *his* city.

It wasn't fair. He'd won their last fight. Sure, he'd pulled out after kicking them around a little, but he'd still won.

He watched as the pixelated image shook. The person holding the camera was far from professional, but the video feed was clear enough to see the Boss's expression. She seemed happy.

The remote burst in his hand, and Kevin swore and shook off the bits of plastic. He'd forgotten to contain his power, and now the remote was shattered like glass. Kevin shook it off, then realized that the TV would be stuck on the news now unless he walked over to it every time he wanted to change the channel.

"Damnit," he swore. The news went on to talk about some economic stuff that he didn't care about.

He got to his feet, took another swig of his beer, then just stood there for a moment. He didn't know what to do next, exactly. He felt like rushing over to the hospital and wrecking the place, but . . . well, he was a Villain, not a monster. Besides, destroying the children's wing of a hospital wasn't like robbing a bank. That kind of thing would get way too much heat on him.

Kevin scoffed. "Enjoy your time, Boss," he muttered under his breath. "We'll see how much this city loves you once it's nothing but ruins."

He didn't finish his beer. Instead, he flung it into the trash and found some sweatpants. Eauclaire wasn't good for him, he was realizing. He'd made a small fortune hitting up the poorly protected banks here, but his dreams of Super Villainy weren't amounting to anything.

Worse, he was getting fat and lazy and complacent here. The room was feeling too small, too constrained, so he left and made his way over to the hotel gym.

It was nearly unoccupied. There was one other guy there, casually pumping iron at the free weights, but he was off in his corner, and Kevin decided to ignore him. He wasn't all that great at the whole exercise thing. He kept up a little, because he had to, but that was it.

Some of the gangs he'd been in had been really into building muscle and doing cardio. Kevin preferred to rely on his power, not his fists, to beat others down.

But if he wanted to rule, then he'd need to lose the gut.

He got onto a treadmill and worked up a sweat. The entire time, he glared straight ahead. It helped if he imagined himself sprinting after that stupid woman and her brats, running toward them to give them a beatdown.

Kevin pounded on the treadmill, each step thudding with the weight of his frustrations. Sweat began to pearl on his forehead, running down in rivulets as he picked up the pace. The mindless rhythm and the mechanical whirring of the machine seemed to mirror the turmoil in his mind. He kept seeing the Boss's smug face, surrounded by her brats, and it fueled his resolve.

He'd had enough of playing small-time. Eauclaire was supposed to be a pit stop on his way to greatness. Instead, he felt stuck here.

There was only one thing to do about it.

Escalate.

Show the city the magnitude of his power.

Kevin cursed under his breath. That would feel fantastic, to finally let loose in a big way. The attention, though . . . He knew he was good. He *was* powerful. But he couldn't take on the entirety of the HRF. If he started collapsing entire streets, then they'd be on him in a big way.

After an hour, he wobbled off the treadmill. The sweat was nice. The feeling in his gut wasn't. He was still annoyed, still frustrated.

He moved to the free weights once the other guy was gone and started pumping. It was so easy to imagine himself crushing this entire city, but even if that was what he wanted to do, he knew it wasn't the right thing.

He needed a plan. He needed a concrete idea of what to do next.

And the first step of that plan would be to crush the competition.

CHAPTER FIFTY-SIX

The Sleepy

Emily woke with a start as her phone rang.

Her phone was not supposed to ring. Not at home. So she muttered something that even she didn't understand and tried to snuggle deeper into her pillows. The motion, of course, unleashed a few elbows and knees, but at this point she was used to it.

The phone rang again.

Some small part of Emily's brain clicked on, remembering a few odd and only vaguely related facts.

She'd asked Maple to make it so that phones wouldn't work in their bunker home. Then she'd asked Maple to make one exception for a burner phone she bought for cash at a gas station, which she planned on leaving plugged in her room.

Maple had made it so that the phone was "untraceable" somehow. Emily wasn't super confident in that, but she was willing enough to gamble on it. Maple had made a machine that was meant to act as a signal relay for the phone and also be very easy to lose. She then proceeded to lose it, and called the entire thing a success, because anyone tracing the call would also get lost.

It was good enough.

And that phone was now ringing, because it was the only phone that *could* ring.

"It's the capitalists, they're trying to sell us stuff," Teddy mumbled sleepily. "Telemarketers. All their fault." She snored, quite loudly, right into Emily's ear, at least until the phone rang again. "Consequence of the Industrial Revolution."

Emily blinked a few times. The room was dark, but her eyes had adapted to it. "Move, please," she asked . . . one of her sisters who was hugging her. The sister moved, and Emily wriggled her way up to the end of the bed.

The phone rang again just as Emily reached it.

She didn't recognize the number at all. What she did recognize was the time.

Someone was calling her at four thirty in the morning, and Emily was strongly considering giving into any Villainous impulses she might have.

Standing up properly, Emily flicked the phone open, then answered. "Yes, hello?" she said before clearing her throat of cobwebs.

"Boss?" a woman asked on the other end of the line. The voice was a familiar one, though it took Emily a moment to place her.

"Melaton?"

"Yeah, it's me," Melaton said. "But this is . . . unofficial stuff, all right?"

"It's four a.m."

"Four thirty."

Emily pulled the phone away from her head and stared at it. Did the distinction *mean* anything? "Okay? It's four thirty. On a weekday. I have . . . a life? Things . . . Why are you calling?"

"All right, yeah, I guess you do. Not everyone is a night owl. Look, we've got trouble here," Melaton said. Now that Emily was a little more awake, she could make out the tension in Melaton's voice.

"Where's *here*?" Emily asked.

"Handshake called me up late last night, said that he'd gotten word from a friend of a friend who knows someone who's a precog of sorts. Not the fancy sort, but the sort that can keep tabs on lots of people for a price?"

Emily didn't know what that meant, exactly, but it did sound a lot like the kind of shady business that Handshake would get himself up to. "All right? Is he in trouble?"

"We're holed up at the café," Melaton said. "The moment we step out, we'll be ambushed."

"Ambushed?" Emily asked. "By whom?"

"Whom?"

"It's . . . it's good grammar," Emily defended. "Do we have time for this?"

"Right. We think it's Rattles. He's making a move, and he's starting it by smacking down anything remotely Villainous within his 'territory.'" The air quotes could be heard in that one.

Emily started to pace her little room. Something in her chest felt constricted and tight. She didn't *want* to face Rattles again. Certainly not at this hour of the morning. The name snuck into enough of her nightmares without her having to actually fight him in the dark.

"What do you want me to do?" Emily asked.

"Well, ideally, ride over with the littlest cavalry and beat the stuffings out of Rattles," Melaton said. "But barring that, do you think you could get some of your less Heroic friends to help?"

"That's not . . . fast," Emily said.

"Oh, right, sorry. I kinda gave you a false impression there. Things aren't great, but they're not devolving too quickly. Rattles is skulking around the area. We know that. Saw him on cameras and everything. But he's not *here*-here. I don't think he knows where Handshake's hiding, just the general area. As long as we stay put, we're safe. At least, that's what Handshake's friend-of-a-friend says. It's the moment we step out that we're screwed."

"Can't you take him?" Emily asked.

"Poor matchup," Melaton said. "Actually, a lot of matchups are poor for me."

Emily sighed and ran a hand through her hair, which was a tangled mess at the moment. She'd need a shower and a few minutes with a brush. She glanced back at the bed. There was a pile of limbs and the sounds of soft, peaceful breathing. It was comforting, at least compared to the impression she was getting from the call with Melaton.

"I don't . . . I need time to think," Emily said.

"Take your time. We're just waiting here, hoping the ass doesn't notice us and decide to bring the ceiling down," Melaton said. It sounded as though she was trying hard to come across as casual.

Emily stopped pacing and took a deep breath. She needed . . . a few things. Rattles gone was on the top of that list, though. "Do you think we could ambush him?" she asked.

"Maybe."

Emily definitely didn't want to face him alone. She'd need allies, even for an ambush. Maybe if this was happening in a week . . . two weeks? A year from now? She didn't know if she'd ever be entirely ready to fight him.

"I can think of a couple of people I could call," Emily said. "But I don't know if they'll want to come. And at this hour, it'll be hard to even get a ride anywhere."

"Yeah, I know, but this might be—"

Emily paused in her pacing to stare at the phone. It hadn't disconnected, but Melaton had stopped mid-sentence. "Hello?"

A few strange noises came over the phone as it changed hands. Someone cleared their throat, then talked. "Boss?"

"Handshake?" Emily asked. She was pretty sure it was him.

"The one and only," Handshake said. "Consider the following, please. I owe you a small but tidy amount at the moment, and you'll never be able to collect if I'm dead. That, and assisting would put me further in your debt. If you remove Rattles from . . . being an issue, I'll pay you two thousand. Half that if you just scare him off for now."

Emily chewed on her lower lip. That did make it significantly more tempting. Two thousand dollars and probably a favor owed wasn't a minor thing, especially not with the way she kept burning through her savings. It was tempting, incredibly so . . . but it would mean fighting Rattles.

"All right," Emily said. "I'll help. *We'll* help. But remember, you owe me, Handshake, and I intend to collect."

There was a relieved chuckle on the other end of the line. "Deal, Boss. And thank you. It's a pleasure doing business."

Emily ended the call, then turned.

She discovered six pairs of eyes staring at her, all of them catching the light in the dimly lit room. "So, who're we beating up?" Teddy asked.

"Rattles," Emily said. "And we're going to win this time. Can you girls get dressed up? Full costumes and everything. Maple, you have your thing?"

Maple nodded. "It's ready," she said.

"Good. I need to make a few calls. Come on, go ahead and get ready, please. Oh, and . . . Athena?"

"Hmm?"

"Can you turn on the coffee machine?" Emily asked. She'd need caffeine for this.

Emily checked the phone again. The number she entered was one she'd meticulously memorized. She pressed call, and held the phone to her ear.

The phone rang twice more before someone answered. "Someone had better be dying," Sam answered on the other end.

"I know," Emily said. "It's late. We need a ride. We've got trouble. It's Rattles."

There was a long silence after, then a sigh. "What do you need?" Sam asked.

"We're planning an ambush. I need a ride there. It's kinda far, especially for this late. I'm calling in a few other favors too."

"Huh, so it's finally going down. All right, I'm in. Lemme get dressed. Text me where you wanna meet."

"Thank you," Emily said. "I'll see you soon."

She hung up, then grabbed her normal phone to look up a number. This time it picked up right away.

"Hey?" a young man said.

"Alea Iacta? Get ready. We're going to take out the city's biggest Villain tonight. I need your help, and your luck."

"Ah, shit. Is this why my sleep schedule got all screwed up?"

Emily had no idea what he was on about, but she told him where to meet anyway.

She punched in another number, and this time it took a while before anyone replied. When they did, it was with the sleepiest voice Emily had heard in a while. "Wazza?"

"Jezebelle?" Emily asked. "Are you awake?"

"Huh?"

That was close enough to a yes. "It's Emily Wright. Remember? I need your help with something . . . work-related. It's urgent."

"Oh," Jezebelle said, coming awake. "Well, shit."

"Yeah," Emily agreed. She explained the situation as quickly as she could, then hung up. The nerves were getting to her. Most of the time, when she called someone, she had to psych herself up for a few days first. Doing it this quickly was like ripping off a Band-Aid.

But it was done, and now she had to prepare herself for trouble.

CHAPTER FIFTY-SEVEN

Jezebelle the Brave

Jezebelle didn't want to leave her apartment.

She found herself frozen by the entrance. The door was open, and all she needed to do was take one step and she'd be outside.

Her car was parked just there, already on, its headlights illuminating the quiet side street a couple of blocks away from the college. She lived in a good part of town, in a pretty nice apartment.

It hadn't always been that way, but the moment she gained powers, things really changed. She went from being the pretty-enough . . . she didn't know how to describe it. She wasn't even the black sheep of the family. To the rest of them, she was just kind of there, riding along and doing her own thing.

Jezebelle didn't have a *rich*-rich family, but it was still a two-vacations-a-year sort of family. Time spent in the south during the summer and up north to ski in the winter. The nice part of middle-class where her family ran a few small, respectable businesses that the younger generation would one day inherit.

Probably not her. She was too young, not part of the most beloved section of the family. She got her college paid for, and that was about it.

But that was before she'd turned into a Heroine. Before she had powers.

Weak, kind of lackluster powers, but still. Her ID as a Mask was open. She'd bought her entire family one of the most valuable things possible: bragging rights. And they had repaid her in kind.

It was nice. The new home, a bigger allowance, a car that had belonged to her uncle that he basically *gave* her. It was barely six years old! A bit . . . midlife-crisis-y, but still, she wasn't about to complain.

And all of that niceness felt like so much dust in her mouth right now.

She urged her leg forward over the threshold, but it was like her body didn't want to listen.

There was a faint ticking coming from behind her. The seconds counting onward on the kitchen clock. A silent recrimination, a reminder that she was wasting *time*.

Her mind kept flashing back to her fight with Rattles. Or rather, the beatdown she'd gotten from the Villain. He hadn't even looked like he was struggling as he smacked her down. For some reason, the look in his eyes was still impossible to forget. It haunted her.

So far, she'd done a good enough job of keeping herself going, even after the hospital stay. There were things Heroes could do other than fighting, and she had taken on every one of those quests she could grab. It meant a lot of volunteer work and time spent doing PR crap, but it was the only way she could really improve herself and her powers.

Burying her fear in self-improvement worked during the day. But now it was four in the morning, and it wasn't going so well.

"You damned coward," Jezebelle muttered to herself.

Right now, the Boss and her brats were going to go and try to fight Rattles, probably all on their own.

She pressed past the doorway, a chill running down her spine as she did so. She was outside in the cool night air. It wasn't even all that dark, not with the streetlights all over. All that worry now felt wasted, though she knew, consciously, that the doorway had only been a metaphorical barrier.

She locked the door behind her, then ran over to her car and slipped into it. Within moments, she was driving along a little bit over the speed limit, heading to the rendezvous point that Emily, the Boss, had set up.

The city flew by until she approached the spot where Emily had told her to meet. It was a 24/7 Im Orton's on the corner of two intersecting streets. There were some parking spots at the back where they might not be as noticeable from the street.

Jezebelle pulled in, then parked at the rear. Her car was the only one there.

She almost bailed before shutting off the engine, but she had made it this far, and she didn't think it was all that likely that Rattles had tricked Emily or anything like that.

So she turned off the car, jumped out, and then went to the trunk, where the rest of her costume was waiting. At the moment, she was only wearing the main suit part and a comfortable pair of running shoes. She ditched those in favor of her costume's armored boots, then pulled on some long gloves made with thick padding and some sort of gadgeteered-up cut-proof material. It wasn't much as far as armor went, but it was better than nothing. The mask came on next, and then she had to rearrange her hair because the mask did awful things to it.

"Nice suit," someone said from behind her, and Jezebelle leapt about ten feet into the air as she spun.

She fell into a wobbly stance, hands raised to punch out, powers almost flaring. There was a guy standing there, dressed like a ren faire reject and holding two coffees.

She blinked. "Wait, you're that Villain that the Boss helped once. Latin-name guy. You asked me out."

"I'm more of a Rogue," the guy said. "And you never said yes, for what little it matters." He took a long sip from one of the cups, then extended the other. "It's, uh, a large double double."

Jezebelle stared. "That's my usual order," she said.

He gestured with the other cup to the coffee shop. "I ordered something else, but they gave me this by accident. Overworked guy at the counter told me to keep it. Guess I'm just lucky like that, you know? Want it? I'll give it to one of the kids otherwise. You know, as payback."

"Payback?"

"For dragging my sorry behind all the way over here," he said. "See this costume? Real silk shirt. And I'm not wearing anything under it. It's cold."

She supposed it was a little cold. "And the payback is?"

"Do you have any idea what this much caffeine and sugar will do to the Boss's kids? They'll be bouncing off the walls. Then the crash will make them all whiney. It's good payback for getting me out of the house at this hour."

Jezebelle took the coffee. "Thanks," she said.

He shrugged. "It was free, Sparkles."

"Glamazon," she corrected. "And you're . . . something Latin?"

"Alea Iacta," he said. "Usually I'd start flirting with you, but I'm cold and tired, so can we just pretend that I put in the old college try?"

Jezebelle laughed despite herself. She hadn't been expecting that. "All right, I think I can do that."

"Nice, nice," he said before cupping his coffee close. He looked around, then at her, then back at the parking lot. "Guess we're early," he said.

"They'll be here," Jezebelle replied. She . . . had a lot of confidence in Emily. Sure, the girl was . . . kind of a hot mess, but she hadn't failed to come through yet. She adjusted her mask. "So . . . been a not-Villain for long?"

"Eh, since last Power Day, same as just about everyone else," Alea Iacta said. "Say, why is it that so many Heroes and not-Heroes around here are so new? That normal?"

"Most Heroes give up within the first three months. It's . . . kind of a thankless job that doesn't pay very well."

"It doesn't?"

"I'd make more serving coffee with the number of hours I put in," she said. "The bonuses are nice, and the hourly pay's great, but for every hour you work, you spend two training."

"Huh," he said. "And the not-Heroes?"

"Jail, mostly," she said.

Alea Iacta's eyebrows rose, then he nodded. "Makes sense."

A van rode into the parking lot, past the drive-through, and parked right up next to Jezebelle's car. The side door crashed open, and then a gaggle of kids came swarming out.

Just six of them, really, but it felt like a lot more. And Jezebelle was pretty sure that there weren't enough belts for all of them in the van.

Then the Boss came around the back, closed the door, and said something to the driver. The van pulled out, then rode around and out of the parking lot.

"Hey," Alea Iacta said.

"It's the lucky idiot!" the beargirl said as she ran over. "Yo! Haven't seen you in a while. Is that hot chocolate?"

"Maybe," he said, sounding pretty defensive about it. "And it's mine. Go away, bear brat."

"I'm Ursa Minor, idiot."

"Ursa, leave Alea Iacta alone," the Boss said as she walked over. "Glamazon, Alea Iacta, I'm happy to see both of you."

"Gotta earn the right to sleep in your train car somehow," Alea Iacta said.

Jezebelle glanced at him and wondered what, exactly, that meant. "What's the situation?" she asked instead. This was already a lot less . . . professional than an HRF operation.

"Rattles was spotted snooping around," the Boss said. "His target's some underground info-broker who's being protected by Melaton. He should still be around. I think . . . we'll try to get him distracted by Melaton, then ambush him. At least, that's the plan so far. I'm, uh, open to suggestions."

CHAPTER FIFTY-EIGHT

Don't Wanna Do It

Emily still didn't want to do this. At this point she was well and properly awake, so she was entering the situation with a clear head and about as much knowledge as she could hope to have, all things considered.

And she still very much didn't want to be here.

But she was here, not in bed, and most of the work of getting her sisters woken up, dressed up, and *here* was already done. The entire bunch was hyped up and ready to go. Even the usually reserved Maple was hugging her toaster cannon to her chest and silently bouncing up and down, like someone burping a baby.

Glamazon and Alea Iacta were standing nearby, but not within touching range of each other. Emily wondered if there was anything going on there, then decided that she was definitely not the person to deal with anything if it *was* going on.

"Okay," she said. Then, louder because Trinity and Teddy were both not paying much attention: "Okay. Everyone. We know more or less where Rattles is. But it's . . . almost five in the morning. We can't sneak around the way we can during the day."

"You sneak around during the day?" Glamazon asked.

Emily ignored the comment. "So, the plan is . . . is to get Rattles to where we want him to be, then ambush him. Glamazon, Maple, you're our only ranged-capable people right now. Ideally, we want to disable him and confuse him as much as possible."

"I—I can do it," Maple said.

Emily nodded, then she fished out a small device from her pocket. Maple had given it to her. A second, better anti-vibration device. It came with the same caveats as the first. This might not work to stop Rattles's power entirely. But it *would* mess with his abilities to some degree, and that might be all that they needed. This one was tougher as well, able to take a hit. Rattles wouldn't get away so easily.

"Ursa Minor, Bandit, you're working to restrain him."

Teddy gave her a thumbs-up, then Trinity added six more. "Can do, Boss."

"Alea Iacta, I want him to be very, very unlucky," Emily continued. "Wait until Bandit and Ursa are holding him down. You need to touch him, right?"

"He sounds unlucky enough already," Alea Iacta said.

"Can you drain his luck or not?" Emily asked. She didn't feel like even trying to muddle her way through small talk.

Alea Iacta stood a little taller. "Uh, yeah, I can do that," he said.

"Great," Emily said. She had a plan. It wasn't a great plan, but it was something to work on. "Owlwatch, you're with me. I need to know what he's thinking, if you can manage that."

"She can read minds?" Glamazon asked with a gesture toward Athena.

"Want me to spill your deepest darkest secrets?" Athena asked.

"She can get impressions," Emily said. "And make people afraid. Anyway, the main goal here is to get Rattles restrained and powerless as quickly as possible. We can't afford to drag this out. Melaton can help once we've got him pinned down."

"What's her gimmick?" Alea Iacta asked.

Glamazon leaned closer to him. "She puts people to sleep."

"Oh. Does she teach math? I think I had a teacher with that power."

Emily cleared her throat. She wanted to chastise Alea Iacta, but he had gotten some of her sisters to laugh and Glamazon to smile. She wished she was able to joke the way he could. Not just because it broke some of the tension, but . . . well, the last time she'd said a joke in public had been in middle school and it had taken all of her bravery to say it.

No one heard except one other girl who repeated it, louder, and got a laugh from everyone. Since then, Emily had avoided humor. Not that she'd been funny to begin with.

"All right," Emily said, trying to get things back on track. "Let's refocus. Once we have him contained, we need to keep him that way. Melaton's good at that, but she might not be able to help. I don't think ropes would work on him. So . . . uh. It'll be tricky."

"We're calling in the HRF?" Glamazon asked.

"I haven't yet," Emily admitted. "But yeah. If we capture him, we're handing him over. Hopefully they have ways of keeping him sedated?" The last was a question aimed at Glamazon.

She nodded. "Yeah. We had training on that. Not much, but still. The troopers have things to knock Villain Masks out. They have canisters of laughing gas too. It's not lethal in smaller doses and it takes most people right out of the fight."

Emily didn't know that, and she was kind of disturbed by the very idea. Still, it wouldn't hurt to make Rattles properly loopy. "Good to know," she said, filing that information away for later. She looked at the team she had assembled. Her sisters and two . . . friends, of sorts. It felt like it was a lot and also too little. "Let's move out," she said.

"I'm going ahead!" Trinity said. Two of her spread her arms out to the sides, then swung them back a little. "Ninja style," she said before she took off running.

Emily considered cutting down her sister's TV time by a lot.

The last Trinity stayed with her while her other bodies darted across the parking lot. "All right. Be quiet if you can, and try not to get noticed," Emily said. Trinity's white-and-black getup was, unfortunately, not the stealthiest of costumes. She'd stick out a little.

"We know more or less where he is, right?" Glamazon asked.

Emily nodded. He certainly wasn't parked in the parking lot of an Im Orton's. "He should be that way. We can start heading toward him, I think. It'll be better to move now than have to run later."

They started walking through the lot at a slow but purposeful pace, and then passed through a fence at the rear that had been bent already so that people could slip by. Emily and Alea Iacta both had lights on their phones, so they lit up the way. Maple had a light, too, but Emily would rather not alert Rattles and also every person in the province to their presence.

The soft light of the phones was barely enough, though her sisters mostly didn't seem to have any trouble. Athena's eyes were two large, glowing disks in the darkness, and Trinity blended in with the dark surprisingly well. Maple was the only one as blind as Emily, and she mostly kept close by grabbing onto Emily's hand.

"I think I found him," Trinity said.

They'd been sticking to alleys and a few back roads just behind the bigger multi-lane streets cutting across the city where most of the shops were. Emily wasn't sure, but she thought they were getting pretty close to the café where Handshake ran his business. It was hard to tell. Eauclaire felt like a different world at night.

"Where did you see him?" Emily asked.

"He's sitting on a bus bench and looking sad," Trinity said.

Emily blinked, then took a moment to process that. "Are you sure?"

"Yeah. It looks like him. He's all in leather with a cool mask and nice hair," Trinity said. "I think he's drinking beer."

"That does sound kind of sad," Glamazon said.

"My guy's not feeling so good, huh?" Alea Iacta said. "Is he alone?"

"Looks like it," Trinity said. "There's a little bike nearby. Uh, one of those not-motorcycles?"

"A scooter?" Glamazon asked.

Trinity shrugged.

"Is he out in the open? Close to the café?" Emily asked. She didn't care about some random scooter.

"Yeah. He's like, right in front of it, a little. There's an alley nearby. If we want to sneak up on him, it wouldn't be that hard," Trinity said. She made some gestures through the air. "We just need to go that way, then around there, then into the alley, then out, and wham!"

Emily did want to see Rattles get "whammed," and she wasn't above attacking him from ambush.

"All right, can you guide us to the end of the alley? Everyone, let's be quiet, please? We might have to turn the lights off, too." There were streetlights, so it wasn't all that bad, and a lot of the apartment buildings they passed had a few lights on inside, which illuminated things enough to see by.

The air felt crisp and cool as they circled around. Trinity gave Emily constant reports. Rattles looked at his phone. He drank another sip. He raised his mask and picked his nose a little. It was mostly useless stuff, but it was good to know that Trinity was paying attention.

They reached the end of the alley. Emily looked at her team. There was a knot in her stomach, but if things went well, then this would be it, the end of her fight with Rattles. The moment where she, inadvertently, became the only real Villain in all of Eauclaire.

"Okay," she said. "Bandit, can one of you bait him into the alley? Everyone else . . . get ready. Fast and hard. We want to win this so fast he won't have time to react."

CHAPTER FIFTY-NINE

Booger Brain

W ell, well, well," Trinity said. She was walking toward Rattles, who looked up at her approach. Her hands were on her hips and she was moving with greatly exaggerated swagger. "If it isn't the great poopy-head himself."

Rattles stood up slowly and scanned the street. Emily moved back slightly, sinking deeper into the shadows of the alleyway. She had to pull Teddy back as well, otherwise the beargirl might move out and into his line of sight.

"What are you doing?" he asked. Emily could just barely hear him.

"I'm making fun of you," Trinity said. She swung her arms out theatrically, then gestured to Rattles. "The poop-head, the crybaby nincompoop, chicken butt . . . uh . . ." She faltered, obviously running out of insults for a moment.

"Booger brain," Maple suggested from the alleyway in a whisper.

"Capitalist," Teddy added.

"I don't know if that kind of insult would work on someone his age," Athena said. "But call him a scatterbrained egghead anyway."

"Oh," Alea Iacta said. "Numpty! Nincompoop two. Uh . . . maybe klutz?"

The girls all nodded, then turned their attention to Emily and Glamazon.

"I'm not participating in whatever this is," Glamazon said.

Emily nodded her agreement.

The Trinity standing out on the street grinned. "You're nothing but a capitalist, booger-brained, numptycompoop."

"I think that last one's wrong," Maple said.

"Eh, I think it gets the message across," a nearby Trinity said quietly with a shrug. And she was right. Rattles looked thoroughly annoyed. He started walking toward Trinity, moving very carefully and slowly.

"You can't be serious," he said. "Of all the useless Masks to show up tonight, it just had to be you? Do you have any idea how much I want to kick someone's ass right now?"

"Pft, you couldn't kick my butt if you tried, old baby," Trinity said. She used her middle finger to pull at the bottom of her eye, then stuck her tongue out at him. "I'm too awesome."

"I've literally beaten you before," he said. "What are you doing here?"

Trinity paused, then stood up straighter and gave him a shrug. "I came here to tell you something."

"Oh? And what's that?" he asked.

"That you're stupid *and* ugly. Not just one or the other, but both, at the same time."

"I should be the one out there," Athena whispered with a shake of her head. "This is just sad. You have no appreciation for the art of insulting people. It doesn't work to just call someone dumb and ugly. You need to really focus on their insecurities."

Trinity blinked at her sister. "Like what?"

"Well, if I were insulting Glamazon, then I wouldn't tell her that she's stupid and ugly, I'd tell her that she doesn't deserve the popularity that she has, that her power isn't nearly as strong as it is flashy, and that her nose is a little long for the size of her face. You need to be *specific*," Athena said.

Emily reached down and patted Athena on the shoulder. "All right, that's enough friendly fire," she said.

Glamazon was touching her nose and looking rather concerned.

"So, what would work on Rattles?" Trinity asked.

"Hmm." Athena leaned forward a little to catch sight of the Villain who was still trading barbs with Trinity. She was making farting noises over him whenever he started talking, which *was*, admittedly, annoying him. "Right, so he's obviously compensating for a lot with that leather jacket and the skull mask. I think he's actually really afraid."

Trinity nodded, and the Trinity out by Rattles stopped blowing raspberries at him. "I know that you're afraid," Trinity said.

"I'm not afraid of you," Rattles snapped.

Athena nodded. "He's not afraid of you. But he *is* afraid. He's afraid that he's going to lose his temper for real, that he'll never amount to anything.

That's why he came here, to Eauclaire, because he was never able to make any real friends in the Villain community. He's alone now, and he's always going to be alone, because no matter what he does, he'll always be both unlikable and yet entirely forgettable."

Glamazon took a small step away from Athena, and Emily could kind of understand the sentiment.

Trinity, though, just grinned and nodded. "Want to know something?" she asked Rattles before she started to move around him. She was keeping a good amount of space between them still. "I know why you're scared."

"Sure you do," Rattles said.

"It's not because you're a coward, or because you're the weakest of the Villains in the Boss's city. It's not even because you're afraid of dying. It's because you know the truth."

"What truth?" Rattles asked.

"You're going to be alone. Forever," Trinity said.

Athena nodded. "Because he's the kind of Villain whose best Villainous skill is hurting the people closest to him first."

Trinity's grin grew. "Because you're the kind of dumb Villain who hurts the people close to him. Like an idiot. You're afraid because you know you'll lose your tempter."

"Temper," Athena corrected.

"And because you know that no matter what you do, or how many cool leather coats you wear, you'll never actually be cool, or make real friends," Trinity continued. Then she stuck her tongue out at him again, for good measure.

"That bike," Athena said, sounding a little excited. "He got nervous when you got closer to it."

"Oh!" a nearby Trinity said. "Well, I'mma give it a kick, then!"

The Trinity near Rattles laughed, then took off toward the bike.

"Hey!" Rattles called out.

It was too late. Trinity had reached the little scooter already. She kicked at its stand, and the whole thing tipped onto its side, then crashed onto the sidewalk. There was a loud *crack* as something plastic broke.

"Oh, you little shit!" Rattles said.

Trinity laughed and took off running.

There was a strange wobbling sensation in the air as Rattles reached a hand out toward her. The ground shook, and just like that, Trinity exploded into ash that quickly faded.

A fresh Trinity appeared next to Emily. "Oops," she said. "He's angry."

"Everyone, in position," Emily hissed. "Bandit, go poke some more fun at him. Everyone else, behind cover."

Putting action to her words, Emily ran back behind cover as well and soon found herself tucked in behind a dumpster along with most of her sisters and her . . . current allies.

Trinity's laughter at the entrance of the alley was accompanied by a vibration shot from Rattles. Emily ducked down lower as the ground below and the dumpster next to her trembled faintly. Even the brick walls lining the sides of the alley shivered a little, and she noticed a small piece of mortar pop out from between two bricks.

"Oh!" the Trinity at the mouth of the alley said before she took off running deeper into the alley.

Rattles stomped after her. Literally. Each step was a big stomp that set the ground trembling and turned Trinity's run into a stumble. She zipped past the dumpster, giving Emily a thumbs-up as she passed.

Rattles followed.

The plan depended on a few things outside of their control. One, that Rattles wouldn't collapse the alley on them, and two, that his night vision was shot from standing in the street.

"Now," Emily said.

Three things happened at once.

Maple activated her Anti-Vibrator, causing the trembling to change in pitch. Glamazon summoned a pair of large, glowing balls of bright light that immediately lit up the alleyway. Finally, Athena rolled out from behind cover deeper within the alley and raised the toaster cannon.

There was a shout of surprise from Rattles as he raised an arm to cover his eyes. He stomped a foot down hard, but while his leg was vibrating, it didn't create the usual big tremor.

Then Athena fired.

She missed, not that Emily could blame her in the chaos. The shot still screamed past, a heavy blow traveling through the air and sending detritus flying.

Rattles ducked a little too late to avoid the blow that had already missed him.

Which was when Alea Iacta reached out of nowhere and touched him on the back. Only his arm was visible. The rest of him was covered by Trinity's ponchos, one over his head like a hood, the other two hanging off him by some duct tape. Along with the partial darkness of the alley, it was enough to cover him from Rattles's vision.

Rattles spun, tripped over his own foot, and completely missed his swing at Alea's face.

Then Glamazon tossed her balls ahead, and they landed around him.

Rattles looked down. Alea Iacta jumped back and spun around.

The balls exploded.

Rattles stumbled back, blind, unlucky, off-balance, more than a little confused, and currently weakened more than Emily had ever seen him.

"Ursa, take him down!" Emily said.

Rattles blinked his eyes just in time to see Teddy's paw come crashing down against his face.

CHAPTER SIXTY

~~~~~~~~~~

Easy Peasy

It had been . . . easy?

Emily couldn't quite bring herself to believe that the plan had worked.

Right now, Rattles was pinned face-down on the ground of the alleyway with one of Teddy's massive paws resting on the back of his head. He wasn't knocked out—because Emily had no idea how to do that to someone without risking their life—but Maple had cuffed his ankles and wrists together with something she'd made that was meant to resist his vibration powers.

He was as incapacitated as Emily could make him.

It was supposed to be a fantastic moment. And it was.

Quest Completed!

Local Villain Removed!

Regional Quest: The Board Ain't Big Enough for the Two of Us, Completed!

You are now the Dominant Villain of the Eauclaire region.

Reward: +1 Skill Slot

This was . . . actually kind of big.

"Oh, that's nice," Athena said.

"Did you just get a Skill Upgrade point?" Glamazon asked. "Because I did, and I don't know if I really earned it."

"Same here," Alea Iacta said. He tapped Rattles's foot with the side of his sneaker. "Seems like taking this guy out was a big deal, huh? Didn't even have a quest for it."

"Yeah," Emily said. She didn't comment on the difference, or the wording. Her . . . quest prompt painted herself as the last big Villain of Eauclaire. She imagined that it wasn't the same for the others.

Nor, apparently, was the reward. Skill Upgrades were nice. A step up, even. But a Skill Slot was a whole other thing. If things went according to pattern, then this would be another sister-creation power. Maybe even her last one? At least for a while?

She wasn't sure if she was ready to use that slot yet.

Rattles started to laugh.

It was so unexpected that Emily jumped, and so did a few of the others. He didn't stop laughing either. It wasn't a full belly laugh, not with Teddy basically shoving him into the ground like that, but it still sounded like Rattles had discovered something that he thought was utterly hilarious.

It was honestly creeping her out. "This explains so much," he said between laughs.

"I think he's finally lost it," Athena said. "We should tape his mouth up, I think."

Emily shook her head. The last thing she needed was for the Villain she'd captured to suffocate. "Melaton will be coming soon. Once she's here, it'll be over. Can everyone keep an eye on him? I'm going to give her a call."

With everyone's agreement, she moved over to the end of the alleyway. One of Trinity's bodies followed her, then leaned up against Emily's side so her big sister could scratch her head while she fished her phone out and made a call.

It took two rings for Melaton to answer. "Boss?" Melaton asked. "You ready for us to move?"

"Um. No? I mean, different plan?" She glanced back to find that her sisters had sat Rattles up. He was on his bum, legs splayed out so that it wouldn't be easy for him to rise, and Teddy was sitting behind him. She imagined that with her proximity, he was feeling bear breath on his neck.

"Different how?" Melaton asked.

"We, ah, captured Rattles," she said.

"You did?" Melaton asked, sounding genuinely surprised.

"Yeah. We're in the alley by, ah . . . " She leaned forward and squinted at the nearest road sign to read it. "Just down the street from where you are, in an alley. I'll have Bandit stay out here to wave you down. Could you come over and use your power on Rattles? His power might make it easy for him to break out."

"Right, I'm on my way. Handshake's pretty happy that he's not getting the secrets beaten out of him, by the way. Remember to charge him for all of this."

"Uh, I will," Emily said. It was more or less a lie. She couldn't imagine herself confronting someone like that on purpose for money. But it would probably give her a little leverage later on, which was nice.

Melaton assured Emily that she was on her way, and then the call went on for an awkwardly long time before Emily said her goodbyes and hung up.

"Hey," she said as she returned. "Melaton will be here in ten minutes."

"We should call the HRF too," Glamazon said.

"After this guy's fully locked up," Alea Iacta said. "I drained all of his luck, so escaping's gonna be tough, but sometimes skill trumps bad luck . . . a little."

"So, you have it all figured out, don't you?" Rattles asked. His shoe scuffed on the ground as he changed his position a little, but a low growl from Teddy stopped him. He smiled anyway, eyes locking on Emily through his mask. His grin was stained red by blood, and she couldn't help the shiver that ran down her spine.

"I . . . I don't know what you mean," Emily said.

"I didn't put it together until just now," he said. He shook his head. "Damn. I was blind, wasn't I? Came here like I was hot stuff, thinking it was some backwater nowhere city I could bend to be what I wanted. Didn't expect any real competition."

"Competition?" Glamazon asked. She sounded dismissive, but was still paying full attention to Rattles as he spoke. There was something about the situation that made it hard not to listen to him. They were in some darkened alley, surrounding the Villain who had hurt every one of them, with the possible exception of Alea Iacta.

"Yeah. For Villainy. I thought there wouldn't be any. Fabien is a petty thief with some flair. That guy's just a loser with a lower power." He nodded to Alea Iacta.

"Ouch," he said.

"Oh, shut up. You know it's true. You're too much of a coward to stand up to any real Villainy." Rattles turned his full attention to Emily. "And then there's *the Boss*. Damn, with a name like that, I should have figured right from the start. But I'm not the only one you're playing for a fool, am I?"

"I don't know what you're talking about," Emily said.

He grinned. "You do. You got the same quest, didn't you? The other side of its coin. Congratulations, you're the last *real* Villain in Eauclaire. The city's all yours. You and your gaggle of brats."

"Boss, what is he talking about?" Glamazon asked. She sounded like she knew, or at least suspected, far more than Emily was comfortable with.

"Nothing," Emily dismissed. "Maple, gag him, please."

"Okay," Maple said. She turned to Trinity. "Give me one of your socks, please."

"But my foot's gonna get cold," Trinity said. "Why don't you use your own?"

"Because I don't want half my feet to be cold, and you have six, so it'll only be one-sixth cold instead of half cold," Maple said.

Trinity frowned, then shrugged. "Okay."

Rattles laughed again. "Hey, Boss. How about before you gag me, you let me go, huh?"

"Let you go?" Emily asked.

"Yeah. You free me, and I'll leave the city. I'll swear it. I'll pick up my crap and leave, go to somewhere less . . . like this place. And, as a bonus, the HRF won't ever learn about you from me."

Emily stared at Rattles. She was conflicted, to the point that she almost considered accepting the offer.

Silence was worth everything. If anyone learned she was a Villain, she'd be ruined.

Then she noticed Glamazon eyeing her suspiciously, and Alea Iacta very obviously not looking her way.

It was Athena that saved the day. She sniffed haughtily, then leaned forward so that she was at eye level with the Villain. "You think anyone will believe you? Idiot. Big Sister Boss is the biggest Hero that's ever Heroed."

"Yeah," Teddy grumbled her agreement. "Boss is a big damned Hero."

Rattles chuckled. "Oh, that's great. The kids believe the lie too?"

"I've never believed no lies," Trinity said. "And it's not a lie that you're lame and stupid."

"Bandit," Emily warned as she pulled Trinity back. "Maple, can you gag him?"

Maple nodded. She'd made . . . something with some tape and Trinity's sock. It didn't look like anything Emily would want in her own mouth, but she was pretty ambivalent about shoving it in Rattles's.

"You can gag me now, but I'll be telling them everything."

"Lie all you want," Emily said. "That's not my problem."

But it was. She could feel the doubt coming from Glamazon. Or maybe she imagined it.

Whatever the case, she had a growing pit of worry in her stomach while Rattles mumbled into the gag her sisters fit around his mouth. If— or when—this all got out, it might spell the end of her career, and of a lot more than that.

The only good thing here was that with Rattles captured, Emily didn't have any real reason to act as a Mask anymore.

Or so she hoped.

CHAPTER SIXTY-ONE

Properly Shook

Emily stood aside, along with all of her sisters, while the entire street was lit up.

There were three HRF vans, two normal police patrol cars, and an ambulance. All that was missing was a fire truck and it would be an EMT party. Right now, the likelihood that firefighters would show up was increasing dramatically as a couple of HRF troopers and some cops were standing by a building, flashlights illuminating the side.

There was a hole there. It was toast-shaped, though Emily suspected that most people would just assume that it was roughly square, especially with the cracks radiating out from around it.

That was . . . not ideal. She hadn't considered what would happen with that toast once it flew past Rattles. But obviously, it had to go *somewhere*, and that happened to be across the street and into the side of an insurance brokerage.

Emily supposed they were covered for Mask-related incidents, at least.

She wasn't going to make a fuss about it, in any case. Let the police and HRF suspect whatever they wanted. As far as she was concerned, it was all Rattles's fault.

It wasn't like his power hadn't led to enough property damage already.

"Oh, more lights!" Maple said. She'd been a little awed by all of the flashing lights already. The red-and-white of the ambulance, red-and-blue of the police, and green-and-white of the HRF were joined by a set of yellow-and-white lights as a tow truck backed up a little ways down the road.

It was here to tow that little scooter, which was illegally parked. Emily felt a little bad for the owner. Not only had Trinity kicked it, but now it was being carried off.

That was kind of Emily's fault, wasn't it? She hoped that whoever had left their bike there wouldn't be too upset once morning came around.

"Right," Alea Iacta said. He was standing a little apart from the rest of the group, notably putting Emily and her sisters between himself and the HRF. "I think this is my cue to scamper away," he said.

"Leaving already?" Glamazon asked.

He shrugged. "The cops and I have a . . . testy relationship. Mostly a recent thing, I assure you."

"Uh-huh," Glamazon said. She didn't sound impressed, but that didn't seem to discourage Alea Iacta.

"Hey, if you want the whole story, I wouldn't mind sharing. Maybe with just the two of us. Over coffee? I remember how you like it. The coffee, I mean."

Emily almost wanted to give him kudos for being semi-charismatic, at least until that fumble at the end. Still, better than she could manage.

"He's trying to rizz her," Teddy said.

Emily turned to Teddy. "What does that even mean? And where did you learn that?"

"On the internet?" Teddy tried.

Emily resisted the urge to pinch the bridge of her nose. She had to stop letting the TV and internet raise her sisters for her.

She turned toward Glamazon, who was eyeing Alea Iacta. "I think I wouldn't mind that."

"Holy sh—crap," Teddy said. "It worked!"

Athena started to golf clap, then Trinity joined in with more enthusiasm, which of course had Alea Iacta blushing up to his ears. "Right, uh, okay. I'll call ya. Bye?" He backed up a few steps, then slipped into a nearby alley. Emily figured that she'd be seeing him again. Especially with the amount of luck he'd stolen from Rattles earlier.

"Are you . . . really?" Emily asked.

Glamazon shrugged. "He's not all bad. Kinda cute? Sorta? Like, a six, at least."

"I guess luck and looks aren't the same thing," Emily muttered.

"Speaking of being bad, can we talk?" Glamazon asked. She nodded to the side before she started walking off. Emily hesitated. Her sisters were mostly behaving, though, and it wasn't far, just enough that they wouldn't all overhear.

She walked after Glamazon, who'd stopped under a streetlight. "Alea's an odd one," she commented.

Emily nodded. Was that what Glamazon wanted to talk about? "Most of us are, I guess," she replied. "But he's on our side, which is what matters."

"Speaking of sides," Glamazon said while turning to Emily. "Are we going to talk about what Rattles said? About you being a Villain?"

"He's wrong," Emily said quickly.

"Emily, you know you can trust me, right?" Glamazon began, her expression serious. "But if you're hiding something, something that could put you or the girls in danger . . ."

Emily tried to meet her gaze, then failed. "I'm not hiding anything that will put us in danger," she lied.

Glamazon's eyes narrowed slightly, and for a moment, Emily thought she might press further. But then, Glamazon exhaled slowly and nodded. "I want to believe you, Boss. I do. You've done a lot of good for this city."

The reassurance was comforting, but Emily still felt the weight of her secrets pressing down on her. "Thank you," she said before forcing a smile. "I, uh, do what I can."

Glamazon reached out, squeezing Emily's shoulder gently. Then her gaze went back to the group. "Are you a Villain, Emily?" she asked. Her voice was pitched low, keeping it between the two of them.

The question came so suddenly that Emily felt like the air had been knocked out of her. "N-no, I'm not a Villain," Emily said.

Glamazon turned and met Emily's eyes. Emily couldn't even begin to guess at the emotions she was seeing there. "I'm . . . I'm not going to turn you in," Glamazon said. She sounded doubtful of her own words. "You'd get the girls caught in the middle of this."

"What? No, I mean. I don't want any of them to be hurt."

Glamazon nodded slowly.

They both fell quiet, and it wasn't comfortable, but neither spoke. The sounds of the police and HRF filled the air, and a breeze passed over them, causing Emily to shiver.

After a minute, Glamazon spoke. "You really do love them, don't you?"

Emily nodded. "I do. They're my sisters. I'd never want to hurt them. And . . . Glamazon, if I were a Villain, I wouldn't be doing these kinds of things, would I? Taking out Rattles, and doing things to help?"

"Maybe," Glamazon said. She turned away from Emily with her arms wrapped around herself. Was she . . . scared?

"I'm not a Villain," Emily said.

Glamazon nodded.

Emily swallowed. She hated this.

Glamazon took a deep breath, then turned back to Emily. "I'm sorry, Emily, but I think I need a little time away. To sort things out."

"O-oh. I . . . okay."

Glamazon nodded again. "Yeah. We'll . . . figure it out, maybe?"

"Yeah," Emily said.

Glamazon hesitantly stepped forward and hugged her, then broke away.

Emily watched her leave, her stomach twisting itself into knots. What did she do now? The answer came a moment later. A hand slipped into her own and she glanced down to see Athena beside her. "Are you okay?

Glamazon was walking over to the HRF troopers, where she was quickly intercepted by a detective.

"I think Glamazon has pieced together that we're not, ah, Heroes," Emily said.

Athena shrugged. "So? We're not. It was going to get out eventually."

"I was kind of hoping it wouldn't," Emily replied.

"Come on, Big Sis, ruling from the shadows is cool and all, but most of us aren't made for that. Did you see how unsubtle Teddy and Trinity are? They're not fit for sneaky mastermind games. We were always going to have to step up eventually."

The two of them stood there, watching the police work for a while, with Athena holding Emily's hand. It was comforting, and the warmth helped Emily calm down a little. Of course, the others came over and immediately shattered any calm, but Emily was used to their brand of chaos already.

"Hey, so, how are we getting home?" Teddy asked.

"I have no idea," Emily said. Then she spotted Melaton standing next to an HRF van with her arms crossed, chatting with an officer. The same van that housed a no doubt sleeping Rattles. "But I think I know who we can bully into giving us a ride," she added.

Emily grabbed two little hands, then led her gaggle of sisters across the street and toward the light show that the emergency responders were making. She had the impression that there were only so many people out because they wanted to make a big deal out of this, and it was working.

The sidewalks were lined with rubbernecking bystanders, some still in pj's, most with phones out.

"Hello, Melaton," Emily said. She was barging into a conversation, but she didn't really care all that much at the moment.

Melaton nodded at her. "Hey, Boss. Kids. Good job out there tonight. I think everyone will be happy to see this jerk off the streets."

Emily smiled. "Yes. Actually, about no longer being on the streets . . . do you own a car?"

Melaton was immediately wary. ". . . Yes?"

"Good, good," Emily said. "Because I think I need to call in a small favor."

CHAPTER SIXTY-TWO

Hollow

Emily was intimately familiar with anxiety.

She'd been feeling stress of one sort or another for what felt like her entire life. Maybe there had been some moments when she was much younger where she wasn't anxious about something, but those moments were a long time ago.

Every meeting was a scenario she had to replay in her mind a thousand times. Every appointment was something she had to worry over until she felt sick to her stomach. Anything that involved talking or meeting with people was . . . Well, she didn't need to go into much detail there. They were their own kind of stress, piled on top of all the rest.

For some reason, the anxiety she was feeling now was entirely . . . hollow.

That was new.

Sure, she had schoolwork to get to, and she knew there would be tasks and assignments that she'd have to work with a group to accomplish. There was that one teacher's assistant that she didn't get along with, and she had a number of small appointments peppered through her agenda that worried at her.

But now they all felt like distant, small stressors, where before each one would be a monolith to face and defeat.

Emily secretly suspected that it was all about tolerance. Since becoming a Villain, she'd had to go through so much anxiety that the things that would have given her ulcers before were now barely more than blips. She was like a thrill-seeker who had discovered that the average roller coaster didn't work for her anymore, not after para-chuteless skydiving.

Not that she had skydived, or would. She liked being alive, thank you very much. And of course, it would set a bad example for her sisters.

The day after Rattles was captured, Emily found herself staying at home. She'd sent a message to the school telling them that she was sick and that she'd be missing the day's classes.

Being up until nearly the crack of dawn didn't suit her sleep schedule at all. Not to mention that getting her sisters to bed after all that excite-ment had been a nightmare.

She was exhausted, and that was after sleeping in until almost noon.

At the moment, she was on the couch, in her walrus pajamas, feet up on the coffee table in exactly the way she'd told her sisters not to do a dozen times. Trinity was tucked in to her left and Teddy on her right, and Maple was humming to herself while playing with something on the table. Athena was . . . Emily looked around and discovered Athena on the far end of the couch, head on Trinity's lap while she watched the TV.

It was nice. They had blankets, and the room was almost uncomfort-ably warm, but not quite. Toasty, from all the body warmth, but not so hot that it was unpleasant.

The TV was turned to the news. A local channel, which mostly cov-ered provincial stuff and news in and around Eauclaire, as well as what-ever big international story was too big not to cover. At that moment, that was mostly a scandal where Apoca-Man had un-Masked a Villain's real identity way down south, revealing that they were the head of some mod-erately big corporation down there.

It wasn't something that would really have an impact on Emily or her friends, but it was still interesting to see what some Villains were up to.

For all that she was . . . reluctantly giving in to the idea of maybe being somewhat Villainous, Emily didn't feel like she was anywhere near the big leagues. Nothing she did was international news.

But it *was* local news.

"Oh, it's us again," Athena said as she sat up.

The story changed to nighttime footage of Rattles's arrest. It was a cell-phone video taken by bystanders, and the video quality was made worse by the flickering lights of emergency services vehicles. First came a grainy video of Rattles being loaded in a van and checked on by some paramed-ics, then a loop of Emily, her sisters, and Glamazon standing off to the side and clearly out of the way.

The newscaster, an attractive enough middle-aged man, smiled into the camera. "Good news this morning for citizens of Eauclaire as small-time Villain Rattles was finally captured. The Villain was responsible for a series of attacks across the city, cumulating in several million dollars of property damage as well as thousands stolen from local banks and businesses."

They cut to some better-quality footage of Rattles hitting a bank, then that money van he'd toppled over.

"The Villain was confronted several times by HRF-associated Heroes, leading to his arrest last night. A team-up by the Eauclaire Brats and local Heroine Glamazon."

"Boo! Boo!" Teddy said to the screen as it split up to show their images.

Glamazon took up a third of the screen. The other two-thirds were split up into small boxes with images of Emily and her sisters, with their Heroic names underneath the images.

"I got in three times!" Trinity said. "Wait . . . That's the same me twice!" She pointed to two of the pictures, which were . . . clearly both Trinity.

"You can tell which you is you?" Athena asked.

"Well, it's all me, but obviously each of me's a little different," Trinity said.

Emily looked at her, then looked at another her. She couldn't see anything that would help. Not to mention, she wasn't sure how often Trinity's bodies had . . . refreshed.

"The team-up led to a successful capture of the Villain early in the morning," the newscaster continued, unaware of their chat. "A statement came in from the HRF thanking local Heroes, associates, and independents for their hard work keeping the streets of Eauclaire safe from Villainous influences."

The camera shifted to the co-anchor, who smiled broadly. "I think that makes us one of the safest cities on the East Coast," she said.

"I think so. Eauclaire was never a place with a strong Villainous presence, but these last few weeks after Power Day have been difficult. It's nice to see the last of these scoundrels put away," the main host said.

"Hehe, they don't know nothing," Teddy said.

Emily patted Teddy's head, and Teddy's smugness only grew. Emily wasn't sure if this was encouraging her or not, but at the moment she was distracted by the way Teddy's ears flicked every time her hand came close. "I guess this means that we've more or less won?" Emily asked.

"Won?" Athena asked. "I mean, I guess. We beat that idiot, so the city's ours now. We just need to kick the Heroes out, and then start spreading."

"Spreading?" Emily asked.

"Our evil influence," Trinity confirmed.

"I can start building bigger things," Maple said.

"And we can start influencing more people. Bring them around to the right way of thinking. Which is our way. Obviously," Teddy said. "But we can also set it up so that the next time some competition comes here, it'll have a much harder time."

Emily was about to dampen her sisters' resolve, but that last bit had her curious. "What do you mean?"

Teddy grinned up at her. It was a surprisingly evil expression. "Because now we have the home turf advantage."

"We *will* have it," Athena said. "We don't yet. We just don't have anyone stopping us from taking it." She shuffled a bit without removing her head from Trinity's lap. "We just need to do some of that stuff Heroes do, where they make themselves all famous and stuff. And get stronger too."

"I got some points for that," Trinity said.

"Me too," Maple added. "From the fight."

That was unsurprising, but Emily was kind of hoping to hold off on using those. Not because they wouldn't be useful, but because she had a hard enough time controlling her sisters when they were this strong. Them being even stronger wouldn't help. "I got some as well," Emily said.

Teddy sat up so quickly that Emily's hand slipped off her head. "Did you get a Skill Slot?" she asked.

"Yes?" Emily replied.

"Wait, does that mean we're getting a new sister?" Trinity asked. She gasped in triplicate.

Emily sighed. "I'm not sure if I'm ready to have another little sister," she said. And wasn't that the truth. She was only just beginning to get used to handling the sisters she had now. Adding another would maybe be the straw that broke her figurative back.

Then again . . . it *was* another sister.

Emily looked over her current sisters, meeting inquisitive, happy gazes, and felt some of that last lingering anxiety melt away. Would it really be all that bad to have just one more?

"Well, maybe," she said.

"Yeah!" Teddy said. "More sisters to boss over."

"Oh, shut up, you can hardly boss yourself," Athena snapped.

Emily let the arguments wash past her, barely listening as her sisters flung pointless barbs at one another. She cleared her throat eventually, calming them down. "If we're going to do this, then we should do it right. Maybe prepare things a little first? That way we can meet our new sister properly."

That sounded like the right thing to do.

CHAPTER SIXTY-THREE

~~~~~~~~~~

Moosin' Around

Emily really hoped that whatever form her newest sister came in, she wasn't someone who cared much for pomp and circumstance. Mostly because their "preparations" weren't all that fancy or impressive.

They'd cleared out a space in the living room, a big circle free of furniture. Then that same furniture had turned into a place to put down offerings.

There were Winkies and Affa Cakes and Os-Louis cakes on a plate. Emily hadn't known about those. She suspected that they'd come from the minions when Maple revealed her stash. There were also a few cookies—which she *had* known about, since they were her go-to bribes—and even some soda. It was enough to start a small party.

The TV was still on, but turned to one of those music-only channels, and they'd all gone through the effort of cleaning up the living room. They'd even cleared out one of the bedrooms. Having an unused room had turned out to be too tempting, and the space had been inadvertently turned into additional storage. Now it was clean and ready for their newest sibling.

"I think . . . that's about the best we can do," Emily said. She pointedly ignored the fact that she was still in her walrus pajamas and that her sisters were in their own lazy-day wear.

Emily checked on her skill sheet again, just to confirm that everything was in order.

Name: Emily Wright		
Alignment: Villain		
Alias: The Boss		
Level: 1		
Powers		
Sister Summoning		
Create Sister	Rank 9	
Sisterportation	Level 3	
Double Trouble	Level Max	
Healpats	Level Max	
Triple Threat	Level Max	
Menagerie Family	Level 1	
Quadruple Quirkiness	Level Max	
Center of Attention	Level 1	
Points		
Power Slots: 0	Skill Upgrades: 0	Skill Slots: 1

"Is everyone ready?" she asked while rereading the skill list. There were some in there that she never really used. Probably for the best, really.

"We're ready," Athena said. Next to her, Maple nodded, and she got a triple thumbs-up from Trinity.

"Get on with it, Boss," Teddy said.

Emily sighed. Then, with a twitch of her will, she spent that point.

New Skill Unlocked!

Quintuple Quake has been added to your Power's Skills!

Emily gulped. That followed the same pattern as all the other skills that had given her a new sister. Now all she needed to do was to drop those two magical words and that would be it.

Quintuple Quake
Sister Summoning
Level Max
Allows you to summon a fifth sister with Create Sister. Instant use.
Activation: Vocal Command
No Cooldown
Max New Sisters: One

That description was the same as well. "It's another Sister Summoning skill," she said. Her sisters cheered, but Emily wasn't sure she felt quite as enthusiastic as they did.

Not only would this be that much more responsibility, but it would also make things a lot more complicated. She was already on thin ice explaining how she'd gotten a group of *four* young girls with animal features together. It probably stretched incredulity. Showing up with a fifth over a month past Power Day? That was improbable to the max.

This was going to be a logistical nightmare, too. One more mouth to feed, one more person to carry around.

She shook her head. No, that didn't matter. It was all trumped by having one more sister to love, one more person to share time with.

Her more practical side pointed out that it would be one more power, one more Mask on her team, and that was valuable all on its own.

"Is everyone ready?" she asked, even if she knew the answer she'd receive.

Confirmations rang across the room, and Emily took in a deep breath. She hoped this would work out.

"Create sister," she said firmly and with more confidence than she felt.

There was a woosh and a tug that she was certain she'd never get used to, then just like that, there was a *pop* and someone new appeared in the middle of the living room, landing with just a faint wobble.

The first thing that Emily noticed was that her newest sister was . . . tall. She was just a hair shorter than Emily herself. She was a redhead, though her hair was quite dark, almost brown? It was only really orange where the light caught it correctly, which was still quite nice.

Emily blinked, then forced herself to meet her new sister's eyes. "H-hello," she said.

The girl smiled. She had a smattering of freckles across the bridge of her nose and her cheeks. "Hey," she said with a confident, upbeat voice.

Emily took just a moment to scan her up and down. She looked . . . older. Not an adult, but definitely in her mid-teens, as opposed to the rest of her sisters, who all more or less looked like they were on the cusp of adolescence. She wore a red plaid shirt with the sleeves rolled up to her elbows and plain blue jeans tucked into sensible hiking boots.

She looked . . . Emily paused to consider the right word, then fell upon it. Outdoorsy. She looked like someone who knew how to start a fire, set up a tent, and navigate through a forest.

"Hmph," Teddy hmphed as she stomped over to stand before her new sister. "All right. Lemme lay the rules down for you. Also, why're you so tall?"

"Uh, I don't know," the new sister said with an awkward shrug. "I was born this way, I guess."

"Huh. Well, it doesn't matter how tall you are, because the pecking order goes Boss, then me, then the rest, then you, and then, if you're real good, the minions."

"Teddy," Emily warned. "Let's not start with bullying."

"It's not bullying," Teddy whined.

The new girl stepped forward, then squatted a little to be at Teddy's eye level. She grinned, a hand extending out. "How about we just be friends, eh?"

Teddy eyed the hand suspiciously, then shook it. "Friends can be subordinates too, you know!"

The new girl chuckled, but she didn't seem too bothered by Teddy's Teddyness. Emily was relieved. "We should do introductions," she said. "So that we're all on the same page. You've met Teddy already. And in order . . . that's Athena over there, those three bodies are Trinity, and the girl hiding behind Trinity is Maple. I'm Emily."

"Hi!" the new girl said with a casual wave. "Don't got a name yet, but it's nice to meet all of y'all!"

Teddy tilted her head. "What are you, anyway?" she asked. "Your ears are all pointy-like."

Emily glanced up, only now noticing the two fuzzy ears on either side of the new sister's head. They were fairly small, and colored the same as her hair, so they didn't stand out all that much. Still, she couldn't begin to guess which animal had ears like that.

The girl grinned. "I'm a cow," she said.

"Huh?" Emily asked.

"A female moose," the girl clarified. She grinned, clearly thinking that catching Emily off guard had been funny. "Look, I've got antlers and all." With a frown of concentration, the girl grew a pair of large, glowing antlers.

They sprouted out of the sides of her head, initially just a nub, but they quickly grew up and out, tines spreading outward and filling in until she had a large rack above her head. One that glowed a ghostly white.

"Are those forcefields?" Maple asked.

"I guess," the new girl said. "I can bash things with them. And I guess I could double as a coat hanger, eh?"

"I don't think I want to have one of my sisters end up as furniture," Emily said. "But . . . they're quite pretty. Is that your power?"

"Yeah!" she said with a nod. A nod that was very impressive, thanks to the antlers that bobbed up and down.

"Can we eat the snacks now?" Trinity asked.

All of her sisters, including the new one, perked up at that, so Emily sighed. "Yes, we can start on the snacks, but! But! New sister first. This *is* her welcoming party."

"That's nice of ya!" the new sister said. "Don't worry, I'll keep a lid on my appetite! Promise."

Emily stared, her mind hard at work. Her power didn't name her sisters, but she figured she'd been doing an all right job of it so far. This one might be tricky, however. She couldn't just rely on puns forever. That was . . . not very mature. "So, you're a moose? I don't think a name like . . . Moosey would be appropriate."

The girl chuckled. "I hope not!"

"We'll think about it," Emily promised. "We can maybe do a bit of power testing?"

"I wanna fight you!" Teddy cheered.

"And I can see what makes her tick," Athena added.

"I'mma see if she's good at not getting stolen from," Trinity added.

"A-ah, um, I can . . . maybe make something to test her forcefields?" Maple tried.

Emily sighed. "Let's not fight, bully, steal from, or torture our new sister, please?"

CHAPTER SIXTY-FOUR

Borealis

She watched as her sisters, her brand-new sisters, of which there were many, pranced around and danced and fought one another.

It was a little overwhelming, but at the same time . . . not? She wasn't nervous, and she wasn't on the verge of panic. She was just sitting there and watching as her many sisters did their own thing. With one another. Without her, because she was new, and didn't know them well.

She wasn't exactly sure how to put it into words, but she did know how it made her feel: envious.

Not extremely so, but . . . Teddy had one arm wrapped around one of Trinity's necks and was burying her knuckles into Trinity's hair. Another Trinity was munching on Teddy's calf while yet another was trying to free her stuck self by tugging Teddy's arm free. Teddy was screaming "Rabies! Rabies!" for the room at large to hear, though she'd occasionally break out into laughter, cutting off her own chant.

Off to the side, Athena was next to Maple, and the two of them were leaning close together, both talking in low tones, sometimes breaking out into giggles. Maple was fussing with something small—a remote? And she sometimes passed it to Athena, who'd inspect it before returning it.

She had no idea what they were doing, but they were doing it together.

Meanwhile, she was sitting on the far end of the couch, separated from all the rest by only a few dozen centimeters, but that gulf felt massive at the moment.

It wasn't just physical. She was . . . not the same as her sisters. They all *felt* younger. Energetic and loud and very silly, but in a fun way. She felt that too, but maybe not as much as they did. She could be silly, if she wanted, but it would be . . . sinking into silliness, as opposed to just being naturally silly.

She wasn't sure if she wanted to do that yet. But maybe she'd have to, if she wanted to fit in with the rest.

And she desperately wanted to.

"Hey."

She looked up and to the side, then smiled as she discovered her only bigger sister coming over. Emily had two cans of soda in hand, both unopened, both a little damp on the outside.

"Want me to scoot over?" she asked.

"Just a little," Emily said. She sat down next to her, then handed one of the cans over. "Here. I don't know what you like yet. It's orange-flavored. Teddy and Athena don't like it, but Maple and Trinity do."

"Oh. Thanks," she said as she took one of the cans. It was cool to the touch. She popped the tab, then sniffed it before taking a swallow. It was fizzy and sweet and . . . she wasn't sure if she liked it right away, but it wasn't all that bad.

"We're going to need to get a bigger couch in here," Emily muttered. She was hip-to-hip with her new sister already, and there was only some space left on the rest of the couch. Just enough for Teddy and maybe one Trinity to squeeze in.

"I can help carry it in," she said before raising an arm. She flexed, and her bicep bulged up a little. "Being strong's not part of my power or any-thing, but I think I should be pretty strong anyway."

"Don't go telling that to Teddy," Emily said with a soft smile. "She'll get jealous."

"I'll keep it to myself, then, eh?"

Emily nodded along, then looked her up and down. "So . . . I guess that leads to a safe subject. Did you want to talk about your powers?"

"Oh, yeah, I can do that. Did you want to see my stats screen?"

Emily considered it, then nodded. "Sure. Though I wouldn't mind an explanation, if you don't mind."

She gestured before her, even if she knew that the gesture was entirely unneeded. It still felt right, and soon there was a small hovering screen for her sister to look at.

Name: ??? Wright		
Alignment: Villain, Little Sister		
Alias: None		
Level: 1		
Powers		
Bastion of the North		
Forceful Antlers	Rank 1	
Points		
Power Slots: 0	Skill Upgrades: 0	Skill Slots: 0

Emily looked it over, then sighed. "We really need to work on your name. I don't like having a sister whose name is nothing. It feels . . . wrong."

"I can think of a few names!" Teddy said. She was still mid-fight with Trinity. "How about Lenin?"

"That's a boy's name," Emily pointed out.

"What about Marx?"

"I . . . don't think so," Emily shot down.

She wasn't so sure about that name either, so she wasn't sad to see it go. "Did you want to see my skill? It's really not much to look at."

"I'd love to," Emily said.

Forceful Antlers		
Bastion of the North		
Rank 1		
Project the strength of the mighty north, indomitable, unstoppable, unyielding.		
No Cooldown		

"I'm not sure what that does, exactly," Emily admitted after reading the screen.

"It lets me summon my antlers when I need them, and I can move them around. I don't think most things can move my antlers, no matter how much they try," she said. There was a bit of pride there. Her antlers were powerful. It might not seem that way at first, she realized, and maybe her sisters had more utility with their powers, but hers wasn't to be underestimated so easily.

"I see. We really will have to do some sort of power testing, then. That might be exciting. I think Sam would like to see that. She seems interested in powers in a way that, ah, I'm not. And some of the other minions would love that too."

She nodded. Power testing seemed like it could be fun. It would give her an opportunity to show what she could do. And impress her family. She might have been sitting in the middle of them, but she still felt like she was a little bit apart.

"Hmm, Bastion of the North," Emily muttered. "Hey, what do you think of a north-themed name?"

"Like . . . Snow?" Maple asked, her head popping up as she joined the discussion.

"Uh, I'm white enough for it, I guess," she said, looking at the skin of her forearm. "But my hair's all wrong."

"We're not going to call the new sister Cold, or Freezing, or Big-Sister forbid, Slush," Athena said.

"I like Slush," Trinity said.

"Then you can call yourself that," Athena snapped.

Trinity—now Slush—blinked in confusion, then all six of her eyes teared up. "But I'm Trinity."

"No you're not, Slush," Teddy said.

"Girls," Emily said warningly. "Trinity, you're still Trinity, not Slush. No one is being named Slush." Emily sighed. "It would probably be best to try for a pretty name. Something like . . . I don't know, Aurora?"

She perked up. "Aurora?"

"Like the northern lights," Emily explained. "They're very pretty lights that shift in the atmosphere. I saw them once, when we went camping in late fall. They're really spectacular in person."

"I like that," she said.

"Really? Well . . . okay then." Emily smiled. "Welcome to the family, Aurora Wright."

"Aurora Wright!" Trinity cheered.

"Aurora Wright!" Teddy followed. She was finally freed from Trinity's grasp as the smaller girl raised her hands above her heads.

They started chanting her new name, soon mushing it together into a long mess of syllables, but Aurora didn't mind. It was nice. Silly, yes, but nice all the same.

The party continued. It wasn't a big one, not with so few people, but it was lively all the same. Maple turned the TV to a channel with loud music, and then Athena dragged Maple into a very enthusiastic and poorly executed dance, which Trinity joined a moment later.

Aurora continued to stay near her big sister, but she didn't feel quite as left out as she had just moments earlier. She had a name now. She was part of this weird, chaotic family.

That niggling worry in her gut? The one that made her wonder if she'd be accepted or not? She was starting to think that maybe it was silly too.

"Right, I think I'm going to go cook something up, I can't have you all eat nothing but sweets. That's too irresponsible, even for me," Emily said.

"I think I can help," Aurora said.

"I'll, uh, help too?" Maple suggested.

And so she found herself in the kitchen, with only two sisters instead of a bunch, preparing a meal with some confusion as she had to look into every drawer and cupboard to find anything, but it was still nice.

Aurora was starting to think that it wasn't just the loud moments that were going to be enjoyable. The small, quiet ones had their place too. And if those moments had a place, then maybe there was room for a wayward moose girl as well.

CHAPTER SIXTY-FIVE

Hover Mode

Emily wasn't used to being worried about the social abilities of *others*. Usually, worrying about her own was a full-time issue already, but at the moment she was discovering that having more sisters wasn't just an issue in the ways she expected it to be.

Yes, Aurora had a healthy appetite, so the food budget would be hit a tiny bit harder than estimated, and yes, it meant more clothes to buy and wash, more cleaning to be done, and more room being taken up in their bunker home, but all of that was expected.

What she hadn't expected were Aurora's initial difficulties in blending in.

So far, the sister who'd had the hardest time socially was Maple, but Maple was just very shy. She liked her sisters, and she liked spending time with them, but she found it hard to speak up for herself. Emily could understand that. Sometimes Emily needed some time to herself, too.

Aurora's situation was different.

It wasn't that she was shy. Aurora had a nice smile, and she was friendly and easy to talk to. She engaged with her sisters without having to be asked, unlike Maple, who was a lot more passive.

Emily was just worried because while the others ran around, made a mess of things, and were having fun with one another, Aurora was constantly standing to the side, apart and alone.

She wasn't sure what to do about it. Her first thought was to go to the park, the same park they'd visited a while ago for Maple to show off her newest inventions. It was a quiet enough space that they'd be able to test out Aurora's powers without interruption, and Emily liked it when her sisters tired themselves out.

It was good for their physical health and great for her mental one.

"All right," Emily said. She clapped her hands, getting all of her sisters' attention. And her mother's.

She had to get to the park somehow, and she didn't want to ask Sam for yet another ride. Emily was very aware of how much of Sam's time she was taking up, and it was kind of humiliating and just rude at this point. Minion or no, Sam had a life, too.

Emily was starting to look into getting a driver's license, something she'd hoped to put off . . . forever. Her dad was happy about it, at least.

So, to get to the park today, she'd gotten her mom to give her and her sisters a ride. The girls liked spending time with Grandma Boss anyway. And Emily suspected that her mom was happy to spend time with the kids, too.

Emily was . . . probably not going to give her mom any grandbabies. That would involve dating. And then marrying someone. She couldn't imagine that ever working out, not when just a couple of months ago the idea of owning a cat felt like it would be a big deal.

Emily shook her head and refocused. She was the center of a lot of sisterly attention at the moment. It was clear that they all wanted to launch themselves into play, so she only had so long to keep their attention.

"All right," she repeated. "We're here to test out Aurora's power. So I guess that's what we'll start with. Does anyone want to help?"

Maple slowly raised a hand. "I can help," she said.

"Yeah, me too!" Teddy said. "I wanna wrestle her!"

Aurora laughed. "Sure, that sounds like it could be fun."

"Uh, wrestling can be . . . one of the tests, I guess," Emily said.

"Want me to take notes?" Athena asked.

"That would be nice, yes," Emily agreed. "How about we start with that forcefield of yours?"

"I'll need something to run into," Aurora said.

"I'll get some sticks!" Trinity cheered.

And just like that, the group broke up, leaving Emily to take a deep breath and try to chill out. She felt a hand gripping her shoulder and glanced to the side, where her mom was smiling at her. "You know, I only had the one daughter to look after, and she was pretty calm," her mom said. "I'd give you a book at that age and wouldn't hear a peep for hours. I'm genuinely impressed by how well you're handling all of this."

"Yeah, thank you," Emily said.

"You did skip some of the harder parts. The terrible twos, the diapers, the—"

"Okay, Mom," Emily cut in. "I get it."

Her mom grinned. "You've grown a lot, sweetie. I'm proud."

It was a blushing Emily who started the tests proper.

The first test had her almost calling things off. It involved Trinity swinging a branch that was longer than she was tall, and which required two of her bodies to lift, right at Aurora's head.

Aurora summoned her antlers, shifted her stance, and met the branch head-on. The stick rammed into her antlers and bounced off with a snap. A second swing had Aurora twisting her head, which wrenched the branch apart and sheared off the end.

Next, Aurora wanted to prove how strong her antlers were by testing them against a tree.

The tree lost.

"Ah," Emily said as she started to catch on.

Her initial assumption was that Aurora's power was . . . not all that strong. A pair of antlers was interesting, and it was a flashy kind of power, but it didn't seem immediately useful. In fact, it seemed like it would make things a lot harder. Simple stuff like walking through doors was a lot more complicated with multi-foot-long branches sticking out of the side of one's head.

But, as it turned out, she hadn't quite understood Aurora's power correctly, not until it was put to the test.

Her antlers were inviolable constructs. When they crashed into something, the antlers would keep moving, regardless of the durability of what they ran into.

Aurora made a smaller tree *bend* as she pushed her antlers against it, because her antlers were unstoppable objects and the tree wasn't immovable.

Eventually the tree creaked, then cracked, then broke apart in the middle.

The antlers didn't have any real cutting or shearing potential. They were just unstoppable.

Emily realized that Aurora wouldn't have problems with doorframes. Doorframes would have problems with her.

Walls, too. And cars. And at the moment, playground equipment and ever-thicker trees.

"Okay, okay," she stepped in as her excited sisters were aiming Aurora at a particularly large tree. "Let's not deforest the entire area, please? The trees didn't do anything to anyone."

The next test was a test of strength. Without her antlers, Aurora was . . . about as strong as a normal girl, if one who seemed physically fit. She was able to wrestle Teddy and pin her down the first time, but Teddy got her in the rematch. Aurora's longer arms gave her some very good leverage.

With her antlers out, there was no way anyone could really stop her.

Only her antlers were fixed and unmovable. The rest of her was only as strong as normal, but having perfect leverage, even if it was just from the head, still meant that Aurora could anchor herself and pin or push others with relative ease.

She could also hover, sorta.

Since her antlers only moved when she wanted them to, Aurora could fold her legs up, grab onto her antlers, and stay hanging in the air.

She had no way of maneuvering once there, since it meant locking her antlers in place, but it was still a neat trick. It made climbing trees easy, since she just needed to pin her head in place, and then she could climb with her legs, get a good grip, and let go of her antlers to reposition.

Of course, Aurora herself wasn't any tougher than a normal person. She had scrapes and a few boo-boos by the end of the day, just like all the other sisters who had roughhoused. So, in theory, she could stop a semi-trailer on the highway from a hundred to zero flat. But the truck wrapping itself around her antlers would still slam into her.

Emily wasn't sure what to do about that.

It was a weird power. Antlers that could only be moved by the person they were stuck to, and nothing else could affect them. Emily didn't know how that would fit into the team's composition, but they'd figure it out.

"Can you change the colors?" Maple asked.

"Eh?" Aurora said.

Maple gestured to the antlers stuck to Aurora's head. "Can you change the colors?"

Aurora turned her eyes up, trying to see her own antlers. "Uh. I don't think so."

"Oh," Maple said, clearly disappointed. Then she perked up. "I can make something for that."

"Are . . . are you trying to give her RGB antlers?" Athena asked.

"It might be helpful. For signaling. And it would be pretty. You could have themed and seasonal colors," Maple defended.

Yeah, Emily really wasn't sure where Aurora would fit, but she hoped that it would work out in the end.

CHAPTER SIXTY-SIX

The Grand Bosses

Uh, hey," Aurora said with a little wave.

The big man looked at her. His expression was . . . neutral, but still quite stern, and just a little bit scary. He would have been very intimidating if Aurora just bumped into him out of nowhere.

At the moment, Trinity was using him like a living jungle gym, which admittedly did help make him a little less intimidating.

"Hey," he said. "You're the new girl?"

Aurora nodded. "I am," she said. "It's nice to meetcha?"

He nodded once. "Likewise. You look older than the rest."

"I guess I'm kinda older, body-wise," Aurora said.

"Nuh-uh, I have three bodies, so I age three times as much in the same time, which makes *me* the oldest," Trinity said from her position atop the man's broad shoulders.

He chuckled, then reached up, grabbed Trinity around the waist, and easily plucked her off his back to place her on the ground. He patted her on the head. "Go and play with the others. I'll chat with Aurora here for a bit," he said.

Trinity perked up, and her other bodies, which were still clinging to him, jumped off. "Okay, Grandpa Boss!" she said with a sloppy salute before she ran off.

Aurora watched her sister scamper off. They were at a Huck and Cheese, a restaurant that Aurora wasn't sure she was fond of. There were some animatronic characters, mostly dressed like Heroes, and a big indoor jungle gym off to one side.

The music was annoying her. It was very loud and obnoxiously upbeat. But her sisters seemed to love it, so Aurora kept her opinion to herself.

"Wanna have a sit?" Grandpa Boss asked. He gestured to the booth they'd been brought to by a pimple-faced, overworked waiter earlier.

Emily and her mom (Grandma Boss) were behind the glass wall between the normal restaurant section and the play area. The rest of her sisters were fighting in a ball pit, Trinity diving in to tackle Teddy under the balls.

Maple was . . . next to one of the animatronics, and Aurora was a little worried about what kind of thoughts were crossing her mind as she stared up at the robotic Hero figure.

"Yeah, let's sit," Aurora said.

"Must be tough, being the new one," he said as he squeezed into the bench across from her. He was a big guy in more than one dimension, and he had to suck in his gut a little to fit into the seat.

"It's a little hard, I guess," Aurora admitted. "But everyone's been nice. It's not a bad family to be part of, eh?"

"I guess not," he said with a soft smile. "My daughter's a good kid. Never figured her for the . . . motherly type, or much of a leader, but she's figuring things out well enough. It helps that you and your sisters seem to respect her."

"She's the Boss," Aurora said with certainty.

"She's Emily first," he said.

"She's Emily first?" Aurora repeated. She didn't quite know what that meant. She supposed that him being Emily's dad meant that he knew the Boss better than even her sisters did. Though some part of Aurora was a little doubtful about that.

"Yeah," he said as he looked across the room. Emily was now *in* the room with the ball pit, wagging a finger at both Trinity and Teddy and telling them to behave. Another kid ran by behind her, bumped into her rear, and sent her sprawling forward with a squawk to crash onto Aurora's sisters. They all disappeared under the balls. "She's always been an . . . interesting kid. Actually, I take back what I said earlier."

"About her being a good leader?" Aurora asked.

He shook his head. "No. About her being good. Did you know that there's a difference between good and good?"

"You just said the same thing twice," Aurora pointed out.

"No, not quite. There's different sorts of good. You know, my wife was surprised and a little shocked when Emily turned out to be a . . . the V-word."

Aurora knew what he meant. Emily had told her—and her sisters—not to use the word Villain out in public if they could avoid it. It was a dangerous thing to say, because being a Villain wasn't something people liked very much.

"Were you?" Aurora asked.

"No, I wasn't," he said as he leaned back into the bench. "Emily was always a quiet, studious kid. She has, well, pretty obvious anxiety when it comes to talking to others and socializing. Don't know where she got that from. Probably my side of the family. We're quiet sorts. It's not from her mom, that's for sure. That woman's a consummate gossip."

"Uh-huh," Aurora said. "And the V-word stuff?"

"Emily's quiet. Quiet doesn't mean good. But a lot of people conflate the two. When someone's good at minding their own business, when they keep to themselves, people seem to think that they're not bad sorts. They're doing their own quiet thing, not breaking any laws, not messing with others. But that doesn't let you see what's going on in their heads."

"Can you see what's going on in people's heads?" Aurora asked. Athena could do that. It was a neat party trick.

He laughed. "No. But I can read my daughter. When she was small, she'd frame the cat for knocking things over. She was quiet, but would use that to her advantage, too. She kept picking books from the older sections of the library, but would just go mum when her teachers talked to her about it. I recall one teacher discovering her in the teacher's lounge one day after she'd gotten a ninety-six on a test instead of a hundred. The teacher just dismissed it, said that Emily wasn't supposed to be there, but Emily was so quiet and nice that no one saw it as a real problem, just something that happened, a kid getting lost. She'd rewritten her exam results to give herself a hundred. She told me about it later, because the teacher had made a mistake while grading her test, and it was easier to break into their room and change the results herself than to correct the teacher."

"Whoa," Aurora said. "How old was she?"

"That was when she was in the . . . third grade, I think? So under ten or so."

Aurora was even more impressed with her big sister now than she had been before, and that was saying something. "She started Vil—uh, the V-word stuff even earlier than I expected."

"Yeah. She's . . . headstrong, in her own way. I think if it weren't for her problems talking and socializing, then my daughter would be a real hellion. Her mother was like that too, when she was younger."

Aurora looked over to the Grand Boss, who was laughing even as she helped Emily out of the ball pit. "She was?"

"Oh yeah. Feisty, that one. She was the sort of woman who others learned to be afraid of. No one bosses her around, lemme tell you. She's not evil or anything, but she can be mean."

"Is that a bad thing?" Aurora asked.

"No, I don't think so. Not when she's being mean on your behalf." He nodded. "It's why I'm not so worried about Emily and this whole V-word thing. Sure, she's got a mean streak in her, just like her mom, and maybe with power and time she'll grow into someone more . . . fearsome. But at the same time, she'll only act to protect herself and what's hers."

"Oh," Aurora said.

She was part of that too, wasn't she? That was a nice feeling to have.

Emily walked out of the playroom and over to their seats, her mom right behind her. Emily's hair was all frizzed up and her cheeks were bright red as she took a seat next to Aurora. "Well, that was something," she said.

"Are you okay?" Aurora asked.

"I'm fine. But I lost my phone in the ball pit."

"Oh . . . you're not looking for it?" Aurora asked.

"I got Trinity and Teddy to compete to find it first," she said. "I give it even odds that they'll either find it or start emptying the ball pit until it's impossible to miss."

Grandma Boss sat down next to her husband, then leaned forward and kissed his cheek. He flushed a little. Aurora thought they were both cute. She wondered if Emily would be looking for someone one day.

A waiter arrived to give them some menus, and that attracted her other sisters back to their table. Maple had . . . what looked like a small part of an animatronic's leg with her, which she tucked under the table, and the others had retrieved Emily's phone and were fighting over who would give it back to her.

It was chaotic, but not in a bad way.

"Huh," Emily said as she grabbed her phone. "Sam sent me a message . . . One sec, I think I need to look into this."

For some reason, what should have been an innocent moment suddenly felt a little more dangerous.

CHAPTER SIXTY-SEVEN

The New Girl

Trinity reached over and tugged on new-and-somewhat-bigger sister's sleeve.

Aurora glanced up. She was sitting on the floor with her back against the couch and one leg folded up. The TV was playing a documentary about bears that Trinity had seen twice already. She was actually watching it now, from another body.

"Yeah?" Aurora asked.

"I need help," Trinity said.

"With that?" Aurora asked.

"I'm in love, and I need help."

"Eh?" Aurora said. Or asked. Trinity wasn't sure what it meant, except that it was Aurora's favorite noise to make.

At the moment, Trinity and her sisters were all alone at home. Emily was off at school, and Mrs. Headerson couldn't do classes today because Steffie had a doctor's appointment. So they had to stay at home and entertain themselves.

Trinity was mostly indoors, so it was okay. The last bit of her was outside, watching her loved one. "I can't get through the barrier," Trinity said.

"The what?" Aurora asked. She turned and then stood. She was a lot taller than Trinity, like a head and a bit. Unless Trinity counted all of her heights all together? That'd make her three times taller than she was now, so technically she was actually way taller than Aurora.

But then she'd need to calculate her weight three times, and that would mean that Athena was allowed to make fat jokes, so Trinity settled on being shorter for the moment.

"All right, you're gonna need to give me a bit more."

"A bit more what?" Trinity asked.

"Information," Aurora said.

"Oh. That makes sense. Uh, okay, so . . . it was like in the movies."

"What movies?" Aurora asked.

"The romance ones. Like Athena likes," Trinity said with a gesture to Athena, who was on the couch with the laptop.

Athena looked up. "No I don't," she lied.

"I genuinely have no idea what you mean," Aurora said.

Trinity reached over the couch with one body and rubbed one of her chins while putting two hands on her hips. "It was love at first sight. I saw him, and I fell in love, and now I need your help getting to him."

"Yeah, all right, and who exactly did you fall in love with?" Aurora asked.

"I also wanna know," Athena said, even though she wasn't looking away from her computer.

"He's a little guy, black, with one eye, and he likes trash too," Trinity said.

"I'm concerned. I think I should be concerned, right?" Aurora asked, and Athena made an "uh-huh" sound.

"Come on," Trinity said as she reached out and grabbed Aurora's hand. "I'll show you."

It wasn't as easy as grabbing Aurora and making her follow. They had to put their shoes on by the entrance, and then Trinity had to go through a whole thing where she convinced Aurora that technically Emily had told all of her sisters *except* Aurora not to leave, and that Trinity was only one-third gone, so she'd only get one-third of a spanking if she was caught, and Mrs. Headerson had explained that some things couldn't be turned into fractions. (Trinity was the best at math. Mrs. Headerson was very impressed with her.)

Then, once they were out of the bunker, it was a short walk to where Trinity's love was waiting. She didn't venture far from home, in case she had to run back for something. This was basically like patrolling the neighborhood.

"Oh, there's your third you," Aurora said as she came up to the other one of Trinity's bodies. This one was pressed up against a fence that blocked off an entire alleyway. It was twice as tall as Trinity and had barbed wires at the top, obviously to protect what was within.

"Is . . . is your love the dumpster?" Aurora asked.

The dumpster was about the only thing in the alleyway. It was behind a jeweler's and an electronics store, which was probably another reason the back was blocked off by a fence and had a bunch of cameras.

"It's him," Trinity said as she pointed.

Aurora followed her pointing finger to the side of the dumpster where the love of Trinity's life was resting. He was so small and shiny and precious.

"Trinity, that's, eh, that's one of those Broomba floor cleaners," Aurora said.

"He's beautiful," Trinity said. "Is that his name?"

"I think you could call it whatever you wanted."

"*Him*," Trinity corrected her.

"How . . . how do you figure it's a him?" Aurora asked.

"Look at the jawline. He's obviously a him," Trinity said. "And I love him."

Broomba stared back at her. He only had one eye, round and exceptionally googly. There was tape where his other eye had been, but it was missing now. It only made him cooler. Like a pirate. For dust. A dust pirate.

"Well, okay, but it's in the trash . . . which isn't a problem for you, but we can't exactly get to that, can we?"

"You could," Trinity said. "Push your horns at the fence."

Aurora looked around, then up the fence. "Yeah . . . that *would* work. One shove and those supports would probably give out first. But I have a better idea."

Aurora then did something very unexpected. She walked around and right into the store. Trinity followed, still holding her taller sister's hand and listening as she explained to a tired-looking counter-person that Trinity really wanted the Broomba in the dumpster out back, and it was in the trash *anyway*.

The clerk shrugged, and five minutes later, Trinity was united with her love.

"He's so pretty!" she cheered.

"You . . . uh, sure she wants that?" the clerk asked.

"Yup, pretty sure," Aurora said. "Thanks, eh."

"You're welcome?"

Trinity skipped back home, hugging Broomba close. He was much smaller than she'd imagined from afar, but heavier too, and he smelled like dust and chewed gum and old plastic, and Trinity loved him a lot.

"We should see if Maple would feel like fixing him," Aurora said. She was still holding onto Trinity's hand, but of the body not holding Broomba.

"I like his one eye," Trinity said.

"No, I meant . . . like, the mechanical parts. Battery's probably dead or something. He looks a bit worn out, too."

"Oh," Trinity said. She held Broomba up before her, then nodded. "Okay."

Maple, when they got back home, was found in her bedroom with a machine that looked a bit like one of those animatronics Trinity had seen a couple of days before, only without the skin and with a lot more spikes.

"Maple, I need help," Trinity said as she turned Broomba around. "Broomba needs help."

Maple blinked, then adjusted her glasses with the heel of her hand. "Huh? Oh, it's a dust-collector. Where did you get it?"

"We're in love," Trinity explained.

Maple didn't seem to get it, but she did take Broomba from Trinity and place him on her workbench. "If only I had plastic explosives," Maple muttered.

"If I find any, I promise to share," Trinity promised.

Maple nodded absently. From the way her eyes looked a little glassy, Trinity knew that her sister was almost in a gadget-making trance. Usually she'd leave Maple to her own devices, but this was Broomba. If he had hands, she'd be holding one while Maple operated on him.

With her tail flapping under her coat, Maple took apart Broomba's skin of plastic shells and set them aside, then started to tug at the motors and computer bits and batteries and other innards of Broomba's body. "Just one little bin?" Maple muttered. "Why only one battery? What's this do? No, that's silly. Hmm. How does he know where he's going with just one googly eye? No depth perception."

"K-keep the one eye!" Trinity said. "It's cute!"

Tools were brought in, then discarded as Maple got to work. There were flashes of light and sparks as she cut into things. The room smelled like melting plastic and inventions.

Finally, after several long hours, it was done.

Broomba came to life with a mechanical whirl. His new eye opened, and a sweep of red lasers scanned the room around him. He now had four little legs, and a little grippy arm from a toy tractor on his tummy, as well as a dust-scooping whirly thing that could move up and down.

"Done," Maple said. "He needs to be fed one battery every seventy-two hours or so. More if he's been active."

"Okay," Trinity said with a serious nod.

"The weapons system will only turn on for intruders and mice . . . hmm, might have to adjust that if we ever get a mouse-sister. Oh, and don't touch the self-destruct button on his belly. It's the red one with Self-Destruct written on it."

Trinity nodded seriously. "Okay. What happens if I do?"

"There's a countdown timer. You'll have ten seconds to double-tap the button to cancel the self-destruct. Otherwise, the dust-dimension in his chest will invert, and all the energy that went into creating a pocket dimension will turn into kinetic energy going outward. Oh, and all the dust will come back, too."

"Okay," Trinity said. "Thank you, Maple, you're the best."

She hugged Maple, who blushed prettily. "I-it's nothing," Maple said. "Back to work for me."

Trinity nodded, then ran out of the room with Broomba, her tail wagging behind her.

She hoped that Big Sister Emily would be okay with the idea of Trinity finding love.

CHAPTER SIXTY-EIGHT

Commiserate

Emily needed someone to commiserate with, and at the moment—not wanting to call her mom, in case she was busy with anything—that meant complaining to her minion-in-chief.

Fortunately, Sam was a good friend, and was more than willing to listen to Emily complain about this and that. In turn, Emily would listen to Sam complain about her far more mundane issues.

Emily was actually a little envious. Not only of Sam's social circle—which seemed to encompass most of the campus—but also Sam's problems and complaints all being about things like gossip and who was doing what with whom.

They were at a coffee shop a block over from the campus, one that was slightly overpriced but actually fairly okay, all things considered. The café had some booths by the windows, which overlooked a fairly busy street.

Emily had just finished commiserating with Sam about the newest gossip in the dorms. Sam had a friend of a friend who started dating this boy, only to break up with him because he was, in her words, "a weak-willed misogynist." Then the same friend started to date her ex-boyfriend's ex-girlfriend, and he got upset about that.

He apparently decided to crash a party where both of his now-exes were while very drunk, and had made a big fool of himself in front of a crowd.

Emily wasn't sure she was actually following the story correctly. But the drama of it all was at least entertaining.

"What about you?" Sam asked as she gestured to Emily with her coffee.

With a groan, Emily launched into her own latest disaster, air-quotes and all. "Trinity came home with a 'boyfriend.'"

Sam choked on her coffee. "A *what*?" she asked, voice rising quite a bit.

"He is a what, yeah," Emily said.

Shaking her head, Sam leaned forward on the table. "No, no, stop doing wordplay and explain. If he's like, any more than a year older than she looks, I'm totally ready to kick some butt. Where did she even find someone? How? Does he know she's got three bodies? Is he actually her boyfriend?"

Emily smiled. "That's what she called it. Him? Uh, it's a Broomba." She made a little humming noise and gestured her hand moving flat over the table.

"One of those little floor-cleaning units?" Sam asked, her immediate anger response changed to one of slight confusion. She spread her hands apart to about the right size. "Small and cute, cleans up floors, self-charging . . . okay, when I put it that way, there are worse boyfriends out there."

"His name's Broomba," Emily said. "And the girls are treating him like a pet. Honestly, it's mostly just cute. I don't know *where* they found it, but I think the trash somewhere. Maple fixed it up and Trinity is adamant that she's in love."

"That sounds about right for Trinity," Sam said. "So, are you taking it for walkies?"

"You say that as a joke," Emily said. "But Maple gave it legs, so . . . yeah, kinda. Now it walks around the bunker and picks up dust here and there. I had to stop Teddy from spreading crumbs around on purpose to have the Broomba pick them up."

"That's not so bad, then," Sam said. "You had me worried when you said Trinity came home with a boy. This seems a lot more tame."

"I hope it stays that way," Emily said. "I measured Teddy's height, you know. She's grown. Not much, just like . . ." She pinched her thumb and forefinger together, then spread them a little bit apart. "But yeah, that seems to be a normal amount of growth for a couple of months. We might have to start buying them all new clothes."

"Just wait until they start hitting growth spurts," Sam said.

"I don't want to wait," Emily said.

"And then they'll be all hormonal, and they'll bring more than just cleaning equipment home. Hmm . . . have they gotten celebrity crushes yet?" Sam asked. Her grin was at best teasing, at worst . . . something less kind.

"Not yet," Emily said. "But Athena does have a *thing* for old Villains."

"Oh my." Sam leaned back into her seat, then blew across the lip of her mug. "You know, your sisters are growing up, which is scary, but so are you."

"Me?"

Sam nodded. "Yeah. You're a lot more confident now than when we met. You hardly stutter anymore, and while you still dress as if you're desperate not to be noticed, you don't carry yourself the same way."

Emily blinked. She . . . had admittedly noticed a few changes in herself, but she thought they were small, not something that others would recognize. "Thank you, I guess."

"Hey, I'm planning on being a shrink one of these days. If you were one of my clients, I'd be pretty proud of your progress."

That warmed Emily's heart up a little. It was nice to have her efforts acknowledged at all. "I'm still a long way from being as confident as someone like you."

"Meh, I'm an extrovert to end all extroverts. Nothing wrong with not being super social. Now all we need is to get you hooked up with someone."

"Wha?"

"Oh yeah, a couple of bad breakups would really get you prepped for life. You're in college. It's practically expected of you to mess up a few relationships, and once your heart's been broken a few times, it'll be a lot harder for other stuff to bother you."

Emily stared at Sam with undisguised horror. "That's *terrible* advice," she said.

Sam shrugged. "Hey, it's part of the experience."

"N-no, no it's not," Emily said. "And don't go giving that kind of advice to my sisters. Can you imagine what a heartbroken Teddy would do? Maple would cry, and Athena . . . would go to jail."

"And Trinity's taste in partners is probably trash," Sam said with a giggle.

Emily didn't want to laugh, but a chuckle escaped her anyway before she could rein it in. "That's mean," she said. It wasn't wrong, but it was still a little mean to Trinity.

"Sorry, sorry," Sam said with a dismissive little wave. "So, I take it there aren't any special someones you have your eyes on?"

Emily shook her head rather vigorously. "I don't think I'd have the brain space for it. Besides, I can't think of anyone that interesting right now."

"Hmm, that's something. What about that Fabien guy?" Sam made a little stabby gesture, as if she were holding a tiny sword.

"The fencer Mask? No, he's too . . . eh. None of the minions either. I mean, some of them are nice-looking, but they're . . . minions."

Sam nodded. "Weird power dynamic. That makes sense."

Emily hadn't considered it too much, but yes, that was more or less accurate. Her minions were her minions first and foremost in her mind. They were also a gaggle of dorks who liked Mask stuff a little too much for their own health.

"What about you?" Emily asked. This was an advanced social technique she had only recently picked up. The "ask a deflecting question" was a small-talk tactic that turned conversations around and made it so that she didn't have to talk as much.

Sam grinned, and Emily worried that she needed more small-talk practice. "Me? Hmm, I wish I had time for dating and such. It's been a wild few weeks, you know? There're a few cute guys and girls around, but not enough time to get to know them. Plus the dating scene is awful right now."

"Uh-huh," Emily agreed.

"You have no idea, do you?"

"Not a clue," Emily admitted. She smiled all the same. This was . . . nice. Classes had finished for the day, and she still had a few minutes before she had to head out to Mrs. Headerson's place to pick up her sisters.

She wondered if Aurora would get along well with the teacher. Probably. Emily's newest sister seemed mature enough to handle herself well.

As per usual when a conversation wound down, they both pulled out their phones from purse and pocket and idly checked their socials. Well, Sam checked hers. Emily was plugged into a rapidly updating 24/7 stream of cute animal pictures that she could tap into on command.

The best part of being so busy lately was that there were tons of new memes she'd missed out on.

She was just about to turn her phone around to share a video of two sleepy kittens who couldn't decide if they wanted to cuddle or fight when she noticed Sam's brows knit together in a frown. "Is . . . is everything okay?" Emily asked.

"Yeah, no," Sam said. "Emily, did you ever let the HRF know about you being on the V-side of things?"

"No," Emily said, her heart sinking. "Why?"

Sam glanced up from her phone. "A couple of friends at school said that people from the HRF were around, and they were looking for you."

CHAPTER SIXTY-NINE

Glowing Betrayal

So, she just waltzes right into the theater, bold as can be, no mask on, little bear ears poking out of her hair, and she walks right up to the manager."

Jezebelle nodded. The story was funny so far. In fact, the boy sitting across from her was . . . actually kind of just funny overall. Not in the traditional way; most of his jokes were self-deprecating, and he was . . .

Well, Alea Iacta was a bit cringy. But he kind of owned up to it, and when he wasn't too self-conscious he could be pretty cute, in a sort of sad, geeky puppy kind of way. For someone with such a dangerous power, he came off as exceptionally inoffensive.

Jezebelle wasn't sure what to think about that. He was not a Villain, but he was certainly on the wrong side of the morality divide.

"Then what?" she asked.

Alea leaned forward. He was maskless. As was she, though she was hiding her status for once, which afforded them a little bit of privacy. They weren't anywhere too special. A kinda crappy pizza place a few blocks over from the school. It was the kind of place that you could smell from halfway down the road.

The kind of place she'd usually avoid, because there was no way she'd stay fit eating here. Still, once, on a date of sorts? She could bend her diet a little for a couple of slices and a can of soda. Alea Iacta seemed to be enjoying it, in any case.

"Right, so she comes right up to me and just straight up threatens me," he said. "My friend just wrote me off, said it was my problem basically. So we went to the costume room, and she has me grab some things. That's where the Boss's costume comes from, by the way. It was an extra costume from . . . urgh, I can't remember the play. Something gangsterish."

"Wait, the Boss's costume is stolen?"

Alea laughed. "I know! I used a bit of luck finding it, which is why I think it fits so well. But yeah, stolen right off the rack."

"Does she know?" Jezebelle asked.

"If she does then she doesn't care. Ted—the bear girl—left with this big pimp coat. I have no idea what happened with that, but I'm kinda glad she didn't use it as part of her costume."

Jezebelle wasn't sure what to focus on there. "A pimp coat?" she finally asked.

"Massive, all purple, fake fur. It came with a feathered hat."

"No," she said.

"Yeah! She was drowning in it. It was kind of cute, actually. But can you imagine a grizzly in that kind of outfit? Terrorizing the neighborhood?"

Jezebelle giggled. It wasn't even hard to laugh.

She . . . was not here for the date. Well, that's what she'd been telling herself all day. She was here to dig up information on the Boss and her kids. Alea Iacta wasn't just giving her everything she wanted to know.

But . . .

Jezebelle tugged the neck of her blouse down a little, laughed again, then leaned her elbows onto the table. "Then what?" she asked.

Alea's eyes dipped for a fraction of a second. He gulped. "Uh? Then . . . I guess that's about when I got recruited. By force. Ursa really didn't give me many options. It was join up or get eaten. Mind you, I think I could have made a run for it, but I don't really regret it. The Boss is . . . actually not the worst boss? Ironically enough."

"I've got to ask," Jezebelle said. "You seem . . . a little scared of her?"

"Huh? Oh, she's not scary once you get to know her. Actually, I think she's a bit of a hot mess. Not hot that way," he hurried to add.

"Uh-huh," she continued.

"Yeah, but she's nice. Mostly to her sisters, but to the rest of her minions, too."

"Minions?" Jezebelle asked. She filed away that "sisters" mention for later. It was just confirmation.

Alea laughed it off. "That's what the brats call the people who work for the Boss. I guess it includes powered people, too."

"Are there that many?" she asked.

"Well, no, but yeah? It feels like every time I go to the bunker there's a couple more minions I haven't met yet."

"I guess she does need a lot of help, with so many sisters."

"Yeah," he said.

Jezebelle backed up on the topic. They started talking about TV shows they liked, then that veered to movies, and then to books. She had a soft spot for the Ord of the Ings series since her dad had read them to her when she was young, and they debated for a bit over whether the movies were better than the books.

In the meantime, she was thinking.

This wasn't an admission that the Boss was a Villain, but . . . well, it was adding to Jezebelle's collection of hints. At this rate, she was almost certain that Rattles hadn't been lying.

She hadn't been able to question him, of course. The Villain was locked away in some HRF facility somewhere, and soon enough he'd stand trial and probably be tossed into some deep, dark hole. There were prisons for Masks out there, and they weren't pretty places. She'd seen the offers to work there. The pay was actually pretty decent, but the work looked awful.

In any case, Jezebelle's suspicions about Emily were all but confirmed.

Emily was on the wrong side of the morality chart.

It made so much more sense. Her rapid growth, her refusal to work with the HRF, her strength, and the way she was so evasive all the time, so cagey.

It was all because she was secretly . . . well, probably not an actual Villain. Maybe a Scoundrel? Jezebelle wasn't entirely familiar with the evil moralities, but she couldn't imagine Emily being near the bottom. She wasn't *that* bad.

Not unless she was secretly influencing those children she was with.

The date ended on a bit of a flat note. Jezebelle looked at her phone and said she had to go. Alea stood, then escorted her out. It looked like he wanted to go for a hug, but he awkwardly shuffled and turned it into a handshake. She was almost laughing as she headed out.

She tugged her blouse back on properly, then zipped her coat up because she didn't plan on catching a cold.

She had plenty of worrying thoughts to keep her company as she made her way back to her car, which was parked a couple of blocks over, and then back through the city.

Jezebelle had been lucky her entire life. She was aware of it, unlike some of her family. Sure, they weren't a big name, nor were they uber-rich, but they were very comfortable, and for the most part, so was she.

It had always been easy to do the right thing. To be a good girl, to help others, to reap the rewards of being *good*. She'd thought of doing some bad things plenty of times, but she would never act on that. Yes, she was a little keen on being the center of attention, but she also tried to help others break out of their shells.

In high school she'd been literally everyone's friend, and she had been in all the clubs. Being a Hero felt like an extension of that. At least initially.

Now . . . now she was driving around with a secret like a millstone around her neck.

Almost without realizing it, she arrived and parked her car. She was out a moment later, after checking herself in the mirror and turning on her status once more. To anyone looking, there was a small piece of text in their language of preference over her head: Glamazon, Hero. It was better proof of identity than any paperwork.

The guard at the door of the HRF headquarters checked her ID, scanned her eyes, and looked at her prints anyway. She even had to give her weekly code word. All measures to stop the trickiest of Villains from getting in.

Once inside, she went to a section of the headquarters that no one wanted to visit but everyone knew the location of. A small office at the very back, where she pressed a buzzer and was let into a room with a chair and a mirrored wall and nothing else.

This was the place to go if any member of the HRF suspected that something was amiss, or had to report something strange, and she had hoped that she would never have to enter this room.

"Glamazon," a neutral voice said over the loudspeakers. Someone likely several cities away listening in. "Do you have anything to report?"

"Yes," she said. "I'd like to report on the identity of a suspected Villain. One who has been masquerading as a Hero."

She hoped that she was still doing the right thing. And that maybe one day Emily would forgive her.

EPILOGUE

~~~~~~~

Things were nice and quiet in the Wright household.

Emily had spent a week expecting . . . something to happen, but no. Things were calm.

Well, things were *relatively* calm. She was trying very hard to do some homework, her laptop on her lap and her legs up on an ottoman that had just appeared in their living room one fine day. The girls were being themselves all over the place, but it was no louder than usual.

"Teddy, stop choking out Athena," Emily said without looking away from the monitor.

"How'd you even know?" Teddy asked from somewhere behind the couch.

Emily sighed. The truth was that Athena hadn't said anything snarky in several minutes, but she wasn't going to say that aloud. "I can hear her choking, and I have Big Sister Magic. Let her go."

"No fun," Teddy muttered. A moment later she yelped, and there was a crash as she landed hard on the floor. Emily imagined that Athena had just kicked her legs out from under her.

Looking up, Emily scanned the room. Trinity was sitting next to her, on both sides. It was actually kind of nice. The girl was watching TV—the volume on low—and chewing on her thumbs while using Emily's sides as a pillow. "Where's your third body?" Emily asked.

"She's with me!" came a call from the kitchen. Aurora, who was even now cooking something.

Having an older girl in the house was a blessing. "Thank you!" Emily called back. That left . . .

Sighing, Emily sat up straighter and turned her head around as much as she could to see into Maple's bedroom. "Maple, what are you up to?" she asked.

It took a few minutes, but Maple's head eventually popped out of the room. Her hair was frazzled, as if she'd been licking a live wire. "Science?"

"What *kind* of science?" Emily asked.

"I made a machine to hide us better," Maple said. "But I'm having a hard time dialing it in."

"What does it do, exactly?" Emily asked.

"It makes people forget the first letter in your name!" Maple said.

"So . . . what, I'd be Eddy instead of Teddy?" Teddy asked.

Maple puffed her cheeks out. "I guess?"

"That's stupid, people would still know who I am!" Teddy said. "Because I'm awesome."

"Does the machine just do it from the point it's activated onward?" Athena asked. "Because then there would still be records, and if a bunch of us suddenly have the same error on our records, then that would just make it obvious that something's up."

"No, no, I made it so that it's retroactive," Maple said. She smiled. "That's why I needed an old clock! I'm trying to make it work on just our names, but I think I set it to everything but names instead?"

Emily blinked. "So . . . what, it would change the name of everything?"

"Uh," Maple said. "I guess?"

"Well, we still live in Anada, so obviously it didn't work," Teddy said.

"I know that!" Maple said. "If it had worked, then it would be super obvious. I mean. Not really, since it's retroactive, but still!"

"I don't get it," Trinity said. "Am I gonna be . . . Rinity from now on?"

"No, sweetie, you won't," Emily said. "Maple, next time, ask before making a machine that changes anything that bit, please? Even if it's for a good cause."

"Ah, okay," Maple said.

Emily shook her head. Sometimes, Maple scared her. But so far she'd been diligent enough to catch the girl before she did anything irreversible. Emily shook her head and returned to her homework.

A few minutes later, Aurora came out of the kitchen with a plate covered in hot dogs, and that had all of Emily's sisters calming right down. She had to clean more than one ketchup stain off the couch and wipe off several messy cheeks, but it wasn't so bad.

She was just resettling herself to work some more when she got a text from Sam. It was labeled *Urgent.*

Frowning, Emily opened it, then looked up at the TV. "Trinity, do you mind if I change the channel? Ah, where's the remote?"

That triggered a fresh remote search. It wasn't between any of the cushions, under the couch, or in the kitchen or bathroom. She ended up discovering it semi-disassembled in Maple's room. Maple focused really hard on the floor and went red in the face, and Emily couldn't find it in herself to chastise her. Instead, she flicked the TV over to the news.

There were commercials playing.

Emily waited impatiently for those to finish and for the breaking story of the hour to come on.

A man was standing in a field somewhere, with several vans behind him and what looked like HRF troopers running about and setting up barricades. He brought a mic up to his face. "It seems as though the cordon is still going up around Saint-Arie now. The city is still early in its evacuation, a process made more difficult by the early stages of the End—"

The newscaster was interrupted as it started to pour.

Not a light drizzle, but an absolute avalanche of water that came down atop the area as if someone had just emptied a lake overhead. He coughed and sputtered, then tugged his coat over his head for cover.

"As I was saying!" he shouted to be heard over the rain. "It seems as if the first Endgame in Anada in several years is starting very soon! The HRF—"

Emily muted the TV.

She stared.

This . . . could mean a lot of trouble. Or it could be an opportunity like none other.

In either case, she had a bad feeling in her gut about it.

About the Author

RavensDagger is a Canadian writer who wants to make people smile. The best way to do that, he has found, is by pecking away at the keyboard and hoping for the best.

RESPAWN YOUR CURIOSITY
follow us on our socials

 podiumentertainment.com

 @podiumentertainment

 /podiumentertainment

 @podium_ent

 @podiumentertainment